THE CADAVER'S BALL

Also by Charles Atkins

Risk Factor

The Portrait

THE
CADAVER'S
BALL

CHARLES ATKINS

THOMAS DUNNE BOOKS

ST. MARTIN'S MINOTAUR   NEW YORK

The Cadaver's Ball is a work of fiction. Any resemblance to persons living or dead is purely coincidental.

THOMAS DUNNE BOOKS.
An imprint of St. Martin's Press.

www.minotaurbooks.com

Book design by Irene Vallye

ISBN 0-312-34204-7
EAN 978-0-312-34204-3

First Edition: October 2005

10 9 8 7 6 5 4 3 2 1

To Al Zuckerman

ACKNOWLEDGMENTS

The author wishes to thank the following for their support, honest criticism, and guidance. While I've dedicated this book to Al Zuckerman, my agent and mentor, that doesn't begin to address the many outlines and drafts of *The Cadaver's Ball* that he patiently read and critiqued. In addition, there are the usual suspects: Gary S. Jayson, who had to suffer the first draft and then say something nice; Stacey Rubin and Elizabeth Fitzgerald, who worked through plot points on the back deck; the Yale writers' group with John Strauss; Ruth Cavin, editor extraordinaire; Toni Plummer; Frances Sayers; Steve Southwick, guru of all things PTSD; Harvey and Cynthia Atkins; my sisters; and, of course, Lisa Hoffman, who's been doing this a lot longer and who constantly reminds me, "You work too hard, why not take a nap?"

Who is this? And what is here?
And in the lighted palace near
Died the sound of royal cheer:
And they crossed themselves for fear,
   All the knights at Camelot:
But Lancelot mused a little space
He said, "she has a lovely face;
God in his mercy lend her grace,
   The Lady of Shalott."

—ALFRED, LORD TENNYSON, *The Lady of Shalott*

Was ever woman in this humor woo'd?
Was ever woman in this humor won?
I'll have her, but I will not keep her long.

—WILLIAM SHAKESPEARE, *Richard III*

THE CADAVER'S BALL

PROLOGUE

1991

"COME ON, BETH." HIS FINGERS entwined in hers, flesh on flesh, holding tight. "I want to show you something."

"What?" she asked, laughing, and followed him down the granite stairs that led to the dissection rooms and the hospital morgue. Careful not to trip on her gown, she didn't think about the stench of death and formalin that curtained the air.

He glanced back, and his breath caught. She was spectacular. Dressed in floor-length white linen, her coppery mane swept up with curls cascading over bare shoulders, she was dressed as the goddess Athena—a tribute to the physician's Hippocratic oath they would take in late spring.

"Why are we here?" she asked. "If you're going to get me all covered with human fat to find Bessie's auriculotemporal nerve, it's not going to happen."

"No." He followed her gaze to the wire-laced window that gave a view of eight oilcloth-covered bodies. "She's sleeping; we shouldn't disturb her."

"That's sick." Her sandaled feet lit gently on the marble floor.

She released his hand and spread her bare arms. "It's cool down here; it feels nice."

She twirled to the vintage Motown that flowed from the Cadaver's Ball two stories above. A yearly bash, it was the closest thing the medical school had to a prom.

Her laced sandal caught and she stumbled. "Wheee!" She looked across at him. "So why are we here? Are you ever going to tell me what you're dressed as?" She sank down on a worn oak bench.

Ed chewed at the overworked wad of cocaine-rich coca leaves tucked in his right cheek. His growing use of narcotics was one of many secrets he'd kept from her. He swept back his black cape and pulled his balled-up mask from the inner pocket. As he did, his fingertips brushed the hard surface of the jewelry box. His stomach lurched and the gag-store rubber smelled like vomit as he pulled it over his face. "You have to guess."

"Okay, although I had to tell everyone who I was. They all thought I was from that *Animal House* movie. Duh, I'm Athena, goddess of wisdom."

"You're beautiful," he blurted, emboldened by his mask and pleasantly intoxicated from the evening's blend: coca leaves brushed with a mixture of hallucinogenic devil's vine and the bruised fronds of a *Psychotria* shrub.

"You're not too shabby yourself," she remarked. "Although . . . not your best look."

There was silence as they stared at each other. Ed's heart pounded, and he wondered how it was possible to love another person to the point that it caused a dull ache in his chest each time he looked at her.

"I know who you are," she said. "You're Death taking a holiday."

"Yes." He removed his mask, a skull to which he'd glued a

pair of Mickey Mouse ears. He crumpled it in his hand and went to her.

"I was sure you would come as that shape-shifter guy," she said.

"Manangee," he whispered, savoring the sound of the jungle spirit's name.

"That's the one."

He sat beside her. He nearly dropped to his knee, but he mustn't scare her; this had to be perfect. "I'd like to take you back there."

She sighed. "No, that was a one-time deal for this small-town girl."

What was she saying? He chewed nervously. "You had a good time."

"I had a wonderful time, but . . ."

And then he remembered; it was the money. But that wouldn't be a problem; everything he had would be hers. The moment had come. He slipped his hand into the pocket of his cape and dropped on bended knee.

She started to laugh, and then her smile fled like a morning mist. She stared at the dark purple velvet box. She gasped as it opened.

He knew that the two-carat, flawless cushion-cut Colombian emerald, far more precious than a diamond, was the perfect choice. "Marry me." Time hung in the air.

She put a hand to her mouth, her slender fingers pressed tightly against her bronze-painted lips. She tore her eyes from the ring and met Ed's expectant gaze. Her head started to shake from side to side.

He didn't understand; he pushed the box toward her.

She edged away. "Oh, no. Oh, God . . ."

"What?" Was it the ring? How could she not like the ring?

3

He'd have to tell her the story of exactly how he had smuggled the uncut stone out of Colombia.

"Ed . . . I can't." Her voice was a whisper.

He heard the words and saw her lips move. What was she saying? It was as though his brain had chosen that moment to forget English. She was saying no. Her mouth was saying no. This wasn't possible. A strangled cry rose from his throat. "Why won't you look at me?"

Like a butterfly pinned to a board, she stopped. Her lip trembled, she shut her eyes. "I can't marry you, Ed."

How could she not want him? "I love you."

She hesitated. "I love you, too, just not that way."

He felt light-headed and frozen. He looked at his outstretched hand, at the velvet box. The emerald sparkled with a dark flame; it was the perfect ring, the green of the jewel not far from the color of her eyes, a color that would be passed to their children. "Please."

She shook her head and wrapped her hand around the box. The warmth of her touch flowed into him. For a moment, he thought that she was going to take it, but then her fingers closed down; the box clicked shut.

"It's lovely, but it's not for me." She rose to her feet.

This was so wrong. He loved her. She loved him; he knew that. "It's someone else." He stood on a throbbing knee. "Who?" His tone was harsh. She flinched as he approached. "Tell me who!"

"Ed, not like this. I can't tell you like this."

Rage surged; he wanted to hit her, to see her fall hard against the marble floor. He bit the flesh of his cheek and tasted blood. "It's okay, Beth." He moved toward her and then stopped. She was frightened . . . of him. It was a look he'd seen before, when she'd found him, covered in blood, with a shrieking three-year-old Indian boy who'd become infested with parasites. The toddler's mother and the village shaman had held the child as Ed had lanced the two-inch fleshy growths under his arms and in his groin to remove the worms and translucent larvae that had grown fat on lymph and blood. The child was frantic, and Beth had screamed at him for not using anesthesia or one of the native brews to numb the pain. She should never have seen that. For the rest of her stay he'd been careful that she never witnessed his experiments—experiments that would lead to discoveries the world desperately wanted. Yes, the child was in pain, but after it reached a white-hot intensity, the body generated its own anesthesia. It was fascinating, and like other things he'd found in the jungle, it needed to be studied, so he had lied and told her that nothing he or the Indians had would have sufficed. She didn't believe him, and something changed in how she looked at him, and now . . . "I guess I look like a real idiot."

"No, Ed." She laid a hand on his shoulder. "This is my fault. I should have told you. I'm so sorry."

"Who is it?" he repeated, wondering if the silent scream rising inside of him would crack the surface of his face.

She looked at the floor, and before she spoke, he knew. "It's Peter," she said.

"Right."

"Are you going to be okay?"

"Fine." A sick tingle spread inside his tightly muscled body. He felt a pressure building as though at any moment he might explode. He wanted to shake her, to kiss her, to hit her. "I . . . I need to be alone."

"Are you sure you're okay?"

He managed a smile that in the dim reflection of a display case, which held antique jars filled with pickled human oddities, appeared wistful. It was the smile of a good loser, of one who takes bad news with grace. "I'll be fine."

"Okay." She moved uncertainly toward the stairs.

Her every step tortured him, her long-legged grace, the familiarity of her naked body beneath her costume, the gold in her hair. She turned on the second step, her perfect profile backlit from above. "It's a lovely ring, Ed. It's just not for me."

He raised his hand, "Don't worry about it, but please, don't mention it."

"I never will." With that she turned and vanished up the stairs.

He waited until her footsteps had gone and all that was left was the music from the party two stories above. It was the Divinyls "I Touch Myself," an obscene song. He heard the hooting and knew that young women, soon-to-be doctors, were being goaded to mimic masturbation as they danced.

A part of him became almost clinical as he stood there. How was it possible to feel so much pain but not to have a physical wound? His fists balled. *How could she do this? Why?* He paced around the two worn oak benches that had long ago been bolted to the floors of the circular room outside of the medical school's anatomy suites and the hospital morgue. *And Peter? Why him? No!* He could hear his sadistic father, the Judge, shout back one of his truisms. *If things don't add up, there's a reason.*

His hands flew to the sides of his head, digging into his close-cropped wheat-blond hair. He pulled, finding comfort in pain. His feet moved faster, his cape billowed. He had been so sure of her, of them, and their future together. This had to be a mistake. But even as he thought that, data leaked in. Like, in the first year of medical school, when they had practically lived in the anatomy rooms dissecting the obese cadaver they had nicknamed "Aunt Bessie," it was Peter who walked Beth home. It had made sense, as they both lived in the East Village, and Ed's apartment was in a much better Fifth Avenue building. Or when the third-year research awards had been given, her smile for Peter's second-place prize seemed brighter than for Ed's winning project. He'd written it off to her wanting to shore up Peter's ego, but perhaps that wasn't it. Still, he'd never seen them kiss or even hold hands. They were all friends, just good friends. *Fuck you, Peter!*

His pace quickened, he pulled fresh coca from a jade inlaid silver box, a gift from a shaman whose wife he'd cured of malaria. He'd win her back. But how? The Judge's voice whispered. *The ends justify the means.* He started to jog and then to run at a killing pace over the cold marble. The room blurred—the cabinets, the darkened doorways—it all became a shapeless whistling hum of color and movement.

He tortured himself with memories of two perfect weeks in the rain forest of northern Brazil. That wasn't his imagination. She had joined him in the Kaiapo village between the third and final year of medical school. It had taken a lot of persuading to get her there, but that was because she had no money. He had told her it didn't matter; he had paid for everything. Once she was there, he saw her excitement, her enthusiasm for the work, her ease with the village women as they painted their naked children for the seamless cycle of ceremonies and rituals. Her instincts were brilliant; she'd even talked about doing a study on gender differences in the use of medicinal plants. And the nights—their bodies were like one. She'd even drunk the ceremonial and highly hallucinogenic ayahuasca with him; under its influence he'd seen the marriage of their spirits. How could she go with Peter after that?

His pace slackened as the worst piece of data forced itself in. Yes, those two weeks had been incredible. They had ended with a kiss as she boarded the single-engine plane, her hair scented with orchids, her lips stained with red achiote berries. However, four weeks later, when he had returned, she had changed. The lipstick kiss on his arrival at JFK was a peck, and his invitations to dinner had been met with a series of plausible excuses—she had to be at the hospital or was on call or was too tired after thirty-six hours straight in the emergency room. He had been stupid and careless.

In the time he had stayed behind in the jungle he had been robbed.

A noise from the top of the stairs brought him to a halt. His heart raced; she had reconsidered. He fumbled for the ring box. He strained as the footfalls descended, waiting expectantly for the hem of her pleated gown to appear. Instead, what landed was a pair of black ballet slippers on short and shapely tights-clad legs. Before him stood a vaguely familiar young woman dressed in a skintight black cat outfit. Her face shone in the hot spot of a recessed light, and she held a plastic wine cup.

She smiled at him. "I had to get out of there," she said. "Guess I wasn't the only one." Emboldened by cheap jug wine, the second-year medical student prattled on. She couldn't believe her luck in having Ed Tyson, senior hunk, class celebrity, and winner of just about any award that could be won, all to herself in the bowels of the medical school. "Kind of a creepy place to be," she offered.

"It's cool down here," he said, feeling the planes of his face snap into place.

"You don't have a drink," she noted, moving close. "Boy, you're really hot." She giggled and quickly amended. "I mean, you look like you've been dancing up a storm."

He said nothing as she handed him her drink.

As though reading his thoughts, she said, "I bet you don't even know my name; it's Miranda, and I'm not usually this brazen."

He smiled and sipped the warm California burgundy. "I'm Ed."

"I know, and what are you doing down here by yourself when all of your classmates are upstairs deciding to get married?"

"What are you talking about?"

"How long have you been down here?" She chuckled.

"I was checking something in my lab," he lied. "What time is it?"

"Boy, you are either extremely dedicated or more out of it than I am." She looked over his head at the large clock with its green glowing radium dial. "It's three fifteen."

He'd come down with Beth more than three hours ago. The plan had been to propose at midnight. She wasn't coming back. This woman in front of him with her ripe body and big brown eyes was talking nonstop, yet he hadn't heard much of what she'd said.

"I don't know what it is about the fourth year," she commented. "It's as though somewhere between the clinical rotations and having to go away for internship, people get this little bit of breathing room, and it's like, 'Okay let's get married, have kids, and do it all in the next two months before our lives become hell.'"

"I missed something." He drained the wine.

"I'll say, you need a scorecard. We've got Linda Farnell and Gupta Singh, Casey Blauer and Jay Hartmann, and Beth Stockton and Peter Grainger. I guess it's sort of a tradition—saying "I do" or at least "I will" on the night of Cadaver's Ball, although I'm not a big fan of the mass proposals, too much like the Unification Church."

As Ed listened, he felt as if he were being lifted out of his body and was staring down on a black-caped man and a pretty, large-breasted woman in a cat outfit. It was a peaceful sensation, like watching marionettes. He could make these characters do or say anything. The man might reach over and wrap his large hands around the woman's throat and squeeze until her trachea cracked and she lay dead on the patterned marble. Instead, he did something else. He leaned over and kissed the woman—Miranda. Her lips were warm and soft, and with his eyes closed, she was Beth. Her body pressed into his, and as they separated the spell held. He watched the blond-haired man reach into the folds of his cape and pull out the velvet box. He cracked it open and showed the jewel. "I'm a firm believer in tradition," he said.

9

The woman seemed frightened, then amused, and then interested as he held her gaze. "You're kidding, right?" she asked.

"Take a chance," he said, his hot wine-sweetened breath landing on her parted lips.

As the blond-haired man proposed to the pretty black cat, he thought of Beth and Peter, and of how they'd lied and betrayed him. He thought of the Judge and the look in his eyes as he fell to his death ten years ago. Yes, he'd win her back. The ends would justify the means.

Holding the ring, he whispered again, "Take a chance."

1

2004

AFTER A YEAR OF INTENSIVE therapy, I know this. I feel it claw at my sanity. Oh, God, make it stop!

My fingers claw at smoldering steel as black smoke burns my eyes. "Come on, Beth!" I can't see. I can't breathe. The smell of gas. Help me! Somebody help me! She's not moving. Is her hair caught in the shoulder strap? I smash the window, but I can't get the door. She's not breathing. I suck in and put my head through the window, my mouth over hers, tasting her lipstick. Headlights come toward us through the fog. I stagger into the road. My hands wave. "Stop!" The whites of a man's eyes stare through the darkened glass. "Please stop." He slows and I grab for the closed window; it's cold against my blistering palm. Why isn't he stopping? I bang my hand against his window. "She's dying! Help me!" My palm print, smeared in blood, slips away; he's speeding up. I scream. A blue sparks turns to flames; it's in her hair. Help me!

I startled and blinked as a hand tapped my shoulder.

"Dr. Grainger. Peter, are you okay?"

I coughed and fought back the nausea that always comes. "I'm fine," I said, not knowing where I was, wondering how long I'd been gone. *Okay, Peter, pull it together. You're in an emergency room, that's what set off the flashback.* I turned toward the voice and found a name to match the concerned face of the short, middle-aged black woman looking up at me. "Grace, I spaced," I told the third-shift aide in the psychiatric emergency room of University Hospital.

"Good thing you're not a surgeon," she quipped. "She must be someone special to drag the big boss out in the middle of the night."

"Aren't they all," I answered, trying to fill in the missing pieces. I was in an emergency room, and it was late at night, which meant I had to be here to evaluate someone. "What do you know about her?"

"Same old, same old," Grace said, leading me into the Plexiglas nurses' station that separated the six patients' cubicles from the staff. "Name's Ann Walsh, twenty-two-year-old sophomore medical student, took a razor to her wrists."

"How bad?" I asked.

"Seen worse, a few sutures on each side, and if she really wanted to kill herself you'd think she'd know to go with the arteries and not against the grain."

"You're a sick woman, Grace. Any idea why?"

"Not that she's telling, but it boils down to a few basic plots."

"Okay . . . and they are?"

"Oh, please." The thirty-year veteran of the emergency room, who knew me when I was a resident, explained. "You've got Romeo and Juliet—young love gone bad. Ophelia—depressed and suicidal. Lady Macbeth—couldn't handle the guilt. And, of course, Lady Ann—'lay one hand on my frilly white under things and I'll kill myself.' Shakespeare covered the bases."

"Which is she?" I asked, remembering that Grace worked the graveyard shift so that she could spend her days pursuing a career as a comic actress.

"Don't know, but I do know she wants out."

"Which will it be? Keep her or let her go?"

"You want me to do your whole job for you?"

"I know you could."

"You know that's right," she answered. "This is how I see it— if they want to go, you need to keep them. If they want to stay, you should kick them out."

"It's a little perverse."

"Am I wrong?" She grinned.

"No." I took the clipboard with Ann Walsh's documentation and leafed through it. She'd arrived before eleven. She'd been drinking. Her alcohol level wasn't that high, but it was just high enough to do something stupid, like cut her wrists. Her roommate had found her and called 911. The questions to be answered were simple—why did she do it? And did she intend to do it again?

Easy stuff, the kind of thing a resident could handle. Why I— the recently appointed medical director for the university's mental health clinic—was here, had to do with a phone call from Ed, my oldest friend and the dean of the medical school. "Peter," he'd said, "I've got a situation with a student that I'd like you to handle . . . personally."

That's why I was here, and that was a big, albeit unstated, part of my job—buffer the students from the real world and keep bad publicity away from the university. Ann Walsh was a problem that needed to be fixed.

I walked the few yards that separated *them*—the patients— from *us*—the staff. She was in cubicle five, and as I knocked on the wall and pulled back the curtain, I had to fight to stay present. ERs and certain other situations, such as crash sites, have a way of setting my brain twitching. But as that curtain slid back, it wasn't just my own memories of lying in one of these cubicles, huddled in a ball and wanting to die, it was something unexpected, and it hit hard. In the filtered light that spilled from the common area

13

into Ann Walsh's cubicle I saw my wife, Beth. She turned and the illusion shattered, just a trick of the light that gave her hair the same coppery gold glimmer, and the way her head tilted on a long slender neck. Her eyes were different, the shape of her chin, her mouth—all different. Beautiful, but different.

"Ann," I said, trying to shake off an irrational bad feeling. "I'm Peter Grainger, Dr. Grainger."

"I'm not crazy," she stated, sizing me up through large blue eyes set in a face that could have been on the cover of *Vogue*.

"So what happened?" I sat on the hard-plastic chair bolted next to the bed.

"Everyone keeps asking me that. Like, why should anyone give two shits?"

"Did you tell anyone why you did it?"

"No." She cracked a smile and tucked a strand of wispy hair behind her ear.

"If you did, we'd stop asking. So yes, you've got to tell me."

"Or what?"

"Or you get trundled up to the psych unit until you're safe to go."

"I'm not going to do anything," she stated. "This was stupid, I was angry, I'd been drinking. You have no idea how much I regret this. Do you know what they've put me through? I could kill her."

"Who?"

"My roommate, Shana. I've been trying to get a private room, but . . ."

"What?"

"There's one way you can get a private room."

"Yes, I'm aware of the 'psycho singles,'" I said, sensing that she was flirting.

"Wouldn't this count—a trip to the emergency room?"

"You sure you want to play this up?"

14

"Good point," she said, wrapping her sheet tight. "So, how do I get out of here?"

"Tell me what happened."

"Jesus, you're persistent. There's no other way?"

"Nope."

"Where will this go?"

"What do you mean?"

"What I tell you . . . who's going to know? And don't tell me that everything is confidential, because I know that's not how this works."

"You're right, it's not that clean. You tried to hurt yourself, maybe to kill yourself; it's in your hospital record. The reasons you did it are inside your head; I need to know what they are. I probably won't have to get into the specifics with anyone else, but . . ."

"There's always a 'but,' isn't there?"

"Right. If you were to tell me that you were thinking of leaving here and stabbing Shana in cold-blooded revenge, I couldn't keep that to myself."

"What if I threatened to mix up her hair scrunchies and nail polish?"

"I'd take it to the grave."

"You know she color codes them?"

"Her nail polish?"

"Everything. That girl needs a shrink. If you so much as touch one of the bottles, she'll know. Plus, she's got bulimia, which—hey live and let live—but our bathroom reeks of puke and Pine-Sol. It's gross."

"Are you trying to tell me you did this to get away from your roommate?"

"Would that work?"

"Nah."

"Why are you so cheerful?" she asked.

Her question caught me off guard; over the past year "cheerful" is not a word I'd have used to describe myself. "Does it bother you?"

"No, I kind of like it, and you don't look much like a shrink."

"Are you trying to get off the subject?"

She sighed and pulled the sheet tightly around her shoulders, looking more like she should be at a spa than a downtown emergency room. "That sounded like a shrink. I suppose I'd better just get this over with."

I waited.

"Long or short version?" she asked.

"Start short; it's late."

"God, you're direct. Okay, it was my father. I was mad at my father."

"What about?" I asked and watched a tear form in the corner of her eye.

"I sometimes wonder why I even bother; it's always the same. You'd think by now I could have figured something out. I'm not a stupid person. I made it into medical school. I should know not to call him, but I had to."

"Because?"

"Because the bursar sent a registered letter telling me that I have two weeks to come up with tuition or I can pack my bags. He'd told me that he'd sent the check."

"He hadn't?"

"He never does, but sometimes I feel like believing him—that maybe he'll act like a normal father. I think I get that from my mom; she was quite the optimist." Ann looked up and I was struck by her expression, so young, so vulnerable, so beautiful.

"She's not around anymore?" I asked, clearing my throat.

"Dead. Berry aneurysm. Do you know what that is?"

I nodded, knowing from personal experience how having your mother die when you're a child changes everything.

"I was ten," she said. "I remember being told that my mother had died from a berry aneurysm. For the longest time I couldn't figure out how a blueberry or a strawberry could get inside her like that."

As she talked, I made dozens of observations, noting the shifts in her mood, the veneer of defensive humor over a sadness whose depth I could only guess. I glimpsed the ten-year-old she had been as she wrapped herself in a cocoon of hospital linen. I thought of my own mother's traumatic death when I was five.

"Are you an only child?"

"There's three of us, and if I don't do something to get them away from him, it's . . . it's not good."

"How old are they?"

"Jen is fourteen. Jason's a year younger than me."

"Does he abuse them?"

"He abuses everything, but not in a way that'll send a social worker to get Jen out of there."

"So what happened on the phone?"

"That's the kicker, because it wasn't any worse than dozens of other times. He'd been drinking—a lot. I'd been drinking a little, which didn't help. I asked him what happened to my tuition. He called me a slut. I told him to fuck off. There was some general screaming, and at some point I slammed the receiver."

"And this is how it goes with your dad?"

"Pretty much."

"So why cut your wrists?"

"You want logic? You're not going to get it, at least not with my dad. This isn't the first time I've seen a shrink about him."

"The other times, was it because you were thinking of killing yourself?"

"Why does it always have to come down to that? It's a pretty big leap from cutting my wrist to saying that I tried to kill myself."

"Good point."

"In fact, if I'd wanted to kill myself, I know what to do."

"Then what were you trying to do?"

"Okay, but you have to promise not to lock me up."

"Sorry." I shook my head.

She shrugged. "I wanted to feel pain. I had no intention of killing myself."

"It's not the first time you've done this?"

"No." She stared at the floor. "I don't do it often, and I don't know what possessed me for the all-out drama fest. I don't usually break the skin; I just bite the inside of my mouth or pinch myself really hard, but after five minutes on the phone with Carter Walsh I needed something to pull me back."

The name instantly registered. "Your father is Carter Walsh, the writer?"

"Used-to-be writer. Now he's just a drunk."

"He knows you're here?"

"I sure didn't tell him, but he'd love to see me locked up. That way everyone would know that I was the fucked-up one and he could play the ministering angel."

I glanced up and saw Grace's outline on the other side of the curtain; it was after four on a Sunday morning. As my dad—a shrink like me—would say, "Time to fish or cut bait." The fishing was almost over. "Ann, let's recap. You cut yourself after a blowup with your dad, you had no intention of killing yourself, and if I let you out of here, you're not going to do anything like that again, at least not tonight."

"You're going to let me out?" She sat up, and the sheet slid back, revealing soft shoulders and, through the gaping straps of a blue paper gown, the tops of perfect breasts. "I swear I'm not going to do anything."

18

I tore my gaze from her nakedness. "There's one condition."

"Name it."

"Follow up. I want to meet with you after you go home and get some sleep. Do you know where the school's mental health clinic is?"

"Yeah. I went there last year; it didn't work out."

"You know what? This is more information than we need now. We'll get into that tomorrow, or rather, later today. Do you have any questions?"

I could see she was going to ask me something, but didn't.

"So I'll see you at the clinic. Say, ten?"

"Four?" She shot back.

"Noon."

"Two?"

"Deal. Then on Monday we'll hook you up with a therapist."

She was all smiles as she rearranged her gown, as if she knew that she'd nearly exposed herself. "I don't want to tell you your business, but me and therapy hasn't worked out real well."

"Let's not make that decision now; let's keep the options open, okay?"

"You bet."

I left her cubicle. Grace was waiting. "Does she stay or does she go?"

"She goes, with an appointment to see me at the clinic." I filled out the ER intake form and completed the narrative with a couple lines of cover-your-ass legalese. *Patient consistently and repeatedly denied any thoughts of wanting to harm herself and was not deemed gravely disabled.*

As I walked to the security door, I glanced at Ann's cubicle. The curtain was drawn. I felt a stab of doubt. *What if she wasn't okay? Why didn't I ask her more about what happened last year at the clinic?* Something in my gut wasn't sitting right. The problem was, I couldn't tell if it had to do with Ann or with me. Glimpsing

19

her bare feet under the curtain, I reran the interview and reminded myself that she was low risk for suicide. *Yeah Peter, but what didn't she tell you?* I felt doubt, paralyzing and irrational. *Fish or cut bait.*

"Grace, I'm out of here. I hope the rest of your night is quiet."

"You too." she unlocked the door. "And get some sleep."

OUTSIDE, IT WAS FACE-NUMBING COLD. Fall had slipped into an early winter and New York had been blasted with an ice storm and six inches of powdery white snow earlier in the week. It had all turned to a frozen mush that made every step an exercise in balance.

I cut through Washington Square Park, where the bare branches painted a black-lace veil against the sky. I was glad for my fur-lined bomber jacket and for the ski cap and gloves I'd tucked in the pockets before heading out. Even so, as I turned east, the wind burned my cheeks. I thought of Ann and how she just wanted to feel the pain. I knew what she meant; there's something grounding about physical pain. In the few minutes I'd spent with her, I'd learned a lot. Apply that to my professional life, which has been spent studying, treating, and writing about trauma, and you get a bit further. Until a year ago I thought that was enough; I was the expert—trust me, I'm a doctor. People published my books; my name was attached to a model for working with trauma survivors—all sorts of good stuff. Then a car went out of control, and my brain, which used to be a good friend of mine, decided it was going to teach me some new tricks.

These were the things that ran through my head as my feet carried me past Astor Place, the newly constructed NYU dormitories, and the faded Punk Rock glory of St. Mark's Place. About halfway down the block between First and Avenue A my ears perked at the sound of voices. There were three men—young and rowdy—and I was on their radar. I quickened my pace to see what they would do. They sped up.

"Shit!" I muttered. When in doubt, I'm a firm believer in running away. Not that I'm a coward; it's just easier. But now, less than two blocks from my loft and my sleeping fourteen-year-old son, Kyle, I had no intention of leading a group of thuggies home. As I hit the center of a streetlight's glow, I stopped and turned. They were closer than I had thought; barely ten feet separated me from the front man, a boy really, with matted hair that jutted out from a filthy-looking cap. At six foot two, I had the height advantage. I made eye contact with each of them and then settled on their leader.

"Give us money," he said.

"No," I told him. I noticed that his nose was dripping and what I really wanted to offer him was a tissue.

"Give us your money." He lunged, brandishing a box cutter.

I pivoted, and my right hand found a particularly painful pressure point in the back of his wrist. I twisted up and back. With my left, I pushed him to the ground, leveraging his shoulder while keeping his buddies in sight. The weapon lay in the gutter.

He shrieked in pain. "Let go of me!"

I eased up without loosening my grip. I held him on the verge of agony as I thought through my options. I didn't have to think long. One of the other boys spotted a patrol car heading down the block. "Shit! Come on, Carl!" Without waiting, they sprinted off.

"Let go of me!"

"There's a cop coming." I gave his arm some play and let him get to his feet, although I kept his wrist trapped—one of the joys of aikido, which I've practiced since elementary school—it offers the practitioner a great deal of control.

"Let me go. Please, let me go."

This seemed to be the evening's theme. First Ann, now this

kid. "Why should I? You tried to mug me." His body trembled beneath the layers of an old army coat, a hooded sweatshirt, and God knows what else. "Where do you live?" I asked, figuring I'd walk him home and let his parents deal with him.

"In a squat. Please, don't let them take me." There was raw fear in his voice.

"Why not?" I asked as the cops spotted us: a tall man in a black leather jacket and a crusty teenager apparently holding hands in the lamplight.

"Please, don't let them take me. They'll lock me up."

I moved him out of the center of the light.

"I can't go back there." He begged.

The patrol car was now even with us. It stopped, and a male officer rolled down the window. "Everything okay here?"

The kid was in a panic, and I knew if I let go, he'd bolt, which would only ensure the cops pursuing him. The smart thing would have been to tell them the truth. *Crusty boy tried to mug me. He's all yours, and have a pleasant night.* "Everything's fine," I lied. "He's a friend of my son's who shouldn't be out. I'm Dr. Grainger. I work at the University. Right now, I'm trying to figure if I'm going to cover for him or just hand him over to his mom." I knew that if the officers got out and took a closer look at the boy, they'd know he was a runaway and I'd look like a pedophile.

"You okay, kid?"

"No problem," he answered. "Please don't tell my mom," he said, improvising on my lie.

Apparently it was good enough, or else it was so cold they didn't want to leave their cruiser. "You'll bring him home, Dr. Grainger?" the officer asked as he rolled up the window.

"I will," I assured him, and watched as they drove off. "If I let go of you, are you going to run?"

"No."

I let go; he bolted. I shouted after him, "Hey, if you want a few bucks for food . . ."

He stopped, looked back at me. "No, but thanks." Then he sprinted away, vanishing quickly.

Overhead, day was breaking, a vivid streak of red against the eastern sky. I walked the last block and a half to Tompkins Square Park. The gates were locked, but I could glimpse the darkened windows of my third-floor loft on the other side. The iron-fronted building had started its life as a tool factory. For a few decades after that it had served as a sweatshop and then it had gone derelict. In the 1980s it had been bought and sold by a series of developers who never did anything with it, and then as the East Village became trendy, it got rehabbed into lofts. I had been fortunate to get such a great apartment, but like so many things in my life now, I had little to do with it. My new job at the university and my loft were gifts from Ed. Not literal gifts—I was more than qualified and the money was mine—it's just . . . it's just, Ed had thrown me a lifeline and had smoothed the way to a new life. So when he had called me up to ask me to see Ann Walsh in the emergency room in the dead of night, there was no question that I'd go.

As I got into the elevator and pulled the gate closed, I thought about how quickly things can change. Just one year ago I was living with my wife and son in Cambridge; we were expecting our second child. It was the happiest time in my life. Everything was in place—my career, Beth's career, Kyle was doing well in school and completely addicted to basketball. It was a very good time. And then, after years of trying and having pretty much accepted the verdict of our fertility specialist, Beth got pregnant—and not just a little pregnant, like the times before when she'd miscarried.

The elevator lurched and hiccoughed to a stop. I yanked back the steel gate and took a slow breath to try to quiet my thoughts.

Beth wasn't a little pregnant; she was a lot pregnant, seven months. A viable child burned to death inside of her, a little girl.

I turned the two locks and slid the bolt on the banded-steel-and-oak door. Inside, the radiators hissed and gurgled. To my right I saw the brightening sky through the windows and the shadowy treetops in the park below. Most of the loft was open. My father—a psychiatrist by trade and carpenter by nature—had helped Kyle and me sheet rock out two bedrooms, a kitchen, a study, and a bathroom. It was the best therapy I could have done. Like Ann with pain, there's something grounding about a pneumatic hammer.

I went toward the back and gently opened Kyle's door. He was dead to the world, his long body sprawled facedown on the diagonal, our tortoiseshell coon cat, Willy, curled at the foot of his bed. I watched him, not moving until I could reassure myself that his chest moved in and out as he breathed. I thought about the street kids. Where were they now? Were they warm? Did they have enough to eat?

I closed the door and looked toward the dark opening of my own bedroom. *Who am I kidding?* No way I'd fall asleep. Whether it was the emergency room or almost getting mugged, my nerves were sizzling. Every creak of the floorboards or clang of the elevator made my head twist. Why even lie down? It would just make it worse. Instead, I went into my cavelike study with its steel-barred fire-escape window. I switched on the light and sat behind the massive rolltop desk, an anniversary present from Beth, and one of the few pieces of furniture I had taken from Cambridge. The walls were covered with bookshelves, and in one corner was a stack of boxes from my publisher, unopened and filled with copies of my books. I was nothing if not prolific. Even now, it was one of the few things that kept me going: my son, my father, and my work. Without meaning to, my hand reached down to a locked cabinet drawer. Inside it were all of my forbidden goodies, the things I needed to stay away from.

I unlocked it, and pulled out the worn manila envelopes, the reams of police reports, and the notarized copy of the fire marshall's findings. There were stacks of photographs taken both the night of the accident and the morning after. There were pictures of the wreckage; there were pictures of Beth. I had the autopsy reports, both Beth's and our unborn little girl's. Then, as I'd done dozens of times before, I searched for answers. Certain things had come back. I knew that we had gone out to talk about something important, that we had wanted to do it away from Kyle. We didn't do that often, only if we thought there might be an argument. I had been driving; there were no skid marks and no signs of mechanical failure. The final finding was that, for some unknown reason, just over a year ago, I had rammed our midnight blue Audi into a granite wall and killed my pregnant wife.

KYLE GRAINGER DRAGGED HIMSELF OUT of bed. His feet found the *wicked good* L.L. Bean slippers that Grandpa Michael had given him last Christmas—the Christmas in hell. He pulled on a Knicks T-shirt and ventured into the chill of the open loft. Morning sun drew a sharp line of light and shadow on the golden-oak floors. He squinted and turned toward his father's bedroom. He knew that Dad had gotten called to the ER late, and as Kyle walked to his door, he said a prayer. "Please God, let him be asleep."

He peered in at the neatly made bed and felt a wave of disappointment. He walked around the granite kitchen counter, back toward the bathroom, and saw light streaming from under the office door. He thought about knocking, but just twisted the handle instead. He stood there, taking it in: his father passed out at his desk, dark stubble sprouting on his face, his arms strewn over a slurry of black-and-white photos. Kyle picked up a photocopied document from the floor; it was his mother's autopsy report. "Fuck!" It dropped from his fingers. He backed out of the room and resisted the urge to slam the door. *No, can't do that, because at least he's sleeping.* He went to the kitchen phone and pressed the first number on the speed dial.

He breathed easier at the sound of the phone being picked up. "Grandpa?"

"Hey kiddo." His grandfather's deep voice entered his ear. "What's up?"

"He's doing it again," Kyle said, trying hard not to cry.

"Details."

"The police stuff, all of it. He's in his office, passed out on top of it."

"Is he taking the medication?"

"I don't know. You want me to check?"

"Not yet, it's probably just a blip. Remember, we talked about how people get better and then fall back a bit. It's not a straight line, like getting over a cold."

"I know, but he was doing good. He's going to work. He's writing again, so . . ."

"So you think he's back to the dad you used to know?"

Kyle gazed up at the stamped-tin ceiling. "No, I don't think he's ever coming back, not all the way. I'm okay with that." Then, with a telltale Grainger guffaw he said, "It's not like anyone's giving me a choice."

"Tell you what, kiddo. Put on a pot of coffee, let him sleep, and I'll be down there in . . . give me forty-five minutes."

"Is Sheila there?" Kyle needled.

"Yes. And?"

"Nothing." Kyle smiled, thinking about his grandfather's lady friend.

"That's what I thought. I'll see you in a bit. And Kyle?"

"Yes?"

"It's going to be all right."

2

DETECTIVE, SECOND GRADE NICOLE SULLIVAN sat rigid in the dark next to Dr. Boris Singer, a child psychiatrist and cofounder of the Garden School. In front of them, on the other side of a two-way mirror, they watched her six-year-old red-headed daughter, Adriana, resist the friendly overtures of a perky female therapist in a brightly lit playroom. The therapist held a rag doll and gestured for Adriana to take it. The girl, dressed in her favorite overalls with an appliquéd penguin, looked fearfully at the toy and then back at the door.

"Thank you for seeing us on a Sunday," Nicole whispered, her features shadowed in the curve of her shoulder-length auburn hair. She watched Adriana, wishing that she'd take the doll.

"It goes with the territory," Dr. Singer commented. "If you work with kids you need hours that parents can live with. Did you look at our brochure?"

"It's impressive," she replied, having not only leafed through the glossy materials for the Garden School, but also done extensive research on anything related to it. What she had learned was that this therapeutic school, nestled close to Gramercy, had a reputation for getting results with badly traumatized children. The kicker was that they didn't take insurance and the annual fees ran around fifty grand—more than her annual take-home salary. She leaned forward as the therapist rolled a wooden dollhouse into the center of the room. At home, Adriana could spend hours playing with Nicole's old dollhouse. If anything would grab her attention, this was it.

Nicole held her breath as Adriana shifted her focus from the door to the wooden house. "You think Adriana would do well here?" she asked, not wanting her desperation to show.

"I do."

She liked the directness of this bespectacled psychiatrist. No hedging, a straight answer to a straight question. Which put the ball back into her court.

"I wonder," he said, "if I could get a bit more of the history. I have some, but . . ."

The attractive, hazel-eyed detective nodded. At least it was dark, in case she started to cry. "Adriana had just turned four when I noticed some changes. She started to go backward. She began to wet her bed and her clothes. Same with talking, she was very verbal, couldn't shut her up, and then she was back to baby sounds, or no sounds, for days. She got clingy, kind of the way she was at two. Every time I came into the house she'd grab on to me and wouldn't let go. If I tried to leave, she'd start screaming—not a little, but shrieking, and shaking. Even now, she gets very upset when I go out."

"And her father?"

Nicole's chest tightened, "Donny? No. She'd cry every time he'd go to pick her up or even touch her."

"That must have been hard for him."

Nicole snuck a sideways glance at the psychiatrist; she wondered how much he knew. Or was it that he'd seen so many Adrianas, he knew how the story went? "It wasn't easy."

"What happened next?"

"I took her to our pediatrician. That's when I learned that my daughter had been molested. That was two years ago."

"I know this is hard, but could you run me through what's happened since?"

She nodded, surprised to see Adriana take a wooden doll from the therapist and begin playing with it in the house. "Okay, our pediatrician—Dr. Bryant—told me that she had to file a report with the Administration for Children's Services. I've done it myself. But when it's your child . . . Donny and I were interviewed, both of us in shock. There was even talk that Adriana would be put in foster care. If we both hadn't been cops that might have happened. In the beginning, Donny didn't believe the allegation."

"But not you?"

"No. It made sense, and there was also some physical stuff I'd noticed, but I hadn't even considered that someone would do that to a four-year-old." Yet even as she said that, Nicole shuddered and thought about another little girl—Tabitha Robinson—whom she and her partner, Hector, had found dead two years ago. The perpetrator had been a serial sexual offender three weeks out of prison. Kid murders were always bad, but Tabitha's had hit harder than any before or since: the timing of it, the girl's age— the same as Adriana's—the fact that her mother, an administrative assistant, had never dreamed that the day-care center would hire a janitor without doing a background check.

"Physical stuff?" Dr. Singer asked.

Nicole tried to will herself numb. "When I bathed her, there was redness. I thought it was irritation from her wetting herself; it wasn't."

"You figured out who was responsible?"

"Yes . . . Uncle Bob. By the end, there was no doubt."

"Can I get you some water?" Dr. Singer asked.

"No, I'll just barrel through; it's easier. Bob was Donny's uncle. He'd baby-sit. I found out later that he'd done things before, and no one had ever said anything."

"You must be very angry."

"I was furious. I still am, but there's nothing more I can do about him. He hung himself in lockup."

"You're lucky," he said, taking her by surprise.

"Yes," she admitted. "It saved us a trial and ACS closed the case based on evidence."

"They did a rape kit?"

"No, his sperm was . . ." Her throat constricted as she remembered the sickening moment when her daughter's panties were examined under a Wood's light and the stains fluoresced a glowing purple, just like Tabitha's.

"I understand," he said. "How did your husband deal with all of this?"

"Not well. We've been separated for nearly a year."

"Will you divorce?"

"I don't know. We talk, but being around Adriana, the way she is now; it's too hard for him."

"Interesting," the doctor commented as he gazed through the two-way mirror.

"My marriage?"

"What Adriana's doing."

Nicole stared into the well-lit playroom. The therapist was kneeling next to the little girl in front of the wooden house; they were both holding dolls.

"You see how every time the therapist tries to make her doll interact with Adriana's, your daughter's doll runs away."

"That's like what happened the few times we tried to send her to regular school. She'd run from the kids and the teachers, and we'd get a call to bring her home. Even with the self-contained classes, she runs away the minute the door opens."

"What have they said at her Parent-Pupil-Teacher meetings?"

"Lots of things, and I always leave feeling like I'm doing it all wrong."

"You're a detective, correct?"

"Yes."

"That's a tough job. What sort of cases do you handle?"

"Homicide."

"Wow! How do you manage to take care of Adriana by yourself? My understanding is that detective work is a tough job with very long hours."

"I moved back in with my mother," Nicole admitted, remembering how hard that had been, like admitting your entire adult life was a failure. "She has a three-family in Park Slope; it's where I grew up. She takes care of Adriana during the day. She's the only other person that Adriana is okay around."

"She'd be able to get her in and out of here?"

"I'm sure she would, but I think you should know . . ."

"That detectives don't make the kind of money that allows their kids to go to a place like this?"

"Right. This all sounds great; I just can't afford it."

"Don't be so sure. You've got a strong case. It's going to take some work, and I'll need a stack of releases to talk with her teachers and the school psychologist. What it boils down to is whether the school system can provide your daughter an education. If they can't, and we can, we've got room to negotiate."

"The school psychologist told me that Adriana had a type of autism and that there wasn't much that could be done for her."

Boris Singer sighed as he looked at the little girl, who was playing a strange game. Once the therapist had realized that Adriana would remove her doll from a room whenever hers entered, she had pushed that further into a raucous game of two dolls frantically chasing after each other through and around the house. Adriana giggled and squealed as she tried to keep her doll one room away from that of the therapist. "No," Doctor Singer reassured, "your daughter is not autistic, but you're going to have to be prepared for a battle. Kids who've been traumatized behave in one of two ways. They either lash out and are totally disruptive in a classroom or, like Adriana, they regress, withdraw, and become depressed. The first group tends to get the resources, because . . . well, because they're so potentially dangerous you have to do something. It's the quiet ones who don't get what they need."

Nicole watched her daughter and listened. The game was getting wilder, and she struggled to hold back the tears; Adriana was giggling and smiling. "If you're telling me that you can get my daughter back to the way she was, I will do whatever it takes," she said, trying to remember the last time she'd seen Adriana happy. She clung to the moment, wondering how long it could last.

"I don't make false promises," Dr. Singer said, "but if we could get her for the rest of this school year and the summer as well, we have a shot at getting her back into the mainstream for second grade."

ADRIANA'S PINK MITTENED HAND HELD tight to her mother's as they walked away from the Garden School. It had been a hard morning and Nicole savored the head-clearing December air. After being told so many horrible things—that Adriana was a hopeless case, autistic, doomed—she felt a surge of hope. "Hey, peanut." She looked down at her daughter in her overalls, rubber boots, and puffy pink parka. "Let's get some lunch." Adriana smiled up, and Nicole stopped. She scooped her little girl into her arms and kissed her on the cheeks. She held her tightly, smelling the sweet fragrance of baby shampoo and thinking through what she'd tell Donny. She remembered their last conversation, when she'd told him about taking Adriana for this evaluation. "When is it going to end?" he'd asked. "How God damn long is my daughter going to have to see all these shrinks! Do they help? All I do is write fucking checks! Is she getting any better? When the hell is this going to end?"

Nicole hugged Adriana tight. *You are going to get better.* Even now, there were nights she didn't wake up crying, and there were days that Nicole could leave the house without a teary scene. Okay, so maybe she couldn't last more than an hour or two at school. This was still a hell of a lot better than where they had started. And if Dr. Singer thought he could get her back to the land of the normal, no one would stop her. She had to get the school psychologist—the one who wanted to diagnose Adriana as autistic—to put in writing that Adriana needed the Garden School. That Nicole loathed the woman, with her condescending kindergarten voice and her office filled with posters of kittens and puppies, was a minor annoyance. At least now she had a clear direction and hope; what she didn't have was time. Everything Nicole had read, which was considerable, talked about the importance of keeping kids on the developmental curve. Two years out of a six-year-old's life was huge.

"Mommy?"

"What, peanut."

"Was that a school?"

"Yes."

"Am I going to go there?"

"Would you like that?" Nicole asked, rubbing her cold nose against her daughter's.

"That lady with the dolls was funny. I told her about my house that Grandpa Henry built."

"Did you?" Nicole marveled, noting that Adriana had more

interaction with the therapist than she'd had with any of the teachers at her school. "I think maybe you will go there."

Adriana pursed her cupid-bow lips, looked intently into her mother's eyes, and said, "Okay."

3

I SAT ACROSS FROM MY father, who, with his salt-and-pepper beard, red flannel shirt, and jeans, looked more like a carpenter than a psychiatrist, and I wondered if there comes a time where you know that you're finally and absolutely an adult. If so, this wasn't it.

Light streamed through my loft windows as I nursed my second mug of coffee. Kyle was nowhere to be seen. "Dad, let's cut to the chase. The kid squealed on me, didn't he?"

"He's worried."

"I know, but I'm nowhere near back to where I was last winter."

"Granted, Peter. It's hard for Kyle; your breakdown short-circuited what he needed to do after Beth's death. He wants things back the way they were."

"Tell me something I don't know," I said, feeling the guilt. "Fathers are supposed to be strong. What did he tell you?"

"That he found you passed out with all of the stuff you'd promised to get rid of."

I really needed to put a lock on my office door. "Dad, I can't, and I don't want to get into a long discussion. It's just—how can I move on when I don't have answers? I lose Beth, our baby, and I have no clue why it happened. I'll throw out the whole morbid lot once I know."

"And if you never know?" he asked. "What then?"

The problem with being a shrink and having one for a father is that we have a way of getting to the questions that are best left alone. "I don't know," I told him, wondering what I could say to make him understand. "Look . . . Dad, I don't tell you enough how grateful I am for all you've done. I mean, dropping everything and coming down here, it's . . ."

"I love you, Peter."

"I know; it's mutual, and Kyle's crazy about you, and I'm a little jealous that you're the one he's come to count on. We can talk later, but right now I need to get it together and meet with a seriously disturbed medical student."

"On a Sunday?"

"Yup, fished her out of the emergency room last night, and before I assign her to a resident, I need to make sure I haven't made some horrible mistake."

"She sounds borderline. You think it's wise meeting when no one's around?"

"I'll see her in the walk-in. There's always somebody there."

"Look, Peter, if you want me to back off, I will."

"Nah, it's okay," I told him, admiring how well he looked with his newly cultivated beard. "I know that you wouldn't be here if you weren't worried. I see it in your eyes, Kyle's, too; it kills me. I wish there were something I could say that would make you feel better, but the truth is I'm still . . ."

"Not yourself."

"Don't complete my sentences," I said, wondering what he would say if he knew that I'd stopped taking my psychiatric medications two months ago.

"Was I wrong?"

I chuckled. "No. It's just annoying."

"Sorry. By the way, I saw your article in the *Green Journal*."

"Which one?"

"The one comparing combat veterans with survivors of 9/11. Your writing's changed."

"Did you like it?"

"Very much, it just seemed more . . ."

"Personal."

"I'm surprised it made it past the reviewers."

"I'm trying something new," I told him as I got up and grabbed my jacket. "We hide behind science. And the one thing I've learned from this god-awful year is that science is supposed to describe life, not the other way. But if you pick up any of those journals, you wouldn't know that they have any relationship to people."

He started to clap.

"Did I get on a soapbox?"

"A little, but you're right."

WE PARTED WITH A BEAR hug on the corner of First Avenue. It reminded me of the times he'd put me on the train to go to college; I half expected him to slip me a twenty. Only back then, I suspect I was more worried about him going home to an empty house than he was about me. Ever since Mom died, he and I had been a self-contained unit. Funny how history was repeating itself with the Grainger men. It turned out I needn't have worried. As Dad later told me, he'd chosen not to remarry or even to date while I was still in school. Once he'd shipped me off to college, that changed, and within two months, Sheila—an Upper West Side widow who I liked entered his life.

As I headed toward the clinic I thought about what he'd said. Yes, my obsession with the accident was unhealthy, but that's the nature of obsessions; they're *not* healthy. Besides, knowing what I did about trauma, I wasn't doing that badly. If it weren't for the flashbacks, the nightmares, and those annoying blackouts—like I'd had in the ER—I'd be back to normal.

When I walked past the giant rotating cube on Astor Place, I spotted a pack of street kids and wondered if Carl, the kid from last night, was among them.

I stopped and really looked, not certain what I would have done had he been there. Probably I would have tried to talk to him and give him some food money, but he wasn't there, or else he saw me first and took off.

I ARRIVED AT THE CLINIC, a five-story 1950s redbrick building just west of Washington Square Park. I breezed past the silver-haired guard with a "Hi George."

"Hey, Doc, what you doing here on a Sunday?"

"Nothing good."

I had wanted to get here before Ann and review her old records. I took the stairs to the fourth floor, shut off the alarm, and went inside. The clinic, which was founded just after World War II, occupied the entire floor. Each year, one-tenth of the student body, both graduate and undergraduate, sought some sort of service here. It was mostly counseling, something that was hard to find in the managed-care world outside the university. That Ann had been here was not earth-shattering. In fact, based on her trip to the ER and what little bit of her story she'd told me, it wouldn't have surprised me if she'd done a whole lot of therapy.

I walked passed the kidney-shaped reception desk and into the hall of a thousand therapists. Actually, it was more like two dozen, an assortment of psychiatry, psychology and social-work trainees, and half a dozen faculty such as myself. At the far end, where I was headed, was the medical records room.

Once inside, I retrieved the keys to the filing cabinets from their hiding place under the transcriptionist's desk. I found the cabinet that contained "U–W," but I couldn't find Ann's records. "That's strange," I muttered, feeling a twinge of frustration. Not many people lie about having seen a therapist; it usually goes the other way. I booted up the computer, typed in my password, and located Ann's account with the health plan. It showed that she'd been registered at the clinic and had come on a weekly basis for a good chunk of last year. "So where are her fucking records?"

I logged off and went back to the drawer, thinking it got misfiled, I leafed through every chart. "Damn!" I checked the drawers above and below. This was bad. There's nothing worse than meeting with a borderline patient without having some history either to corroborate or discount the stories that get twisted through a chaotic psyche. What made it stranger was that according to the computer, she'd been coming for a while. Which . . . Why the hell didn't Ed say anything when he'd called me about her? Not that I'd know every patient, but as the clinic's director, which up until August had been Ed's job, I would have been familiar with the names.

Although . . . was that true? As I locked up and headed toward the stairwell, I realized that I knew about all of the *problem* students. If Ann had come for therapy and been a bread-and-butter case, Ed might never have heard about her. That thought was quickly beaten down by the memory of the beautiful blonde whose father was Carter Walsh, author of one of the most powerful Vietnam novels ever written. Ann Walsh was a girl who'd get noticed.

Back on the ground floor, I walked past George toward the walk-in clinic. This was a sort of twenty-four-hour alternative to the ER. I stopped and looked around the waiting area. Ann wasn't there, and it was now five past two. I felt a pang of anxiety—maybe she was worse off than she'd let on in the emergency room.

I went back to the treatment area, said hello to the internist, and found a suitable room for meeting with Ann. I leafed through a couple safe-sex brochures and one entitled *Know Your Crab Lice*, and then went back out to see if she'd arrived; she hadn't. It was now time for a round of catastrophic *what ifs?* What if I shouldn't have let her leave the ER? What if she were floating in a bathtub full of blood, having slit her wrists?

"Dr. Grainger?"

"Ann." I turned and immediately felt better.

"Am I late?"

"Not really." It took me a moment to recognize the striking young woman before me. She was dressed in jeans, black T-shirt, boots, and a leather jacket. Her eyes were clear and a lighter blue than I remembered. Her face was unlined, her symmetrical features framed by a curtain of honey blond hair. It was easy to imagine her as the dream date of her medical school class. "We can meet in back," I told her.

"We're not going to the fourth floor?"

"It's pretty deserted on the weekends."

"Scared to be alone with me?" Her tone was light and flirtatious.

I led her back to the small conference room, with its orange plastic chairs and a laminated faux wood table in the center. As we settled, I asked, "How are you doing?"

"Better. I wanted to thank you. Someone else might have locked me up."

"Have you ever been admitted to a psychiatric unit?"

"Not yet, but I'm still young."

"Did you see your roommate when you got back?"

"She was asleep. I heard her this morning. I don't think she was happy to see me."

"Is she also a medical student?"

"Thank God, no. Although I'm sure by tomorrow everyone will know."

"How will you handle that?" I asked.

"I don't know; I'm pretty good at dropping the blinders."

"The what?"

"Mental blinders. I used to ride horses, and after my mom died I found that if I pretended to wear blinders, things didn't hurt so much. It's kind of evolved; now it's more like steel shutters. You just drop them down, plant a smile on your face, and everyone thinks that Ann is a happy person."

I wondered if she was doing that now. "So, when you walk into class, you'll be wearing steel shutters?"

"Pretty much."

"What about friends? People you can talk to?"

"No. I don't make friends easily."

"A boyfriend?"

She snorted, "How do you define boyfriend?"

"Someone you're romantically involved with?"

"Sure, why not?"

"That's cryptic."

"It's complicated and not something I want to go into, at least not yet."

"Fair enough . . . it sounds like you're pretty much on your own."

She looked directly at me. "I like it that way. I don't trust people."

I felt her testing me, wondering if I'd be someone else who'd let her down. "Last night you'd mentioned coming to the clinic before."

She rolled her eyes.

"You've got to give me more than that. What happened?"

"It was a bad fit. I don't think I'm a beginner patient."

"You were working with a resident?"

"Yes."

I thought through my roster of trainees. "Who?"

"I don't think he's here anymore, but I don't want to talk about that."

I thought about her steel-shutter analogy; it was apt. I felt myself banging up against one closed door after another, and considering the concerns I had about her, that wasn't good. I decided to go long. "Ann, have you always been depressed like this?"

She stared at me, about to refute what I'd just said. I held her gaze, and for several moments neither one of us spoke. Finally, she broke the silence. Her shoulders slumped, and she turned in her chair. "Ever since my mom died."

Her steel shutters cracked, and something resonated with my own empty lump of what it means to lose your mother. "Tell me about her."

"I miss her so much. None of this would have happened if she were alive. She had a way of keeping everything together."

"Including your father?" I asked, seeing her fragility, her sadness.

"She could handle him. He was different with her. I mean, he drank, but it was parties and summers in the Hamptons. He was even writing. It was something of a joke—his next novel—but he did publish some stuff, enough to keep the illusion alive."

"What was she like?"

"I have a picture of her, of all of us on a boat. She's holding Jen, Jason looks normal, and everyone is smiling . . . and it's real. I have to look at that picture to remind myself that she was there; it's like she's slipping away, and one day she'll be gone."

"How did things change when she died?" I asked, remembering my mother's funeral, Dad never once letting go of my hand.

"It's funny, but there's a lot I can't remember, and I don't know when it was that I realized he was drinking so much. There was always booze around, but now there was no pretense about no drinking before five. Which, if he were a happy drunk, might be okay, but any noise, any problem, can set him off and he starts screaming. Jason got the worst of it; he'd really lay into him. Sometimes he'd apologize, but even that stopped. It's like a war zone."

"What about other family? Did anyone try to help?"

"They might have, but it wouldn't have worked. He wouldn't let them."

"I don't understand."

"It's hard to describe, but Carter has a talent for pissing people off. Even if someone wanted to help, he wouldn't let them, and he'd do it in a way that they wouldn't try again. And there's some sort of bad blood between him and my mom's family. I rarely saw my grandparents when she was alive, and then not at all." Ann looked at me. "I think they thought Carter wasn't good enough for her. They were right."

"So you have no one."

She shook her head.

"What about your brother?"

"Jason." Tears started. "I hardly ever cry," she said. "I feel like such an idiot." She wiped her eyes with her sleeve. As she did, I glimpsed the bandages from last night. "Jason has problems," she continued. "I think he has schizophrenia."

I was about to caution her against diagnosing family members as part of her intro to psychiatry course, but instead I asked, "What makes you say that?"

"He's not right. He used to be okay. I remember the two of us working together at a restaurant in Montauk. I must have been seventeen, so he would have been sixteen. That summer he was okay, and then I went to college. When I came home on break, he was strange, like something in his eyes. He'd stare at the wall, and when you asked him what he was looking at, he wouldn't tell you. Then I started getting calls from Carter, asking me if I'd seen Jason. He just started disappearing, which I didn't think all that much about, considering how Dad treated him. And then one day

I was walking through the park, and I don't know why, but I stopped and looked behind me, and there he was. I didn't see him at first; it was bizarre, like he was hiding."

"What did you do?"

"I asked him why he was following me, and he started talking nonsense. I told him that he was scaring me. I thought he was on drugs."

"Was he?"

"Maybe. I tried to bring him to the emergency room, but he ran away. I told Dad what had happened. I told him that Jason needed professional help."

"And?"

"He told me to shut up. That was four years ago, and every so often I turn around or I look across the street, and there's Jason. It's like he's watching me, but whenever I try to talk to him he mostly runs away."

"That's very strange," I said, struggling for words and wanting to comfort her.

She laughed. "No shit!"

"It doesn't seem to bother you that much. Am I missing something?"

"It's not like he's hurting anybody, and at least I can see him and know that he's okay. I mean, it's weird, and he needs help, but it's . . . I like seeing him."

"Okay . . ." I didn't know where to go next. If she were telling the truth, her life was a nightmare. "Last night you told me that it was because of a fight with your father that you cut yourself. You said it had something to do with his not paying the tuition."

"That's right."

"How do you cope with that? It seems like a big deal."

"I'll figure something out," she said, clearly not telling me everything. "This isn't the first time he's pulled this. Last night he just got the better of me."

"It really does sound like a war zone. These constant battles with your dad, the screaming on the telephone—it must be horrible."

"It's not that bad," she said, dabbing the corner of her eye with a fingertip. "Or if it is, I'm so used to it that I don't think about it. You know," she said with a wry smile, "when I was growing up, there was a TV show that I loved. It was a sitcom with a family that had two girls and a boy, and I used to wonder what it would be like to be part of that family. Years later I saw one of those 'Whatever Happened to?' shows and the oldest daughter was on it. Turns out she had anorexia and had nearly died. They were even thinking about replacing her on the show because her weight was so out of control."

"What made you think of that?"

"It's like my life; on the outside, it looks okay. My dad has a nice house, which he'll eventually lose. I'm smart, I'm pretty, I'm going to be a doctor. It looks okay."

"But it doesn't feel that way," I offered.

"No."

"Ann, I'm going to recommend that you start back in therapy. What do you think about that?"

"I guess. I have to do something. But no pills—at least not yet."

"You've been on antidepressants?" I asked.

"Not really. They've been prescribed, but I've never taken them for more than a day or two. They make me jumpy."

"We don't have to go there yet. Any chance you could come back tomorrow? I'd like to see you one more time before deciding which therapist to have you work with."

"Not again. Can't you see me?" There was a pleading look in her eyes.

"Probably not." But as I said that I had a number of competing thoughts. Ann, as she had so correctly identified, was not a "beginning patient" and shouldn't go to one of the trainees. Beyond that, her story had hit me hard; I wasn't certain if it was our shared experience or that this was a young woman I knew I could help. Or was it because she was the daughter of a man who wrote one of my favorite books?

"I feel comfortable with you," she explained. "I'm not sure I would with somebody else."

"Let me think about it," I told her, making eye contact, wanting her to know that things would work out. "We'll decide tomorrow. Okay?"

She looked away.

"Is that okay?" I repeated, knowing that I had somehow let her down.

She nodded, but wouldn't look at me. "Sure."

As she walked out the door I couldn't quiet the feeling that something bad was brewing.

4

ED TYSON SWIVELED BACK IN a black-leather Eames chair. His corner office, part of a penthouse suite overlooking Washington Square Park, was a well-composed mix of tribal artifacts from his expeditions to the Amazon and mid-twentieth-century furniture, mostly from the Cincinnati School of Design. On the floor lay an antique Sarouk, its background faded to pale rose by the sunlight that streamed through the floor-to-ceiling windows lining two walls. Outside, a massive Marcel Breuer desk fronted his reception room, and the walls were lined with display cases filled with proof of his achievements. While waiting to meet with him, visitors could read the plaques for his research awards or leaf through his books, which included two crossover bestsellers. But most impressive, and the thing that had the university president looking anxiously back over his shoulder, was the glass case in the center of the room. It contained an architect's model of the two-hundred-million-dollar renovation to University Hospital that was nearly completed and included the Sonja E. Tyson Cancer Center, both funded entirely through grant money that Ed had secured.

However, Ed's thoughts weren't on any of that as he watched the activity of the antlike people in the city below. He wasn't thinking about the rumors he'd been nominated for the Nobel Prize for his discovery of a curare derivative that paralyzed without affecting the diaphragm, thus allowing surgeons to operate without placing the patient on a ventilator. He wasn't thinking about his discoveries in tumor reversal or about his two children, Camille and Blake, who smiled broadly from a black-lacquer frame on his desk, nor about his wife, Miranda, a pediatric cardiologist with a manic devotion to charitable causes. No, as he pulled out his Peruvian silver box and removed a treated coca leaf, placing it between gum and cheek, he chanted softly and conjured Beth. It was a form of waking dream he'd been taught years back in the jungles of Brazil, where the Kaiapo shaman viewed the dream world as more solid than the chair he was sitting on. It was a topic he had discussed in his latest book, how crafting drug-induced dreams and then moving within them was where the shaman worked their magic.

For Ed, it brought back Beth, dressed in shimmering white. Her cool, green eyes smiled at him, filled with love. It was moments like this, so peaceful, when he let himself believe that she was really here and still alive. But like a worm, whose poisonous saliva spreads rot to an entire piece of fruit, the thought of her death, of what Peter did to her, shattered the illusion. Tightness spread through his body, his jaw clenched, and his vision of Beth faded. Her place was stolen by a memory, a phone call from his wife, just over a year ago. "I just heard the most horrible news," Miranda had said. "Beth is dead." He'd tried to speak, to ask questions. "Some kind of car accident . . . Peter's still in the hospital; they say he's going to make it." After she'd hung up, Ed had his secretary cancel his appointments and hold his calls. He'd then locked his office, turned off the lights, and spent the next twenty-four hours in a sea of pain. At times he'd lain curled in a ball, clutching his knees, and silently howling and sobbing into his chest. More than once he'd contemplated taking the single flight of metal stairs to the roof and diving off. By nine the following morning, he'd tracked down the number to Peter's hospital room in Boston. Michael Grainger had picked up.

"What happened?" Ed had asked.

Peter's father told him that the car had driven into a stone embankment.

"Who was driving?" Ed's voice had rung hollow in his ears.

"Peter."

He'd listened and heard the unspoken. Both Michael Grainger and Ed were psychiatrists. They both knew that driving into trees, off cliffs, and into stone walls was not always an accident, but a blameless way of committing suicide—or in this case, homicide. In that moment, he knew the truth: Peter had murdered Beth and had taken the only thing in Ed's life that mattered.

Until then, he had never lost hope that one day, with careful planning, she would wake to the horrible mistake that she had made in choosing Peter. Ed had always believed that moment would arrive, and when it did they would both shed their other lives, their half existences.

As the ant people continued their dance below, he flicked open his cell and entered a number from memory. The phone was picked up after the fourth ring.

A man answered, "Hello." His tone was harsh.

Ed sank into his chair and pitched his voice to match perfectly that of the Pakistani waiter who'd served him lunch earlier that day. "Could I please speak to Mr. Carter Walsh?" His mimicry was flawless.

"Yes?"

"Mr. Walsh?"

"Yes. What?"

Ed wondered how much Walsh had already had to drink. It was midafternoon, but the man's syllables had slurry edges. "I am calling from University Hospital to see if your daughter made it to her follow-up appointment."

"Huh? What are you talking about?"

"I'm sorry, do you have a daughter, Ann? Ann Walsh?"

"Yes, but what follow-up appointment?"

"Your daughter gave your name as the contact person on her paperwork. You did not know that she was in our emergency room last night?"

"What's wrong with her? Is she sick?"

"Oh, I'm sorry I would have thought she would have told you. Oh, dear."

"Is this some sort of joke?"

"No joke. I'm very sorry."

"Look, just tell me what she was doing there. Is she all right?"

"Yes, fine. I'm just supposed to find out if she made it to her follow-up appointment. That's all I'm supposed to do." Ed felt Carter's rage; he remembered the man well.

"Look, Bub. You call me in the middle of my Sunday afternoon and tell me my daughter was in the fucking emergency room and now you're not going to tell me what she was doing there? Get me your supervisor."

"I'm sorry. I'm just supposed to see if she made it to her appointment."

"Get me your supervisor."

"Oh, please, sir. I think I might have made a mistake."

"You can say that again. Tell you what, you tell me what my daughter was doing there, and I won't tell your supervisor that he's got a total boob working for him. Deal?"

Ed lowered his voice. "Okay, sir, but please, this is irregular."

"I won't tell a soul."

Ed heard the clink of ice against crystal; he could almost smell the bourbon. "Your daughter tried to cut her wrists, she had stitches and was seen by the psychiatrist."

There was silence, and then, "They fucking let her go! What idiot was responsible for that?"

"Sir . . . please, sir. Try to calm yourself. She was supposed to meet with her psychiatrist today."

"What! Who?"

"A Dr. Peter Grainger. I think he's a very good doctor; he came to see her in the middle of the night."

"Yeah, she has a way with the good doctors. So where is she supposed to meet with the good Dr. Grainger?"

"The University Clinic. That's all I wanted to find out—if she made it to her appointment."

"Give me their number and I'll find out for you."

"Oh, sir, please don't get me in trouble."

"Give me the fucking number!"

"Okay, sir. I'm looking at the discharge instruction sheet. Here's a number for the doctor. Please don't tell him that I gave it to you."

"Shut the fuck up!" Carter Walsh slammed down the receiver.

Ed clicked his tongue against the roof of his mouth. Last year, when he still ran the clinic, he'd had plenty of time to observe Walsh. The unfortunate business with his daughter had given him all the information he needed; the man's rage was never far from the surface, and once he'd latched on to something—or someone—he wouldn't let go. The girl, Ann, was something else. He knew that his initial attraction had to do with the physical; in certain lights Ann Walsh looked like Beth, only Ann was damaged goods, and below her perfect exterior lay despair and a frantic hunger to be loved. She was the kind whom men trashed their careers and families over as they tried to rescue her and to possess her. As he did with her father, Ed had plans for her.

Peter would not see it coming; it would happen in stages. All that he had stolen from Ed would be returned: the years of waiting, the love he'd lost, and the thing he couldn't bring himself to think about—the gift that he'd given Beth that she had so desperately wanted and that would have brought her back to him. It was a fantasy he'd played over and over in his mind during those golden months when he knew she was pregnant. He had planned to be there at the birth. As she nursed, he would reveal that he was the true father. She would be forced to see Peter's inadequacies, his impotence a metaphor for his failings as a man. Ed had thought through all of the details: Miranda could take Blake and Camille; he'd make sure they didn't want for money. And as for Kyle Grainger, Peter could have him, although his fantasy at times had included the boy suffering an unfortunate and tragic accident, effectively severing the last link between Beth and Peter.

In the pain-filled days and weeks after her murder, he'd asked himself why Peter had done it. What finally came to him was that it was his gift, that he had found out and had killed her.

Beth's shadowy image re-formed and floated before the windows. He let his focus soften and saw her lips move. He relaxed further, letting his weight sink into his chair and allowing the vision to gain strength. She was trying to speak.

Her voice soft inside his head. "You will avenge me."

"Yes."

She turned in the streaming sun, a green glow spread from her eyes, filling the room and warming Ed. She smiled, and try as he might to hold her, she drifted through the windows, lost shape, and was gone.

5

NICOLE EASED HER ARM FROM around her sleeping daughter in careful increments. As she lay there, her thoughts had drifted. Tomorrow was Monday and she and Hector would have to drive to the forensic hospital where Tabitha Robinson's murderer—Victor Cranshaw—was due for his fourth six-month review hearing.

She checked to see that Adriana's breathing hadn't changed, that she wasn't being wakened. She glanced at the glowing Thomas the Train clock; it was after midnight. She didn't want to think about the hearing or about how she'd been operating on four hours of sleep a night, since . . . She pictured Cranshaw's dim-witted smile, his bad teeth, and lumbering Baby Huey body that had not meant to kill Tabitha. She knew that for years to come, she'd have to make these twice-yearly visits to the hospital to ensure that no well-intentioned review board ever let him out. Victor Cranshaw had the IQ of a six-year-old. He'd been born premature to a crack-addicted mother and was raised by the state of New York in a series of foster homes in two of which, he had been raped. He'd been found incompetent to stand trial for what he'd done to Tabitha, whose body he had left to rot in the basement of his seventy-five-dollar-a-week rooming house.

At the door to Adriana's bedroom, Nicole stopped and looked back. It had taken more than an hour to get her to sleep. Then, two hours later, the screaming had started. Maybe she'd make it through the rest of the night.

Nicole, on the other hand, doubted that her thoughts would let her rest. She walked across the narrow hallway into her bedroom. Through the open door she could see her daughter, while below her she heard her mother's television. She thought about phoning down, but lately her mother, Jeanine, was pushing her in a bad direction. It did, however, feel familiar, being back in the Park Slope home where she had grown up. The top floor she and Adriana now occupied had, in her childhood, typically been rented out to a string of young couples; the husband was always a cop. They'd stay for a couple years, her father keeping the rent low so that the couple could pull together money for a down payment. The two lower floors of the turn-of-the-twentieth-century home, which was identical to half the other houses on the block, comprised the Luria household.

"Jesus," Nicole muttered, trying to figure out what to do as she thought about Tabitha's mother, Gail, who'd be at the hearing tomorrow. The smart thing would be to have a whiskey and try to get some sleep. Instead, she went over to a small door built into the eaves of the house and went into the attic room, her retreat. She reached into the dark, pulled a string, and a bare bulb lit the triangular space that ran the length of the house. In the center sat an overstuffed armchair covered with a purple-and-white afghan that her grandmother had crocheted. Beside it was a lift-top child's desk that Nicole had rescued from the garbage. From inside of it she pulled out a sketch pad, some charcoal, and a rag.

55

She poured herself a whiskey and sat back. She took a sip and felt the tension start to go. Her hand touched down on a fresh page and she began to draw.

Time slipped away as it always did when she did this, her first passion. Line and shadow took form as her fingers smudged and shaped the charcoal, creating the image of a laughing Adriana holding out a doll, her entire body in motion.

Then she heard the familiar cry; it started like a bird chirping and quickly grew in intensity, its pitch rising to a shriek.

"Mommy! Mommy! Mommy!"

Tonight would go a third round. That's how Donny referred to it, as though their daughter's misery were a boxing match.

"Coming," she said, knowing that Adriana couldn't hear her through the door. Nicole lifted herself from the warmth of the chair and turned off the light. Back in her bedroom she heard a knock at the kitchen door. Reinforcements.

"I'm here, peanut," she told her daughter, showing her face. "I'm going to let Grandma in; I'll be right back. Okay?"

She jogged down the hallway to the kitchen and the back door. Through the window she could see the wings of her mother's red and silver hair. She turned the bolt.

"Thought you could use some help," Jeanine offered, belting her yellow quilted robe snug around her slender middle. "Were you sleeping?" Jeanine's eye's sought out her daughter's.

"Not yet."

"I didn't think so. Were you in the attic?" she asked as they moved toward Adriana, whose cries had transformed into a muffled sobbing.

"Yeah."

"What are you doing in there?"

"I've been drawing some."

"I didn't know you still did that," she said, her expression a bit off, as though she'd just discovered some unsavory fact about her daughter.

Nicole said nothing as she watched her mother go to comfort Adriana. "What's the matter, sweetie? Bad dream?"

Like a drowning child Adriana threw her arms around her grandmother and buried her tear-streaked face in the quilting of her robe.

"It's okay," Jeanine cooed, smoothing her fingers through Adriana's hair. "Grandma's here. It's just a bad dream." Jeanine caught her daughter's eye. "You went to see that school today?"

"Yes," Nicole said, noting how the light cut a swath across her mother's face. "It looks like what we need."

"They had dolls," Adriana snuffled.

"Dolls are nice," Jeanine whispered as she rocked her granddaughter, gently sending her back to sleep. After a time she looked at Nicole. "How much?"

Nicole rubbed her thumb and fingers together. "Much."

"And Donny?"

She shook her head, not wanting to continue in earshot of Adriana.

Jeanine nodded and eased the sleeping child back to her crumpled nest of Wonder Woman sheets.

They padded down the hallway to the kitchen. Jeanine filled the kettle. "Tea?"

"Sure."

"So, you spoke to Donny. Today?"

"Yeah. He thinks that if we put her back into normal classes she'll 'snap out of it.' Or if I let her scream through the night she'll get tired and go to sleep."

"He doesn't mean to be cruel," Jeanine said, fishing chamomile tea bags out of a blue ceramic canister.

"He barely looks at her."

"Men aren't good with this stuff. If it was something he could fix, he'd be okay, but it's not, and he doesn't know what he's supposed to do." Jeanine handed her the mug. "I don't know if I should tell you this, but Dottie Scanlon saw Donny having dinner with Meg Capshaw's daughter, Liz. You know they used to date back in high school."

"They're friends."

"Uh-uh."

"What are you saying?"

"Nicole, what are you going to do? You're welcome to stay here as long as you like, but is this the life you want? You know he wants to get back together."

"That's what he says."

Jeanine shook her head. "You're thirty-five, you work too much, and you have a child who needs a father. I know your father would never have let Donny walk out."

"I left him," Nicole said, feeling sad and hollow.

"That's not the point. Adriana needs a father . . . more than some special school. You have to make a choice, Nicole; he's not going to wait."

"Mom, I'm tired. I'm going to sleep," Nicole said, getting to her feet.

"I don't mean to argue, it's just that I love you and I see where this is going."

"I know you do, it's just . . ." She looked at her mother, whose hair was askew, her expression worried. Nicole knew these things that twisted in her gut were said out of love, but how could she explain not wanting to live in a dead marriage to a woman whose husband and children had been everything? She couldn't find the words. "Good night, Mom." Nicole turned away, knowing that her mom would let herself out and that this conversation would be picked up again and again.

As she brushed her teeth, she looked in the mirror. There

were fine lines around the hazel eyes that were the color of her French Canadian father's. Her body was in shape, although she rarely had time to use the police gym, and while she'd never considered herself a beauty, she'd also never lacked for dates. That a man as good-looking as Donny Sullivan, with his jet-black hair, blue-green eyes and almost feminine features should have fallen for her was no big stretch.

Nicole stared at her reflection. She didn't want to get back with Donny, and she wondered why she had married him in the first place. For most of her life, Nicole had struggled with a profound sense of not belonging. As a little girl she was convinced that someone had switched her at birth and that her real family had nothing in common with the boisterous, mostly male world that she had landed in. Her father and most of her uncles were cops. Her two older brothers were on the force, and it seemed preordained that Nicole would either join the force or marry into it; eventually she had done both. Before that, however, there had been a detour, which was never spoken of.

Nicole knew that there was another person inside of her, one who rarely saw the light of day. Years back, that girl had been accepted on a full scholarship to a fine-arts program in Manhattan. There'd been a strange pride in her father's eyes when she had received the acceptance letter, as though he was happy for her but couldn't quite understand why and how someone would make a living as an artist.

Her two years at the university held the happiest and—until the events with Adriana—the worst days of her life. She had lived in Greenwich Village and had grown as an artist, surrounded by people to whom such things mattered. She'd fallen in love with an author in residence at the Expansion School—a married man—although it wasn't until later that she'd learn about his wife and children in Connecticut. She'd find that out the same day she'd learn that she was pregnant. In the weeks that followed, she'd

59

learn many things. Such as men who say, "I love you" may not be telling the truth, and that good Catholic girls *do* have abortions.

Nicole heard the kitchen door close and footsteps descend the back stairs.

No, she thought, wandering to her bedroom, *I don't want to get back with Donny. If he wants Liz Capshaw, good for him.*

As she sank beneath the covers, the sheets cool against her skin, she wondered if she'd married Donny to make her father happy. She'd certainly been attracted to him—it was hard not to be—but love? No, although she had tried.

Her final thought, before a fitful dream-filled sleep overtook her, was that her mother was wrong; Boris Singer's school would be better than a father who couldn't bear to look at his daughter.

6

"DR. GRAINGER, AM I LATE?" Ann asked as I crossed the deserted waiting room. She was seated in one of the green plastic chairs, a bulging book bag by her feet, her hair tied back. Her face, free from makeup, glowed.

"No." I led her back to the hall of a thousand therapists.

"Do you always come in this early?"

"Sometimes. But few students want an eight o'clock appointment."

"It's the only way. I have a microbiology lab at nine thirty."

I opened the door to my office.

"So, you're the head honcho now?"

"For what it's worth."

She looked around before settling into one of the two olive green armchairs.

"You never told me whom you met with when you came here before," I commented, having just spent another frustrating half hour hunting through medical records.

"He's gone. . . . His name was Keith Taylor." She watched me for a response.

"I don't know him." I took the opposite chair. She seemed poised today, as though the events of the weekend hadn't happened. She wore a black ribbed turtleneck and jeans and looked more like a model or a ballet dancer than a woman heading to a microbiology lab to plate out mold spores. "Do you want to talk about him?"

"No."

"And you've been in therapy other times?"

"Once, when I was a teenager, after my mom died. I was with him for years."

"Who?"

"Dr. Green. Robert Green." She looked out one of the two small windows and bit the corner of her lips. "I don't think this is a good idea."

"What?"

"This. Coming to see you—or anyone for that matter."

Okay, I thought, *we go from Dr. Green to not wanting to be here at all. What happened?* "Things didn't go well with Dr. Green?"

"I'm not talking about that."

"It's okay. This isn't the Spanish Inquisition; you talk about things when you're ready. I'm just trying to cover the basics."

"I'm sorry, but I've been thinking about this a lot. My life is complicated. I don't have time for this, and I can't risk things with some shrink in training."

"You're worried about confidentiality."

"You told me yourself it's kind of iffy."

"Sure, if you were thinking of hurting yourself, your therapist might need to take some action to keep you safe."

"I understand that, but don't you talk about cases with each other? Isn't that part of the training? So, even though I'm talking to one person, there's someone else or maybe whole rooms of people who hear my stuff. I don't want that."

"Understandable, but supervisors are bound by the same rules of confidentiality."

She swept her bangs back from her forehead. "People don't always follow the rules. Look, I feel comfortable with you. I'd be willing to do this if you were my therapist, but I can't deal with someone who doesn't know what they're doing."

She obviously understood the behind-the-scenes reality of the training program; cases did get discussed. So why was I reluctant to see her? It's not that I had a huge caseload. As the director, I had a couple dozen patients, mostly VIPs or faculty in the midst of mental meltdowns. I had thought of pairing Ann with Felicia Jones, my chief resident and a highly capable therapist. Why was I hesitating? "Okay," I told her, not seeing a choice.

"Thank you, and what we'll talk about will stay in this room?"

"Yes, with the exception . . ."

"I'll be sure to bring my bags if I'm thinking of offing myself. Maybe you guys should put a notice on your doors, like everything you say will be confidential with the exception of blah blah blah." She threw her head back. "I can't believe it's Monday."

"Did you clear things up with your dad about the money?" I asked, knowing that I needed to keep an eye on the crisis that had landed her in the emergency room.

"No. I won't call him."

"I thought you were being given warnings from the bursar's office."

"I'll take care of it."

"This is a different tune from the other night. You have the money?"

She picked at the arm of the chair. "You need new furniture."

"It comes with the office. So what about the money? You have other resources?"

"You could say that."

"Are we heading into another area you don't want to talk about?"

"This is why I can't meet with a trainee. If I tell you stuff, you can't repeat it."

"I'm assuming—and tell me if I'm wrong—that's happened to you before."

"You got it."

"Here?"

"Yes."

"And with your first therapist?"

"Even worse, my father's insurance was paying for it, and I was a minor."

"This isn't going anywhere," I assured her.

She twirled a lime green thread on the arm of the chair. "I'm doing things that are making me crazy." She stared at her boots. "I'll have the money, because I'm working for an escort service."

Silence blossomed. We both knew that she had dropped a bomb in the middle of the room. "Do you want to talk about that?"

"Not really, but I think I need to. I started when I was a sophomore in premed."

"Because you needed money?"

"Yeah. I tried some other things. I waited tables, even thought about doing porn videos, but those you can't leave behind. I could have gotten five thousand dollars a shoot. Instead, I do this three or four nights a week—it pays the bills."

"Because your father won't." I looked at her perfect face, unlined and almost expressionless. I did the math: she'd been doing this for more than two and a half years, times three or four a week. She'd potentially sold herself to hundreds of men.

"You see, I'm doubly screwed." She groaned. "No pun intended. On paper, my dad has too much money. The house is worth a couple million. What people don't know is that a few years back he stopped paying taxes. Eventually, they'll foreclose. I thought about emancipation, but then they're going to wonder how I've managed to pay tuition for the last three years. So I figure whatever he pays, great, and everything else I'll take care of. The other night when I told you about us fighting, that's part of it. Remember I said that he called me a slut?"

"Yes."

She shook her head. "That's the thing that pisses him off. Not that I turn tricks, but that I got out from under him. It makes him crazy. And when he finally spirals down the toilet, I want to watch. I just have to get Jen out of there before it's too late."

"Too late for what?"

The intensity of her gaze startled me. "I don't want her to be like me. I think I'm really fucked up. I'm not even sure, because I feel so numb, like dead inside." She looked away. I thought she might cry, but no tears came.

"Does turning tricks have anything to do with that?"

"It doesn't help." She looked up. "In fact, I'm about to quit."

"You found another way to get the money?"

"Yeah, but I think this is enough trust for one day. And no, I'm not going to mug anyone."

"I wasn't going there, but you do take a lot of risks."

"I don't have a choice. I have to finish medical school. All I have to do is figure out how do I get from point A to point B, and what better way than to land an all-expense-paid scholarship."

"A Goddard Fellowship?"

"You know about those?" She sounded surprised.

"Sure. There are two a year and they're extremely competitive."

Her eyes narrowed. "You went to medical school here?"

"Yes." I admitted.

"Don't tell me you were a Goddard Fellow."

"I was."

"Huh, I wouldn't have figured you for a research head. . . . How many years were you a fellow?"

"All four, and that's enough about me."

"No, shit! You made it through medical school without paying anything?"

I nodded.

"Ain't that a kick in the pants, and you didn't even have to sleep with anybody. Although, don't get me wrong"—her smile was electric—"I do enjoy sex. I don't want you to think that I'm some poor abused woman. Most of the time I like it."

"What aspects of it?" I asked, wondering at her sudden shift in mood. And what did she mean by "sleep with somebody"? Was she talking about turning tricks or something else?

"Power. You'd think it'd be the other way around, that the man has the power, but it's really me. . . . It's kind of like being a psychiatrist. Most of my regulars I see weekly. I get paid better than you do and I make them feel good, make them forget about their frigid wives and bad jobs. A couple have even offered to pay for school."

"You turned them down?" I asked, surprised by her inconsistency.

"I was tempted, but right now, I see them when I want and on my own terms. The minute they feel that they've bought more than the hour or the evening . . ."

"You lose the power."

"Yes." She looked across the room at the clock on my paper-strewn desk. "I need to get to class. Is this time good for you?" she asked, beating me to my usual line.

"It's fine. So, same time next week?"

"I'd like that," she said. "You're easy to talk to, but please . . . no students."

AS I TOOK MY USUAL seat at the head of the scarred Formica table in the windowless conference room, I thought back through the session. Ann was up to something, some scheme to get a Goddard. Plus, there was the unresolved issue of her missing chart, which if it didn't turn up soon had serious implications. Medical records aren't supposed to go missing, and if they do, it's a huge compliance issue, the kind of thing that results in six-figure fines from the board of health. For somebody like Ann, with her concerns over confidentiality, they needed to turn up, and quick.

I sipped my second large Dunkin' Donuts coffee of the morning and watched the staff crowd in for the Monday meeting. They were a mixture of twenty-somethings combined with a few faculty. There was the usual good-natured banter as people compared notes about the weekend, what movies and plays they'd been to see, what restaurant was especially good or interesting or really bad.

Felicia Jones, the chief resident and the woman I had wanted to do therapy with Ann, plunked her coffee down and sat next to me. "Morning, Peter," she said, fixing me with her large brown eyes. "Rough weekend?"

"I look that bad?" I asked, taking in her all-black outfit, which made her thin, pale, and lightly freckled face glow from under a wild mop of chestnut curls.

"You look tired," she offered, holding my gaze.

"Felicia, you were here last year, right?"

"Uh-huh."

I hunted for the name of Ann's prior therapist. "Did you know a . . . Keith Taylor?"

A hush fell over the crowded room as though all the air had been sucked out. "Okay, what am I missing?" I looked around at the faces. Most of the trainees appeared as clueless as I. It was the faculty who seemed uncomfortable. "Who was he?"

Felicia was visibly upset. "I would have thought that Dr. Tyson would have told you about what happened last year."

"Obviously not," I said, curious as hell.

"Keith Taylor was a third-year resident who was expelled."

"Because?"

"Boundary violations," she said, clearly not wanting to go into details in a room full of people. "He was also my friend . . . it was very ugly."

"Okay," I said, and added under my breath, "you'll give me the details later?"

She nodded. "So," she said, trying to regain her composure. "Who had the wretched on-call beeper for the weekend?"

Gerard Bingham, a second-year resident who couldn't have been more than five feet tall and had the cheeky face of a junior high student, started in on the events of his weekend. It was the standard stuff, stressed out graduate students wanting a sleeping pill, a homesick freshman who just needed to talk.

"But," he said, "—and for this I'm eternally grateful—I did not have to go to the emergency room to deal with the suicidal medical student—praise be."

Felicia perked, "Why not? You know it's policy that any student in the emergency room gets seen by the clinic."

Before Gerard could defend himself, I spoke up. "I saw her."

"Okay," Felicia said, assuming the tone of a jealous woman. "What made her so special?"

"It was a favor for Ed Tyson." I sensed glances being exchanged among the senior faculty. "What?"

Felicia had a worried look on her face, "Who was this medical student?"

In light of what I'd just learned about her friend and expelled resident, Keith Taylor, I could see where this was heading. I wanted to pull Felicia aside and tell her in private. I had promised

Ann that her business—so to speak—would remain confidential. Then again, she hadn't been all that forthcoming with me.

Felicia leaned in and whispered, "Please tell me it wasn't Ann Walsh."

I looked at her and didn't need to say a word.

"Fuck! I feel sick," she said, and she wasn't kidding; she looked green.

"Obviously, I have some catching up to do," I whispered back. "Let's finish rounds, and Felicia . . . we need to talk."

I could tell she was seriously upset. So I stepped in, went through the list of intakes, divided them up, and sent the minions out to do battle against mental illness.

As we walked to my office, I could hear the doors closing as we passed. It was maddening; everyone knew something about Ann Walsh that I didn't, and if they knew, Ed, who had been the clinic director for the last five years, would certainly know. So why didn't he tell me?

I unlocked my office and let Felicia in. "Have a seat."

She looked back at me. "When did you see her?"

"Late Saturday night, actually more like Sunday morning. Then I did a follow-up with her in the walk-in and I saw her first thing this morning. I was thinking of assigning her to you," I said, as I sat across from her.

"I'd turn it down."

"That's not like you. It's that big?"

"I can't believe she showed up again. I feel so sick. You'd think after last year she wouldn't have had the nerve."

"It wasn't her fault. She landed in the emergency room."

"Because?"

"A little cutting."

"Figures."

"You think she's borderline?" I asked, referring to the diagnosis of borderline personality disorder, a condition characterized by chaotic relationships, depression, self-mutilation, a frantic fear of abandonment, and suicide attempts.

"With a capital *B*."

"You've met her?" I asked.

"No, but I've seen her. She's a dangerous-looking girl."

"What do you mean?"

"Please, you're male, you're breathing. Give me a break. Girls like that know at a very young age what they do to men. Between the perfect skin, face, and body every intelligent man turns into a drooling idiot, and she knows it. Peter, you've got to be very careful with that one."

If this weren't Felicia, with whom I'd felt a bond almost immediately upon coming to the clinic, I might have been offended. "You think I could get into boundary problems with her?"

"Well, you're off to a good start. When's the last time you went to the ER to do an evaluation? It should have been Gerard. And then you see her in the walk-in clinic the next day . . . Why?"

"I was worried; I wanted to make sure she was okay."

"How considerate." Her tone was sarcastic. "And then this morning, I bet you got here early just to see her."

"I'm here early anyway, but point taken."

"And that," she said, slapping her hand against the chair, "is how the rot begins. Let me quote from a lecture given by the wise and wonderful Dr. Peter Grainger on the topic of boundary violations. I will paraphrase. . . . "The most common case of a therapist getting into trouble is of a male between the ages of thirty and fifty, and it starts slowly. It happens in stages, often with a seductive patient who has a positive transference to the therapist—"

"Nice to know someone listens."

"If you tell me you're not attracted to her," Felicia said, "I will be much relieved."

I pictured Ann and remembered my first shock on seeing her

in the ER and how much she had looked like Beth. "I would never act on it."

"Great. So, let me tell you about another really wonderful doctor who would never do such a thing. Keith and I were in med school together. A sweet man who would have made a wonderful psychiatrist. He was seeing Ann in individual therapy. I don't know all the details, but they had a sexual relationship, and it was discovered. . . . It was pretty awful. Keith was terminated, and there was no way another program would accept him. He owes more than two hundred thousand dollars in school loans and now he's a waiter."

"Do you still see him?" I asked.

She shook her head, and swallowed back tears. "No."

"She did tell me that she had been here before," I commented, feeling a need to defend Ann. "She was reluctant when I suggested that she do therapy here."

"Hurray for her."

"I couldn't find her records," I added.

"What?"

"They weren't in the file and there was no indication that someone had removed them. All I could find was her registry on the computer, nothing else."

"You know . . . last year Dr. Tyson mentioned that if there's a chance of litigation the charts go to the attorney. . . . That's the only thing I can think of."

"Good point. I'll check." I hoped she was right, but the mention of litigation got my stomach churning.

"So if you're not assigning her to me, who did you give her to?"

"Me."

"Jesus!" She put a hand between her eyes and rubbed as if she were in pain.

"Felicia?"

"What?" She sounded numb.

71

"One last question, and it's slightly odd; I don't want it leaving the room."

"Okay."

"Dr. Tyson would have known about Ann, correct?"

"Of course. He had a lot to do with Keith's termination."

"Okay, taking into account that Ed knew about Ann, why wouldn't he have given me this information?"

Her eyes widened. "What? He didn't tell you about her?"

"No."

"So he called you up, asked you to meet with this borderline on wheels, and he didn't even give you a clue?"

I shook my head.

"I thought he was your friend."

"He is."

"Good friend." She gave me a funny sidewise glance.

"What?"

"Some other time. Just be careful," she said. "And please, don't see her without someone else around. You know," she said, getting to her feet, "it's been a lot nicer these last few months having you here."

"Thanks."

"No, I mean it, and I know the faculty feels the same. I don't want to say anything, but your friend Ed is an odd person to work for."

"What do you mean?"

I could see she wanted to say more, but something held her tongue. "Some other time."

AFTER SHE LEFT, I COULDN'T ignore the tightness her words had planted in my chest. I'd felt as though I'd been played for a fool, and I couldn't tell who was responsible, Ann, Ed, or was I overreacting? One thing was certain: I needed to see her records.

I was hunting for the university attorney's number when Peggy, my secretary and the clinic's silver-haired den mother, called me on the intercom.

"Peter?" she said, a slight Irish lilt giving evidence to her Galway birthplace.

"Yes."

"You've got a call on line two; it's a parent and he's not happy."

"Do you know who?"

"Unfortunately, yes."

"And?"

"His name is Carter Walsh. He's the father of a student who was here last year."

This was unreal. "And this morning."

"What?" She sounded shocked.

"I saw Ann Walsh this morning."

"I don't see any record of it."

"I couldn't find her chart. I just wrote a note on her and was planning to drop it in the box on the way out." Even Peggy was making me defensive.

"Peter, it's none of my business, but be careful. Do you want to talk to him?"

"From the tone of your voice, probably not. But I will." The line clicked. "Hello?" I said.

"Is this Dr. Grainger?" the voice was male, deep, and raspy. The intonation on the word *doctor* was loaded, as if *doctor* were another way of saying *scum-sucking bastard*.

"This is Peter Grainger," I replied.

"You saw my daughter?"

His directness caught me by surprise. "I'm not at liberty to say."

"The fuck you aren't. Listen, bub, I know you've been seeing her, so don't play the fucking prince with me. I know all about my darling daughter and her doctors. She tell you that one of them did jail time?"

I said nothing.

"Didn't think so. And don't believe the shit she says about her family. Ann is a pathological liar."

Actually, based on this brief interaction with Carter Walsh, I was thinking that Ann had given an accurate assessment of her father. Years back I had read *The Jersey Boy*, a brutal account of his years in Vietnam. It was a tribute to the savagery of war, but more than that it showed how severe and persistent combat trauma can forever alter the course of a man's life. "Is there something you wanted to tell me about your daughter?" I asked, using the strategy of "people can tell you stuff, you just can't tell them stuff."

"You're fucked," he said. "So why didn't she get admitted to the hospital? I heard she tried to off herself. Isn't that what you're supposed to do? I guess it's just another in a long line of fuckups."

Based on how his words slurred together, I sensed he'd been drinking. Reasoning wasn't going to work. "Mr. Walsh, if your daughter was coming to the clinic and if she signed a release of information, I'd be happy to talk with you, but without those two things, I can't say much. I'd suggest you call your daughter and discuss this with her."

There was a slight pause and then a throaty laugh. "I suggest you fuck yourself." The line clicked dead.

As I held the receiver the other line flashed. I pressed down.

"How bad was it?" Peggy asked.

"Bad. So it sounds like everyone knew about Ann Walsh except me."

"Sorry, Peter. I'd hoped that was out of our hands and into the attorneys'."

"Is that where her records are?"

"Yes. . . . I feel terrible about this."

"Do you have the number?"

"Hold on . . . here it is. . . . I know this isn't my place, but someone should have told you . . . which reminds me . . . you're supposed to have dinner with Ed and Miranda Tyson tonight?"

"Cute segue."

"Thanks, but he should have warned you about Ann Walsh."

"Are there other cases like this?" I asked, trying to keep the anger from my voice. This wasn't Peggy's fault, but it felt as though there was a conspiracy to keep me in the dark.

"Not that I'm aware, and I've been here since the dawn of time."

"Thanks, Peggy." I hung up. I was royally pissed at Ed. Why didn't he tell me about Ann or her crazy father or the resident who was terminated? Shouldn't he have mentioned that? A distant memory popped into my head. At the time I'd accepted Ed's explanation—he'd wanted to teach the medical student a lesson—*of course* he would have stopped him. But what if I hadn't walked in on Ed and the second-year student who was about to inject an elderly woman with concentrated potassium chloride instead of diluting it with intravenous fluid? She would have died. Would Ed really have stopped him?

I felt the creeping edges of paranoia. I thought of my medications, which for the past two months I'd been flushing. *This is crazy. Ed's your friend.*

Yeah, right. I had to do something. I needed to know what was going on. I looked again at the number for the university's lawyer; I dialed.

7

"IT'S GOING TO BE OKAY." Ed soothed over the phone in his penthouse office. "The final decision rests with me."

"What if someone finds out?" she asked.

"That's not going to happen, Ann. Not unless you tell. You haven't done that, have you?"

"Of course not."

"Not even your new psychiatrist?"

"No."

"Good, because that *would* complicate things. The Goddard Fellowships carry a lot of prestige. I won't let a scandal develop, even for you."

"You said I deserve it."

"You do, but even with the highest GPA in your class, no one can know about us."

"What are you saying? You sound like you regret it."

Ed smiled, enjoying the interplay with Ann, like a fish on the line; he could reel her in and then let her out again, make her think she was in control. "Of course not."

"Because if you changed your mind, I swear . . ."

"Calm down. You know how I feel about you. Don't you believe me?"

"I do. . . . Say it. I need to hear it."

"I love you, Ann." He pictured Beth. "I want to be with you."

"You'll leave your wife?"

As if he were reciting his daughter's favorite fairy tale, Ed supplied the magic response. "Yes, I'll leave my wife, and the two of us will be together . . . forever." *And they lived happily ever after,* he thought.

"I love you, Ed."

"I love you, too. And soon all of this will be behind us. I'll see you tonight? Where we agreed?" he asked, needing to make certain that there were no last-minute improvisations.

"Yes, I'll keep the room."

"Good. And Ann," he said. "I do love you very much."

"I love you, too."

He hung up and looked out at the darkening city. His secretary had left for the day; he was alone. He pulled out his silver box and tucked a coca leaf into his cheek. He had little time and much to do.

Ed strode through his office suite and toward the elevators. Once inside, he pulled out the key card that allowed him access to B2. As he descended, he thought of Don Carlos Jortega, the shaman who had first introduced him to ayahuasca—the vine of the dead. It had been in payment for healing his sister's malaria, and it had been the start of Ed's training in the way of the shaman—the wizard. A watered-down version had found its way into his books and into the scientific papers that kept the military and the pharmaceutical companies vying for exclusive rights to the drugs he had since developed.

The elevator stopped at subbasement B2. It was here, outside of what had once been the medical school's anatomy suites, that he'd proposed to Beth. Little had changed, other than that this was now his domain. Students were no longer allowed here and the morgue for University Hospital, the only remaining suite he didn't yet occupy, was being moved into the hospital's main building thanks to a discretionary grant that Ed had procured from the Pentagon. It was part of a much larger funding stream, a backroom cigar-and-brandy deal, where in exchange for first rights to new compounds, the defense department gave him access to nearly unlimited, and mostly unrestricted, grant funds. While paralytic drugs usually fell under the domain of surgeons, their potential for use as weapons and espionage tools was not lost on a number of high-ranking officials.

To the outside world, the money Ed had brought into the university had been nothing but good. With it, he'd proposed and pushed through a plan to save the aging University Hospital—a turn-of-the-twentieth-century brownstone elephant of a building at risk of losing its accreditation. Ed had become a hero in Greenwich Village, saving the structure, while bringing the facility into the twenty-first century. His efforts had landed him on the cover of both *New York* magazine and *The Village Voice*. The president of the university, an aging Pulitzer Prize winner, had taken to glancing anxiously in Ed's direction. There were rumblings that he would step down, and Ed's name was first off the tongue whenever successors were discussed.

B2, which still reeked of formalin, was circular, with three corridors that radiated out like spokes on a wheel. In the center was the oak bench where he'd held out a ring and asked Beth to marry him; she sat there now, dressed in white.

He turned from her, knowing that she would follow, and headed down the hall to his main complex. It had started with two small rooms—one not much larger than a supply closet—that he'd been grudgingly given after he'd obtained his first NIH grant to research the structure of compounds used by the Kaiapo Indians in Brazil. It was on the basis of this that he'd been awarded a Goddard Fellowship as a sophomore. It had roused intense jealousy among his classmates. If he'd cared what they thought, he might have told them it was never about the money. It was always about her. Peter had one fellowship; Ed would have the other. If Peter published, Ed would publish ten times that and make it onto the bestseller list. To the best man belonged the best woman.

As Ed became the greatest breadwinner for the university, he'd been offered bigger and more modern facilities; he'd always turned them down. The reason he gave was that moving all of his files, his hydroponic greenhouse, and equipment was too daunting. There was some truth to that, but as he opened the door into his laboratory there was a feeling of being home.

"Ed!" Ralph White, his longtime assistant, wearing a lab coat and smiling broadly, came toward him.

"Still here, Ralph." Ed said, wondering how he could ease him toward the door. "What are you working on? Shouldn't you be home with the wife and kids?"

"Let me show you."

Ed was torn, he didn't have time for this, but Doctor Ralph White, with his savantlike facility with chemical manipulations, was the best assistant he'd ever had. He followed him to the wall of cages.

"You got to see this," Ralph said, his dark face alive with excitement. "Remember when I was talking about esterification of compound T2745?"

"Right," Ed said, having set Ralph to the task of taking his curare derivative and figuring out every possible chemical manipulation. "What have you got?"

"Check this out."

Ed watched as Ralph reached in and grabbed a large Norwegian rat by the scruff of its neck. Holding it steady, he injected the animal with a metered dose of the paralytic drug. In the time it takes blood to circulate through the rat's body, the animal lay flat and motionless. Ed saw the slow movement of the animal's diaphragm—the key effect of T2745—paralyzed, but still breathing. "So what's the difference?" Ed asked, feeling time slip away.

"You'll see. I was thinking that this might happen, but until you actually try it, you never know." With the animal still flaccid, Ralph pierced its flesh with a small needle and drew a couple cc's of blood. He then squirted it into a test tube and held up a small beaker. "This is the curare antibody."

Ed nodded, familiar with the test about to be run in which the animal's blood was mixed with the antibody and a color-changing reagent, shaken, and the whole mixture turned blue. It was a standard check to make sure the drug was actually in the animal.

Ralph shook vigorously; the vial did not change color.

"You checked to make sure the antibody is still good?" Ed asked.

"I did it with three separate batches and they all worked with regular T2745. And . . . that's not even the best part."

Ed marveled at his excitement. "You going to tell me?"

"I've run every standard test, even spectroscopy. And you know what?"

"No."

"All that shows up is blood. Something's going on where the body is breaking down the compound into pieces that are completely undetectable."

"Like succinyl choline," Ed commented, referring to another paralytic drug.

"Yup."

"Okay, Ralph it's interesting, but what applications do you see for this?"

". . . I don't know." The younger man faltered, his initial excitement dampened.

"Well"—Ed marveled at how easily he could alter Ralph's mood—"it's good work."

As if a switch had been hit, Ralph beamed. "Thanks, Ed."

"Don't mention it. You should get out of here. It's getting late."

"I don't mind."

"No," Ed said. "I insist."

"Are you going to work on the tumor project?" Ralph asked, not wanting to miss out.

"I'm not ready to show this to anybody, including you, my best assistant ever."

"When are we going public?" he asked. "This stuff is going to turn the world on its head." His excitement was infectious. "We have two complete generations of a thousand animals without a single tumor; this is FDA fast track for certain."

"Soon," Ed said, feeling a surge of affection. "And you, my friend, are going to be very famous."

If Ralph had been a cat he would have purred, "Okay . . . I'll see you tomorrow."

"Great, see you tomorrow," Ed said, modulating his voice to match Ralph's, a trick he'd been taught by a native sorcerer along the Xingu River. The idea was to mirror the person you wished to influence without their awareness. It was highly effective, as people tend to do the bidding of those who sound like themselves.

Finally alone, Ed locked the outer doors, so even if Ralph were to return, he'd be unable to get in. It was time to get to work.

"For you," he told the glowing image of Beth, who had been watching from beside the wall of rat cages. He lit a burner and removed a Baggie from his pocket. Inside it were three dried pieces of fruit from the *datura innoxia*. He took out a ceramic mortar and pestle, macerated the cucumber-looking vegetable into a paste, dumped that into a beaker, poured in distilled alcohol, and stirred. He topped the beaker with a Pyrex reflux chimney and let it boil.

As that cooked he went in search of the latest batch of T2745. When he got to the locked cabinet where the product was kept, he stopped.

"Ralphie, you might have something." He went back to Ralph's workbench and looked at the flagon of esterified T2745. He tapped a fingernail against his front tooth, weighing the pros and cons. Judging by the experiment with the rat, the stuff worked, so that wasn't the problem. Dosing might be different. T2745 was in its third and final stage of human experimentation; the dosing was clear. But with anything new—even a minor variant—dosing could be significantly different, not to mention side effects and all of the other possibilities of introducing strange chemicals into the human body. The attraction of Ralph's new variant was clear—it would leave no trace.

He pulled out a glass pipette and siphoned out the drug and then injected it into two rubber-topped self-sealing ampoules.

Like a gourmet chef who handles many tasks simultaneously, Ed returned to his *Datura* just as the mixture started to boil off the alcohol, which now contained the potent amnesiac and hallucinatory drug. Taking the amber-colored liqueur, he placed it in a fresh bottle and let it simmer. To this he added dried coca leaves. While that cooked, he hunted through a set of stainless-steel cabinets for a small root-beer colored bottle, as the mixture was light-sensitive and easily destroyed.

The last time he had made this potion, an adaptation of an Amerindian ceremonial drink, it had been with Beth, whose apparition hovered near. As he waited patiently for the product to drip through the glass apparatus, he spoke to her. "You remember New Orleans?"

"Of course," she said, standing next to him.

It had been more than a year and a half ago, they were both

there for the annual New Discoveries in Pharmacology convention. Ed was presenting, and Beth had been invited to give a series of lectures on the use of psychiatric medications by internists.

"You know I got you there," he said, having arranged her invitation to present.

"I know that now," she said. "It wasn't the first time, was it?"

"No," he said, having managed to separate her from Peter before. Over the years there had been other conventions and other dinners. After all, they were friends and colleagues. "New Orleans was different."

"It was," she agreed.

It had been a night that he had dreamed about. Over drinks, she had admitted that her life hadn't turned out exactly as she had thought it would. "Not that I'm complaining," she had said. There was a sadness in her lovely face, still unlined by the years.

He had seen tears in her eyes. "What is it?" he had asked.

"I can't have any more children."

It wasn't the response Ed had wanted. But the pain in her expression held him in thrall. How could he comfort her? He desperately wanted her to be happy. If nothing else, Beth had to be happy. If not, what was all the sacrifice for? The years of watching from a distance were difficult, but because he truly loved her, her happiness had to be enough.

Over dinner, she had revealed how, after Kyle's birth, her body had developed antibodies to Peter's sperm. It was the kind of conversation that only doctors could have, couching painfully intimate matters in clinical language.

As she had sipped her martini the words tumbled from her beautiful lips. "I've had five miscarriages in twelve years. My clock is ticking down. I don't know why this should matter so much, but I love being a mother. It's like—and this will lose me any credibility as a feminist—a big part of me wants to stay home and be Mom. Remember the Mekranoti?" she had asked, referring to the tribe of Indians known for its intricate designs in body paint, one of several Amerindian groups that Ed had worked with.

"Of course."

"Those two weeks we were together. Do you ever think about that?"

"Yes." He could barely breathe.

"Me, too. Of course, I would never tell Peter about . . ."

"Don't worry, I gave you my word."

"But the women," she had said, "that one, Anika, whose youngest was having his naming ceremony. There's something that she asked me. At the time I laughed it off, but . . . she asked me where my children were. I was what? Twenty-four? But I was older than half of them. Now it's the end of my reproductive life. Where are my children?"

"You have Kyle," he had offered, not letting her see how even mentioning his rival's offspring brought the taste of bile to his mouth.

"Of course, and I shouldn't complain. It's probably the booze . . . and seeing you. You've done so well, Ed. I hope you know how proud I've been to see all you've accomplished. People say that you'll win a Nobel Prize. It's wonderful."

What he didn't say as he had glowed in the light of her approval, was that everything he had done, he had done for her. They agreed to meet the following night, the last of the convention. In his hotel room he had assembled the ingredients necessary, and using a small alcohol lamp and a cheap set of cooking Pyrex he'd purchased on Canal Street, he had brewed his mixture.

When they had met, she apologized for having been so maudlin. She loved her husband, her son, and her life. "Maybe I'm premenopausal."

He had listened, seeing the pain behind her words; she wanted another child. When she went to the ladies room, he let five drops of the alcohol-based *datura* and *banisteriopsis* mixture dissolve in her drink. An hour later he had taken her back to his hotel room. Her eyes, dilated by the brew, were lustrous and bright. If she had told him to stop, he would have, but she didn't.

"I can hear the drums," she had said at one point.

"I will give you a child," he had told her.

She had said nothing as the powerful drug carried her through a dimension that is best described as dreaming while awake. That night Ed saw that she still loved him, had always loved him.

He had returned her to her room, and knew that in the morning she would not remember. He had no way of knowing if she would conceive. He discovered the truth four months later when Miranda had told him that Peter and Beth were going to have a baby.

He gasped at the memory now and almost let his mixture boil away. "Beth," he whispered, needing her near him, "I'm so sorry."

He stoppered the bottle and deposited it in his briefcase. Satisfied that he had ample quantities, Ed cleared away all traces of his activities and went back to his basement office, his private sanctum. Neither the cleaning crew nor Ralph was allowed in here without his presence.

It wasn't much to look at. What artwork there was—also Amazonian—contained none of the elaborate feather- and beadwork found in the masks and ceremonial shields that decorated his penthouse suite. But to the initiate, the few pieces over his massive gray steel desk and its three computer monitors were far more rare. All had been gifts from shamans and *curanderos* for whom Ed had performed significant favors. When asked what it was that he wanted as payment for his medical services, he was clear. It was the secrets of the shamans, their potions, their chants, the heart of their magic; this knowledge was the only currency he would accept. For tribes such as the Krago, still hidden deep within the jungle, these were their most treasured possessions. But one by one, they handed over the secrets. The objects in Ed's office—the rattles, fetishes, and swords woven from umbilical cords, and the ancient amulets containing human remains harvested from slain warriors—were the sole province of the shamans; they were rare and they were priceless.

Ed had intended to write another book, dedicated to Beth, focusing on the shamans. He would have called it *The Garden* because to the true shamans—not the ones who fed hallucinogens to thrill-seeking tourists—but the ones who were part of a lineage that spanned back to the Inca, the Toltec, and the Olmec, the jungle was not a jungle; it was a garden. Its fruits were the tools the shamans needed in their travels between worlds. In its pages he would have told the story of his greatest discovery, the cure for cancer. He was so close, and the tumor project to which Ralph had alluded was the culmination of many years' work.

His first observation was that within the Krago village there was not a single incidence of cancer, even among the animals. Over two subsequent visits, he had calculated the probability of such a finding until the conclusion was irrefutable—something in the Krago diet or medicines protected them from cancer. Next came the painstaking work of itemizing their food, determining the composition of their cooking implements and every ingredient and step in their shamans' medicines. Ed gathered quantities of everything, and through hazardous single-engine lifts out of the jungle and bribes to customs officials on both sides, he got the materials back to his labs for analysis. What came next would not find its way into a book, but to Ed, his ends clearly justified the means. The Sonja E. Tyson Cancer Center, barely three years old, had a growing reputation for miraculous cures. What the public would never know was that the cancer center patients provided Ed the single most critical component, human test subjects. Yes, there had been mishaps, even deaths. But based on the incredible remissions of eight women with advanced breast cancer, he knew that he'd found the answer in a saprophytic fungus that grew only on the *Maquira sclerophylla*—a latex-producing mulberry tree. Without revealing the source of the substance he'd named Tumoren, he'd had Ralph set up the first animal study, the results of which were conclusive—it worked. Now he was close to going to the FDA with his miracle in a bottle. It was too late to save his mother, but millions of others would be spared the devastation that she'd endured—the surgeries, the chemo, the radiation, the final months on higher and higher doses of morphine. It would all vanish into the past, leaving future generations to marvel at the barbarity.

Ed unlocked his desk, pulled out a small MP3 player, and plugged it into his computer. After typing a series of passwords, he pulled up a folder labeled "Emerald," opened it and looked at the long list of new files. He started with a short one labeled "Ceiling 2" stamped with the time and the date; it contained the sounds of Peter's cat meowing. He listened for a couple seconds, and then went to a longer file time-stamped "kitchen phone" from late Saturday night. It started with the message on Peter's answering machine; then came the sound of Ed's own voice.

"Peter?"

"Hey, Ed."

"I have a favor to ask," Ed had said. "And I hate to do this so late and on your weekend, but we have a situation down at the ER. I'd like you to handle it personally."

"What is it?"

"One of the medical students." Heavy sigh. "She's apparently tried to kill herself, and I'd rather you see her yourself. No offense to the residents, but . . ."

"Not a problem," Peter had said; just one friend doing a favor for another.

Ed deleted it.

The next file contained Kyle's distress call to his grandfather. Ed listened closely, sorting through the nuance of intonation. Kyle was close to tears, and his grandfather's voice was similar in pitch and tone to Peter's. He pressed pause and mimicked Michael Grainger's voice into a microphone hooked into the computer. As he spoke, his voice was converted into a glowing green sinusoidal image on the monitor. He played a portion of the file back and studied the pattern. He paused and tried again, and after three attempts the pattern his voice produced was a perfect copy of Michael Grainger's. "Kyle," he said, his mimicry choked with emotion. "Your father's been arrested. I'm at the courthouse. Dr. Tyson is coming to pick you up."

8

AS I OPENED MY OFFICE door to let out my last patient for the day—a doctoral student whose supervisor had morphed into his punitive father, effectively paralyzing his attempts to complete his dissertation—I saw Felicia head toward me.

She waited for the patient to pass. "You're still here. Peggy said you were leaving early. . . . She mentioned that you were going to look at Ann's records." Her gaze was searching. "You want company?"

I was going to say no, but then realized that Felicia knew more about what had happened with Ann and her previous therapist than she had told me. I also trusted her. "You sure you don't want to get out of here?"

"Not really." She appeared pensive.

"What is it?"

She whispered, "Since this morning, it's all I can think about. I have a horrible feeling about her showing up again, and I don't know if it's just because I lived through last year and saw one of my best friends reamed out by this system."

"How involved were you?" I asked, grabbing my jacket.

"Enough for a four-hour deposition."

We didn't speak until we were on the street. "What happened to the case?" I asked.

"I don't know; it's nine months and I keep waiting for the lawyer to call."

"Did you ask Ed?"

"Are you kidding?"

"What?"

"I know he's your friend, but I don't care for Dr. Tyson."

"How come?" I asked as we came to the four-story brownstone in which many of the university's administrative offices were housed.

"You have to promise not to tell him what I'm about to tell you."

"Okay."

"I can't prove any of this," she said slowly, "which makes it worse. But last year Keith was crucified, and Ed Tyson had everything to do with it."

"You don't think Keith had an affair with Ann?"

"I didn't say that . . . but it wasn't so cut and dried."

I wanted to press her further; I knew there was more, but the afternoon was slipping away and I needed to look at Ann's chart.

The law offices were on the first floor, where a redheaded secretary in a too-tight white angora sweater buzzed us in. I showed her my ID and Felicia did the same.

"Clarence Green is at a conference," she informed us, "but he said as the clinic director you can review the records. However, you can't copy or remove any portion."

"That's fine," I told her.

"And who's she?" the secretary asked, her gaze raking over Felicia's wild hair and witchy outfit.

"My assistant," I said, realizing that by all rights I shouldn't have brought Felicia, and that having her review Ann's records was not kosher.

"I suppose that's okay," the secretary conceded, getting up and showing us into a small meeting room with a polished mahogany table, leather swivel chairs, and a window that faced out over a brick-walled courtyard. In the center of the table was an unbound chart held together with two thick rubber bands.

"Could I get you some coffee or anything to drink?" she asked.

We each said no and waited for her to leave.

When the door clicked shut I peeled off the rubber bands and started to flip through the pages.

The first few were copies of correspondence to the court and requests for records on the attorney's letterhead. I could see that a civil case had been brought and Carter Walsh was the plaintiff.

"That's odd," Felicia said, her forefinger moving across the page. "I just assumed Ann would have brought the suit. After all, she wasn't a minor."

"Good point. Maybe she wasn't the one who was upset."

"Maybe . . . but for malpractice you have to prove damages, don't you?"

"Of course."

"So how could the father be damaged? He wasn't seeing Keith; Ann was."

"Doesn't matter," I told her. "Families can bring civil suits on behalf of family members. It happens all the time with wrongful death."

"She's not dead."

"Even so, as long as she didn't object, a judge would probably have let it go. It's a good point, though," I commented, as I read through the pages. "Did Keith tell you about any of this?"

"No. When this hit, he dropped out of sight. I tried to stay in touch, but he didn't want to talk to me or anyone. For a while I kept calling. . . . I was afraid he might do something stupid. The last time I spoke to him, he thanked me for being his friend and asked me to stop calling. Said he'd be okay."

"Are you all right?" I asked, realizing that the ghosts we stirred held painful memories.

"I guess. . . . Thanks for asking."

"So what makes you think Ed had something to do with this?"

She looked at me. "He was Keith's clinical supervisor."

Stunned, I let go of the chart. "What?"

"Yup."

Here was something else Ed had neglected to mention. "Maybe Keith never told him about Ann."

"Maybe." She sounded unconvinced.

For several minutes we read the files in silence. Keith Taylor's progress notes on his sessions with Ann were written in the bland expository style that we teach the trainees. The goal is to write just the facts—the person showed up, he was improving, or not—sign it and date it. Keep it dull and short—*Client showed for appointment on time. She discussed issues related to her family and unresolved conflict with her father and residual grief over the loss of her mother. Again raised antidepressant therapy as an option, which she continues to decline. Denied any thoughts of wanting to harm herself. Scheduled to return in one week.*

"I bet that's where it started," Felicia said.

"What are you looking at?"

"There," she pointed to the note in my hand. "Look at the time."

In the margin was written "5:30 P.M." With the exception of evening group therapy, the clinic would have been deserted. I looked at the next several notes and saw that they were all from either late in the afternoon or early in the evening.

"Don't you think he would have seen that?" Felicia asked.

"Who?"

"Peter, you've told us *many* times not to see patients outside the regular hours."

"So?"

"You don't think Ed would have known? That Peggy wouldn't have mentioned that one of the male residents was seeing a female patient in the evening?"

I still wanted to defend Ed. After all, he had arranged my job, my apartment, getting Kyle into Stuyvesant; I owed him. So he probably wasn't the best supervisor. "Maybe he knew," I admitted, "but knowing Ed, it probably didn't register. I imagine he was usually out of the office and either in the field or in his laboratory." Even as I gave plausible excuses, I didn't believe them. Ed never let details slide. Rather than quieting my anxiety, Ann's records were making things worse.

"Have it your way," Felicia said.

We had come to the end of the progress notes when I encountered a battered manila envelope that contained a stack of ragged-edged pages ripped from a notebook. "These don't belong here," I said.

"Process notes," Felicia said.

"Yup. I wonder how they got here."

"They probably got subpoenaed along with everything else."

"Maybe," I said, "but most people—attorneys included—wouldn't even know they existed." Process notes are a learning tool that student therapists bring to supervision to dissect their work. They're a detailed account of each session that includes the therapist's thoughts and feelings; they don't belong in the medical record.

It was clear from the first note that Keith was headed into hot water. *If she wasn't my patient, Ann is the sort of woman over whom I would become obsessed—my unobtainable, the woman I fantasize about but never get.* At the end, he summarized the session. *Ann is a highly troubled woman who elicits strong feelings inside of me. When she cried, it was all I could do not to reach across the space and tell her that everything would be okay. While I would never do such a thing, I felt a strong impulse to play the hero, to let her know that she could be saved and she could be protected. When she left, I sensed that she did not want to go, that if I could have extended the session, she would have liked that. If such a thing were appropriate, I would have happily obliged.*

"Okay," Felicia said, finishing the note a couple seconds after me. "If you had a trainee come in with a first session like that, what would you tell him?"

"You don't know that Ed didn't," I said.

"You're right. . . . I don't know that for sure. But don't you think that as a supervisor you would be keeping a very close eye on this therapy?"

"Of course." I started in on the second note. There was something fascinating and horrible about these. It didn't happen all at once, but the boundaries, the invisible walls of safety that keep therapy different from the rest of life, were being slowly dismantled. Keith's attraction to Ann, though understandable, was the kind of thing good therapists learn to handle.

In his third session he wrote, *She asked me if I was this kind outside of therapy. She wanted to know if there are men like me in the real world. I felt like saying of course there are, but didn't. She told me that she'd had a dream, and I was in it. We were driving in a car together in some foreign land. We got lost and she wouldn't let me stop for directions. She told me that she could figure out the way because she'd been there before. She said that the dream became erotic and that in it she reached across the seat and started to touch my thigh and then my penis.*

I became aroused in the session. I crossed my legs so that she wouldn't notice my erection. I asked her what she thought the dream was about. She said it was obvious—that she was attracted to me, and "didn't that just suck." That the "one man she couldn't have was the one man she could see falling in love with." What came next stopped me cold.

I thought about Dr. Tyson's advice, that I should let things go their course, that to interfere with her erotic transference would be to shut down the therapy. So I said nothing. It's my thoughts I found a concern: I wondered what it would feel like to stroke her hair, to hold her, to kiss her.

"So Ed didn't know?" Felicia cocked an eyebrow. " 'Let things go their course.' What kind of supervision is that? Why not just tell him to jump in the sack with her?"

"You don't know," I told her. "There was probably more to the supervision." But was there? While Ed paid attention to the details, his genius was in putting things together in novel ways. Was the therapy with Keith and Ann an experiment? Was Ed playing with the formula to see what would happen?

"Right," she said, unconvinced. "Let's keep reading."

It was obvious from the next few notes that Keith Taylor was doing everything in his power to keep his feelings in check. There was an occasional mention of his supervision by Ed, so the case *was* getting reviewed.

On the pages for the eighth session a yellow Post-it had been affixed, and someone—probably the attorney—had written *"Res ipsa loquitur."*

"What's that?" Felicia asked.

"It's Latin legalese: 'The thing speaks for itself.' It's used in malpractice cases when the guilt is obvious, like cutting off the wrong leg."

We read the note.

Ann just left. It's after nine and the clinic closed hours ago. I can't believe what I've just done. I couldn't stop it. She was so unhappy. Did she really throw herself at me? A part of me can't get over having a girl that beautiful be attracted to me. This is so wrong. I knew it when she got out of her chair. I should have told her to stop, but I didn't. I couldn't. I thought it would stop when she put her arms around my neck. She was crying, but it didn't stop. She looked sad when it was over. She asked me if she should come back the same time. I told her yes.

What have I done?

Felicia was crying. "Can you see why I blame Ed?" She brushed tears from her eyes before they could fall. "We all have to deal with this stuff, and that's why we have supervision. I mean, let's face it, most of us aren't much older than our patients. Sometimes we're even younger, and we have some mighty attractive people sitting in our offices. I've had gorgeous men tell me how they've fantasized about making love to me. It would be like shooting fish in a barrel. I think in the first week you were here"—she continued, her rage barely in check—"we had more than four hours of seminars on maintaining boundaries. You know what I think?" she asked, stabbing her forefinger onto the page with the Post-it. She didn't wait for my reply. "I think not only could Ed Tyson have stopped this, but that he *wanted* to see what would happen."

"Oh, please. Why? Why would he do that?" What if she were right?

"He's a manipulator. And he thinks most of us are too stupid to see it. Keith told him all about his sessions with Ann; it's in his notes."

"You're making him sound like the puppet master."

"That's what he is."

There was a knock, and the secretary entered. "We're going to need this room in fifteen minutes, sorry."

"Not a problem." I pushed back from the table. "We've seen what we needed."

We left without speaking to each other. I told the secretary that I'd call her boss in the morning to check on the status of the case. It was the kind of scandal that was so cut-and-dried I suspected the university would have settled rather than run the risk of such a damning case going to trial. If it had settled, who got the money? If it was Ann, none of this made sense.

Outside a light snow had started to fall. Felicia drew her ankle-length wool coat closed around her neck and turned toward me. "I've got to get home. . . . Peter, I know you think I'm overreacting, but I'm worried. If you can't see Tyson's involvement . . . I don't know. Just please be careful. Okay?"

"Okay." I fought back the impulse to give her a hug. Normally, I might have acted on it, but considering what we'd just been through, it felt kind, but wrong.

She flashed a quirky smile and then hurried toward the PATH train and Hoboken. I pulled my ski cap out of my coat pocket and put on gloves. Snowflakes sparkled on the sidewalk and in the air as they drifted through the lamplight.

I needed to get home, but a part of me resisted. I was angry and confused. I thought about Felicia's accusations. She was right; Ed should have stopped things. Why hadn't he?

I thought back through the past couple days, starting with his phone call asking me to see Ann in the ER. Based on what I now knew, it was understandable that he'd wanted me instead of one of the trainees, especially if there'd already been a lawsuit. But—and this was what I couldn't see—why didn't he tell me about her? I'd been telling myself that it was an oversight, which, if Ann's case were only a little out of the ordinary, would be understandable. However, this was a great big whopping catastrophe. How could he *not* tell me? Why would he send me into the ER with a high-profile case without giving me the details? It felt like a setup. But for what? To see if I'd be the kind of psychiatrist to sleep with Ann Walsh?

There had been times in school when Ed and I had been in fierce competition with each other for grants and research awards. We had flip-flopped back and forth between being ranked first and second. But the closest I'd ever been to distrusting Ed had been the summer that Beth had spent two weeks with him in Brazil. I was so jealous that it made me ashamed. Beth had been hesitant about going, but the three of us had been such close friends for so long that she took him up on the offer, even letting him pay. If anyone had reason not to trust, it would have been Ed, because during the second half of our second year, Beth and I had moved beyond friendship. However, on account of the gossipy nature of medical school, we had wanted to keep things quiet—at least until we knew where we were going. I'd felt bad that we hadn't told Ed.

BY THE TIME I MADE it home, I felt drained and nerved up. I was confused by all the mystery around Ann. How the hell did she think that she could get a Goddard? Not to be a snob, but those awards go to the top two students in the class. Of course, I hadn't asked her if she had a 4.0 average. Why would Ed give her that scholarship? Something was seriously fucked.

As I opened the door I saw Kyle perched on a kitchen barstool sharing a can of tuna with Willy. Willy glanced at me, realized that I wasn't going to shoo him off the counter—something Beth would have done with a sharp clap of her hands—and resumed his feast.

"You're going out tonight, right?" Kyle asked.

"Right."

"Okay if I get pizza?"

"Fine, just don't give any to Willy; you know he can't have tomatoes. How was school?"

"Okay."

"Anything more than that?" I asked, wondering if he'd ever bring up yesterday's fiasco with my father.

"It was fine."

"Aren't you almost at the end of the marking period?"

"Yeah."

"Well, how's it going?" I asked, knowing that he wouldn't lie to me.

"I'll do okay. B's mostly."

"Good." I wanted to say more, like that I was glad things were kind of working out for him, and I was glad that he was away from the group he had started to hang with after Beth's death. Our move from Cambridge was, in part, for him. Kyle had always been a straight A kid; we'd kind of taken it for granted. Then his mother died and his father had a breakdown. He pretty much stopped going to school, started smoking pot, and didn't talk. It was my dad who'd picked up on it. He'd laid it all out while I was psychotic and hospitalized. He'd told me I had a choice: either pull it together—if not for my sake, then for Kyle's—or make some other plan for my son. If I couldn't be a parent, he'd said, someone else would have to take over. I had needed to hear that. Sometimes the completely nontherapeutic advice to knock it off and pull it together is just the ticket.

I was relieved Kyle was doing better in school. What was killing me was this wall between us. I wanted to hug him and tell him that everything was going to work out, but I felt as though I'd lost that privilege. Now we were like two people who were related but not close.

By seven, I was shaved, showered, and dressed in chinos, a button-down blue shirt, and a navy jacket. I'd been dreading this evening, the thought of light conversation not high on my list. At least now I had a reason to go. I needed to find out what Ed was up to. He had a lot of explaining to do, and I intended to get answers.

On the way out, I glanced into our slotted metal mailbox. I stopped, my mouth went dry, and a tightness spread from the back of my throat down to my belly. "Shit." Just when I'd thought the day couldn't get worse . . . the smell of smoke filled my nostrils. I watched my hand put the key in the mailbox and lift the flap. *Beth's face stares back from the off-white surface of the envelope. I taste blood and lipstick as I try to breathe life back into her.*

"Stop it, Peter." I imagined a steel screen dropping down in front of the flashback. *Please, God, don't let Kyle see.* My heart pounded as I steadied myself against the wall and shoved the envelope back in the slot. I'd try not to think about it—and the fact that whoever had sent the two previous envelopes to me back in Cambridge now knew where we lived. I had thought I was done with that, that whoever it was would leave me alone. I was wrong.

9

ANN HELD THE RECEIVER TO her ear; if she'd known it was her father, she wouldn't have picked up. "So what?" she spat at him. "So I'm seeing a shrink. It's none of your fucking business. How did you even find out?"

"They called me," he told her.

"Who did?"

"Some towelhead at the hospital."

"Why would they do that?" she asked, feeling a familiar dread.

"Said they wanted to know if you made it to your appointment. Said you had a real dedicated doctor who came in the middle of the night. . . . I'm sure he did."

"Why are you calling?"

"I thought you wanted your tuition."

"Sure, I want the money. Are you planning to send it?"

"Maybe. It's just I'm real curious how you've been getting by all these semesters. Looking back, I can see that I've forgotten maybe one or two checks."

"Try five, but who's counting? Look Carter, if you want to try to be my father, send the money. If you're not going to do that, just don't call."

"So that's all I am, a checkbook. I wonder what your mother would say if she knew how you were paying your bills."

"If she were still alive," Ann said, "I wouldn't have to do any of this, asshole!"

"Look, slut . . ."

Before he could say more, she hung up. She didn't slam the receiver down; it hadn't gone that far, but enough was enough. She glared at her roommate, Shana, who had recently undergone foot surgery to have webbing removed from between her toes. Their three months together had been miserable, and Ann's image of the frizz-headed girl with her gauze-wrapped frog feet was of some human toad perched on a Laura Ashley knockoff comforter. It was Shana who had ratted her out to the dorm master, a deceit that had ended in her night in the emergency room; there would be payback. If Shana weren't careful, her twice-daily visits to the vomitorium would become public knowledge—all out of concern, of course. Saturday night had been a nightmare, but at least Ed had intervened by having his friend bail her out. However, why had they called her father? It's not as if she were a minor. Letting Carter know was bad.

She glanced at the clock. It was nearly nine, and she had to get ready.

Shana looked up from her book as Ann headed toward their shared bathroom. "You have a date tonight?" she asked.

"Yes," Ann said, shutting the bathroom door. She felt as though her every move was scrutinized by this chronically regurgitating frog girl.

When they had first started rooming together Shana had been a bundle of questions, and Ann had felt like some exotic creature to be studied. Then the weirdness had crept in. This last intrusion—calling 911—was the final straw. The girl could not be trusted, and this weekend had confirmed that.

Ann locked the door, reached back into one of her two closet shelves, and pulled out a large cologne bottle. She turned on the faucet, uncorked the stopper, and took a deep swig of slightly warm Ketel One vodka. She felt the burn as it slid down. She took another long draw and set the bottle on the edge of the white porcelain.

She looked across at the pretty girl in the mirror—straight blond hair, blue eyes, skin that needed no makeup, and long dark lashes, a tribute to some Northern Italian blood. She pulled her hair up and back, twisting it into a French knot with a few tendrils falling free on either side, the whole thing held in place with an antique jet comb. Next, she unscrewed a tube of mascara and stroked up, remembering her mother saying, "You can never be too rich, too thin, or wear too much mascara." Then came lipstick—two tubes and a final gloss applied with a brush, and a hint of color to the apples of her cheeks and the face that emerged was flawless. She never overdid it. "Too much makeup," her mother had told her, "corresponds to too little class . . . unless we're talking about mascara." And then she'd laugh and say, "you get dispensation for that." It was getting hard to remember the laugh, other than it warmed her like the sun on a summer's day or a good shot of vodka before her swan song with the Imperial Escort Service.

Ann turned and studied her reflection in the floor-length mirror that hung on the back of the linen closet. She wore a strapless black Donna Karan cocktail dress that she'd hidden in a bin at Loehmann's, swooping down to retrieve it the day it went on final markdown. The scooped neckline showed the full curve of her breasts, and the hem fell just above the knee in a soft drape that drew attention to her long swimmer's legs. She wore silk stockings and four-inch heels, and beneath her dress she was a wet dream of black lace and garter belts—johns' favorites. She took a last drag on the cologne bottle, recapped it, and pushed it to the back of the closet. She was sure that Shana knew it was there, but after tonight that wouldn't matter. She'd do this last date and then it would be just Ed. He loved her. He said that the Goddard Fellowship was hers. He could probably even swing a single at the dorm. Plus, if for some reason Ed couldn't keep his promises . . . well, she wasn't going to be messed with. If word ever leaked that he was sleeping with one of the students, it wouldn't go well for him. It was all about control, and she was in the driver's seat.

Back in their bedroom, Ann ignored Shana. She grabbed a crushed black velvet and beaded wrap, draped it around her bare shoulders, and picked up a small black purse, which contained, among other things, condoms, lubricant, and an envelope addressed to the reporter who'd been interviewing her and a few of her classmates. Then, not looking at all like a medical student, she dropped the envelope down the mail chute and went out.

THE CAB DEPOSITED ANN IN front of the Park South Hotel across from Central Park. She strode confidently through the revolving door and smiled at the doorman. She didn't stop at the desk, but went straight up to the tenth floor. Tonight she'd see one of her regulars, and so she was on autopilot. She knocked on 1001. It opened, and a short balding man in his fifties who wore a two-thousand-dollar suit greeted her.

"Good evening, Veronica." He stepped back to let her enter. "Could I get you a drink?" he asked, taking her wrap and letting his eyes rest on the creamy perfection of her skin and the graceful curves of her shoulders and breasts.

"That would be lovely, John," she said as she turned into him, letting him feel her softness as his lips met hers and they kissed.

OUTSIDE THE HOTEL, A YOUNG blond man stood hidden in the shadows of an African Plane tree. He knew from experience that it would be at least two hours until she emerged. He muttered "Watch out for Ann" as voices whispered and laughed inside his head. They called her names and at times told him to do bad things. To drown them out he put on earphones and listened to an R.E.M. CD.

Passersby occasionally noted his presence, but quickly looked away when they realized that the man, wearing headphones and standing in the cold staring up at the hotel, was repeating a single phrase. "Watch out for Ann. Watch out for Ann. Watch out for Ann. . . ."

10

I ARRIVED AT ED AND and Miranda's lower Fifth Avenue building with two bottles of cabernet and a determination to get answers. I felt torn by my growing distrust. I thought about Keith
Taylor and Felicia. *Ed hung him out to dry.*

I got off on the eighteenth floor and checked my reflection in
a mirror outside their apartment. I looked tall, dark, and gaunt,
but otherwise normal, something that I found odd. I pictured
Ann and how pretty she looked on the outside. What a mess she
was on the inside; I could relate. So I looked good and I had wine.
I pressed the buzzer. As I did, I realized that the door was ajar, and
so I walked into the marble foyer. There was a spotlit bronze
Rodin bust to my right and a Miró oil hanging to my left. I
looked through the archway and spotted Ed, dressed in black, in
the living room in front of the grand piano. His back was toward
me and he appeared to be in a heated argument with a voluptuous
blonde in a low-cut red dress.

He must have heard the bell, as he turned and called out to
me, "Peter. You made it. I was sure you were going to come up

with some lame excuse." He said it with a smile on his broad Scandinavian face, but I heard a barb behind his words.

As I walked in, my feet sank into the carpet. "Am I that obvious?" I asked as he shook my hand.

He turned to the woman, "Gretchen, this is the illustrious Dr. Peter Grainger. Peter, this is Gretchen Becker, my second cousin."

"How do you do?" I asked, knowing a setup when I see one.

Gretchen extended her hand and smiled, revealing gleaming white teeth. "I've been looking forward to this." Her voice had a slight accent, probably German. I figured her age to be close to mine, and she was very attractive. Her fingers lingered, and I smelled jasmine. "I'm a huge fan of yours. I've read *The Road Back* so many times it's falling apart."

"Thank you," I said, curious as to why she'd be so interested in my book on recovery.

"You work at the mental health clinic now?" she asked.

"I do. I have Ed's old job."

"Fascinating, all those young people trying to figure out who they are."

"It's interesting," I admitted.

Ed broke in. "I should warn you that Gretchen is a journalist. What you think is harmless conversation can and will be used against you. In fact, she's doing a piece on our medical students for *New York* magazine. It's going to be a stunning exposé."

"My cousin teases," Gretchen said, fixing me with her china-blue eyes. "But I'd love to hear about the work you did with the police and fire departments after 9/11."

"You really want to know? It's like asking a grad student to talk about his thesis."

She laughed. "I don't think you could ever bore me."

"Thanks." I wondered how she knew so much about me. "You

know if you're really interested, I'm giving a lecture on trauma tomorrow for the med students; you're more than welcome."

"I'd like that, and perhaps we could find some time for an interview?"

"Maybe," I said, pleasantly distracted by her cleavage and the curve of her neck.

"Peter." Miranda appeared from the other side of the hallway, a tray of appetizers in either hand. "I thought I heard your voice. How are you?" Her smile was warm and genuine, and she looked adorable and chic in a green silk dress over which she'd tied a checked apron. Not for the first time I was struck by the contrast between her and Ed. Where he was tall, athletic, pale, and blond, she was short, curvy, and dark. Her hair was cut in a geometric bob that framed her face and accentuated her large brown eyes.

"I'm good," I told her.

"Are you?" Then, as if embarrassed by her assumption that I was ready to crumble, she added, "Of course, you are. And you brought wine." She smiled as though I had accomplished some especially wonderful feat. "So why is everyone standing around?" she asked. "Sit, be comfortable; I'll bring drinks. I've got a fabulous recipe for mojitos that, after I finish squeezing two dozen limes, I will be thrilled to share."

"Can I help?" Gretchen asked.

"Absolutely not," Miranda said, arranging a baked Brie on the coffee table.

"Where's Camille?" I asked Ed, wondering about his energetic eight-year-old who looked so much like Miranda.

"I heard something to the effect of a Brownie sleepover."

"And when does Blake get back from the Yucatán?"

Ed smiled over even white teeth. "In our last call, he was lobbying to stay the year."

"Isn't he young for that?" I asked, knowing that Blake was younger than Kyle.

"The apple doesn't fall far. He wants to learn Spanish, and the only way you do it is by being there," Ed said. "And frankly, the best thing to do with adolescent boys is have them hit the road. Think how many cultures send their young men on walkabouts."

"Is that what you did?" Gretchen asked. "You always seemed to be traveling."

"It was better than staying home," Ed answered. "At least Blake doesn't have to deal with an insane father the way I did."

"Oh, come on . . . you *are* insane." Gretchen chuckled, and directed a curious smile at Ed. "Aren't you being a little dramatic? The Judge was a sweetheart."

"To little girls, my dear," Ed replied. "He wasn't a fan of little boys; thought we all harbored the devil." He spoke through his trademark smile, the resting point of his broad face.

"I'd forgotten how much you didn't care for him," I said.

"He was a sadist," Ed said. "He derived pleasure from seeing other people suffer. Considering his career choices as an attorney and then judge, he had ample opportunity to make people squirm."

"I've never really heard you talk about him," I said.

He shrugged. "Not my favorite topic. Although to be fair, it was my need to get away from him that started me out. I wanted to be an anthropologist—that or an archeologist. He considered both unsuitable."

"He met with a horrible death," Gretchen added, her eyes on Ed as she spread melted Brie over a cracker.

Ed met her gaze. "No . . . it wasn't pretty."

"You were there," she said, not looking away.

"Yes. I was fifteen."

"What happened?" I asked, wondering at this connection between Ed and his cousin, almost as though they were playing a game. Clearly, his father was a subject that despite his smile, he didn't want to discuss. So why was she pushing?

Miranda reappeared, wheeling a hostess cart. On it was a frosty pitcher of mojitos swirling with crushed wedges of lime and macerated mint. She stood in the doorway as Ed told the story.

"We were on a miserable family vacation to the British Isles," he began. "One morning, before we took the ferry from Wales to Ireland, the Judge decides he wants to see some stone circles up near an old lighthouse on Holyhead Island. My mother and I got dragged along; neither of us wanted to go, but it wasn't worth arguing. It was raining that soft misty haze, not really coming down, just hanging in the air. When we got to the cliffs it was so thick that you couldn't see more than a few feet. The smart thing to do would have been to turn around, but he was determined to see these ruins—kind of a small-scale Stonehenge. Somewhere along the way we lost him. To get to the punch line, he fell off a cliff. We ended up getting to know the Island of Anglesey really well. It took two days to retrieve the body and another week to deal with the officials who needed to be certain that no one had pushed him."

Miranda left the drink cart and stood behind Ed's chair. She rested her hands on his shoulders, leaned down, and kissed his cheek. "I've never heard you tell that story like that," she said. "You must have been devastated."

"Not really. And this is where I lose all sympathy: I was glad. He had made my mother's life hell. I couldn't stand being around him, and I couldn't stand the way he treated her, which is why I got out as soon as I could. I started doing exchange programs when I was in seventh grade. But Mom . . . she had no escape. She'd never have divorced him. When he died, it was like she became another person."

"I wish I could have met her," Miranda said, handing her husband a cocktail.

Gretchen turned to me and whispered, "Breast cancer."

"So," Ed said, "that's my sad story. Who's next? Peter? Gretchen?"

"I didn't know," I said, feeling a pang of guilt over my suspicions.

"It wasn't pleasant," he admitted. "We weren't even certain if he was dead. The mist was so thick that we couldn't see the bottom of the cliffs to know where he'd landed. Even trying to find our way back to the car took hours. When I read your first book on trauma, aside from being pea-green with envy that you'd published before me, it reminded me of that walk. I remember Mom asking me, 'Do you think he's dead?' I told her, 'I don't know,' and we kept walking in this strange fog. Then, when we finally found the car, we had to decide what to do. Do we look for him? Do we go back to town? I think that was one of the hardest things for Mom. Without the Judge around *she* was now the adult. It used to be that every decision she made he questioned, ridiculed, and tore apart. When we got to the police station I saw a side of her I'd never known."

Miranda quietly poured drinks as Ed continued.

"I was proud of her, the way she repeated the story to the constables, never changing it. Yes, I was glad he was dead, and glad that she got a few good years without him."

"You really loved her," Miranda said, perching on the arm of his leather chair.

"Of course. I just wish her life could have been happier."

"So, Gretchen," Ed said, clearly trying to shift the attention, "how's your exposé going? Will I still have a job when you're done?"

"It's not an exposé, Ed." She turned to me. "You ask your

111

cousin to do you a favor, and . . . I should have used Cornell or NYU."

"Okay," Ed conceded, "so it's not an exposé. What is it?"

"It's the next in a long line of pieces that do well and pay my rent." She laughed. "This one focuses on how much money people make and the kind of lifestyle they can expect, all with a New York slant. And it's not just medical students. I've been given the green light for a four-part piece. I'm going to hit Wall Street, NYU Law, the medical school, and something more touchy-feely like teaching, where you make no money. All of my subjects are in their twenties, intelligent, and articulate. It'll be about the choices people make and their reasons for doing so."

"Who do you write for?" I asked, intrigued.

"Anyone who pays. This piece is for *New York*, but if I do it right, I'll rework it and then sell it to half a dozen of my regulars."

"Gretchen does a lot of publishing overseas," Miranda said.

"Yes," she said. "Europeans have a fascination with Americans. I'm not certain it's healthy, but a piece about young driven Americans pursuing the almighty dollar—there will be several takers."

"Is that what you and Ed were talking about when I came in?" I asked.

Ed's smile wavered over clenched teeth. "Gretchen and I are in disagreement over her choice of subjects."

"You said that I could pick whomever I wanted, as long as they were willing, and as long as I didn't mention my connection to you."

"True, but I had assumed you would show some judgment."

"All of the students you suggested, were, well . . . dull." She sipped her drink. "Either that or they were so unphotogenic it would have made it unsellable."

"You do what you have to," he said, still smiling, but clearly displeased.

"You gave me free rein."

A vein pulsed on his forehead. I immediately thought of Ann. Was that who they were arguing over?

"Okay," Miranda said, sensing the tension as she refilled our glasses. "*Now* you can help me." She looked at Gretchen. "Come along."

"I guess that's my cue." She got to her feet.

After they'd left, Ed turned to me. "What do you think of Gretchen?"

"I think you're sorry that you let her into the medical school."

"That's nothing. She's just focusing on the most unbalanced members of the student body. Thinks they'll make good reading. If it's too inflammatory I'll have the attorneys stop it."

"What if they can't? Couldn't that be a problem for the school? For you?"

"*If* she pushes too far; I don't think she will. We go way back. I stayed with her family in Frankfurt when I was sixteen. She's like a sister. So do you like her?"

"She seems nice," I commented, noticing how he was trying to shift the topic.

"Jesus, Peter." He sucked back his drink. "She's gorgeous."

"She is," I admitted, smiling in spite of myself.

"Just checking," he said. "I thought maybe the accident had damaged more than your memory."

I stopped smiling and stared at him.

"Sorry," he said. "My God, man, it's been a year." He got up from his chair and walked to the drink cart. "At some point you're going to have to think about dating. . . . Aren't you?" With his back toward me, he poured two tumblers of Miranda's concoction and then stopped. "You know, I have some freakishly expensive tequila, care to try?"

"Sure."

"So what about Gretchen? Interested?" he persisted, handing me a snifter with a hefty shot of a dark amber liquor.

"It's too soon," I said, wishing that he'd back off.

"I bet she'd go out with you if you asked her."

"Don't push me, Ed."

"You need a push," he said. "But hey, your choice. Beautiful woman, smart, funny, neither one of you attached . . ."

"Speaking of beautiful women," I said, my voice low. "You didn't tell me about the mess I was stepping into with Ann Walsh."

"What do you mean?"

I sipped the tequila, letting it smolder on my tongue. "Where to start? You could have told me about her history."

"I could have," he admitted without pause. "And I probably should have told you something before you went to see her . . . and thank you for doing that. It's just . . . the whole thing was a frigging nightmare. The girl is a train wreck. When you came in and saw me talking to Gretchen, that's who we were discussing."

"She wants to interview Ann?"

"You got it."

"I can see why you'd be upset."

"I can also see why Gretchen wants to use her; it's great copy. The daughter of a famous author, she's beautiful, and depending on how much she tells Gretchen, it could be quite the tawdry tale, as I'm sure you know."

"You should have told me," I repeated. "And about her father. He called me at the clinic this afternoon."

"Did he? What did Carter have to say for himself?"

"Mostly he yelled at me. By the way, he said that one of her psychiatrists ended up doing time. Was he talking about Keith Taylor?"

Ed's expression wavered as though surprised I knew about him. "No. That was a miserable business . . . good resident, but no way could we keep him. The attorney was clear that if we didn't want to end up with a mammoth settlement, he had to go." He glanced toward the kitchen. "The jail thing was when she was

a teenager. She was seeing some older psychiatrist in the Westport area and . . . he made some stupid mistakes."

"What happened to him?"

"Carter brought charges. Probably statutory rape; she was a
minor. When I got the call that she was in the emergency room,
all I could think was, Oh shit, here it comes again. Which is why
I called you."

"Ed, buddy, pal, next time . . . don't spare the details. . . . You
were Taylor's supervisor."

"Yes. And?"

I took a swig of tequila; the liquor helped lubricate my tongue.
"Why didn't you stop it?"

"If I'd known, I most certainly would have," he replied tersely.

I was dumbstruck as Ed's lie batted up against Taylor's notes.
You did know. I stupidly blurted, "Are you really planning on giving her a Goddard?"

"Who told you that?" he hissed.

Shit, here I was breaking Ann's confidentiality for the second
time after she'd pleaded with me not to. "It doesn't matter. But
why?"

"None of your concern."

"What aren't you telling me?"

"I don't know what you're talking about."

What came to mind was outrageous—either she was blackmailing him for his complicity in the Taylor scandal or . . . "Are
you sleeping with her?"

His expression was unreadable. He swirled his tequila and
looked me in the eye. "Peter, that is slander. And the only reason
I won't kick you out of my house is because I know what you've
been through. But it worries me. Are you taking your medication? Because I have to tell you that these fantasies verge on
paranoia."

He was trying to turn the tables, but I knew what I'd seen,

what I'd read. "What are you trying to do to me? You deliberately set me up."

"You should hear yourself. . . . Are you even fit to work? Who else have you said these things to? I've got a reputation, and I won't have you spreading this garbage."

There it was. I had put my faith, my livelihood, and my career in his hands. I'd trusted him as one of my oldest friends, and now I heard threats to remove me from my job, to destroy my career. "No one," I said, glimpsing a side of him I'd never seen and wondering what the hell I'd signed on for and how fast I could get out of it.

"I hope not. And I don't expect to hear it again . . . ever. Now I suggest you forget about this, and we rejoin the ladies."

AS MIRANDA SERVED UP A candlelit feast, it was all I could do to stay. I'd just been very stupid and needed to make certain that whatever plans I made would not be shared with Ed. I also felt bad for Miranda, whom I truly liked; I didn't want to ruin her evening. Beth, who'd been no slouch in the woman-of-the-twenty-first-century department, used to joke about Miranda's over-the-top competence. Mother of two, a leading pediatric cardiologist, a board member of three charitable organizations—including one where she went yearly with Ed to South America to perform pro bono surgery—but she also prided herself on whipping up gourmet meals for her family. Tonight was no exception. With the help of Betty, a young Brazilian woman whom they were helping to get her green card, she produced a splendid supper for which I had no appetite. We started with lobster bisque served with freshly baked bread and herb-infused butter. Then prime rib with gravy, glazed carrots, twice-stuffed potatoes, and a Caesar salad.

"So this is the healthy heart diet?" I asked, keeping my anxieties to myself and forcing down even more food, as Miranda had insisted I take seconds.

"It's all lies," she said. "Eat what you like; it's all about portion control."

I looked at my second thick slab of prime rib and the gravy that trailed from the butter-drenched potato. "This is moderation?"

"Sweetheart, you need to gain weight. Mother's merely looking after you."

"I think Mother's looking to drum up business," I replied, thinking I could get a position at Columbia or even get reinstated back in Cambridge—although I didn't want to pull Kyle out of Stuyvesant. Either way, I could get out with a month's notice.

"You're hurting my feelings. Besides, I only work with kids."

"It's delicious," I said, unable to taste it. I wondered what would happen if I went to the board of directors with Taylor's process notes. Would they understand the implications? Would they even care, in light of the massive grant dollars Ed had brought in?

"So how long have you all known each other?" Gretchen asked.

"Long time," I said, thinking how that was true, but that I didn't really *know* Ed—and that no matter what, I would not meet with Ann Walsh again, at least not alone.

"Ed and Peter were the Frick and Frack of their class," Miranda added.

"Which was I?" Ed asked. "Frick or Frack?"

"Definitely the Frack," Gretchen said. "So you all went to school together?"

"Pretty much," Miranda answered. "They were two years ahead of me. And the stars of their class."

I looked at Gretchen, whose porcelain-white skin glowed in the candlelight. "She's exaggerating."

"I most certainly am not. Peter came into medical school having already done a huge amount of research on trauma survivors. You published your first book when you were what, a freshman?"

"It's not that big a deal," I said, feeling put on the spot. Like a five-year-old who's pushed in front of company to play the *Moonlight Sonata*. "I was in the school of public health before medical school. My master's thesis just turned into something bigger."

"Uh-uh," Miranda said. "You couldn't turn around without finding his name on some publication, and every issue of the university bulletin had some mention of the young soon-to-be-doctor Grainger's accomplishments. Naturally, we hated him."

"Naturally," Gretchen offered, catching my eye and smiling. "And cousin Ed?"

"He took the Indiana Jones route, and you'd swear that the two of them were in this constant competition. Ed was off on these incredible jaunts to the Amazon where he'd come back with plants and toad venoms that had never been analyzed. And then he started writing. When *The Jaguar's Bride* was published it was like the rest of us were left in the dust. What do you do when you're going to school with someone who gets on *Oprah* and *The Tonight Show*? And look at them. It would have been okay if they'd been dogs. But no, they were the two best-looking men in their class."

"Were?" Ed asked, dryly.

"Men are so vain," Miranda replied. "Yes, my love, you are still beautiful."

He turned to me, his expression pleasant. "It's good to know."

Years back, this would have been a great night, the kind Beth would have loved. Now, it seemed discordant and scary. When Gretchen cajoled Ed into a round of his uncanny imitations, a skill he'd picked up in the jungle, where he'd learned to mimic everything from the mating cries of birds, to Miranda yelling at their teenage son to pick up his room, I was more frightened than amused.

"It just takes practice," he said after perfectly imitating Gretchen. The experience of watching her voice come through his mouth sent a chill. And then the conversation turned to the curious events of the Cadaver's Ball.

"Everyone was proposing to everyone," Miranda explained to Gretchen. "We all got engaged on the same night. Thinking back," she said, looking wistfully at her emerald, "it's almost cultish . . . but, stranger things have happened." She turned to her husband. "Do they still have it?"

"Yes." He blew her a kiss. "And people still get drunk on cheap wine and propose to women they've never met."

I forced a smile, but my head had started to throb. I needed air, so after dessert—shoofly pie—I made my excuses. "Miranda, it was wonderful, but I've got an early morning."

"You sure you wouldn't like to stay for a brandy?" Ed asked.

"No." I tried to match his tone, as though our prior discussion had never occurred. "One more drink and you'll have to pour me into a taxi." I felt strange. Normally I don't have to worry about flashbacks when I drink, but there was a trippy quality to my head that must have been from the mixture of mojitos, a couple glasses of wine, and the shot of five-hundred-dollars-a-bottle tequila. So either I was drunker than I thought or I was heading toward one great big daddy of a flashback.

"I think it's time," Gretchen agreed. "Heading east?" she asked.

"Yes."

"Maybe you could walk me home?"

"Sure." I felt the room start to spin.

We said our good-byes, and I draped my heavy coat over my arm.

"Aren't you going to be cold?" Miranda asked.

"I'll put it on outside." Heat pulsed through my skin. I forced a smile and kissed her on the cheek. "It was wonderful, thanks."

Ed came over and shook my hand, his grip tight as he stared at me. It was weird; his features were like a mask, and behind that contempt burned in his eyes. "Have fun," he said.

He released my hand and I stumbled back.

"Come," Gretchen said, snaking her arm through mine to steady me. "Take me home."

11

ED STEPPED OUT ONTO THE terrace that faced Fifth Avenue. Behind him, he sensed Miranda as she busied herself with the cleanup. He'd sent Betty home before Miranda could offer her the guest room as she often did.

The air held a wintry snap, and his breath streamed frosty tendrils. He spotted Gretchen and Peter. From this height it almost looked as though it were Beth and Peter, a sight he'd watched with bitterness on many occasions—like the night a month after the Cadaver's Ball, when, at Miranda's urging, Ed had hosted the agonizing "Everyone's Getting Married" party. Afterward, Peter and Beth had walked away together, no longer hiding their treachery as they held hands and kissed in the streetlight.

Gretchen turned back and looked up; it was unlikely that she could see him, but he smiled anyway. He'd spent the night observing Peter. The man clung to his guilt like Lady Macbeth. He had fooled the others—the police, the fire marshal—but not Ed. What to most passed as the trappings of grief, Ed saw for what it was—the face of the sinner. The only wrong notes in the evening—and they worried him—were Peter's accusations.

Somcone had talked. He immediately suspected Felicia Jones, remembering how she'd confronted him in his office after he'd broken the news that Taylor was being expelled. She'd accused him of incompetence and of deliberately setting Taylor up. She'd had no proof, however, and backed down when he'd pointed out that her allegations were unfounded, insubordinate, and grounds for disciplinary action. After tonight, none of that would matter. Still, he worried; had Ann said more than she should have? That business about the Goddard was a mistake. Plus, why would Peter have made the jump from that to . . . *What have I missed?*

He went inside and poured two snifters of sambuca. From his breast pocket he removed the *Datura* mix and added eight drops to one of the glasses.

Miranda came up from behind. "Is one of those for me?" she asked.

"No." he smiled. "I thought now was a good time to become an alcoholic."

"Peter's too thin," she said, taking the snifter. "You think he liked Gretchen? She looked gorgeous tonight, and it would be nice to see her with a decent guy for a change."

"You never know."

"No," she said, as she looked around the living room and sipped her drink. "I suppose Betty can finish up in the morning."

"Absolutely," he said, knowing that the drug would hit her hard and fast. "You've done more than enough for one night."

"Thanks, handsome." She put down the snifter and wrapped her arms around his waist leaned her head on his chest. "I'm a lucky woman. I often wonder what would have happened if there'd been another girl hanging outside the dissection rooms that night."

"No." He stroked her hair, anxious to get on with things and tormented by the thought that something critical had been forgotten. "I was waiting for you."

12

NICOLE SULLIVAN WAS HAVING A miserable night. Three in the morning and the crime scene in room 1001 at the Park South was getting ugly. When she'd first been paged it had been reported as a homicide, the first in a series of errors that had left her and her partner, Detective, Third Grade Hector Vega, with a bad situation.

As she surveyed the room where Ann Walsh had been found, Nicole felt the integrity of the scene slipping away. Her artist's eye took in how things were now, about an hour after the girl's discovery, and how they had probably been before the paramedics and a host of well-intentioned others had traipsed through.

When she'd arrived, she'd found a pissed-off medical examiner, Fred Corley, chewing out the medics as they loaded the woman onto a stretcher. "Did you even put a stethoscope on her chest?" the balding pit bull of a man had asked. "How long did you leave her bleeding? Is that what they teach you—leave someone long enough and you can bypass the hospital and go straight to the morgue?"

Nicole got a good look as they strapped Ann to the stretcher.

It wasn't hard to see why they'd taken her for dead. She hadn't appeared to be breathing; pale, young, blond, beautiful, and looked dead, but wasn't. Her blood was everywhere—on the sage-and-rose bedspread, the carpet, the wheels of the stretcher, and on the thick rubber-soled shoes of the paramedics, who had tracked all around.

Hector, who had arrived shortly after she did—unshaven, his dark hair mussed, and wearing a leather jacket and faded jeans—took one look at the mess of footprints and said, "That's not good."

"No kidding," she said, glad to have her buddy beside her. She then turned to the medical examiner, "So Fred, it's not a homicide. . . . Is it going to be?"

"Hard to call, she's lost a lot of blood. It looks like she did a recent hack job on her wrists and someone else wanted to finish the job."

"You're sure of that?"

"Yup, angles all wrong for self-inflicted. But, whoever did it wanted it to look like a suicide."

"Anyone get pictures?" She made eye contact with both of the responding officers. Neither met her gaze. She pulled her auburn hair back off her face and counted to ten. It had been less than an hour from the time of the call. But that was all it took to royally screw up the scene.

When she'd first received the call, there hadn't been much information. Two 911 calls had been made fifteen minutes apart. The first silent, just the sound of something, or someone, falling, and the second a whack job, a male caller babbling "Watch out for Ann" over and over. They were traced to the hotel, but not to the room.

Now wearing gloves, Nicole systematically went through the place as Hector snapped pictures. "Is this how the lights were when you arrived?" she asked.

"I don't think so," the older of the two officers said. "Just the lamp by the bed."

"You're sure?" she asked.

"Yes, ma'am."

"Okay, Hector, kill the rest of the lights and do a series like that. How was the body . . . the victim?"

For the next forty-five minutes Nicole labored to reconstruct the scene, mentally dividing the room into quadrants and ensuring that every inch had been examined at least once. She knew that she had a reputation for being a bitch and for, as her father put it, "not being able to suffer fools." She couldn't help it. So much evidence could be destroyed early on. All the intangibles could be lost—how the room smelled, the lighting. That she could live with, but having the body . . . not be a body. In fact, had the call been phoned in properly as an assault and battery, she'd still be at home.

But as usual, Jeanine had come up to look after Adriana. Nicole knew that Mom would get a good breakfast into Adriana, take her to school, and then, if Nicole couldn't get away, she'd drive Adriana to the therapist of whom she so disapproved in the afternoon.

Nicole shuddered as she looked around. She felt a lurking unease about this case. For starters, the girl carried an identification card for the university Nicole had attended. Added to that, the victim's last name was Walsh, which just happened to be the name of the man who had betrayed Nicole.

"You want to go through her purse?" Hector asked.

"Sure," she said, as she bagged and tagged a blood-smeared razor blade she'd found under the bedside table.

"So what do you think she was doing here?" he asked as she spilled the contents of the black satin purse onto a white garbage bag.

Nicole looked at the brightly packaged condoms and tubes of

spermicidal lubricant. She'd already found a used rubber in the bedside pail. "Maybe a hooker."

"Could be. The room's registered to a John Johnson." Hector said.

"Cute . . . so she comes up for her trick, and then what?"

"John doesn't like her or is into something rough and it goes bad."

"But slashing her wrists? No. And why isn't there more sign of a struggle? One of us is going to have to check on her at the hospital. Life would be so much easier if she'd wake up and tell us who did this. And if our perp finds out she's not dead, and he wanted her that way, we could have a problem. She'll need a guard."

"You pick," Hector said. "I could stay or go."

This was one of the many things she liked about Hector; he was easy. She knew after three years together, the feelings were mutual. Hector was a smart hard-working detective who repeatedly got the shit end of the stick for being both Puerto Rican and openly gay. Very little pissed him off, and when Nicole needed to sneak away for a parent-teacher conference, or got a call in the middle of the morning that Adriana was freaking out, he never complained.

"I'll go," she said as her stomach churned at the thought of setting foot in the downtown hospital. Her fear, she knew, was irrational, a throwback to another person, one who was going to become a painter and spend her life with a man who'd written a wonderful book and who loved her.

None of that, she told herself, could touch her now.

13

BY THE TIME I MADE it home, I thought my head was going to explode. My throat was parched, and all I wanted was a fistful of aspirin. I glanced at the clock. How could it have gotten so late? The answering machine light was blinking, and when I looked down at my pager, clipped to my belt, I realized that it was off. *Shit.* I picked it up and saw that my service had called after midnight. "So where were you at midnight?" I asked, realizing that I couldn't remember much since leaving Ed and Miranda's . . . other than I now had a huge problem with Ed. I vaguely recollected walking with Gretchen, and then . . . nothing. *So where were you for the past four hours?*

I pressed the play button on the phone and my stomach lurched at the sound of Ed's voice, "Peter, if you're there pick up . . . We've got a situation. . . . give me a call."

"Now what?" I grabbed the aspirin, swallowed four dry, and then called my service. "This is Dr. Grainger, you were trying to reach me earlier tonight."

"Nothing new, sir," the operator said.

"But my pager shows that I got a call at around midnight."

"Yes sir, and I have it logged in that you got the message."

"Right, thanks . . . Would you mind repeating that message?"

"It was from an Ann, no last name, but insisting that you call her."

"Could you give me the number again?" I scribbled it on a napkin. "Thanks." I hung up with the service and dialed the number. I got a busy signal. This was bad.

I then looked up Ed's number. I didn't want to talk to him, but I called anyway.

Miranda, sounding groggy, picked up after several rings.

"Sorry to wake you," I said, "but Ed left a message; it sounded important."

"Okay." I heard her call out. "He's not here, but he left a note, says he had to go to the hospital for something school-related. That's probably why he called."

"Thanks." I hung up and had a horrible feeling that Ann had done something.

The phone rang and I started.

"Peter?" It was Ed; he sounded surprised.

"What's up?"

"Where you been, man?"

"Long story," I said, hoping to not get questioned beyond that. "I called Miranda and she said you were at the hospital. What's happened?"

"It's Ann Walsh . . . of course. Although I shouldn't say anything."

"Tell me she's not dead."

"Not yet, although they're not giving great odds for her making it through the night."

"Shit . . . what did she do?" I felt the acid hit my gut. *What had I missed?*

"That's just it. They don't think she did it to herself."

"What? I'll be there in twenty minutes."

"No need. There's nothing that either one of us can do."

"I'll be right there."

"Peter, there's nothing you can do. Stay home."

"I know," I said, noticing how my head hurt less if I held it still, "but there's no way I'm going to be able to sleep without knowing what's going on." What I didn't say was that I didn't trust him alone with her.

"Suit yourself." He hung up.

I threw my coat back on and thought about Ed's call. He sounded pissed off that I was going to the hospital. *So why call?* Like he was checking in on me.

Kyle staggered out of his bedroom with the cat brushing between his ankles.

"Where were you?" he asked.

"Ed and Miranda's."

"No, after. Dr. Tyson called an hour ago."

"Just out . . . walking," I said, aware of the lie as it slipped through my lips. "And now I've got to go to the hospital."

"When are you going to sleep?" he asked.

"I'll figure something out. You get back to bed."

"Okay." He picked up the cat. "I'll see you for dinner?"

"Sure. And Kyle . . ." I said, heading out and feeling spooked.

"What?"

He looked so young with his crumpled boxers and sleep-mussed hair. "Bolt the door after me, and don't open it for anybody."

14

NICOLE STOOD OUTSIDE TRAUMA CUBICLE two staring in at the comatose girl. Her thoughts were jangled, and she wanted to unload this case, fast. It was four in the morning, and her past was closing in. *Just do your job*, she reminded herself.

When she'd arrived, she'd checked on the girl—comatose and no one laying odds on her survival. Next, she'd bullied the triage nurse into letting her look at Ann Walsh's chart. There, on the line for next of kin was "Carter Walsh, father."

Yeah, thousands of Walshes, but how many with the name Carter? One of the first rules of being a cop is to step away from cases where you're personally involved; it's bad business. You can't be objective, and if it progresses to trial you'll be shredded on the stand. She told herself that at the first possible moment, say around ten, she'd hand off the case. But how? What reason could she give to her immediate supervisor, Frank Plimpton, a man who believed that women cops should be crossing guards or prostitutes in vice stings? And that's what she was anxiously mulling as she listened to the steady in-and-out of Ann's ventilator. She'd have to tell the truth, but not go into stuff that Plimpton could use against her. She could admit that as a girl she'd had an affair with Carter, a married man. People would talk, but it wasn't grounds for anything. However, the problem with cops, and with Plimpton in particular, was they nosed out the truth; he wouldn't stop until he had the whole story. That she'd had an abortion would make for gossip, but it couldn't get her fired. The piece that was bad was that after the abortion she'd become severely depressed, and one afternoon she'd taken a lethal dose of antidepressants. While an episode of mental illness wasn't grounds for dismissal—at least in principle—leaving it off her police force application was.

Lost in thought, it took her a moment to register that she was no longer alone. There was a tall man staring in at Ann Walsh. His dark wavy hair was tousled as though he'd just gotten out of bed. She figured him to be in his late thirties.

"You know her?" she asked.

"Yes," he strode into the cubicle, looked at the monitor, and then back to the girl who had a tube taped to her mouth and two intravenous lines, one transfusing blood and the other labeled "Ringer's Lactated."

"You're her doctor?" Nicole asked.

He looked across at her. "And you are?"

"Sorry, Detective Nicole Sullivan." She pulled out her shield.

"I'm Peter Grainger, her psychiatrist." He extended his hand across the bed.

"At the university?" Nicole asked, feeling a need to be anywhere but here.

"Yes."

"Do I know you from somewhere?" she asked bluntly.

"I consult with the NYPD. Been doing it for a few years."

"You did the 9/11 groups."

"Some of them. What happened to her?" he asked.

"It's not clear; someone tried to have it look like a suicide."

"But it wasn't," he said.

"You sound relieved."

"I probably shouldn't be. I mean, this is horrible, but as a psychiatrist . . ."

"Got you, it's bad for business. She *had* tried to kill herself," Nicole commented. "Recently."

"Yes."

"Why?"

His deep brown eyes looked squarely back. "This is tricky. . . . Well, I suppose this counts as an emergency. She told me it was over a fight with her father."

Nicole swallowed. "What about?"

"It's complicated; I've only met with her three times, but she's a member of one of the saddest families I've ever encountered. For starters, her father is a bit of a celebrity. Remember a book called *The Jersey Boy*?"

The blood drained from her face. "Sure . . . so that's her father?"

"Yup, and from what I can tell, he's a mean drunk."

"You've met him?"

"No, just one nasty phone conversation."

"So she and her father were fighting?" Nicole struggled to keep a game face.

"Right." His eyes searched out hers. "Are you okay?"

"It's been a long night. So what was the fight about?"

"I'm not clear. . . . You should know that Ann was turning tricks; I'm pretty sure that's something she threw in her father's face."

"Why would she do that?"

"Her story is that he wouldn't pay her tuition and she needed the money."

"You don't buy that?"

132

"Maybe." He paused, weighing his words. "It's hard to say. . . ."

Despite her near panic, Nicole found it easy to talk with this attractive man with his square jaw, dark eyes, and deep voice. "Any chance she told you *who* she was meeting tonight?"

"No . . . although she said something strange this morning."

"What was it?"

"Some sort of scheme she was working on. Something so that she wouldn't have to turn tricks anymore."

"Was there more?"

"Yes." He looked at Ann. "Every year the school gives two full scholarships; she thought she was getting one."

"You sound skeptical."

"The Goddard Fellowships usually go to researchers. Maybe she did that, too, and I didn't know about it."

"I'll check. Anything else," she asked.

"Yes . . . and I should check with the university attorney before talking."

"That bad? You know it all comes out anyway. Especially if . . ."

"She dies?"

Nicole nodded. "All the secrets come out."

"I don't have all the details," Peter said, "but Ann had a sexual relationship with her therapist at the clinic last year."

"That can't be good," Nicole said, using Hector's pet phrase.

"No, I just looked at the records today. The resident was kicked out."

Nicole was about to ask for the resident's name when his pager beeped.

"Excuse me." He checked the readout. "It's the clinic."

She watched as he stepped behind the nurse's station to find a phone. He looked across at her as he spoke. He nodded and rubbed two fingers between his eyebrows.

"What's the matter?" she asked when he came back.

"Apparently, there's a crazed student tearing up the clinic's lobby."

"Why call you? Shouldn't they call the cops?"

"You'd think, but as I'm learning, things are a little different where the students are concerned. Got to protect our kids or something like that."

"Sounds like you've got to go." She reached into her pocket and pulled out her card. She glanced in Ann's direction. "I'll want to talk with you some more."

"Sure, although if we're going to talk about her old business, I should get some sort of blessing from the attorney."

"Always best," she said. "Could you at least give me the name of the resident?"

His eyes met hers. "It's Taylor. Keith Taylor."

"Do you know where I can find him?"

"I don't." He shook his head and glanced back in Ann's direction. He looked worried. "I've got to go. . . . Don't let anything happen to her."

She wanted to ask him what he meant by that, but he was already weaving his way through the ER.

Her attention was pulled to a commotion by the triage desk, where officers in blue had surrounded a shouting man.

"Where is she?" His voice rose in pitch and fury. She saw the man's back as he tried to barrel through.

One of the security people warned him, "Sir, you're going to have to calm down or you're going to have to leave."

"Fuck you!"

Her body froze and her heart raced. She remembered the last time she'd heard that voice and what it had said. *Why did you have to go and spoil things? I thought we were having fun.*

"Where's my daughter? I'll sue the lot of you! Get the fuck off me!"

It was all happening in slow motion. She saw Peter Grainger move past the melee. He stared at the man and then across at Nicole. He shrugged and then disappeared.

She watched as the guards pulled plastic gloves out of their back pockets.

Her breath caught when she saw Carter's face, red and contorted with rage. Spittle flew from his mouth. "Keep the fuck away from me!"

"Sir, you're going to have to leave."

"Or what, fuck face?" He attempted to bull his way through.

Someone shouted "Take him down!" The circle tightened around Carter and the officers brought him thrashing to the ground. There was a guard on each limb and one holding his head. The leader told him, "Sir, you're drunk. You can sue us in the morning, but right now you either leave or you spend the night in the drunk tank. You decide."

"You can't keep me from my daughter!"

"Yes, sir, I can do exactly that. You're not coming back in this emergency room."

"Get off of me!"

"Glad to, but are you going to leave?"

"Sure," Carter said, his tone much calmer.

"Okay," the lead guard skeptically said. "Release his legs."

Nicole saw their mistake as it happened. The man holding Carter's left was leaning such that when he released the limb, the booted foot kicked him in the head.

"That's it!" The lead guy said. "Into the tank!"

They moved with a practiced efficiency, strapping him to a steel-framed stretcher.

As they wheeled him across the room, Nicole got a good look. The years had not been kind. Carter's nose had the orange-peel quality of a hard drinker, and even with his still full head of steel-gray hair, it was hard to see the lyrical man she had fallen in love with, even if that man had existed only in her mind.

She wondered if he would recognize her and thought to turn away. Curiosity held her gaze, however. His head was locked in the steady grip of a guard, but even so, he bucked and thrashed. When he was directly even with Nicole, he turned in her direction. There was no spark of recognition, just blind fury.

As the procession retreated, she glanced at Ann and tried to catch her breath. She stared at the blood dripping through the IV and frantically hunted for the plausible excuse that would fly with Plimpton to get herself off this case.

15

WHAT WENT WRONG? ED SEETHED as he watched them bundle the swearing and struggling Carter Walsh through the emergency room.

From where he stood, holding a foam cup of coffee in the center of the nurse's station, he could see all the players yet remain hidden. *What went wrong?* Why had Peter left so suddenly? How was he even able to stand after the dose of Ralph's T2745 he'd been given in the hotel? He was supposed to have been found passed out with a very dead Ann Walsh and his fingerprints on the razor blade. He should have been on his way to lock-up, while he, Ed, let fall the sword laying waste to everything Peter loved. *Kyle, your father's been arrested. Dr. Tyson will pick you up.*

But this? This was maddening.

On the panel in front of him he watched Ann's heart monitor. *Why aren't you dead?*

It had gone well . . . to a point. The players had followed their lines. Ann had sobbed when he'd told her, "Of course I love you. It's just . . ." and he had explained the things that his good friend Peter Grainger had said about her, things that made him doubt her love. After all, if he was going to leave his wife and children, he had to be certain that she wasn't just some girl trying to sleep her way to the Goddard Fellowship. Ann was furious and had jumped at his suggestion to get Peter to come to the hotel so that they could "clear the whole thing up." She had said exactly what Ed had suggested when she called Peter's service, telling them she desperately needed to speak to him and no one else. The note he had her write for the bellboy, to be delivered when Peter arrived, was, likewise, letter-perfect.

What went wrong?

He stared at the auburn-haired detective in front of Ann's cubicle and, having poured a second cup of coffee, he backed through the swinging door and moved toward her.

"You look like you could use this," he said, offering her the coffee. "I'm Ed Tyson, dean of the medical school."

"Nicole Sullivan, detective . . . That's something." She put the coffee on a side table.

"What's that?" he asked, moving into the doorway to get a clearer look at Ann.

"Her psychiatrist was just here and now the dean of the medical school. This is standard procedure?"

Ed turned to her and smiled wistfully, dimples forming in his broad cheeks. "When students get in trouble we try to run interception, but this . . ." he sighed, relieved that Ann was unconscious and had a tube down her throat. "She doesn't look good."

"No," Nicole agreed, walking with him to the bedside. "They say they'll move her into the intensive care unit as soon as they have a bed."

"Do you know what happened?" Ed asked, desperate to know how the story was being pieced together.

"Not yet," the detective answered. "You know her?"

"I know all the students," he said, running an inventory of

Ann's life-support equipment and the various routes of access into her fragile body.

"Tell me about her."

"She's a good student, a hard worker," he added, noting the two separate lines, one for blood and the other for Ringer's lactated.

"You know that she tried to kill herself earlier this week?"

"Is that what happened?" he asked, pointing to a freshly bandaged wrist.

"No."

He found this woman infuriating; he needed details. With his voice pitched low and his face fixed with an expression of paternal concern, he switched tactics. "I knew she was having personal problems. . . . It's a school policy that any student who voices suicidal thought—or actually tries something—gets referred to our clinic. They don't always go," he admitted, "but we make the effort."

"I understand she saw Dr. Grainger, that he's her psychiatrist."

"That's right." Ed's ears perked up, glad that she'd identified the man who had to become her prime suspect.

"Recently?"

"I believe so."

"She'd been seen at the clinic before. Who did she see?" she persisted.

"A resident," he did not like this line of inquiry.

"His name?"

Ed faltered; she wasn't leaving him time to think. "I can't recall. . . ."

"I thought you said you knew all of the students."

"It'll come to me," he said, "and residents aren't students."

"But they are considered part of the medical school, aren't they?"

"Yes."

"They were lovers?" she asked.

"It shouldn't have happened," he said, realizing that Peter had told her about last year. *What else had he said? What else did he know?* And then it hit him, the thing he'd forgotten—Taylor's fucking process notes—somehow, Peter had gotten his hands on them.

"Was she still seeing him?" she asked. "Was he her boyfriend?"

"I tend to doubt it."

"Because?"

"Because he was kicked out of the program."

"And you can't remember his name?" Her tone incredulous.

"It's Keith Taylor," he admitted, furious that she had trapped him into a stupid lie and realizing he needed to destroy the notes before this detective laid eyes on them.

"So what happened to Mr. Taylor?"

"I don't know. I hear he's still living in the city, but I'm not sure."

"Seems like he might have reason to be upset with her."

"Perhaps."

"Perhaps? The man's future as a doctor was destroyed because of her."

"It wasn't good," Ed admitted. "But he's young. People move on."

"Is it a dead issue?"

"What do you mean?" he asked, battling frustration and feeling defensive.

"Is anyone taking it to court? Doesn't sleeping with a patient constitute malpractice?"

"There are lawyers involved," he said, visualizing the locked closet in the law office where the records were stored.

"Who's pressing the issue?"

"Her father," Ed said, and as he did, he noticed the detective look away, her interrogative stride broken. *Interesting.* And like testing a piece of ice to see if it could hold weight, he pushed. "Her father is a famous author."

"Yes, I'm aware of that."

The hint of a blush spread across her cheeks and her nostrils flared slightly. "Carter Walsh. Perhaps you saw them hauling him into the drunk tank?"

"I did."

He smelled the adrenaline and noted the dilation of her pupils. What was it about Mr. Walsh that made this woman squirm? "Have we met? You look familiar."

"I don't think so."

"You never went to the university?"

She paused before answering. "I was here as an undergraduate."

He was about to ask which school she'd been enrolled in when a young Latino man in jeans and a black leather jacket approached them.

"Nicole."

"What's up, Hector?"

"I got the hotel room sealed off; I thought you might want to get a second look."

"Thanks." She turned back to Ed. "I'll need to talk with you some more."

"Of course." They exchanged cards. He noticed she was wearing a wedding ring and realized he'd need her maiden name if he intended to look up her school records.

"What's the status of the girl?" Hector asked within earshot of Ed.

"She's starting to stabilize," she replied.

"She said anything yet?"

"No, and she's not going to be able to until they get her off the ventilator." Nicole glanced at Ed, and then her eyes darted past the locked door of the drunk tank. "Let's get a uniform outside her door," she said. "At least until we know what's going on."

"Already called for," Detective Vega replied. "I'll stay with her till then."

"Thanks Hector." She took off.

Standing beside Detective Vega, Ed watched her leave, taking the path farthest from the drunk tank. "Smart woman," he commented.

"That she is," Hector replied as he flipped open his cell.

"You can't use that in here," Ed told him, and pointed to a poster that prohibited cell phones in the hospital. "You can use the one at the nurse's station."

"Thanks, man."

"Don't mention it." Ed listened as Vega's footsteps were swallowed in the hum of the ER. Everything was falling to shit, but maybe it wasn't so bad. As for Taylor's notes, even if Peter had seen them, the only others who knew of their existence were Taylor, himself, and the attorney. If they went missing, everything in them would be hearsay. But first . . . he looked at Ann; furious at her for still breathing. That needed to change; the only question was . . . how to do it?

16

IT WAS STILL DARK OUT when I arrived, feeling both exhausted and wired, at the walk-in clinic. There, an overweight, out-of-breath, and near-retirement guard—Martin Stuckey—was trying to reason with a young man who was talking to himself while pacing tight circles inside a wall of upended tables and chairs. It reminded me of the bedroom forts that Kyle used to build when he was six.

"Come on, son," Martin coaxed. "Why don't you go with that nice doctor," indicating the on-call physician, who had a syringe of Haldol drawn up and waiting.

The kid, who looked to be about twenty, with matted blond hair, good teeth, and a hunted expression, wasn't biting. I wished that Martin had called 911, but I knew that he, like the rest of us, was encouraged to handle things internally before calling the cops.

Martin spotted me. "Doc, am I glad to see you."

At the same instant the boy stopped circling and turned to face me. "Watch out for Ann." He pointed at me.

I stopped and looked at him. He hadn't shaved in a few days

and his clothes were a rumpled assortment of two jackets, baggy jeans, and a hooded sweatshirt. I moved toward him slowly. Something felt wrong.

"Watch out for Ann." His index finger stabbed the air between us.

"That's all he says," Martin added. "I thought he might be one of yours."

"I don't know him," I said, although there was something familiar about him. *What's on his hands?* At first I thought it was dirt, but it had the reddish brown color of dried blood.

The boy's gaze darted across my face. "Watch out for Ann."

Of course, I thought, *that makes it perfect. She's in a coma, her father's in the drunk tank.* This had to be the brother. "Jason," I said.

He started to rock on the heels of his grimy sneakers. "Watch out for Ann."

I continued my cautious approach. I caught an acrid whiff of body odor and noticed dark stains on his pant leg and the cuffs of his sleeves. It was blood, but whose?

"Watch out for Ann." He backed away and began to pace laps inside his fortress of toppled furniture. "Watch out for Ann." There was a look of intense concentration on his face.

I knew he was trying to say something beyond those words. He stopped, and his eyes darted from a chair, to me, and then to his bloodstained hands. "Watch out for Ann. Watch out for Ann."

I generated a diagnostic differential to explain what I was seeing. The most likely choices were either that this kid had a psychotic disorder, such as schizophrenia, or he was high on hallucinogens—perhaps a bad batch of LSD.

"What about Ann?" I asked.

"Watch out for Ann."

Right. This was going nowhere. I felt the eyes of the night staff watching me. "He's not a student," I told Martin.

"He seems to know you," the guard replied.

"His sister's a student. She's in the hospital."

"The girl they found in the hotel?" he asked, bad news having traveled fast.

"Yes."

Jason stopped rocking. He stared at the floor, then at me. He sucked in a giant breath and blew out. "Watchoutforannwatchoutforann." Over and over, faster and faster. His face was red, and it was like watching an engine rev. I backed away, having seen this kind of thing before and knowing that nothing I said would slow him down.

"What you got drawn up?" I asked the doctor who had been cowering behind the reception desk.

"Ten of Haldol. Two of Ativan."

Not a bad thought; I just didn't know how we'd be able to get close enough without someone getting hurt.

I abandoned the idea entirely when Jason grabbed the metal legs of a chair. He pulled it free from where he had thrown it earlier and began to spin in circles. The vinyl covered chair banged against other furniture and against the floor. I could imagine that in his psychotic state the chair was like a force field, holding us back. In fact, it wasn't doing a half-bad job.

"Call 911," I told Martin. "He's got to go in."

"Whatever you say, Doc."

Jason abandoned the chair, now little more than twisted ribs and shredded vinyl. He flung it over a similarly demolished armchair and started in on an orange love seat. He picked it up by one edge and then slammed it to the floor repeatedly, splintering the stubby wooden legs one by one.

When the ambulance and the cops arrived, I gave them what information I could. "I think his name is Jason Walsh, but I'm not certain." I pulled out Nicole Sullivan's card and gave them her name and number, as I assumed she'd want to know about this.

With the cops and the medics behind me, I again approached. "Jason," I said, "I want you to go to the hospital."

Perhaps it was the show of force, but he stopped banging a mustard-colored chair against the floor. He looked at me. "Watch out for Ann."

"Ann's at the hospital," I told him. "We need to go there."

He slowed. "Watch out for Ann."

"She's at the hospital."

He stopped and let the mangled chair fall to the ground. He looked at me, and then at the police and the EMTs. "Watch out for Ann."

"Yes, we will. You need to come with us." I felt my heart going out to this kid while I wondered what he had done tonight. *Why is there blood on your hands, Jason?*

"Watch out for Ann." He walked toward me, and our little group parted, allowing me to lead him to the waiting ambulance.

Outside, the flashing lights painted his face with garish splotches of blue and red.

"You want to come with us?" the female EMT asked. "He seems to like you."

"Sure," I said, motioning for Jason to step up into the back of the truck.

The woman whispered to me, "You think he'd let me strap him down?"

"I think he'll be okay," I said. "But if you're going to restrain him, do it while you've got the manpower. I'll ride in back with him."

She hesitated. "Okay . . . I'm not supposed to do it like this, but see if you can get him to at least wear a seat belt."

I climbed in next to Jason and sat on the vinyl bench, our legs wedged up against the empty stretcher.

"You need to put a seat belt on," I told him.

"Watch out for Ann," he muttered quietly.

"I'll put it on for you."

The EMT climbed in and closed the door. She called to her partner, "Let's roll." She asked me, "Where do you want us to take him?"

"University Hospital," I said, figuring we may as well have the entire family under one roof. "Tell the driver to pull into the psych bay; it'll save us having to go through the main ER."

On the drive through the Village I listened to Jason's soft chanting. I smelled blood, and in the red light from the ambulance cabinets I saw his palms painted with the stuff, like the natives in Ed's books. He didn't appear to be injured, and I wondered what he knew about the attack on his sister. Could he have done it?

The ambulance pulled to a stop and through the back windows I glimpsed the emergency room's electronic doors.

We went in through the psych entrance, and for the second time in less than a week I saw Grace's smiling face.

"What are you doing here?" she asked, taking the paperwork from the paramedic. "I thought you were a big shot."

"He showed up at the clinic. . . . Don't ask why I was there. He's still a John Doe, but I think he's Ann's brother—the girl from the other night."

"Really? You don't see that every day."

"So who's the resident on call?"

"My new favorite, and she'll be thrilled to see you," Grace said, directing Jason to the bolted-down chairs outside the nurse's station. "It's Felicia. I hate to wake the poor thing; she's had a rough night. Ten so far. Your boy makes eleven." As she chatted, she helped Jason off with his coats and had him roll up his sleeve. The boy appeared docile in her no-nonsense hands. Grace put a blood pressure cuff on him, pumped it up, and stuck a stethoscope in her ears. "That's fine," she commented, writing down his pressure. "What you got on your hands, sweetheart?" she asked.

"Watch out for Ann?"

She looked up at me. "Looks like blood, should he be on the medical side?"

"I don't think it's his." I turned at the sound of a rapping on the security door. Through the wire-laced window I saw Felicia in green scrubs and a white coat.

Her first words were, "What are you doing here?"

"Long story." I took her into the back room, where we watched Grace get Jason into a Johnny coat. I told her about the attack on Ann and Jason's subsequent destruction of the clinic waiting room.

"You think they're connected?" she asked, flashing a worried look.

"I'd hate for that to be true, but . . . she said something about how her brother used to follow her around. Mostly she liked it, like having a guardian angel."

"I'd call it stalking. She never did anything about it?"

"I don't think so."

"Great . . . how long has he been psychotic?"

"Probably years. If it is Jason, which I'd put money on, the father has a real problem with psychiatrists, can't stand us."

"Wonder why?"

"Read his book. There are a couple chapters on how he ended up on a VA psych unit. He was shell-shocked and they misdiagnosed him as schizophrenic."

"Shit!"

"Yeah, and in those days it was whopping doses of Haldol and Mellaril, you'd keep pushing until they'd shake, drool, and couldn't walk."

"Ours," Felicia commented, "is a proud history."

"So you need anything else from me?" I asked, just wanting to get out of there. "I know I don't have to tell you this, but be extra careful how you document."

"Absolutely," she said. "You think I should medicate him?"

"Yeah, but gently. I don't think he's ever been on anything. Maybe just a whiff of Risperidone, but chase it down with a stiff dose of Ativan to calm him."

"And if he refuses?"

"As long as he's not tearing the place up, that's his right. Don't push unless you have to."

I wandered back to the ER to where Ann had been; she was gone. My heart skipped as I thought the worst—that she was dead.

I scanned the patient board; Ann's name had been lined out with "ICU" written in the final box. "Thank God." Farther down, I saw that her father was still in the tank, and Jason had just made it up as a John Doe.

It was five in the morning, and I was still in the clothes I'd worn to Ed and Miranda's. I knew I should go home, get an hour's rest, but I couldn't. I had to see Ann, to know that she was okay.

I took the elevator to the fourth-floor ICU. It was dark and strangely calm with the rhythmic whoosh and pulse of the ventilators. The only light streamed from the waist-high central workstation, giving the aides and nurses an eerie under-lit glow.

I was relieved to see a uniformed officer sitting outside one of the rooms. I walked toward him. "How's she doing?"

"Hasn't changed," he said. "You a friend?"

"I'm her shrink."

"Oh . . . I heard one of them say that if she recovers from the blood loss, she'll probably make it."

"Thanks." I looked in, not able to see much in the dim light, just her profile with a tube running down her throat and her chest rising and falling with the ventilator. On a rational level, I knew that there was nothing I could have done—or was there? She had called me around midnight, I'd gotten the message. So what did I do with it? Why couldn't I remember? And why was my head still pounding? I pictured Ed, his back to me—*. . . freakishly expensive tequila. Care to try?* A day ago I would never have thought such a thing, now I couldn't stop. *Did he drug me?*

I looked around, and spotted what I needed—the supply room. I tried the door, but it was locked. I fished out my wallet, grabbed my ID tag, and went to the nurse's station.

"Excuse me," I said to a morbidly obese night clerk reading a romance novel in the dim light. "I'm Dr. Grainger, and I need to get into the supply room for a dressing change." From over the counter I glimpsed her swollen ankles, and a pair of pancake-flat loafers.

She looked up, scanned my ID, and seemed perturbed that I had disturbed her reading time.

"If you give me the key," I offered, "I can find it myself."

"Knock yourself out," she said, relieved that she wouldn't have to get up.

Before she changed her mind, I took the keycard and was soon ferreting for needles, a rubber tourniquet, syringe, and tubes. When I returned the keycard, she barely looked up. "Where are the lab slips?" I asked.

She sighed and pointed behind her.

"Thanks." I was grateful that it was third shift—the land that time forgot. There was no questioning as to why I, a psychiatrist, was doing a dressing change. I locked myself in a patient bathroom, took off my jacket, and rolled up my sleeve. Using my teeth and my left hand I got the tourniquet on tight, saw the veins pop, and with a 23 needle got two tubes of blood. Using the sink as a desk, I filled out the triplicate lab slip. I thought of using a patient name, but if I was actually right and had been drugged, I didn't want to muddy the water. Right or wrong, it was going to look mighty odd that I was running a toxicology screen on myself.

I put the slip and labeled blood into a Ziploc bag, and went back to the nursing station. I saw what I needed, and without bothering the clerk, who was pretending not to see me, I put the bag into the vacuum transport, pressed the button, and sent it on its way.

I copped a last peek at Ann's monitor—her pulse looked strong and her blood pressure was holding. *Please, let her make it.* I wandered out of the ICU and sank down into a wonderfully inviting chair in the deserted conference room. I needed to think. What I did, though, was fall asleep.

I dreamed that I was back in med school. It was late at night, and I was outside the anatomy labs. A classmate had just told me that I had to present a dissection in the morning; I hadn't even started. I'd be there for hours, but it had to be done. No one was around, and I heard a noise, like a drum. I turned and saw a janitor splashing water on the floor and swirling it with a filthy mop. It made a squishing noise, and I saw thick pieces of yellow fat. He was using human fat to clean the floors.

"That's how they make soap," he told me, "fat and lye."

"Right," I said, having read that somewhere. I pushed into the anatomy lab and again heard the beating noise. *Boom chucka boom chucka.* It grew louder, but I couldn't find its source in the room filled with partially dissected cadavers beneath shiny white oilcloth.

Boom chucka boom chucka.

I spun around, hunting for the drummer. The beat persisted, getting louder.

I stared at the concealed body in front of me, I thought I saw it move. I stepped closer and reached for the oilcloth. As I did, the slick plastic fabric flew back and a half-dissected man sat bolt upright. He looked away from me. Strands of muscle and milk-white tendon dangled from his cheek.

"Hey, Joe!" he called out. The drum continued to beat.

The cadaver on the next table slid back his oilcloth and sat up. "What, Moe?"

"Do you hear that beat? That crazy beat?" He raised a hand with muscles that hung from the bone, snapped his skeletal fingers in time to the drum, and started to sing in a sweet Motown tenor, "My baby came a-calling. Looking for her man . . ."

I sensed others moving and shifting. The room was coming to life as bodies slithered off their tables.

"I had to take her dancing. I took her by the hand."

A stainless-steel box flew open and eight partially dissected heads joined in a perfect four-part harmony. "Baby got to dance. Baby got to dance."

I felt a tap on my shoulder and turned to face my assigned cadaver, Bessie, an old woman who had given her body to medicine. "What's the matter, darling?" she asked, with a warm southern accent. "Cat got your tongue?"

I didn't know what to say; I was grateful to her for letting me cut her apart, but I wasn't prepared to meet her like this.

"Dance with me," she said, stretching a bony finger toward me. She placed her hand on my shoulder drawing me closer. "Come on, darlin', dance with me."

The room closed in. She gripped me hard. I didn't want to hurt her, yet I desperately wanted to get free.

She brought her face close. I saw the bones of her jaw and the metal of her bridgework.

"Kiss me." Before I could break away, her lips were on mine.

I pulled back. The music stopped; it was just Bessie and I. She shook her head as the muscles, the layers of fat, and the tendons knitted themselves into place. New skin formed, her hair changed from wispy and white to lustrous and blond. "Kiss me," she said, and this time I didn't resist. I couldn't. Her tongue entered my mouth; it was warm. I felt repulsed and aroused. She pulled away; it was Ann.

"I've got to go," she said, pushing me back, but letting her fingers linger.

"Wait!" I called out as she moved into darkness.

"You can't follow." Then she was gone. I looked around; there was nothing. I started to run, I tripped, and I fell into blackness.

I WAS WAKENED BY MY pager's electronic bleep. It seemed to be tied directly to my adrenal glands. My pulse jumped and I had a horrible feeling that something bad was about to happen. I couldn't believe I'd fallen asleep here. *Shit.* I glanced at the clock, it was after nine. *What day is it?* I had to get my bearings. It was Tuesday. *Do you know what you're supposed to be doing today?*

Around me I heard the hustle of the unit, as a group of white-coated physicians wheeled by the doorway with their cups of coffee as they did their morning rounds. I remembered snippets of my dream and of chasing Ann. I didn't catch her, at least I didn't think I had. The pager sounded again; it was Peggy.

I picked up the phone in the conference room and dialed. "Hey Peggy."

"Where are you?" she asked.

"The hospital."

"Are you okay?"

"It was a rough night."

"That's what Felicia said."

"You saw her already?"

"She came in to see you. Said she wanted to talk about the patient you brought in last night. . . . Have you gotten *any* sleep?"

"Some . . . not much. What's on my schedule?"

"Let me pull it up . . ." I heard her tongue click against the roof of her mouth. "Oh, dear . . ."

"What?"

"Did you know you're giving a lecture at ten?"

"Shit!"

"Uh-huh . . . do you want me to cancel?"

Despite my decision to get away from Ed, I still had to be careful about how many screwups I had; word gets around. And I didn't want to put Peggy in the position of having to lie for me. I'd known about this for months; it was to be a basic talk on trauma for the medical students. "No, I'll be there. Any messages?" I asked.

"A Detective Nicole Sullivan called."

"If she calls again, page me, unless I'm in the middle of the lecture. So what else?"

By the time I hung up, Peggy had talked me into canceling two afternoon meetings so that I could leave early. Then I called home, expecting to get the machine.

Kyle picked up.

"Why aren't you at school?" I asked as I walked out of the room, stretching the cord to where I could see into the ICU to reassure myself that Ann was still alive.

"Where are you?"

"I'm at the hospital. I had to admit a student last night." The same cop from last night gave me a tired nod. Behind him, I could see the foot of Ann's bed and her heartbeat pulsing red across the monitor. *Thank God.*

"Why didn't you call?"

At that moment, hearing my son's voice and how frightened he was, I felt myself sink through the floor. "Look, Kyle, I should have called. I'll try to be home early. Can you still make it to school on time?"

"I'll probably need a note."

"Have them page me." I made him write down the number.

"Okay . . . I didn't call Grandpa this time," he added.

I felt tears well, "It's okay, Kyle. If you want to call Grandpa Michael, it's okay . . . I'm really sorry."

"I know you are, Dad."

"I love you, son."

"I love you, too, Dad."

I hung up and put my hands on either side of my head. Somehow, I would make this up to him. I felt stubble and I wondered if I smelled as rank as I felt. "Just move," I told myself, remembering a quote from someone, probably Emerson, about how you know you're a man when you get up and go to work even when you don't want to.

I left the hospital, squinting against the blinding sun. I stopped in at a deli and bought a disposable razor, a small can of green shaving gel, deodorant, a sixteen-ounce cup of coffee, and a pair of eight-dollar sunglasses.

It was ten to ten when I got to the Fleming Building and entered the cool lobby, which had been renovated in the 1920s with a somber black marble that covered the floors and shot up to the vaulted ceiling. The arches overhead were white, and the whole effect was like being in church.

I was slotted to speak to the second-year students—Ann's class. I wondered if they knew what had happened to her. Did any of them know she had nearly died? Would anyone care?

I stuck to the periphery, inside the shadows of the columns that ran around three sides of the massive room, and snuck down to the basement. One floor below, behind an electronic security door, was Ed's sprawling maze of labs, also the location of my dream. I could still see Ann. *You can't follow me.* Where was she going?

No place good, I speculated, as I pushed open the door to the men's room. I flicked on the light and latched the door, grateful for the quiet, the solitude, and the eight minutes before the lecture was to start. I cracked open the plastic lid on the coffee and took that first wonderful sip, like sparking a motor back to life. I caught my reflection in the mirror. My eyes seemed to have retreated back into my skull. My cheeks—covered with stubble— had a hollow, almost tubercular look. I wondered if I'd lost even more weight. When Beth was alive, I'd achieved what she referred to as my front porch, a pooching around my midsection that no amount of sit-ups, crunches, or working out at the aikido dojo could remove. I'd been more than 220 pounds, which wasn't tragic considering I'm six foot two, she liked to cook, and I liked to eat.

I peeled off my shirt. The front porch was gone, and while I should have been proud of the six-pack abs that had been hiding beneath my extra weight, it just made me sad; another piece of Beth—the effects of her cooking—gone.

"Okay, bone boy." I filled the sink with hot water, dropped in a blue disposable razor, and with only a couple nicks, scraped my face clean. I grabbed a handful of brown paper towels and soaped and sponged off my torso.

"Well, that's as good as it's going to get." I took long sips of the rapidly cooling coffee, dressed, and left the safety of the bathroom. As I glanced at the keypad by the door to the subbasement, I wondered if Ed were here. His choice to keep his laboratories deep underground had always struck me as quirky. We used to crack jokes about his proximity to the morgue. Now I couldn't remember why that was funny. He was up to something with Ann, and had tried to suck me into it. And while I wouldn't voice it—not without proof—I bet he'd had something to do with her attack.

I punched the elevator button and soon found myself surrounded by a noisy throng of students outside the two main lecture halls. According to the printed notice I had been given the bigger of the two: Craft Auditorium, your basic intimate setting with a capacity of five hundred. I had expected to find a smattering of attendees and was surprised to see that the place was filling up, and not just with medical students. There were cops and firefighters with whom I had worked a couple years back. Beyond that, I wasn't certain who these folks were. The second-year class had a hundred students, so even if they were all here, the auditorium should have been mostly empty. A professor I'd met during a meet and greet waved. Behind her was Gretchen Becker, who had a tape recorder trained on the podium.

"Dr. Grainger?" A man in blue workpants and a university logo shirt approached me.

"Yes."

"I didn't hear back about your A/V requirements. . . ."

"I don't need anything," I told him, having long ago dispensed with slides.

"Any handouts?"

"No. Besides, they're going to tape this. Any questions for the exam will come directly from the lecture."

"Great." he smiled. "If only they were all this easy. How about a refill on the coffee?"

"Thanks."

I felt the attention focus on me as I walked down the aisle. The moderator, the bearded and bespectacled Dr. Albert Goldwin came over.

"Quite the turnout," he said. "My office has been getting calls ever since your name came out on the syllabus."

I didn't know what to say; I used to do a ton of lecturing, but almost nothing in the past year. My books continued to sell, but mostly because they were mandatory in many curricula.

"Do you have an introduction you want me to use?" he asked.

"No, just show me the mike."

"Right." He climbed the stage and the room quieted.

With my back to the wall, I stared at my shoes as he made the introduction. He was effusive, and I would have been happier with less.

". . . and now, I give you Dr. Peter Grainger."

There was clapping, and I felt as if I were supposed to launch into a medley of my favorite tunes, more like a performance and less like a lecture.

Dr. Goldwin shook my hand as we passed on the stairs. "Good luck," he said, unhooking the lavalier microphone from his shirt and passing it to me.

"Thanks."

I took a deep breath and the first thing I noticed was a university logo mug filled with steaming black coffee. I picked it up and looked out; it was standing room only. This was supposed to be your basic introductory lecture about trauma. I'd given this talk hundreds of times. I could do it with my eyes closed, but as I looked out at these faces who'd come here for something more, I knew that I didn't want to do this on autopilot.

"Where to start?" I heard my voice echo through the cavernous hall. I put down my coffee and stepped out from behind the podium. "For years I've been studying trauma and its effects on people. Why would I do such a thing? My father, who's also a shrink, thinks it has to do with something very bad that happened to me when I was five: I witnessed the death of my mother." I made eye contact with an old friend from the fire department. "I was playing in the driveway, and she'd gone out to get a few things for supper. There was a tall hedge that lined our driveway, so she couldn't see me. At the last minute she swerved to avoid hitting me, the car went into a tree, she wasn't wearing a seat belt—because she'd just run out for a few things—and I saw my mother die. I don't remember much after that. My dad tells me that I had many of the classic symptoms of children who've experienced traumatic events—night terrors, some regressed behavior, fights at school, that kind of stuff. Although, as he's quick to point out, this wasn't the best time in his life either, having just lost the woman he loved. So point one: Trauma hits *families*."

My eye caught some movement at the back of the room, and I

noticed Detective Sullivan wedging in against the door. There were no empty seats.

"So then what? We both got on with our lives. I stopped having nightmares, I got really good at fighting, and other than needing to turn off the television when they're showing especially gruesome car wrecks, I was mostly scarred over. Not better, not back to the way I was, but good enough. Kind of like when you break a bone and it heals, it's never one hundred percent. So point two: People do recover; we get better, but there's always a scar. It fades; but it's there. And for some, with severe PTSD, it may never fade.

"Then I got older and went to college, swearing that I'd never become a psychiatrist like my father." The audience chuckled.

"I've since learned that when I say I'll never do something, I can pretty much bet I'm going to end up doing it. . . . Anyway, I started out as a biochem major, very interested in what goes on between our ears, chemically. As I got more involved with brain chemistry, neurotransmitters, etc., I became fascinated with conditions where you could identify changes before and after some event . . . like trauma. That was my entry into the field. I began to work with Dr. John Borkman, who had a lot of expensive scanning equipment and a huge cohort of Vietnam veterans with severe post-traumatic stress disorder. What we've learned since that time is that the brain is changed by traumatic events. We produce different chemicals in different quantities, and when we're rechallenged by a stress, we start pumping adrenaline, cortisol, glucose and all sorts of juice, which either make us want to punch somebody's lights out or get the hell out of there as fast as we can. It's fight or flight, and it's the underpinning for everything we're going to talk about today. Point three: There's a good evolutionary reason why we freak out in dangerous situations; it keeps us alive. If our cave-people ancestors hadn't had this response they would have seen the saber-toothed tiger and said, 'here kitty

kitty.' Chomp. End of species. You do not progress to the next level."

I took a sip of coffee and waited for the laughter to subside. "Along the way we learned other stuff, like, among a large number of vets who'd seen a significant amount of combat, all but a couple developed post-traumatic symptoms. Anyone want to guess what those folks had in common?"

One of the cops shouted out, "Sociopaths."

"Correct. The only people who weren't affected by the killing and the bloodshed were sociopaths, people with no ability to empathize with the suffering of others. Which begs a question . . . if sociopaths deal so well with stress and don't freak out like the rest of us, aren't they more suited for survival in the long run? Their brains work differently from ours." I paused. "Of course, I'm making the assumption that there are no sociopaths in the audience, which . . . having gone through medical school myself, might be the wrong assumption."

I waited for the room to quiet, and while I'd meant it as a joke, I was thinking of Ed. "So where were we? . . . trauma." I looked around. I wanted them to get the real point, the big message, and in that moment I knew there was only one way to do that. "The truth about trauma is that for most people who've never worried about mental illness—'it's not for me, thanks'—it's the way in."

I gripped the podium. "About a year ago I was in a car accident; I was driving, it was late at night. To this day I can't remember exactly what happened, but the car went into an embankment, and my wife, who was pregnant at the time, was trapped inside. I can remember trying to free her from the burning car; I was unsuccessful, and she died."

The silence in the auditorium was total and heavy.

"After the accident, I experienced a number of post-traumatic symptoms." I looked out at the audience and made eye contact with several of the students. "Having always considered my thoughts to be somewhat under my control, I was a little freaked to find that I could be standing in the supermarket, but inside my head I was back at the scene of the accident trying to pull my wife from the burning car." I was on dangerous ice as I told the story, trying to keep it together, not wanting to overwhelm them with the details—my lips on Beth's trying to breathe for her, the smoke everywhere.

"Here's my situation—I was supposed to be the expert on trauma, but I found that until you actually experience a flashback, it's academic. I started to lose chunks of time; I dissociated. I became severely depressed, and for the first time in my life, I thought about death and how it might be preferable. I thought about suicide, and on more than one occasion, while I was driving my car—something I now avoid, but had to do—I resisted strong urges to turn the wheel, push my foot down on the gas, and end it.

"It progressed to where I had to be admitted to a psychiatric hospital. . . . So, why am I telling you all this? First, it's because regardless of the kind of physician you become, you are going to work with people who have been in, or who have witnessed, life-threatening experiences. With the exception of sociopaths, these people have been changed. We know this from the research, and I know it from the reality of finding my brain turned into an unpredictable jack-in-the-box.

"But my final point—and where we'll spend the rest of our time—is that people do recover. . . . Things can get back to normal. So now let's talk about treatment, and how we get folks to come out on the other side. . . ."

17

AS PETER LECTURED, ED SHUT down his computer and emerged from his underground office. These past few hours, anxiously monitoring Ann's progress from the ER to the ICU had been hell. At any moment she might have wakened, but there'd been no safe opportunity to take care of her; she was shuttled from x-ray to CT scan. Finally settled in her room, she needed to die, and it had to be now.

"Ralph, I'm going to get coffee. You want anything?" he asked, as his assistant busily recorded the vital signs of test rats.

"I'm good, thanks."

"I won't be long," Ed said, appearing calm. "I just want to clear my head." Without further discussion he took off, glancing back to be sure he wasn't being observed. He held still, making certain that there were no workmen in the morgue, which was in the final stage of its move. Satisfied, he headed away from the elevators and toward the labyrinthine tunnels that connected Fleming to University Hospital. It was also the only remaining entrance to this section of the medical school that didn't require a pass code. That, too, would change in a few days.

The tunnels were the domain of the janitorial, kitchen, and maintenance staffs. When Ed had been a student, the on-call rooms had been on the fourth floor of Fleming, so every resident and student knew these underground passages that allowed you to get from building to building—a handy thing in the dead of winter.

Over the years, Ed had explored these tunnels; he knew where to duck when the pipes cut the headroom down to less than five feet or which door led to the maintenance floors' staircase—part of the novel infrastructure he'd conceived of and had funded for University Hospital and the attached cancer center. Architects from around the world now flocked to the hundred-year-old structure, which fifteen years ago had been written off as not viable. The maintenance floors—all his idea—with their five-foot ceilings, had been built above the patient wards. In the newly created spaces, all of the internal systems—ductwork, sprinklers, electric, oxygen, computer cable, etc.—could be upgraded and concealed. It had been dubbed "room wrapping" and had become an industry model.

What Ed had never shared with the architects was his real purpose. These spaces allowed him unobserved access to patients. Every day, he had his pick of four hundred human subjects already hooked to monitoring equipment. All he needed was to select the appropriate candidate by scanning the hospital's census data. If he needed three forty-year-old males to study the cardiac effects of a new compound, they were just a couple clicks away. If he had to study the combination of two drugs in an elderly woman, no problem—her name's Hattie Field—she's on Eight West. And when he had needed to determine the lethal dose of T2745, what better way than with a young hoodlum—John C. Carroll—shot in the leg by a cop following a vicious attack on a female store clerk. In cases like that he would think of his father, and realize that on top of everything else, he was providing a service to the community. No expensive trials or the cost of jail, no subjecting the victim to the terror of facing her attacker. A worthless life had been ended and redeemed by its value to science.

Ed's competitors wondered how he was able to push his drugs through the FDA faster than anyone else. He had a reputation for getting it right, for knowing the side effects and safety profile of each compound well before it went into human studies. The answer was simple: By the time he got FDA approval for human investigation, he'd already run the tests.

Now, however, his thoughts were far from experimental medicine as he ran up the metal stairs, skipping every other step, his footfalls sure and silent. His ears, like sonar, scanned for any human presence.

As he got to the fourth floor—one of his favorites, specifically because of the ICU and the superb ability to monitor human subjects—Ed crouched through a four-foot door and found his way to the space above Ann's room.

He bent down and looked through a crack between an outflow vent and a ceiling tile and felt a rush of relief as he saw that she was still on the ventilator and alone. As he eased up the tile, he glimpsed a uniformed policeman's back through her open door; his chest tightened. He knew that from the waist up, she was invisible from the nursing station. Only someone in the room or standing in the door could see what he was about to do, but if the officer should turn or if he had mistimed the nurse's fifteen-minute checks . . . disaster.

He glanced at Ann's face. She looked younger without makeup, almost innocent. His eyes traced her two intravenous lines. They had stopped giving her blood, so the line on the left was now stoppered with a heparin lock. The one on the right was dripping, and it appeared that an antibiotic had been added to the bag. Perhaps she'd developed pneumonia. Maybe she'd die on her own.

A fluttering of her lids caught his attention, and then they opened; she stared up at the ceiling, up at him.

His breath caught, at first thinking there was no way she could see him hidden in the shadows. Her eyes bulged, raw fear was in her face.

He started to panic. If she moved or made a commotion the guard would be in. He'd get away, but how long before they took the tube out and she started to blab? However, she didn't move; she just stared. "Oh, Ann," he whispered, realizing that they had paralyzed her to keep her from bucking the ventilator. She couldn't move.

He reached into his pocket and pulled out a coiled-steel angioplasty catheter. Normally, this would be snaked up a patient's femoral artery and into the heart or carotid artery either to inject dye or to blast open a blockage. The beauty of the hollow-tube design was that it allowed for a variety of functions, everything from taking pictures with a fiber-optic camera to drilling through cartilage. For Ed, the eight-foot instrument was perfect for other things, such as administering drugs from a distance.

Lying flat, he swung the catheter toward the rubber-capped heparin lock embedded in Ann's arm. He brushed against it on the first try and attempted to grab it with the clawlike surgical clamp on the tip. The metal teeth closed on empty air.

He swore as he swung it back for a second try. His hands, one bracing the other, started to tremble. He maneuvered through empty space, trying to slow the distant end of the instrument; he hovered by the heparin lock, opened the clamp, and just as he pressed to release the teeth, her arm moved. "No," he hissed, feeling the seconds slip away. He glanced anxiously at the officer's back, it didn't budge. Then he looked at Ann directly below him. Her blue eyes were wide open, tears streamed, and she was trembling, trying to move, trying to save herself.

No. Rage built. He swung the catheter into position. The

clamp encircled the heparin lock, he pressed the release, and grabbed on to the rubber tip. *Yes.* He fished out the syringe loaded with an ampoule of concentrated potassium chloride.

Ed stared into her eyes; he could hear her silent scream. He paused briefly, remembering how, when he had made love to her, she had become Beth.

"Die," he mouthed and depressed the plunger, sending the KC1 as a rapid push down the catheter and into her arm. He counted to two and released the clamp. As her bedside monitor started to beep, he yanked the wire, replaced the ceiling tile, and ran.

He reminded himself to stop at Starbucks, and he was back in his laboratory with a double latte, all in the span of a longish coffee break.

"So how's the esterified compound coming?" he asked Ralph, his expression bland.

"You know," his assistant admitted, "one tiny change and it throws everything off."

Ed nodded, picturing Ann's blue eyes staring up at him. "It happens that way. What's the problem? Dosing? Duration?"

"All of the above," Ralph said. "It works great with some of the rats, but others seem to shake it off."

"You might want to stabilize it with a methyl group," he commented, knowing that even as he spoke the ICU staff would be performing CPR on Ann. They would pump her full of drugs and try to restart her heart with jolts of electricity. In the end, they would fail, and at autopsy they would report that she had died of a massive coronary secondary to blood loss. Her death was now a homicide.

"Huh, I hadn't thought of that," Ralph said.

"It'll put less stress on the chemical bond; it won't break apart as easily. Of course, it might not break apart at all, but it's at least worth trying."

"Thanks."

"Don't mention it," Ed said, and satisfied that he'd made his presence real, he retreated to his office and booted up his computer, desperate to access Ann's monitor, to know that she was finally dead.

18

NICOLE SULLIVAN STOOD IN THE back of the packed auditorium, her attention riveted. Peter Grainger's deep voice filled the space; his words resonated. She thought of Adriana as he talked about stages in the healing process. She also thought about Donny and her marriage. As Peter talked about critical decision points, to stay frozen in fear or screw up your courage and move forward, she knew that she was at such a point. It was just a matter of taking action. If not, she'd be worn down by her mother, Donny, and her own uncertainties. So what if she was alone? She'd known love—that had been Carter. She'd gone the secure route with Donny, and that hadn't worked, either. As she mulled over this, her right hand played with her wedding band. She felt its hardness and its worn edges, she pulled. It stuck at the knuckle, and then came off. She stared at it, feeling its weight in her palm. Then she clicked open her purse and dropped it in.

Peter took questions at the end of his talk. Hands shot up. It was apparent that she wasn't the only one who had been touched.

As one girl tearfully asked about nightmares she'd had since the death of a baby brother, his answers were kind and understanding.

A Vietnam veteran stood up and asked about the role of drugs and alcohol that had been such a factor in his own life and in that of many of his buddies.

"Good point," Peter said, "and a whole other lecture. But boiled down, drugs and alcohol make sense with trauma. People are in pain, and drugs and alcohol numb pain. Why this becomes another big topic is that when you work with trauma survivors and drugs and alcohol are also an issue, you can't work on one without the other. It used to be that people were told they had to be clean and sober before starting therapy. That usually won't work, because the substance use is in some ways protective; it's like a chemically induced defense mechanism. So you can't take it away without replacing it with something else, such as some of the coping skills I touched on in the lecture. But those skills don't come in a week, or even a month; it's a long process. And that's a hard choice—bourbon makes you feel good in five seconds, this other stuff takes practice."

Eventually, Peter had to stop. The room erupted into applause, and Nicole observed both men and women drying their eyes on sleeves and crumpled tissues.

At a couple points in the lecture, Peter had made eye contact with her. It was a strange feeling, and she wondered if he sensed how close to the bone his talk had come. She stayed back as the room emptied, and the cluster of students and others who hadn't been able to ask their questions slowly thinned. The last to go was a tall blonde in black slacks, high-heeled boots, and a vibrant silk blouse who'd been taping the lecture. From behind, Nicole had assumed the woman was a student, but now, each footstep added years. The woman's body language was wide open—a finger to her throat, her chest—and Nicole felt a pang of disappointment; this must be his girlfriend.

Peter looked past the blonde, spotted her, and smiled. "Peggy must have told you where I was. I wish she had also told you that I was going to be giving a lecture."

"She did," Nicole said, making eye contact with him and then the woman. "I wanted to hear it. . . . You're a wonderful speaker."

"Magnificent," the blonde agreed. "I was in tears."

"Detective Sullivan," Peter said, "This is Gretchen Becker."

"How do you do?" Nicole asked, taking the woman's hand and reestimating her age as late thirties. She noted the absence of a wedding ring and that Gretchen's striped mauve-and-turquoise blouse revealed more than it covered.

"Detective?" Gretchen repeated. "There were a number of police here, weren't there?" She turned toward Peter.

Her tone struck Nicole as proprietary, as though he were a tract of land to which she'd laid claim.

"Gretchen, I'm going to need to speak with the detective."

"Is something wrong?" she asked, picking a bit of lint off his lapel.

He hesitated. "It's one of the students, and I can't go into it."

"Ann Walsh," Gretchen shot back.

"You know Ann?" Nicole asked, wondering who this woman was and thinking her face familiar.

"I've met her," Gretchen replied. "Is she in trouble?"

Peter looked across at Nicole and shook his head a fraction of an inch, as though warning her to say no more. She noticed Gretchen's hand reach under her coat and into her shoulder bag. For a moment she had the ridiculous notion that this high-wattage blonde with the German accent was going to pull a gun; she heard a click.

"Gretchen's a reporter," Peter said. "She's been interviewing some of the medical students, including Ann."

Suddenly Nicole placed the face, one she'd seen among throngs of reporters at news conferences she'd either given or attended.

"You were recording Dr. Grainger's lecture?"

"I'm a big fan," she said, raking her eyes over Nicole's off-the-rack navy suit and drab olive raincoat. "So what's going on with Ann?"

Nicole chose her words carefully. "She's been the victim of an attack." She watched Gretchen's face, noting the response, the finger to her lips.

"That's horrible," she said. "Is she all right?"

"It's not clear."

"Do you know who's responsible?"

"We're conducting an investigation." Just as at a news conference, Nicole mouthed responses the PR department could be proud of. "We're following all leads."

"I'd love to interview you about this."

"I'm afraid that's not possible. However, since you know Ann, I'll want a number where you can be reached."

"Of course," Gretchen said. She pulled out a thick black wallet and gave Nicole her card. "It's best to use my cell. Well . . ." she looked at Peter. "I can see that you and the detective need to talk. Call me later," she said, freeing her black wool cape from the straps of her pocketbook.

"Sure," he replied.

Nicole watched as Gretchen exited up the middle aisle. "Girlfriend?" she asked.

"No," he replied without pause. "I met her last night at a dinner party at Dean Tyson's house."

"Is she doing a story on you?"

"Possibly . . . I don't really know why she was here."

Nicole kept her thoughts to herself, that Gretchen Becker—judging by what she'd just seen—had come for more than the talk. She looked at him closer. "You haven't been home yet, have you?"

"No," he admitted. "It's been a weird night. I even left a message for you."

"You had breakfast?" she asked.

"No. You?"

"No, I had to run home to Brooklyn. . . ." She stopped herself, realizing she was about to get more personal than she had intended.

"What?" he asked.

"It's nothing," she said, thinking how easy it would be to talk to this brilliant man with his sad stories and haunted eyes. She also didn't want to tell him that when she went home she had pulled Peter's book on traumatized children off the shelf and read through his bio several times. "You want to go to a diner?" she suggested. "There's one around the corner, and the booths are quiet."

"The Acropolis."

"Yeah . . . you've lived around here long?" she asked as they walked up the aisle.

"I went to medical school here."

"That story about your wife . . . I'm so sorry."

"I don't know what possessed me; I've never done *that* before." He looked at her, and there was a questioning expression on his face. "I've bored you with this stuff."

"You haven't. . . . What were you going to say?" she asked, noting that he wore no wedding ring, and feeling the strangeness of her own bare finger.

They walked out into the daylight and each put on sunglasses.

"It's kind of where I am with my work . . . not the stuff at the university—that pays the bills. But like that lecture, and why I talked about Beth. Before the accident I was very clear about what I was doing. I actually thought I knew something. I designed experiments, I collected data, I developed treatments. . . ."

"What's wrong with that? Sounds like science."

"That's the problem. Science makes models to try and describe life, but it misses. Do you know what I'm saying?" he asked.

"Of course," she said. "How do you put a number on human despair?"

"Exactly." He stopped outside the door of the diner and held it open.

They took a booth in the back, ordered coffee, and took laminated menus from the waiter.

"You have French toast?" Peter asked the waiter.

"Of course," he said. "Would you like that with meat or fruit?"

They both ordered French toast with blueberries and large glasses of orange juice.

"I did get your message," she said after the waiter left. "I went to the hospital to try to get a statement from him."

"Carter?"

She looked away. "No, they let him go." Her stomach churned. All the way to and from her mother's house she'd ruminated about dropping the case. However, the facts remained: She was the first detective on the scene, her name was all over the evidence, and the first reports would be hers and Hector's. All she could do was try to minimize the risk and pray that Ann Walsh didn't become a homicide. "I did get to see Jason Walsh," she finally said. "And by the way, thanks for having his clothing bagged."

"It seemed the thing to do . . . considering."

"Most people wouldn't have done that. Pity they cleaned him up before getting some pictures. I spoke with the night-duty aide. She said he was pretty bloody when he came in."

"His hands," Peter said. "The palms, almost like they were painted with it."

"He's pretty crazy," she said. "Is it an act?"

"No . . . but I *can* be fooled. It's just Ann's story matched the way he looked, like somebody with untreated schizophrenia."

"That's what I thought," she said, about to ask a follow-up question when the waiter returned with their French toast.

She waited till he was gone, the silence affording her the chance to sneak glances at Peter, who unlike many good-looking men, such as Donny, seemed oblivious to it. This wasn't to say he was a slob—rumpled clothes and bad shave aside—but he carried himself with an easy grace. She imagined that the kindness and lack of bullshit he had shown in the lecture were no act and had everything to do with the attendance of several members of the force, who typically have zero tolerance for anything touchy-feely. As she mentally sketched his soulful eyes and full lips, she realized that she was attracted to him. *Great, Nicole, just what you need.* She struggled to retrieve the thread of their conversation. "So, all he said was, 'watch out for Ann'?"

"That's about it," Peter said. He took a drink of orange juice and his eyes met hers. "There was more he wanted to say. He just couldn't get it out. The other thing I'd love to figure out is why did he go to the clinic?"

"Good point. He'd never been there before?"

"No, it's just for students."

Nicole flicked the two-inch scoop of whipped butter off her breakfast and scraped away a portion of the thick syrup. "But Ann had been there. Maybe he connected her with the clinic?"

"Maybe, but if he had a habit of following her, the same thing could be said of a lot of places."

"Right . . . which leaves you." Nicole said, again finding herself caught in his gaze.

"What do you mean?"

"You said that it felt like he was trying to tell you something. Maybe he went there looking for you."

"Huh . . . this was the first I'd seen him." Peter said.

174

"You look like you're not sure of that. What are you thinking?"

"I'm telling you that I've never seen the kid before, but something in the back of my mind . . . I can't put my finger on it."

A pager sounded, and both Nicole and Peter reached for their beepers.

"It's mine," she said. She pulled out her cell.

"You want privacy?"

"It's okay, I don't want your breakfast to get cold," she said, realizing that he'd barely eaten. "Hector, what's up?" She listened as her partner filled her in.

"For starters," he said, "Ann Walsh is now a homicide. Word from the hospital is that she died about thirty minutes ago."

"Shit." She looked across at Peter and shook her head. "What are they giving as the cause of death?"

"Preliminary is cardiac failure secondary to massive blood loss. She should be on her way to the ME's for the autopsy."

Nicole's chest tightened, and just looking at her food, brought the taste of bile.

"And lucky me," Hector continued, "I've been in the snow-covered fields of Connecticut meeting with her father."

Nicole felt the room spin. "What did he say?"

"Not much. Called his daughter a whore. Yelled a lot, needed a couple belts of bourbon to keep down the shakes."

"Does he know yet?"

"I'm figuring the hospital will do that. At least I hope so, but I do have one little ray of sunshine."

"Let me have it." She said, hoping that somehow Hector would have come up with something that could tie this up fast.

"The clothing that went to the lab . . ."

"Yes."

"They haven't run the confirmatory yet, but it looks like a match.

Nicole made eye contact with Peter. "So the brother did it."

"Looks like."

"Hector . . . have you seen him?"

"Just briefly. You interviewed him, right?"

"If you want to call it that," she said. He's completely out of his head."

"That's not good."

"Right . . . you know what the judge is going to say."

"Yup," Hector said, "been there, done that. . . . What do you suggest?"

"Do it by the book. You get the warrant, and then we start hunting down a couple psychiatrists for the evaluation. In fact"—she smiled at Peter—"I'm with one now."

"Really? Which one?"

"Ann Walsh's psychiatrist, Dr. Peter Grainger."

"Is he the blond dude? Or tall, dark, and handsome?"

Nicole snuck a glance across the table and felt heat tingle in her cheeks. "The second. The blond guy's the dean."

"Maybe he could do the other interview." Hector suggested.

"No," she said with more force than she'd intended, recalling her strange conversation with the concerned-appearing Dr. Tyson, and how he'd deliberately tried to conceal the name of Ann Walsh's prior therapist. "We'll need an outsider. Dr. Grainger saw the boy last night, so I think he can get further with him."

"Whatever you say, boss. I'll give you a call after I get the warrant."

She clicked the phone closed and pushed her plate away, her breakfast mostly uneaten. "So what do you think?" she asked.

"About which part?" He made no pretense about having overheard the conversation. He placed a napkin over his uneaten breakfast and pushed it away.

"Would you be willing to interview Jason Walsh for the court?"

176

"Of course . . . Oh, God," he closed his eyes, visibly shaken by the news.

"You okay?"

"Not really . . . You don't think it's going to create a boundary problem having me interview him?"

She felt like telling him that his boundary issues were tiny in comparison to hers. "If it is, I can always get a third. But if Jason went to the clinic because of you, then maybe he'll tell us something useful."

"Like why he did it?" Peter asked.

"That would be nice," she said, but years of working cases had taught her not to jump to conclusions. Other threads needed to be pulled, like the ex-resident who'd been fired. "Think you could help me get a look at Ann's old clinic records?"

"They're with the attorney." There was something odd in his expression. "Make sure you get all of them."

"What do you mean by that?"

He pushed his coffee and empty juice glass aside and leaned across. He lowered his voice. "There was something horribly wrong about Ann's therapy with Keith Taylor, and I'm not talking about the obvious."

"I'm not following. What are you trying to tell me?"

"I don't have proof, so I need to be careful. But if you look at the record . . ."

A cell phone rang.

"Me again," she said, not wanting to stop Peter, and thinking it was Hector. But when she looked at the number in the caller ID . . . "Damn!" She flicked it open. "Hello?"

"Mrs. Sullivan?" a young woman spoke tentatively.

"Yes?"

"This is Penny. I'm the aide working with Adriana today. Mrs. Scolevski wanted me to call you and tell you that someone needs to come and get Adriana."

"What happened?" Nicole asked, dreading the answer.

The aide whispered, "She's been displaying behavior that's upsetting the other children."

"What did she do, specifically?"

"I'd rather not say on the telephone."

"Fine . . . did you try to see if my mother could pick up Adriana? I'm at work."

"Mrs. Scolevski wanted me to have you pick up Adriana. She needs to speak with you. She told me that if I couldn't reach you I was to get in touch with Adriana's father. Would you rather he come?"

If Nicole's hands could have reached through the phone, they would have wrung the life out of the well-meaning Penny. "Where is Mrs. Scolevski? Let me talk to her."

"She can't come to the phone," the girl sounded scared. "She's in the middle of a PPT. But she said that she'll be out by the time you get here."

"Where's Adriana?" Nicole asked.

"She's right here," Penny said.

Nicole blanched as she realized that her daughter had overheard all this. "I'll be there in forty-five minutes," she said, wondering how they let incompetents like this Penny around troubled children.

"You okay?" Peter asked.

"Absolutely not." She looked at him and knew she was about to cross a line. The first rule of police work—don't mix your personal life with your professional life—was about to go out the window. "Do you know anything about the Garden School?"

"Sure, I know a great deal about it. You have a child who goes there? Was that them?"

"No. I have a daughter. . . . That was her school calling. I'm going to have to go. . . . Does it work? Does it help?"

"The Garden School?"

She nodded, desperately wanting some advice, but knowing that every minute her daughter waited in some office with that aide was not good.

"When you have some time," he said, "I'd be happy to tell you about the Garden School. But bottom line, if I had a child who'd been seriously traumatized, that's where I'd send them. Boris Singer is the best in the business."

She got to her feet and pulled a wallet out of her bag. "That's what I needed to hear. Sorry to run like this; you've been a lot of help."

He tried to wave away the money she threw on the table.

"No, it's on me." She tore the receipt off the bottom of the check. "Get some sleep."

"You, too," he said.

As she hurried away Nicole was already prioritizing how she'd keep all the balls in the air. She was determined that by the time she left her meeting with Mrs. Scolevski, she would have a referral to the Garden School. She'd touch base with Hector as she drove to Brooklyn, make arrangements with her mom to stay with Adriana, and with any luck be back in her office by four. She thought about Peter's suggestion to give him a call so he could tell her about the Garden School; she'd do that, too. It was strange, but when she'd walked out of the restaurant, a part of her wanted to ask him to go with her. She thought about his eyes and how when he looked at her she felt stirrings of something old and mostly forgotten. It was his voice, though, that stayed with her—the way it resonated and how when he laughed it was like something deep inside him was released, and others couldn't help but laugh along. Even when he was talking about difficult and horrible things in his lecture, he could crack a joke, and the tension flew from the room. *Don't even think it*, she told herself, realizing that she was one step away from a full-blown crush. She'd ask him about the Garden School, and she'd ask him to interview Jason Walsh, and that would be the end of it.

19

TRUE TO HER WORD, PEGGY had cleared my afternoon, although the snow squall that descended after brunch would have
achieved the same. I holed up in my clinic office and tried not to
think about Ann, which was impossible. She was dead, apparently
at the hands of her brother. That didn't sit right.

I forced myself to make calls, still resolved to get away from
Ed and whatever strange games he was playing. By one o'clock I'd
spoken with my old department chair, who was thrilled that I
might return. Likewise, I'd had promising conversations with
Cornell and Columbia. The next step would be to have a heart-
to-heart with Kyle about whether to move back to Cambridge or
to stay. It felt like running, but I couldn't risk my reputation and
my ability to bring home the bacon and take care of my son.

I was set to leave when the phone rang.

"Dr. Grainger?"

"Yes?" I didn't recognize the voice.

"This is George Langley; I'm the director of laboratory services at University Hospital. I have your results, and I wanted to
make certain you got them."

"Right." My mouth went dry.

"I'm getting set to fax them, but I wanted to call first."

"What's wrong?" I sensed his hesitation.

"A number of substances showed up, some of which I can't identify."

"Like what?"

"For starters, scopolamine, hyosyamine, someatropine, and some alkaloids I've never seen. My guess is they're of plant origin. We're getting quite a mix, and I'm getting set to do a gas separation. That is, if you want me to."

As I listened, all I could think was *Ed drugged me.* "Absolutely. Do you have enough blood?" I asked, remembering the second tube I'd dropped into my pocket.

"I think so, but you do realize how strange this is, to have one of our medical staff run a toxicology screen on themselves."

"I know." I wondered how many rules I was breaking.

"May I ask why?"

"I think I was drugged at a party," I admitted.

"Have you contacted the police?"

"Not yet, but anything else you can tell me would be helpful."

"Of course, but now that you tell me this, what I didn't want to say was that some of the alkaloids look similar to strychnine, which is found in hallucinogenic mushrooms. A little makes you see things, too much is rat poison. . . . It's going to take at least a couple days to complete the analysis."

"Call me the minute it's done." I gave him my numbers.

My first impulse was to hunt down Ed and ask him point-blank what the fuck he was up to . . . and then I'd beat the crap out of him. I pictured his smiling face, and it made me sick. But as I thought it through, a head-on attack would be dead wrong. I needed proof, something that would directly tie him to whatever shit he had poured into me. I knew that he had a large underground greenhouse and rooms filled with cataloged specimens brought back from the Amazon. I could only imagine what he'd given me. But why? How was I going to get the evidence I needed? His laboratory had a sophisticated security system, plus he was probably there right now.

The only other place I could think of . . . I grabbed my coat. Outside, the snow was blinding as I headed into the wind toward Fifth Avenue and Ed's building. In his lobby, the concierge was on the phone, and without stopping, I went to the elevators.

As I rode up, I concocted an excuse for my visit; I wondered what I would do if Ed opened the door. Punching out his lights seemed a reasonable option.

I rang the bell and expected the Brazilian au pair to answer, but it was Miranda who came.

"Jesus," I said, taking in her bathrobe, disheveled hair, and hooded eyes. "You look like hell."

"Thanks," she coughed. "I've been puking all morning. What time is it?"

"About two," I told her.

"God, I must have picked up something from one of my patients. I feel terrible. Betty?" She called out toward the kitchen.

I waited for the broad-built Brazilian woman to appear. "Betty?" she called again. "That's odd." She shuffled toward the kitchen and I followed.

My first thought was that maybe somebody should draw *her* blood, but as much as I liked Miranda, I couldn't get sidetracked. "I think I left my reading glasses. Okay if I look around?" I asked.

"Of course," she said, finding a note from Betty telling her that she'd gone to pick up Camille. School was letting out early and Gymboree had been canceled.

"Can I get you anything?" I asked.

"No, I just need to sleep, but thanks." She retreated toward their bedroom.

I quickly took in my surroundings. Through the kitchen I

glimpsed the vivid foliage in the conservatory that overlooked the city. It was a beautiful room constructed of thick glass framed in steel. Inside, tropical plants spilled off the shelves and woody vines twined overhead. I recognized a few of them and quickly pinched off buds, leaves, and flowers. Unfortunately, Ed's real storehouse was two stories underground; these specimens were mostly for show. I needed something better than this kind of shotgun approach, and I didn't have a lot of time.

I popped back through the kitchen and headed toward the bar in the living room, from where he'd taken the tequila. I looked at the bottle, reminded myself that he'd had some, so it must have been something in my glass. I looked at the rows of crystal snifters, all in their place; Betty must have already washed and put them back. This was getting me nowhere. *Think, man.*

My gaze fell on the hall that led to the bedrooms and Ed's study. The master suite was at the end and the door was shut. Ed's study was on the right, across from his son's bedroom. I tried the door, expecting to find it locked, but it wasn't. I snuck in, closed the door, and turned on a lamp. His study was dark, windowless, and lined with shelves. In the center stood an imposing mahogany desk that had belonged to his father. I walked around it. His computer was on. I tapped the mouse and instantly confronted a security window unlike any I'd ever seen before. I knew that Ed had contracts with the military, and I suspected that whatever measures he'd taken to protect his files were more than I'd be able to figure out. And then my eyes fell to a bit of ripped paper peeking from his top drawer. I reached down to open it—locked. I pulled the paper, careful not to rip it. My pulse quickened as I glimpsed the handwriting. He'd stolen Taylor's process notes.

I got on my knees and examined the antique lock. I grabbed a silver letter opener and started to work away at it. I felt a little play in the catch and began to jimmy it down millimeter by millimeter. I tried the drawer again, adrenaline surged as it slid open, revealing the notes still in the folder from the lawyer's. My impulse was to grab them and run, but then I'd lose my chance to catch him unawares. I spotted a fax machine behind his desk, figured there were about twenty pages of notes, and proceeded to copy them. I was nearly done when voices drifted down the hallway.

I grabbed the last page as it was going through and pulled back, trying not to tear the ragged edges. I folded and stuffed the copies into my breast pocket, and put the originals back. Using the letter opener and my thumbnail I got the catch started up, shut the drawer, and tried to jimmy the lock back into place.

I was rounding the desk when the door opened.

I froze.

"Daddy?" Camille, dressed in her blue-and-gray plaid school uniform, appeared in the doorway. "Where's Daddy?"

"He's still at work." I told the eight-year-old. "I needed to get something I left last night," I told her.

"Oh," she looked behind me; I felt my heart beating in my ears. "I'm not supposed to be in here when he's not home."

"I won't tell him," I said. "Okay?"

She smiled, "Okay."

I closed the door behind us and knocked on Miranda's door. "Don't get up," I said, "but I found them, thanks." And with my imaginary glasses back in my possession, I left.

I WAS HOME BY FIVE, my nerves fried, and my thoughts whipping fast. I could see why he'd want Taylor's notes, but to steal them? Although, in contrast to drugging me, that was probably a minor crime. Which led to the big question . . . why? As I walked up my stoop and into the doorway shaking the snow from my coat, my eyes fell on the mailbox and the envelope stuffed inside. "Damn!" I pulled it out along with a couple of bills, two journals, and a credit card application. Inside my loft, I called out, "Kyle."

No answer, just a note propped against a bowl on the kitchen counter.

I'm at Grandpa's. Call me. And don't forget to feed Willy.

As if to reinforce the message the cat appeared from Kyle's bedroom and began to brush his furry flank against my ankles.

I put the mail on the counter, reached into the cabinet, and pulled out a can of Fancy Feast. I shook it into his bowl, and then called my father. Kyle picked up.

"Hey, Dad."

"Hey, kiddo. I got your note. What are you doing up there?"

"I didn't know when you were going to come home, and so Grandpa asked me if I wanted to stay over."

I tried not to hear the reproach. Like, what kind of father doesn't let his kid know when he's coming home? "You have your stuff for school?" I asked.

"Yeah."

Remembering our earlier conversation, I said, "You still need a note? I forgot to call the school."

"Grandpa said he'd give me one . . . if that's okay."

"Sure."

"Are you okay?" he asked.

"I'm fine." I was lying; I was far from fine as I stared at the envelope.

After we hung up I poured myself a glass of wine, took the package, and headed back to my study. I ripped it open and spilled the contents onto the desk. I ran my hand over the glossy black-and-white photographs, spreading the gory images like a fortune-teller with a tarot deck. They were so familiar, even the word *Murderer* written in red nail polish over the accident photos. This was the third set. The first time, I'd brought them to the Cambridge police. They couldn't track down the sender, and the officer assigned had even suggested, albeit gently, that perhaps I had sent them to myself. The second time they came, I'd told no one.

I looked inside the envelope to see if there was anything else, perhaps a letter, something to reveal the sender's identity; there was nothing. The only difference was that this time it was a New York postmark instead of Cambridge. I turned them over to see if there was anything on the back—just the Kodak logo. I stared at the bright red lettering. *Murderer.* Not my handwriting. *Could it be Ed's?* I slid the pictures back into the envelope and put my copies of Taylor's notes on top.

My gaze drifted to the locked bottom drawer. Like an addict, I couldn't stop myself. I pulled out the medical examiner's six-page autopsy report. Almost like playing a game with myself, I read it word for word. I hadn't made it halfway through the first page when I stopped, bothered by something I'd never noticed. It was the blood analysis of Beth and the baby. It sent me over to my shelf of medical textbooks, most of which dated back to my school days. What struck me was that both Beth and I were in the A grouping, as was Kyle, which meant that our child either had to be A or, if we both carried a recessive gene for "O," there was a 25 percent chance the baby could be O. However, written next to the fetus was AB, a genetic impossibility considering the parents.

It had to be a mistake.

I glanced at the clock. It was still early, around dinnertime . . . and Tuesday, which meant there was a good chance that Pat would still be in her office. I flipped through my phone book and found her name—Dr. Patricia Hayes—a woman who had become more of a friend than a doctor as she got us through the years of trying to have a second child.

Her secretary picked up and told me that she was finishing up with a patient.

I held as a Mozart string quartet came over the line.

"Peter." Pat's husky voice, which I hadn't heard since before the accident, brought memories surging.

"Sorry to bother you."

"Not a problem. What's on your mind?"

"It's probably nothing," I said, trying to convince myself. "By the time a fetus is six months old, you can pretty much tell its blood type, can't you?"

"Mostly. There're a lot of immature cells, but if you're talking about groupings, sure . . ." I felt her hedge.

"I've been looking at Beth's autopsy report, and there's something I don't understand. The baby's blood type is listed as AB . . . That's not possible if both Beth and I are A . . . is it?"

There was silence.

"Pat?" I wondered if we'd been disconnected.

"Yes, Peter."

"It's not possible, is it?"

"No . . . She never told you," Pat said. "I wondered about that."

"Told me what?"

"Hold on." The line clicked and Vivaldi's *Four Seasons* played. The music stopped. "I closed the door," she explained. "You're sure you want to hear this?'

"It's important. . . ."

"Okay, you know that Beth had an amnio a couple weeks before the accident."

"Yes."

"I thought that perhaps the lab had made a mistake, so when the results came in, I had them run a second time."

"What are you talking about?"

"I thought she had told you. . . . The child wasn't yours; it couldn't have been. I'm very sorry."

I couldn't speak. I sat there listening to this woman I'd known in another life tell me from two hundred miles away that the basic assumption of my life—my relationship with Beth—was not what I had thought. "Did she say who the father was?" I blurted out.

"No . . ."

"There has to be more. What is it you're not telling me?"

"Beth didn't believe me. She said it wasn't possible. She wanted me to redo it."

"I thought you did."

"No, I had them run the *sample* again. She wanted another amnio, which I wouldn't do considering her history of miscarriage."

"Could the samples have gotten mixed up?"

"I was going to have them run Western blots to verify the DNA; that's why I thought she would have told you. I would have needed cells from both of you."

"Right . . . How long before the accident did you tell her?"

"Two days."

"Thanks, Pat," I told her. I picked away at a memory.

"I'm sorry, Peter."

"Not your fault." I hung up and found myself slipping back to the day of the accident. A piece of the puzzle had just clicked. It was Beth who had wanted to take the drive. Something she needed to tell me. I now knew; the child wasn't mine.

I stared at the autopsy report and regretted that Pat hadn't gone ahead and done the DNA verification. I weighed the possibilities. Sure, I knew that more than fifty percent of marriages involved at least one episode of infidelity, but that wasn't *my* marriage, or my Beth. She was almost seven months pregnant; the accident was in October. I counted back; she would have conceived in the beginning of April or end of March. We had always assumed—although I guess it was just me—that it was during our night of reunion after she'd returned from New Orleans.

The autopsy fell from my hand. It was a conference we both liked to attend, but invariably only one of us could go; someone

had to stay with Kyle. It was her turn, plus she was presenting. . . .
It was also the year that Ed was the keynote speaker.

I felt dizzy. I could hear Felicia hammering away at Ed, accusing him of setting up Taylor. I tried to remember the week that Beth was away. We spoke nightly. I knew that she had dinner with Ed; I would have been surprised if she hadn't. In all our years, I'd never felt jealous, with the exception of that trip to Brazil. I'd seen other men eye her, but she'd always made it clear that I had nothing to fear. She'd even joked that if I strayed, she'd be forced to kill me "It's neater that way. No messy divorce, no dividing assets . . . just make it look like an accident."

Like her accident. The child wasn't mine. . . . Was it Ed's? Bile rose. No, not possible, not the thoughts of a sane man. However, I was already figuring how I could access his medical files to check his blood type when the phone rang.

I hoped it was Pat calling to tell me that she'd been confused and that none of what she'd said was accurate.

"Peter?" It was Gretchen Becker.

"Hi." It was hard to speak, why was she calling?

"I heard about Ann."

"And?" I was instantly leery.

"You were seeing her. I thought maybe you could give me a little information."

"Why?"

"She was one of the students I was interviewing. And now that she's dead . . ."

"She'll make better press? Look, Gretchen, I know this is your job, but I can't talk about this."

"Why? It's not like the rules of confidentiality apply to dead people. Did you know that she was a prostitute?" she persisted.

I said nothing, my emotions too knotted.

"This can all be off the record."

"I'm sorry," I said, "I've had a long day . . . actually two, and I can't talk about this." I felt like my head might explode as my focus drifted to the autopsy report.

"You sound like you've had some bad news."

"Something like that." God, what would it take to get her off the phone?

"You want to talk about it?" she asked.

"No, but maybe Ed could tell you about Ann."

"Fat chance," she said. "Ed didn't want me to interview her in the first place."

"Why not?"

"That's not fair. You want information, but you're not giving me anything."

"Okay," I racked my brain, trying not to think about Beth, trying to focus on Ann. "Yes, I knew Ann turned tricks. Was that why Ed didn't want you to interview her?"

"This can't ever get back to him. . . ."

"It won't. You sound scared." What was she playing at?

"Not scared, just . . . I've known Ed a long time. It's never good to cross him. If he knew I'd met with her more than once, he'd be upset. If he knew I was talking with you about her, he'd be very upset."

"Why would he care?" I asked, eyeing my copy of Taylor's notes.

"Just a hunch," she said, "based on knowing him and some things Ann said."

"Like what?"

"This isn't fair," she complained again. "I'm the one who's trying to pull a story together. . . . Ann told me that she thought she was going to get some kind of scholarship, and that people in high places would help her out. That she'd make sure they would."

"I already know this," I said, but I was curious to see that Ann had told someone else. "It makes no sense. The Goddard Fellowships are worth about fifty thousand a year. They go to the very top students. Ed, as the dean, makes the final decision. So why Ann? What do you know about this?"

"I wanted to discuss Ann, not my cousin," she said.

"Was he having an affair with her?"

"This was a mistake," Gretchen said. "I'm sorry to have bothered you."

"Wait!" I said, before she could hang up. "Last night?"

"Yes?"

"When I left you outside your apartment, do you remember which way I went?"

"You don't?" she asked.

Why did she sound so sad? "No."

"That's very odd, Peter. How much don't you remember?"

"Just that," I said, not about to admit to my four-hour blank.

"You went north," she offered abruptly, as though I had pissed her off. "You left my apartment and went north."

God, could something have happened between Gretchen and me? Was I missing the real reason she had called and why she had come to my lecture?

"What else don't you remember?" her words held an accusation.

I punted, something I've gotten skilled at since the accident. "I had a good time."

There was a pause. "I was hoping we could get together again."

The ball landed in my court. Was I interested? My nostrils caught the scent of jasmine. Had I made love to her and been left with no recollection? "I'd like that," I said, not certain what I felt, other than a cold fear at being unable to remember.

"Me, too. Only next time, you call me."

20

THE FOLLOWING MORNING, TWO STORIES below ground, Ed hunched over his computer and replayed Peter and Gretchen's conversation. *Traitor.* So she knew more about Ann than she'd let on. Did she have more than hunches?

Damn her. It was Gretchen who had asked Miranda for the introduction to Peter, apparently a fan of his simplistic salves for the psyche. Which, considering her history of bouncing from one abusive man to the next, including two that she'd married, made sense. He'd found it titillating to see his cousin, with whom he'd had an on-again off-again relationship since they were teens, go after Peter. This, however, was too risky.

Unsettled, he clicked on the next file, the one between Peter and Dr. Hayes. Peter acted as though he didn't know the child wasn't his. Bullshit! So what was that call about? Unless he wasn't giving Peter enough credit. Perhaps he'd underestimated him. After all, when Peter would go on trial for Ann's murder, the death of his wife would be scrutinized; they'd discover that the child Beth was carrying wasn't Peter's. The call to that doctor could be part of an alibi.

At least the *Datura* had worked. From Peter's questions, it seemed clear that the drugged tequila took effect not long after he'd left Ed's apartment. He'd have no recollection of anything that occurred for hours; Ed was banking on it. Now that Ann was dead, he could set about repairing the damage to his plans. He whispered into the microphone, *"Kyle, your father's been arrested, Dr. Tyson will come . . ."*

The phone rang.

"Yes?"

"Dr. Tyson," his secretary said, "there's a police detective here. She'd like to speak with you."

"I'll be right up." He pictured the intense detective from the ER. What did she want? Careful to lock his office, he went out through his laboratory, where Ralph was teaching two assistants proper pipette technique.

Ralph was beaming, having gotten the go-ahead from Ed to publish the results of the rat studies using Tumoren. The wheels were starting to turn.

ON HIS WAY FROM THE elevator to his offices, he got a brief unobserved view of the detective. She stood in his waiting area studying the architect's model of University Hospital. She wore a navy skirt suit and he imagined she had her firearm either in her handbag or in a shoulder holster.

"Detective Sullivan." He crossed toward her, his voice tinged with sadness. "I wish I could say that I was glad to see you. Won't you come in?" He offered his hand and noticed the slightest hesitation before she accepted.

"Could I offer you a cup of coffee, some water?" he asked, as he led her into his office.

"No, thank you."

Ed regretted their meeting in the ER; he'd struck the wrong

note. He studied her, noting the small gold earrings and sensible low-heeled black pumps. He pictured her background—blue-collar, Irish Catholic, family probably in Brooklyn. A bit odd that she was a cop, and a detective to boot. What was notable, in the natural light of his office, was that even without the benefit of makeup, Detective Sullivan, with her thick shoulder-length hair, pale skin, and hazel eyes, was extremely attractive.

He directed her toward a seating area.

"You have an interesting office," she commented.

"Thanks, I think."

"Is the furniture Eames?"

"Some of it . . . you have a good eye."

"And the artwork is from your travels?"

"Yes."

"It's quite beautiful."

"Thank you," he said, wondering when she was going to get down to business and knowing that it would be best to let her steer the conversation. He sat across from her with his hands in his lap. He waited.

She looked him squarely in the eye. He held her gaze and then looked away, letting her stay in control, but also feeling an uncomfortable uncertainty. Had he missed something? Why was she looking at him like . . . like a suspect?

"Now that this is a homicide," she said, "I need access to Ann's classmates. I wondered if you have any kind of assembly where I could address the students."

"Not typically," he said, "but something could be arranged.

"That would be helpful. And Keith Taylor's address?"

Bitch, he thought, not letting his smile fade. "The university attorney—Clarence Green—he should have it."

"So there was a lawsuit," she said.

"Yes," he admitted, hoping to lead her out of this quickly. "I believe it was settled."

"Really? So not only did Keith Taylor lose his ability to practice medicine, but she also sued him?"

This woman was like a dog with a bone. He'd have to be careful "Keith, like all trainees, was covered by the clinic's malpractice. Because of the nature of the complaint we could have left him out on his own; we didn't."

"Who else was named in the suit?"

"The clinic and the medical school."

"In which case," she continued, "it wouldn't have been in your best interest to leave him in the cold. By supplying his counsel, didn't you ensure his loyalty?"

"Correct," he admitted. "As ugly as it was, things could have turned worse. It was the attorney's suggestion not to split from Keith."

"Smart, and I imagine Mr. Taylor was relieved."

"He had no money anyway," Ed said, realizing just how clever this detective was. "In the end they always go for the deeper pocket, which, in this case, was the school."

"How deep did she go?" she asked.

"She wasn't the complainant. It was her father." He looked up, noting her reaction at the mention of Carter.

"How much did he get?"

"I don't think any of it's been paid out, but again you'll need to check with the attorney . . . or Mr. Walsh," he said deliberately. "I think the sum was around one hundred thousand."

"In exchange for?"

"I'm sure there's language stipulating silence. If he takes the money he can't write about it or go to the press. The university is paying him off. For the record, I was not in agreement with that."

"It doesn't seem like a very large sum," she commented.

"True." He noticed that she wasn't backing down even though she was clearly uncomfortable. "It would have been higher had

Ann brought the suit. It's difficult for the father to prove damages. But she was unwilling to testify against Keith."

"Was she in love with him?"

"I couldn't say. I don't think she wanted to hurt him."

"My understanding is that she desperately needed money. It seems like this kind of settlement would have taken care of that."

"It does, doesn't it. I don't know what her reasons were," Ed said. "I'm also not certain that they were completely rational."

"I don't understand."

"Ann's father . . . he was the one making the fuss. The more angry and obnoxious he got, the less she wanted to do with any of it. Which, for the university, was a good thing. She wouldn't even talk to the attorney."

"It doesn't quite make sense."

"I suppose it doesn't," he said, "But I imagine the person who could fill in those pieces would be her father."

"Perhaps," she averted her eyes.

"I don't know if I should tell you this, but you'll come upon it anyway . . . It's my understanding that this wasn't the first time Ann had slept with her psychiatrist."

"Here?"

"Not that I'm aware, but as a teenager, and no, I don't have the details."

"How well did you know her?"

"Not well."

"The night she tried to kill herself you called Dr. Peter Grainger and specifically asked for him to see her."

"I did."

"Why?"

"Because of all this, I didn't want to risk an inexperienced resident getting involved with her." He was pleased. Finally she was getting around to Peter.

"Makes sense . . . Did you know about her brother?"

"No," he said. *Damn! Why is she so quick to let go of Peter?*

"She never mentioned being stalked by her brother?"

"I didn't really know her. If that was going on, I was unaware. Is he somehow involved?"

She hesitated, "It's possible."

What the fuck is going on? He knew Ann had a brother. She'd mentioned him, but never as someone she was frightened of. It was also clear that Peter wasn't even on this detective's radar. How could this be? He told himself he had to be careful; now was not the time to push, but he desperately needed to know what he was missing.

"When you had Dr. Grainger meet with Ann, did he know about her earlier history at the clinic?" she asked.

"I'm not certain," Ed said.

"But he would have known about Keith Taylor . . ."

"Possibly not."

"I thought the two of you were friends," she said.

What was she insinuating? "We are."

"You knew each other in medical school?"

"Correct."

"It seems like a *friend* would have told another friend about Ann's habit of seducing doctors."

"It was late," he said with a shrug. "I should have told him. I was just relieved that he'd see her instead of one of the residents."

"So it was out of the ordinary for him to go to the emergency room."

"Somewhat, but it happens."

"You used to have his job."

"I did."

"How did he get it?"

"I recruited him when I was offered the dean's position." This was all wrong. Why was she interrogating him this way?

"I see. . . . Why?"

Ed seized the opening. "He's more than qualified. . . ." He pitched his voice lower, sadder. "I also thought he could use it."

"Because?"

"You know about his wife's . . . accident?"

"Yes."

"It left him changed. He wasn't able to work for a while, and . . ." Ed's voice trailed.

"What?"

"You'd better ask him," he said, not wanting to plant more than the tiniest whiff of suspicion. She was too quick, and he mustn't push.

"I will," she said, letting her gaze rest on him.

He smiled and waited. He knew that she was engaging in a game of verbal chicken: Who would speak first? He couldn't appear too strong. "Is there anything else I can help you with?"

"Not at the moment" she said, still watching him. "Oh wait, there was something."

"Yes?"

"The Goddard Fellowships, was Ann going to get one?"

He felt her eyes on him. "Of course not."

"That's interesting," she said, getting up. "She thought she was."

"If she did," Ed said, feeling a strong desire to wrap his hands around this bitch's throat, "she was mistaken."

"Perhaps."

"Anything else?"

"Not at the moment, but I'm sure there will be. . . . Your secretary can get me the names and numbers for all of the students?"

"Of course." He led her out and instructed his secretary, "Give the detective whatever she needs."

Detective Sullivan faced him. "You've been very helpful. Thank you."

"You're welcome." He heard overtones of sarcasm and distrust in her words.

He retreated to his office, chewing on the encounter. It had left him with a clawing pit in his stomach. Why had she looked at him that way? *Shit!* Who had Ann told about the Goddard? He looked at the street below and saw her exit the building.

He remembered how she had flinched at the mention of Carter Walsh, not just now, but in the emergency room the night Ann was brought in. *What are you hiding?* He saw her head west and then vanish around the corner.

He turned back to his desk, flicked the mouse, and sat down. He clicked on the admissions-program icon and searched on "Nicole Sullivan." He got pages of Sullivans, but not a Nicole. He recalled that in the ER she was wearing a wedding band; strangely, he couldn't remember seeing one today. In fact, he'd put money down that she hadn't been wearing it.

He entered the single name "Nicole" and was again confronted with pages of names. He drew parameters around her date of birth, estimating that she was in her midthirties, but allowing himself a range from thirty to forty-two. He was now down to fewer than a hundred. In the ER she'd said that she'd been an undergraduate, so he eliminated the graduate and professional schools, leaving him fifty-four possibilities. One by one he went down the list. Some he eliminated based on race; others he had to open their files for more information. Her accent was relatively neutral, but Ed had discerned the sound of Brooklyn and some of the more blue-collar towns of Long Island. By the time he'd factored in height and eye color, he was left with two candidates—an English major and an art student. The interest she'd taken in his office furniture and tribal artwork led him to pick the art student, Nicole Luria, first.

If indeed this was she, she'd be thirty-five which sounded

right. She'd been enrolled for two years in one of the fine arts programs, an interesting start for a cop. How do you go from fine arts to the NYPD? He scanned the information, which gave her address as Park Slope, Brooklyn—not too Brooklyn. Mother, Jeanine—housewife—father, Henry—detective. *Like father like daughter.* He scrolled to the end and wanted more. He trilled two fingers on the edge of his desk. "Let's try . . ." He closed admissions and went into the drive for the bursar. He entered his password and "Nicole Luria." Her transcript popped up. *Interesting.* She had the basic undergraduate requirements—English and a gut math—but everything else was in one of the extremely competitive studio programs. These required a portfolio critique for acceptance. These art programs enrolled only those few who the instructors believed might actually make a living in the arts. In their flyers, they made no bones about the fact that they took less than 2 percent from their pool of applicants. He knew there was a story here: straight A's for her first three semesters; her fourth and final one was incomplete. The marks, with the exception of a C minus in advanced life drawing were all I's—incompletes.

He reread her course titles. It wasn't just that she was getting A's and then took a nosedive, but . . . He counted the credits; she was averaging twenty-four a semester, essentially doing one and a half times a full course load. Nicole Luria was no slouch, and it appeared as though she was assembling a double major, with English as the second. She had even taken night courses at the Expansion School back when the university had had a reciprocal arrangement with it. Ed rubbed his temples. *So what happened?*

He toggled back and entered the health plan database. Perhaps she took ill, or . . . what he was actually hoping for. When students experienced a sharp change in performance, it tended to be boyfriend/girlfriend trouble, sexual-identity questions, illness, mental illness, or family problems. All of which might bring someone to . . . and there she was . . . at the mental health clinic. *Now what?*

It was one thing to know she was there, but something else to know why. Fifteen-year-old charts would be archived on microfilm; he'd need to sneak a look at those. He went back into her transcripts. Her third semester was something of a departure; one course was conversational Spanish and the other was called "Writers on Writing," part of a series at the Expansion School, their most famous being the televised "Actors on Acting." It grabbed him for two reasons. First, something happened either third semester or at the beginning of her fourth, and second, there was some reason that Detective Luria-Sullivan had a visible stress reaction each time Carter Walsh was mentioned. Ed intended to find out why. If the bitch wanted to play with him, she'd soon discover that she was way out of her league.

21

FOR THE SECOND TIME IN a week Nicole was on the viewing side of a two-way mirror, this time on the psych ward at University Hospital. Alone in the dark, she watched Peter as he prepared to evaluate Jason Walsh.

In her pocketbook was the judge's signed order; Hector had obtained it, along with a subpoena for Ann's records and an arrest warrant, while she was meeting with Tyson. Best of all, Hector's name, not hers, was on the paperwork.

She just wanted this case to be over. On the plus side, it looked like they had their perp. Based on Jason's bloodstained clothing and fiber samples from the hotel room that matched ones on the soles of his shoes, they had more than enough for an arrest.

She watched as Jason, dressed in hospital pajamas and medicated with a powerful tranquilizer, sat in his chair and rocked. He hadn't shaved, and his blond hair was matted like unintended dreads. Across from him sat Peter.

"Jason," Peter said, his voice rumbling through the speakers. "I want to talk with you today, but this isn't a normal interview. Things you say will be looked at by the judge and by the court.

They could be used for or against you in determining the outcome of your case."

Jason stopped rocking and looked at Peter.

"Do you understand?" Peter continued.

Jason shook his head from side to side and then up and down.

Nicole edged closer to the glass.

"For the record," Peter spoke into the microphone on the table, "it's unclear whether the subject comprehends the purpose of this evaluation."

"Watch out for Ann." Jason's eyes were wide; he looked at Peter and then down at a spot on the floor and then back at Peter.

"That's what I want to talk about," Peter said, "and what we talk about today is not private or confidential. Do you understand?"

"Where's Ann? Watch out for Ann."

"Your sister is dead," Peter stated softly.

Nicole knew that it wasn't the first time that Jason had been told of his sister's death. She inched forward on her chair. "Something," she whispered. "Give me something." The finger twitching and the rocking stopped briefly, but other than the momentary pause, she could see no change in Jason.

"Watch out for Ann," Jason repeated and abruptly resumed his rocking.

Peter sat back and said nothing for a moment. "Jason . . . Jason." he waited until he had the boy's attention. "Why do you watch out for Ann?"

His lips started to move.

Peter leaned in. "What was that? What did you say?"

The rocking stopped. Jason struggled to speak, each word an effort. "Mother . . . told me . . . to."

"Your mother told you to watch out for Ann?"

Like some great burden had been lifted, Jason bobbed his head. "Yes. Yes. Mother told me. Watch out for Ann. Watch out for Ann."

"Does your mother still talk to you?"

Jason stopped, his eyes fixed on something above Peter's head.

"No," Jason said. "I can't hear her. Watch out for Ann."

"Do you hear other voices?" Peter asked.

Jason's eyes shifted to another spot. To Nicole, it looked as though he were focused in midair halfway between Peter and the chalk-white wall.

"Do you hear voices?" Peter repeated.

Jason nodded and gently rocked back and forth in his chair.

"What do they say?"

"Mumbling," Jason said. "Mumbling now. Laughing."

"Are they always there?"

"Always. Almost always. Watch out for Ann."

"Do they ever tell you to do things?"

"Things," Jason said, parroting Peter.

"What kind of things?"

"Kind things. Kind things."

As Nicole watched, doubts crept in. Jason Walsh was so disorganized; how could he have pulled it together to murder his sister? Where was the motive? All they had was some strong evidence that placed him at the scene. So either he did it, or . . . he knows who did. This was not an open-and-close case. *Shit.*

"Kind things. Kind things."

"Jason . . . Jason, listen to me." Peter's voice was stronger. "Do you know that Ann is dead?"

Jason swung his head faster. "Watch out for Ann." He shouted, "Watch out for Ann! Watch out for Ann!"

Peter tried to calm him. "It's okay, Jason. It's okay."

"Watch out for Ann! Watch out for Ann!"

Peter turned toward the mirror and shrugged. He looked at the shouting boy and after about thirty seconds, he shook his head and got out of his chair.

Jason's face had turned red. It reminded Nicole of how Carter had looked as they dragged him into the drunk tank. Tears streamed down the young man's face.

Peter stopped and looked at him, "It's going to be okay," he said.

"Watch out for Ann," Jason sobbed. The sound of the boy's wailing filled the observation room. It was primitive and powerful; it brought tears to Nicole's eyes, and through the glass she could see that it was affecting Peter as well.

"It's okay, Jason." Peter walked back and cautiously approached the boy, who was doubled over, racked by waves of convulsive sobs. He put a hand on his shoulder.

Jason raised his head, tears flowed. He gasped, "Watch out for Ann." He twisted in his chair and looked up at Peter. He started to cough and choke.

"Sshhh," Peter said, his tone like that of a parent comforting a child.

Nicole sat transfixed as Peter crouched down and put his arms around Jason. It's not what she had expected. He held Jason as he cried, and the two of them rocked in that awkward position. Minutes passed, and Peter helped Jason to his feet. He leaned down as Jason mumbled something that wasn't clear through the speakers. She hoped Peter would get him to repeat it, but they were already heading through the door.

She retrieved her blazer and met up with Peter in the hallway as he took Jason back to the nurse's station.

"You might want to give him something to help him calm down," Peter instructed a nurse.

To Nicole, Jason looked exhausted as he stared up at Peter. His face was tear-streaked and he didn't seem to mind as Peter grabbed tissues out of the box and wiped the snot from his nose. She framed the images, the composition, in her mind. So beautiful. One person caring for another.

Peter turned and caught her looking. "Sorry," he said.

"Don't be."

He tossed the soiled wad into a basket and placed a handful of clean tissues in Jason's hand. "You okay?" he asked.

Jason nodded, seemingly spent. His lips moved, and as Nicole got closer she heard a steady mumbling, like a chant.

". . . Watch out for Ann. Watch out for Ann. . . ."

The nurse came out from behind the counter with a pair of pale blue pills. He gave them to Jason and watched him swallow them.

"You all done with him?" the nurse asked.

Peter looked at Nicole.

"I think we've gotten all there was to get," she said.

"I think so," Peter agreed. "Jason . . . Jason." He waited till the boy made eye contact. "Thank you for meeting with me. If you have any questions I'll leave my number with the nurse, okay?"

Jason stared at Peter and took three decisive steps toward him.

For a tense moment Nicole wondered if he were going to strike.

Instead, he stopped within inches of the psychiatrist, and as though he were saying something of great import, stated, "Blood . . . flowers."

"OKAY," NICOLE SAID, AS THEY exited the unit. "What are blood flowers?"

"No clue," Peter admitted. "But it's the second time he said it. As we left the room, he mumbled something about bloody flowers or blood flowers."

"So he's crazy, right?"

"You have to ask?"

"Not really," she admitted, feeling desperate.

"So what happens to him now?" he asked, pressing the button for the elevator.

"The judge will declare him incompetent and send him to a forensic unit. Then he'll go the not-guilty-by-reason-of-mental-defect route. I normally think it's a bunch of crap, no offense intended."

"Why should I take offense?"

"I don't know," she said, noticing that one of his front teeth was chipped and that his upper lip formed a perfect bow. "In this case, I think it's warranted. Unless, of course, you think meds will bring him back to the land of the normal."

"Part of the way, but they're not magic. So you really think he killed her?"

"There's some strong evidence."

The elevator arrived. Inside was a patient holding on to her IV pole and a friend with whom she was chatting.

Nicole and Peter rode down in silence listening as the patient described how, the previous night, her roommate had suffered a cardiac arrest. "I didn't know what to do." she told her friend. "They were all over the place. I just buried my face in my pillow; it was horrible."

"Was she okay?"

"No, they took her to the intensive care unit. I asked the nurse this morning how she was. . . . She'd died!"

"Jesus!"

The bell dinged and the doors opened onto the lobby. The woman wheeled out. Her intravenous pole momentarily stuck in the crack.

After they were out of earshot Nicole whispered, "A whole lot of people seem to die in your intensive care unit."

"That's what they're for," he said.

"What?"

207

"Forgive my cynicism, but it's the most expensive care in the hospital and a lot of times, absolutely futile, like sending a terminal cancer patient to intensive care . . . Why?"

"Was Ann's stay futile?" she asked.

His face clouded. "No . . . I thought she was going to make it. . . . There's something I need to talk to you about. Do you have to be anywhere right now?"

"No, what is it?"

He glanced around. "Not here. You want to get coffee?"

"Sure." She wondered at his jumpiness. They headed through the revolving doors and stepped out into an unseasonably warm December day. The sky was a vivid robin's-egg blue and the mid-afternoon sun had turned the gray piles of snow from yesterday's storm into slush that dribbled dark puddles into the pockmarked streets. They stopped at an umbrella-topped coffee cart, and then walked north toward the park.

"You cold?" he asked.

"No, it feels good to be walking. Of course, I keep spilling my coffee."

"I know a place that's pretty quiet. We can talk there."

"Lead on," she said, and they turned up Sixth Avenue.

So how did things go with the Garden School?" he asked.

"Funny you should ask." She smiled, thinking about how many bits and pieces of her life were in motion at the same time. "How much did I tell you about my daughter?"

"Not much," he said and turned west on Tenth.

Nicole stalled as she looked down the block toward the Expansion School. That would be just the cruel sort of joke that fate would play. He'd take her to the place where she had first met Carter.

"How old is she?" Peter asked, stopping in front of a cast-iron gate outside a squat Norman-style church.

"She's six," Nicole said.

He reached in and undid the gate. "We don't have to talk about it."

"No, you're one of the few people who'd understand . . . This is lovely." She stopped where a weathered stone walkway split into paths that encircled the church. A dense evergreen hedge shut out the noise and a massive beech tree towered over them. "I don't know how many times I've walked by this church but never come in."

"Beth and I used to come here when we were in school. We each had tiny apartments in Alphabet City and finding places to be alone . . . it was nice. This was our favorite. In the spring this entire yard is covered with daffodils."

Nicole sat on a stone bench and sipped her coffee. She wondered how he would have looked as a younger man and why he had selected this place that was filled with so many memories. "I've managed it so that Adriana can start at the Garden School on Monday."

"That's wonderful." He settled beside her. He was pensive. "It's best not to let too much time go by."

"Too late for that," she blurted.

"How long ago was it?"

"Almost two years since we found out . . . Had I told you what happened?" she asked, wondering how it was he seemed to know so much.

"No, it's just that kids go to the Garden School for very few reasons. . . . None of them things that kids should ever have to go through."

"What you said yesterday . . . about trauma affecting families. It's true."

Peter leaned forward, sipped his coffee, and stared ahead.

"My daughter was sexually molested by an uncle," Nicole said. "It's only in the past couple months she's begun to talk with anyone other than me or her grandmother."

"What about her dad?"

Nicole's throat tightened. "Very little . . . We're separated."

"Because of this?"

"Donny can't deal with Adriana being strange, and that's how he sees her."

"So you had to choose?"

"I did. . . . We're not divorced yet, but when I contacted our attorney about having a chat with the school superintendent to give the written go-ahead for Adriana, I asked him to serve the divorce papers. Donny wants to get on with his life."

"And you?"

"I'm all right," she said. "Of course, if you'd asked me earlier this week, it might have been different. It's like I've been treading water for months, but now. . . . I'm just going to get the decisions made and do it. I'll call him when I get home. I think he'll be relieved."

"You've turned a corner."

"I have," she admitted, meeting his gaze. "And you've been helpful."

"Me?"

"Yes, you. Your lecture, letting me know what you thought of the Garden School. It's been helpful. When it first hit the fan with Adriana, I didn't want to talk about it; I just wanted everything to go back to normal, but that doesn't work, does it?"

"Not usually." He laughed. "It would be nice if it did."

Nicole found herself laughing with him. "Why is this funny?"

"Because it's sad and pathetic and sometimes that's the best way to deal with it. I had someone turn to me once in a session after she'd just told me all of this horrible stuff that had happened to her ever since she was a child. Through the telling she was cracking jokes. So I asked her about her sense of humor, and she very seriously told me that's what had kept her going. Those few occasions when she'd not been able to laugh and to make a joke—those were the times when she had wanted to die."

"You can laugh or you can cry," Nicole added. She looked at him. "You had something you needed to tell me, and I've been rambling."

"Occupational hazard," he said, smiling, but clearly anxious. He reached into his inside pocket and pulled out a wad of folded pages. "These are Keith Taylor's process notes. On Monday they were with Ann's chart at the attorney's—I went to see her records with my chief resident. Yesterday afternoon I found these in Ed Tyson's apartment."

"I don't understand. Why would he have copies?" she asked.

"That's just it: The originals are in his top desk drawer. I ran them through a fax to make copies. You need to read these. For starters, did you know he was Taylor's supervisor?"

"What?"

"Yup. It's true . . ." His pager went off. "What time do you have?" he asked.

She looked at her watch. "It's five to four."

"I've got a patient," he said, not sounding happy about it. "I'll try to dictate something on Jason by tomorrow. When would you like it?"

"The sooner the better." She said, holding the pages and trying to digest the information he was throwing at her. She looked at him dead-on. "You don't think Jason did it, do you?"

"No, he's too psychotic. I had the feeling that he just realized—I mean, really made the connection—that his sister is dead." He swung open the iron gate.

"It doesn't look good for him; there's a lot of evidence." She followed him out onto Tenth. "Although it would be nice to have a motive. Why does he keep saying 'Watch out for Ann'?"

"That sort of makes sense," Peter said. He took one last sip of coffee and tossed the cup in a trash bin. "His mother told him to, and he took it literally. Concrete thinking is common in schizophrenia."

Nicole walked with him. She didn't want to keep him from his appointment, but she also wanted to hear his take on these unanswered questions. "Like a deathbed thing? 'Keep an eye on your sister'."

"That's what it sounded like," Peter agreed. "Ann needed watching."

"No kidding. So if you don't think he killed her, what was he doing at the hotel?"

"Watching over her. She told me that he followed her, but that she never felt threatened by him. I only met with her three times, but when she talked about Jason, it was positive. She had this fantasy that she could somehow save him and her sister from their father."

"Let's say you're right, and that maybe he was trying to save his sister—then who killed her?"

A pager sounded. Peter flinched. "That will be Peggy, wondering where the hell I am. I've got to run." He stopped and looked at Nicole.

"Peter, what is it you aren't saying? Obviously, you think Tyson is involved."

He shook his head. "I think Ann had an affair with Ed. I think she was blackmailing him into a Goddard Fellowship."

It was unexpected, and it left her stunned.

His beeper went off a third time. "I have to go."

"I'll call you," she said. "We need to talk about this."

"I have no proof." He reached out his hand and took hers.

The touch was electric.

"Something strange happened last year. . . . Ed was in the middle of it." His voice vibrated inside of her. He gave a half smile. "All this aside, I liked our walk."

"Me, too," and for a moment it felt as though he might kiss her. Instead, he let go of her hand. "Got to run."

"Bye." She felt a pang as Peter darted into the building, and she thought of the White Rabbit in *Alice in Wonderland*. She was also shaken by his comments. Yes, Jason was at the hotel, yes he was covered in his sister's blood. The emotion that came through in the interview, however, was grief—raw gaping grief. And that bombshell about Tyson—easy to say, hard to prove, and just the thing to bump an already high-profile case onto the front page. On top of that she had two supposed friends clearly out to get each other. And the cherry on top—she was attracted to Peter. How absurd.

She wondered who he was meeting with, and remembered the way the clinic had looked when she'd been a student and had met with a young psychiatrist—Dr. Priscilla Barnes. She'd had a total of six sessions and could still picture the heavyset therapist with her flowing skirts and her ability to get Nicole to say the things she didn't want to, like, "No, I don't want to have this child."

Old feelings stirred, like embers poked in a fire.

She pulled out her cell and dialed. "Hector."

"Hey Nic, how's it going?"

"Fair. I'm in the Village and trying to decide whether to come back to the office. What have you got on the Walsh case?"

"Weirdness," he said.

"Weird how?" she asked, not wanting to hear it.

"Weird as in two hours ago I got a call from the manager of the Park South. Seems there was a doorman—Jimmy Bishop—on that night, who was given a message from a pretty blonde in a black dress."

"And?"

"Well, it's one of those everything-that-can-go-wrong deals. He gets off work right after delivering the message and doesn't realize anything has happened until he comes back two days later.

So he tells the manager about the message and wonders if it could be the girl who was killed on the tenth floor."

"And was it?"

"Yup. He took one look at the picture, and said, 'That's her.' . . . You sitting down?"

"No, just spill it."

"He didn't read her note, but the instructions were clear. He was to give it to a tall dark-haired man, and on the outside of the note she'd written 'Dr. Grainger.' "

"He's sure of that?" Blood drained from her head.

"I just got back from taking his statement. You're going to want to read it."

"I'll be right there." She felt a dull tingle in her fingers and her toes. "What about the note? Does he know where it is?"

"I asked him that. He thought the man who took it—Dr. Grainger—put it in his pocket."

"Has he positively identified Peter Grainger?"

"I didn't have a photo. Any chance you have one?"

She was about to say no and then realized. "Just grab one of his books out of the resource center. There's a picture on the back."

"Right. Bishop's on duty tonight, so I can run it over and have him make the ID. Kind of throws a monkey wrench, don't you think?"

"I'm not sure what it does, but good work," she said, not wanting him to know that she was finding it hard to breathe. "Any luck with her escort agency?"

"Not much. I was hoping we could double-team them."

"Okay, give me forty-five minutes."

She ended the call and stood outside the clinic. A part of her wanted to barge in on Peter to ask him what kind of game he was playing. *Damn him.* She felt like an idiot for being taken in by his rumbling voice and his caring eyes.

She started toward the precinct where she'd parked her car, but switched directions and strode quickly back to the gated churchyard. She went over to the garbage can and fished out Peter's coffee cup. She took an evidence bag from her pocketbook and dropped the cup inside. With luck, they'd get both fingerprints and enough saliva for DNA. If either matched anything in the room at the Park South Hotel, Peter Grainger would be in serious trouble.

She looked around the quiet churchyard and wondered if it had all been an elaborate line. What didn't make sense is that she hadn't seen it coming. *Yeah right*, she told herself. *Like you can't be played by a man.*

22

KYLE KNOCKED AT MY STUDY door. I started and clicked off the recorder. "Yes?"

He popped his head in. His hair was slicked back as if he'd put gel in it. His eyes darted toward the surface of my desk, probably expecting to see my accident collection. Relief crossed his face. "What are you working on?"

"Trying to get a dictation done."

"Oh . . . any chance you'd want to see a movie tonight?"

"No, but don't let that stop you." As soon as the words left my mouth I knew I'd been had. What fourteen-year-old wants to be seen with his father at the movies? And what occasion warranted his brand-new Knicks jersey?

"Can I have twenty bucks, then?"

"Sure," I said. "Who are you *really* going with?

He smiled. "Just some girl."

"She have a name?"

"Kyra."

"What would have happened if I'd said yes?" I fished a twenty out of my wallet.

"I knew you wouldn't."

"Hey, maybe I'd like to see a movie with my son and his new friend Kyra."

"Don't even think about it." He laughed.

As I handed over the cash, I said, "This isn't enough for both of you."

"She'll pay for her own, everyone does."

"Really? You're sure?"

He hesitated.

I pulled out a second twenty. "Look, you decide. But I'd be willing to bet that Kyra would love it if you bought the tickets and a bucket of popcorn. You'll be back by eleven. Yes?"

"No problem."

"Kyle?"

"What, Dad?"

"There's something we need to talk about. . . . The job isn't working out. I need to get out of there."

He looked across at me, and I suddenly realized that when he stood up straight he had an inch advantage on me. *When did that happen?*

"I kind of figured," he said. "You're at the hospital in the middle of the night, you're not getting any sleep, they're always paging me. So what does this mean?"

"That's what I wanted to talk about. We can go wherever we want. Back to Cambridge, stay here . . . someplace else. I wanted to know what you thought."

He looked down at his size-twelve Nike's and then back at me. "I like it here. School's okay, the city's cool. . . . I like seeing Grandpa."

"And Kyra . . ."

He grinned. "Hey."

"Come here, you." I said.

"What?"

217

Before he could escape, I wrapped him in a bear hug. "You have fun . . . and be careful."

"Dad." He squirmed free, his face crimson, but smiling from ear to ear.

Shit. Among everything else that was happening, my fourteen-year-old, who looked seventeen, was going on his first real date. I pictured Beth and how she'd joked that when Kyle started with girls, she was going to keep a basket of condoms next to the clothes dryer and put them in the pockets of all his pants. "You know what I mean," I said.

"It's just a movie."

"Uh-huh."

"Before I could launch into an embarrassing discussion of safe sex and "no means no," he said, "Catch ya later," and beat a quick retreat.

ALONE AGAIN, I TURNED BACK to my notes on Jason Walsh, not an easy dictation, but I was looking forward to getting it done, if for no other reason than to see Nicole again. I clicked the recorder on. "This is Dr. Peter Grainger dictating a court-requested psychiatric evaluation on Jason Walsh. Identifying data: This is a twenty-one-year-old never-married Caucasian male who was interviewed on the inpatient psychiatric unit at University Hospital. The interview was videotaped and the patient was advised of his rights. His attorney, through the public defender's office, declined to attend on the condition that he would have access to the videotaped record."

I clicked it off. Problem. I don't think Jason understood a word of what I had told him, which was the punch line of the whole evaluation. He was too crazy to know what was going on. No way he could process a court hearing or work in his own defense.

As I got further into it, clicking the Dictaphone on and off and reviewing what history I had, I realized that Jason Walsh was incapable of murdering his sister. I thought about what Nicole had said, that they had strong physical evidence. I imagined that the blood on his clothing and on his hands had been Ann's. What if he had tried to save her, to protect her? After all, that one thing was clear—Jason was watching out for Ann.

I didn't doubt that Nicole knew her job, but what if something had been missed?

Not your problem, I reminded myself, and I organized my thoughts for the final run. The legal assessment of insanity is totally different from the psychiatric definition. The law demands two things—does the person have a mental illness, and, if he does, could he have known that the act of which he is accused was wrong?

I answered the second question first. "Impression: One. In my medical opinion Mr. Walsh's judgment is globally and severely impaired based on his level of cognitive disorganization and psychosis. Specifically, when asked about the details of the crime of which he is being charged, he was unable to formulate a cogent response. When pressed to acknowledge the death of his sister, Mr. Walsh did provide what can be construed as an emotionally appropriate response by becoming profoundly tearful."

The first question was easy. "Impression two: Ruling out the unlikely possibility that Mr. Walsh could be malingering psychotic symptoms to avoid prosecution, my medical opinion is that his severe psychosis would preempt him from being able to effectively participate in his own defense." I finished up, figuring I'd give the tape to Peggy in the morning, have her transcribe it, make my corrections, and get it to Nicole by the afternoon. Maybe I could hand deliver it.

I opened my door. The loft was dark save for a light over the stove. "Kyle?" There was no answer; I hadn't heard him leave. I smiled, thinking about him at the movies with Kyra. I wondered what she looked like, but mostly I was thrilled that she existed.

Again, I pictured Nicole. What did it mean that the one place I could think to take her was the church where Beth and I used to sneak away between classes? I reminded myself that she was just doing her job, but why did she tell me about her personal life. . . . Why was I so interested? Why was I remembering the flecks of gold in her hazel eyes or the color of her hair? I was glad that she'd managed to get her daughter into the Garden School; I thought about giving Boris a call, just to let him know that she was . . . a friend.

Standing in the darkened loft, I thought how destructive my obsession with the accident had become. What if all I did was ruin Beth's memory? Sure, I wanted to pin down what caused it, but at what cost?

The phone rang, and I nearly jumped. I checked the caller ID; the number was familiar, but it wasn't until I picked up that I could place it.

"Dr. Grainger?"

"Detective Sullivan." I was surprised at the formality in her voice. "What's up?"

"Jason Walsh eloped from the inpatient unit."

"When?" My stomach lurched.

"Somewhere between six and eight. Have you been home all evening?"

"Yes," I said, wondering if she thought I had something to do with this.

"Are you alone?"

"At the moment. Kyle went out to the movies. It's kind of a date."

"When did he leave?" Her tone was curt.

"I didn't look at the clock. I was doing Jason's dictation . . . If it's important, you can ask him when he gets back. Why are you asking me these questions?"

"Where were you the night of Ann Walsh's attack? Where were you from the time you left Dr. Tyson's house to the time we met in the emergency room?"

"I wondered when you'd ask me that." I said, wishing that we weren't doing this on the phone.

"Why is that?" She sounded angry.

"Because I can't remember." As the words left my mouth, I knew they sounded bad.

"Don't you find that odd?" She persisted.

"I think I was drugged," I said. "But in the past, since the accident, I have had blackouts. Just not recently and not this long."

There was silence. "What makes you think you were drugged?"

I told her about drawing my own blood and about the toxicology report.

"I see." Her only comment.

I could tell that she didn't. Why was she so pissed at me? And why did her questions sound like what you'd ask a suspect?

"Any ideas how Jason escaped?" she asked.

"No, the only elopements I know of have been through the front door."

"How did they do it?"

"One guy curled up in the food cart, someone else went out in the laundry. The usual way is a patient attaches himself to a visitor on the way out the door."

"No other way?"

"There's a fire exit, but that's locked and alarmed."

"Where do you think he went?" she asked, sounding less pissed.

"I don't know. Maybe back home . . . I mean, his whole reason for existing centers on Ann. Maybe he'd try to get to her body."

"Interesting thought. I'll have someone check it out. . . . Peter, I need to get a statement from you."

I heard a hesitation and knew there was more.

"I'm also going to ask you for a DNA sample."

"Ask" was a polite way of saying I was a suspect. A chill shot through me. "When?"

"Tomorrow. The earlier the better. And Peter . . . you might want to have an attorney."

She hung up and I stood holding the phone with one hand and gripping the granite countertop with the other. Where was I Monday night? *Shit!* Why hadn't I told her about the drug screen? Or about my blackouts? Although they're not the easiest thing to talk about—Oh, by the way, I'm bonkers and every so often my brain hiccoughs and I can't remember a damn thing—it's especially not the kind of icebreaker to use with a woman whom . . . whom I was interested in.

The phone rang again. Figuring it was Nicole I picked up without checking the caller ID. "Hello?"

No answer.

"Hello? Who's there?" I heard breathing over the line, and a woman's faint voice. "I can't hear you." It was soft, but it landed like a rock-tight fist to my belly.

"Peter, why?"

I froze.

"Why, Peter?"

"Who is this?" There was no denying who it was but it was not possible.

"Why did you do it?" she asked.

"Beth?"

"Why, Peter? Why?"

I stared at the caller ID box; it read "number unavailable." "Who is this?"

"Why? Why? Why?"

222

"Who is this? What do you want?"

I strained to hear, but there was just breathing and then she hung up.

Like Grace's emergency-room theory on who belonged on a psych unit, I had my own corollary: If you thought you were crazy, you probably weren't, and the people who thought they're the most normal were total whack jobs. At that moment, I had to believe the whole thing was in my head. I had just had a hallucination, brought on by stress, but why was I holding the phone? I hit the first button on speed dial.

"Dad?"

"What's up, Peter?"

"You got a few minutes?" I asked, the sound of his voice was like a lifeline.

"Sure," he said. "You sound strange."

"I feel strange. Promise you won't send the guys in the white coats."

"That bad?"

"Yup." I wondered if getting my father worried was such a great move, but I needed someone to hang on to, because I'd been over the edge, and hearing Beth on the phone was not a sign of mental health.

"What's going on?"

"I got another package," I began. "It came Saturday."

"Same as the others?" He sounded disappointed. "Okay . . . we've been through that before. What was the postmark on this one?"

"Manhattan."

"Downtown?"

"Yes . . . you think I sent it to myself, don't you?"

I pictured him on the other side, wanting to be honest, yet trying to be kind. "Peter, when you got the first one, the cops did a good job. The only fingerprints were yours, and they came from post offices near you. But let me ask you this, of all the emotions you've felt since the accident, what's the worst?"

A no-brainer. "Guilt," I answered.

"Right. Every time we've talked about the accident, you've not been able to get past your feelings of being responsible."

"But I was."

"You were driving, Peter. Accidents happen."

"Of course. I'm not stupid." I sounded harsher than I'd intended. "I've always been a good driver. There was no mechanical failure, yet for some reason I drove into a rock wall. Why did I do that? Was I trying to kill both of us?"

"No. You and Beth had a great relationship, and I don't believe you faked that."

"I found out something," I said, not wanting to share my discovery. "The child she was carrying wasn't mine."

"Jesus, Peter! What are you talking about?"

I heard his exasperation, like "Oh, God, here we go again." I told him about the blood types. "It's in black and white. So maybe she went ahead with a sperm donor . . . but why wouldn't she tell me?"

"What else have you been thinking?"

"The obvious . . . What if she'd been having an affair?"

"Even if she was, which I doubt, what would that have to do with the accident?"

"That there was something she had to tell me. What if it was so terrible that I deliberately crashed the car? What if the reason I can't remember is because I am guilty and the rest of my brain can't deal with that?"

"Okay, Peter. Let's do a reality check. The reason your memory is messed up is because when they got you to the hospital you nearly died. You had a massive subdural hematoma and went into a grand mal seizure. If they hadn't drilled two holes into your skull to get the blood out, you would have died. People with that kind of head trauma don't remember what happened to them; it has nothing to do with guilt."

As he spoke, the burr-hole scars on the right side of my head tingled.

"Then let's go through some of the other points," he continued. "I can't comment about the blood types, other than to say, so what? Beth is dead, the child she was carrying is dead, and knowing the two of you, even if she had gone on her own to be inseminated, that would have worked out. As to why she didn't tell you, maybe she wanted to spare you from getting your hopes up in case she miscarried, but now that she was far enough along, where . . . maybe that is what she wanted to talk about. And even if she did have an affair, Beth loved you. Do you doubt that?"

"No." His words washed over me, and I pictured Beth, her body nested in mine as we'd try to decide who'd be the first out of bed on a cold winter morning.

"Good . . . as to why the car crashed, Peter, you're going to have to let go."

"There's something else," I said. "The girl who was murdered . . ."

"You mentioned her. You were going to evaluate her brother."

"I did that. I don't think he's responsible, but I might be a suspect."

"What?"

I told him everything, including the maddening piece about not being able to remember a sizable chunk of that night. "I think Ed slipped something in my drink."

"Why would he do that?"

"I have suspicions, nothing solid."

"You're making me nervous, Peter. Do you have a lawyer?"

"Not yet. But you're the second person who's told me I need one."

"Who was the first?"

"The police detective."

"Damn! What about Kyle?" he asked. "Does he know any of this?"

"No, and up until now I didn't think this was going to affect me directly. Other than Ann was my patient and . . ." My ears perked at the banging of the elevator gate. "Speaking of Kyle, I think he's back from his date. That does not bode well. It's not even ten thirty."

I held the phone and looked across at the security door. I heard the elevator clang open and close repeatedly. "That's strange, I'll call you right back."

"What's happening?"

"It sounds like the elevator's stuck."

I hung up. "Kyle?" I called out through the door. There was no answer, just the bang of the elevator doors. I stuck my head out. "Kyle?"

There was something heaped on the floor of the elevator; from thirty feet away it looked like a pile of clothing. Two steps closer and I saw a hand. I ran. "Kyle!" There was blood on the wall, and as I knelt I saw a polished steel kitchen knife stuck in his belly. He was curled in a ball, as though he were trying to protect his middle. Then I saw blond hair and a face; it wasn't my son. His eyes were open. "Jason . . ."

He said nothing; I felt for a pulse. "Jason, can you hear me?"

His eyes fixed on mine, but nothing came out of his mouth. "It's going to be okay," I said as the door banged into my side. I felt around the blade to see how much blood he had lost . . . was losing. His coat was open, revealing hospital pajamas soaked with blood. I didn't want to move him for fear of making things worse.

"Dad." Kyle had come up the stairs.

I started. "Call 911!" I shouted. "Get into the loft and dial 911."

I stayed with Jason, feeling his pulse weaken with every beat. I looked for other wounds. "Don't die, please." Still, every time the elevator door slammed half shut and then opened I felt him worsen.

Kyle returned with the cell phone.

"They want to know a name," he said.

I felt him staring at me. "It's Jason Walsh," I said. "Go downstairs and unlock the front door. . . . Tell the paramedics to take the stairs. And then get right back up here and stay in the loft. I don't want you seeing this."

"Okay."

I placed my hands around the blade, careful to not cut myself. I immediately recognized the knife, it was a Global vanadium steel chef's knife—Beth's favorite. All I could think was that this was an eight-inch blade, and judging by how much had entered Jason's body, it wasn't the outside bleeding that would be the issue. It was a horrible wound, the kind that keeps someone alive for hours, but ultimately, because of damage to the intestines and internal organs, will mean death from peritonitis and sepsis.

I heard the wail of sirens as the ambulance came across Tenth Street, growing louder as they passed by the park. My eyes were fixed on Jason. I watched for the faintest sign of air moving in and out of his open mouth. Tears slid from his eyes. He was staring at me without moving, perfectly still save for the increasingly spastic movement in his chest as he struggled for every breath. He was dying. I smoothed his bangs from his forehead. "It's okay," I said, knowing that it wasn't.

I heard the outside door crash open and the sound of feet running up the stairs.

"Up here!" I shouted. "Third floor."

I looked back and saw the medics in their navy uniforms lugging their stretcher with a green oxygen tank strapped on top. They ran toward me. "What happened?" the first one asked, kneeling beside me and shining a light into Jason's eyes.

"He's been stabbed. He has a pulse," I offered, "but it's weak."

"Did you see what happened?" his partner asked as she snapped an oxygen mask over Jason's nose and mouth.

"No, I heard the elevator slamming and I came out to see what was wrong."

"Do you know him?" she asked, cracking open the valve on the oxygen.

"His name is Jason Walsh. He's supposed to be a patient at University Hospital. He eloped from their psych unit."

"Oh."

I turned at the sound of more footsteps and saw two uniformed officers clear the landing. One of them stepped into the elevator and, leaning over the stretcher, took a good look at Jason and the knife in his belly. "Is he going to make it?" he asked, as one of the paramedics gingerly felt Jason's back to see if the knife had gone through.

"Don't know," he said, shaking his head.

His partner placed a backboard inside the elevator. She cradled Jason's head, and the two of them gently rolled him onto the board being careful not to twist his spine.

"Let's get him out of here," the woman said.

Both officers stepped inside the elevator and helped hoist Jason onto the stretcher. "You need help?" one of them offered.

"Naah," the woman said, "I may be short, but I'm strong." They wheeled Jason down the hall, and moving in unison, they disappeared from view.

As they left, I saw Kyle. He'd watched the entire thing.

The taller of the two officers looked at me. "You Kyle Grainger?"

"No, that's my son. I had him call 911."

"You saw what happened?" he asked.

"No, I was on the phone when I heard the elevator. I came out to see what was wrong and I found Jason in the elevator."

"You know the victim?"

"I do."

"How do you know him?"

"His sister was my patient. I work for the university. His sister, Ann Walsh, was murdered." I heard the words leave my mouth, strange and disjointed. *Why did Jason come here?* "The detective in charge of her case is Nicole Sullivan. She called me to tell me that Jason had escaped from the hospital a couple hours ago."

"You got her number?"

"Yes." I led him back into my loft.

Kyle was sitting cross-legged on the floor, his back to a pillar, holding the cat on his lap; the phone to his ear. He looked up. "Grandpa wants to talk to you."

"Just a second," I said, trying to figure out where I'd left my wallet. It was on the kitchen counter next to my pager and my cell phone. As I picked it up, I glanced at the steel knife block on the counter. It was in its place between the toaster and the mixer. What wasn't there was the chef's knife. *Oh, God.*

I checked the sink to see if the knife was there, but I knew it wouldn't be. Beth had trained both Kyle and me to not leave the high-tech Japanese knives in water. They had to be toweled dry immediately after every use. The knife buried in Jason Walsh's belly had come from my kitchen. I felt numb as I handed Nicole's card to the cop.

"Grandpa wants to talk to you," Kyle said. He handed me the phone.

"Peter, what's going on? Kyle said that somebody was attacked in your elevator. Are they okay?"

"I don't think so," not daring to say more in earshot of the police.

One of the officers came over to me, "Dr. Grainger, Detective Sullivan is on her way. She doesn't want you to leave."

"I won't."

"Other than the front door," he asked, "are there other ways into this building?"

"Yes . . . there's a back door to the alley, and a pair of bulkhead gates in the sidewalk that lead to the basement . . . And you can get in through the roof, but it should be locked. Sometimes the neighbors have parties there."

"How many people live in this building?"

"Just us and the Richards, but they're in Sweden until Christmas. The other two floors are commercial."

"How many people have keys?"

"I don't know," I said. "It could be a fair number."

"We'll need you to make a list."

"Okay," I said, still holding the phone.

"Peter?"

"Yeah, Dad."

"I'll be right down. And Peter . . ."

"Yes?"

"Be very careful what you say."

23

HIDDEN IN THE SHADOWS OF Tompkins Square Park—a ten-and-a-half-acre rectangle of iron-fenced Victorian strolling paths—Ed Tyson tugged the collar of his black cashmere coat. Despite the cold, the park was dotted with homeless men and women sleeping one and two to a bench. Away from them, in a fenced playground on the east side, he leaned against a ginkgo tree and listened through a tiny audio receiver in his ear. In his pocket was the cigarette-pack-sized control, which he had dialed up to its loudest setting. The reception from Peter's phone was perfect; the problem was with the three bugs planted in the ceiling. He could pick up snippets, but understanding Peter's deep voice was impossible. He heard the cop ask who else had keys to the loft, but couldn't make out the response. Would Peter mention him? When Peter and Kyle had moved in, Ed had made a show of handing over two sets. It wouldn't take a rocket scientist to realize that he'd kept one.

Beth's shadowy image hovered. He glanced at her and caught the glimmer of approval. It was going well. Even the challenge of getting a full-grown male out of the psych ward. So many things might have soured. He'd almost aborted the plan when, from the maintenance floor above Jason's room, he'd noticed the second bed—it was supposed to have been a private room. Fortunately, no one was in it. Trickier still was the distance from the ceiling to the ground. Unlike the other floors, the psych unit had twelve-foot ceilings, a deterrent for patients who might try to hang themselves. From his hideaway, it had been a long way down.

He'd shot a blow dart tipped with T2745 into an already-sedated Jason Walsh; the youth was paralyzed in less than a minute. Then Ed had lowered himself from the ceiling using a winch, harnessed the boy, and hoisted him up. The whole process was similar to techniques used by the Krago to raise and lower slain prey from the jungle canopy. At every step it could have gone south—a nurse coming to check, the roommate returning, an aide coming to mop the floor.

As it was, he'd only just replaced the ceiling panel when he'd heard the nurse. As she called out for Jason, he'd held his breath. He'd heard her check the bathroom and then run back out into the hall. Throwing Jason's limp arms around his neck, Ed had dragged him in a hobbling fireman's carry. By the time the alarm sounded, he'd made it to the stairs.

Chewing on coca, he mused about the timing. He was already in Peter's basement when he'd heard the phone conversation with Detective Sullivan through his earpiece; she had finally made the connection between Peter and Ann's murder. The part that alarmed him was Peter's allegation that he had been drugged and had actually had the balls to draw a toxicology screen. While Ralph's modified T2745 was completely undetectable, the same wasn't true for the *Datura* and Cagé he'd dosed Jason with. It was unfortunate, but who was to say that Peter hadn't taken them himself?

It was all about calculated risks, and while it would have been easier to kill Jason at the hospital, his *elopement* from the unit and his murder cleaned up loose ends. Peter's fingerprints on the knife were gravy.

Now, waiting for the arrival of the detective, Ed felt a delicious anticipation. It had been worth it. Would she cuff him right there? He pictured Peter being led away, Kyle sobbing, the wheels of justice finally starting to move. Then he'd go after the boy; his body would never be found, just a puff of smoke high above the city.

"Hey, mister."

Ed turned and saw a scraggly youth not two yards away.

"Go away," he said, identifying the boy as one of the runaways who flocked to the East Village.

"Give me some money," the kid said, moving closer.

Ed looked down and saw something glint in the kid's hand. "Scum." He feinted to the left.

The kid lunged predictably, and Ed, with the speed of a pit viper, was behind him, his left arm around the youth's throat and his right hand now firmly in possession of the cheap switchblade, which he sank it into the flesh of the teenager's hand.

The kid shrieked, "Help! He's . . ."

Ed squeezed on his windpipe, shutting off his air. "Shut up," he hissed, his arm coiled like a boa around his trachea.

The boy thrashed, desperate for air.

Ed pondered feeling the boy's futile struggle. Two murders this close would create a problem. He kept up the pressure, and when he felt the kid go limp, he held for an additional count of ten and let him slip to the ground. Ed kicked him over with his foot and let him flop against a grimy snow bank.

He looked back up at Peter's windows. No detective yet. He was torn—he desperately wanting to watch, to see the puppets dance. Frustrated, he looked at the unconscious boy. *No.* He wiped the blade in the snow and stuck it in his pocket. He glanced at his watch; it was near midnight. In minutes the cops would sweep the park, kick out the homeless, and lock the gates. Normally, he'd stay behind, concealed on the flat roof of the ladies' restroom, but not with this. Would the boy be able to recognize him? He should kill him. No one would mind. Just one less filthy mugger.

His ears pricked at the sound of voices. He glimpsed the distant silhouettes of two officers crossing the park. Beth's specter whispered in his ear, "you'd better leave."

He looked down at the filthy kid and felt the plastic-handled switchblade in his pocket. The patrol was getting closer. "All right," he said, hating this loose end. As he left through the south gate, he consoled himself with the thought that the cops wouldn't find the boy, and more than likely he'd freeze to death before morning.

24

NICOLE BYPASSED THE ELEVATOR—IT was crisscrossed with
crime-scene tape—and climbed the worn steps to Peter's loft. *In
for a penny, in for a pound,* she thought, knowing this case could
get her kicked off the force. Ultimately, that's why she'd kept it;
she'd rather see it coming. So when she got the call about Jason
Walsh stabbed outside Grainger's loft, she'd said, "Yeah, sure, I'll
take it."

On the drive from Brooklyn she'd called the hospital and
learned that Jason was DOA. She'd then called Hector and told
him to assemble the crime-scene team.

At the top of the stairs she saw the photographer setting up by
the elevator. To her right a young officer stood casually outside an
open door.

She flashed her shield. "Has Detective Vega arrived?"

"No, ma'am."

She pushed inside. Her first impression of Peter's loft was that
it was huge; it was also dark, and she could see three men seated in
a living area toward the front, their faces lit by moonlight. Some
sort of kitchen was to her left, doorways behind that, probably

leading to bedrooms, but the rest of the space was just big and open.

One of the three saw her and stood. "Detective Sullivan."

"Dr. Grainger," she answered as his deep voice rumbled through her. She wanted to trust him, and she hated that she couldn't. As she approached, the other two men stood. Something about that struck her as Old World. They were all over six feet; one was a teenager—his son. The other man she couldn't place.

"Detective Sullivan, this is my father, Michael, and my son, Kyle."

The older bearded man extended his hand. Kyle kept his at his sides.

Good for him, she thought, shaking Michael Grainger's hand. *At least he's got family; he's going to need it.* "Who found Jason?" she asked.

"I did," Peter said, still standing. "About a quarter after ten."

"You're certain of the time?"

"I was on the phone with my dad and I thought that it was Kyle. His curfew is eleven."

"He was on the phone with you?" she asked the elder Grainger.

"That's right."

"How did he sound?" she asked, wondering at the coincidence of Peter having a partial alibi in his father.

"Fine."

She heard a set of footsteps behind her. "Hey, Nic."

She introduced Hector, glad to have her partner there. "Would you mind if he took your son aside and asked him some questions?"

Peter hesitated. "Can my father go with him?"

"Of course," she said, knowing that any information they'd get from the boy would be the first thing an attorney would attack. She felt bad for the quiet boy; he had witnessed something horrible and his life might be primed for another huge upheaval.

She watched as Hector led Kyle and Michael Grainger away.

"Would you like to sit down?" Peter offered.

"Thanks." She sat across from him. "You hear the elevator and you find what?"

"I thought it was Kyle." He stared at his hands. "And then I saw the blond hair and the knife. He was still alive; he had a pulse."

"Who called 911?" she asked, knowing the answer.

"Kyle. He'd just gotten home."

"Before the phone call with your father, what had you been doing?"

He looked up at her. "I'm a suspect, aren't I?"

She met his gaze. A part of her wanted to reach across the space and tell him that it was going to be all right, but the evidence was piling up. "Yes," she said.

"Then I should have a lawyer before I answer any more questions."

"That's your choice," she said. "You've not been formally charged." Nor would he be, she thought, until she had all of her evidentiary ducks in a row. Plimpton would ream her out if she got it wrong a second time. "I need your statement for tonight and the night of Ann Walsh's murder. How soon can you round up your attorney?"

"I don't have one." He looked down at the floor and then back at her. "You already know the worst of it. . . . I can't remember what happened the night Ann was killed. I walked Gretchen home from Ed's apartment and then there's a gap."

"What's the next thing you remember?" she asked, feeling a twinge of jealousy at the mention of the blond reporter.

"Coming home and checking my answering machine."

"What were the messages?"

"Just the one from Ed—that something bad had happened to a student. I suspected it was Ann even before I called."

"Why's that?"

"Just a feeling. It's like, ever since Saturday, when he first called me, all I've been doing is dealing with Ann Walsh or Jason. Her father even called and screamed at me; I have no idea how he knew that I'd seen his daughter. And then I find out he habitually sues his daughter's psychiatrists after she's slept with them."

"Did you sleep with her?" Nicole asked, sickeningly curious.

"That would make sense, but no, although I could see how it would happen."

"She was very beautiful."

"It's not that." He met her gaze. "There was a quality to her— it came and went—but when it was there, it's not so much that I wanted to have sex with her, but I wanted to protect her. That's a powerful aphrodisiac. That's what drew in Keith Taylor."

"You knew him?"

"No, but my chief resident, Felicia Jones, was good friends with him."

"Does she know where he is?"

"I don't think so. . . . Did you read his notes? The ones I copied?"

"I did, and that's another issue. The university attorney is saying you stole them and that's why he didn't give the originals to us."

"That's not true. Felicia was with me when I first saw them. Talk to her."

"I will, but you have to admit your story of finding them in Tyson's apartment . . ."

"Can't you see why he'd want them gone?"

"Not really. He was a lousy supervisor, maybe even set the kid up, but there's no proof of anything more." Although, they *did* confirm that Tyson had lied to her in the ER.

He shook his head. "This feels so unreal. I'd just finished dictating my report on Jason. I guess you won't need it."

"I might," Nicole said.

"Do you want me to have it transcribed?"

"That won't be necessary, but I'm going to want to take the clothes you were wearing both the night of Ann's murder and tonight."

"And if I don't agree?"

"I'll be back in an hour with a warrant."

"Doesn't seem like a choice . . . Take what you need."

"Thanks. I'm going to need you to sign a few forms." She pulled her pocketbook into the light and fished out the papers.

Michael Grainger walked back toward them. "What's going on?" he asked.

"Detective Sullivan needs to take a few things as evidence."

"May I talk to my son in private?"

"Of course."

"Where's Kyle?" Peter asked.

"I told him to stay in his room. He doesn't need to see this."

Nicole watched as the two men went into the corner. Moonlight fell across their faces. The father was clearly worried, and Peter . . . What was it about him? Even with this weirdness, she was drawn to him. He glanced over and caught her watching. She heard him say, "No, I don't care," and he walked toward her.

"Peter." His father trailed after him. "You need to think this through. Think about Kyle." He turned to Nicole. "Please tell my son he needs a lawyer."

"I already have."

"Are you charging him?"

"Not at the moment, but I need a complete statement, and

soon." She looked at Peter. "You really should have an attorney with you."

"I wish I could say that there was nothing to hide. But that's the problem with blackouts—you just don't know." Peter turned to his father. "Although there's one thing I could do to get my memory back."

"You've *got* to be kidding." Michael replied.

"What are you talking about?" Nicole asked.

"Hypnosis," Peter said.

She realized he wasn't joking. "That's pretty unreliable," she commented.

"It can be . . . but."

"Don't even think about it," Michael told his son. "Is your memory that short?"

"No," Peter said. "At least think about it."

"What I think," Michael Grainger said, "is let the detective do her job, and I'll give Harold Beckerman a call to see whom he'd recommend."

"You've been hypnotized before?" she asked, wondering at how things were shifting from strange to stranger.

"Yes, once . . . I needed to know what had happened. I couldn't remember much."

His father interjected, "You had a head injury, Peter. What do you expect?" He looked at Nicole. "He was comatose for weeks and they had to drill holes to relieve the pressure on his brain."

"My father's trying to tell you that I have holes in my head and I should shut up, but why try to cover up any of this? It'll all come out. I had a colleague who'd done a lot of work with retrieved memories, do the hypnosis. I figured it was worth a shot."

"The man was a quack," his father said.

"What happened?" she asked.

"I don't really know," Peter admitted. "Maybe it was too soon, or I was too depressed, but I became psychotic . . . as in, certifiable. The hypnosis triggered a flashback that wouldn't stop. I was cycling over and over through the accident. It wouldn't stop."

"That sounds horrible." She wondered why he was telling her this.

"It wasn't good. . . . All I wanted was to have it stop. I didn't care how."

"He ended up in the hospital," Michael said.

"Really?" she said, thinking how this might be the opening salvo in an insanity defense. . . . all the more reason to take things slowly. "If you'd rather I get a search warrant? . . ."

"No," Peter said, signing his name to the forms on the table. "It'll all come out anyway."

25

"IT'S QUITE THE STEW YOU'RE in, Peter," Harold Beckerman commented as we cleared the lobby of the grungy precinct where we'd been since eleven that morning. The seventy-year-old attorney, who looked fifty with his exquisitely draped suit, twinkly blue eyes, and obvious enjoyment in his work, held the door.

I squinted against the sun; my head felt fuzzy. "What time is it?"

"Almost four," he said, taking a deep breath.

"Is it always like that?" I asked, feeling as though my insides had been slowly dissected over the last five hours.

"Only when they're not sure . . ." He looked at me, his bushy white eyebrows knitted. "You're lucky to be walking out of there."

"I know." All day long I'd been waiting for Nicole to say, "Enough is enough," and read me my Miranda rights. "So what do you think?"

"They're being careful. If they charge you with murder, they have some procedural abnormalities to deal with."

"Like what?"

"For starters, they had you evaluate Jason Walsh. Which, if for the sake of argument you did kill his sister and he was a witness, then it might appear that they unwittingly helped, or even incited, you to murder him."

"Oh, please."

"Just some thoughts. Cute detective, don't you think?" Then my father's poker buddy, one of the top criminal lawyers in Manhattan, gave me a searching glance before he stepped over a muddy snowbank to hail a taxi.

"What do I do now?" I asked as a cab swerved across the avenue and stopped.

"That's easy. Don't do anything. Got it?"

"Got it."

"I'll have my secretary call you. I want to see you tomorrow so we can try to fix some of the mess you've made. But remember, no talking to the pretty detective."

"Got it."

"Uh-huh." He opened the cab door and looked back at me. "It's a mess, Peter, but it's a mess on both sides. That's going to buy us a little time . . . but not much. I need you to think things through between now and tomorrow. For me to work with you and do my job, you'll need to tell me everything. Understand? Everything."

"I will," I said, realizing that he didn't believe me.

"Good." He gave me a hearty handshake. "I've seen worse."

I watched his cab pull away; the back of his balding head was visible for a whole block. I wondered if having a friend of the family as an attorney was the way to go, but there had been something comforting in having him next to me as those detectives had asked me the same questions over and over.

I felt beat and scared shitless, but it wasn't the cops. Although seeing myself in the crosshairs was unnerving; it wasn't that. I believed Nicole and her partner would do the right thing, and if, in fact, I had murdered Ann Walsh in some bizarre fugue state, then I needed to be locked up. That wasn't the issue.

What was freaking me out was Jason, who had either found his way or been taken into my building. There, someone had gotten into my loft, taken one of Beth's knives, and had killed him within spitting distance of my front door. What if Kyle had come home? What if he'd come upon the murderer? The thought of my boy trying to defend himself against an armed psychopath was killing me. And what about Jason? According to Nicole, there were no signs of a struggle. Like a lamb to the slaughter, Jason had just stood there while an eight-inch vanadium-steel blade was buried in his gut. I pictured his eyes staring into mine, alive but unmoving.

I stopped and looked down Fifth, past Ed's building and through the arch of Washington Square. A horrible thought flashed to mind.

I pulled out my cell and called my dad.

"Peter? Where are you?"

"I just got out of the station. I owe you big for sending me Harold. Is Kyle with you?" I asked, trying to keep my fear in check.

"Yes."

"I don't want him going back to the loft. Can he stay with you?"

"Of course. What about you?"

I paused. "I'll be okay. . . . Someone has to look after the cat."

"The cat can stay here, you know."

"I know, Dad. . . . Someone was in the loft. There's no other explanation. They took a knife out of the kitchen, and there were no signs of a break-in. I need to change the locks, and I don't want Kyle back until I'm sure it's safe."

"You want to speak to him?"

"Sure, put him on." I shifted gears as Kyle picked up.

"You okay, Dad?"

"I'm fine, kiddo. They just wanted to ask me some questions."

"You knew the man in the elevator."

"He was the brother of a patient of mine."

"The girl who was murdered."

"That's right." I wondered what else he knew or thought he knew.

"You were trying to help him," he said.

I heard an uncertain edge to his voice and pictured how it must have appeared to him coming up those stairs. His father crouched over a dying man. Did he see the knife? If he had, he would have recognized it. "That's right," I told him. "I was trying to save him." I felt his unasked question hanging. *Dad, did you kill him?* "I can't imagine what you're thinking right now."

"I know you didn't do it, Dad."

I bit back the urge to ask how he was so certain and would he mind sharing that knowledge with the cops. "I told Grandpa that I want you to stay with him until I'm sure everything's okay at home."

"What about Willy?"

"I'll make sure he doesn't starve."

"He's gotten really fat," Kyle remarked, and we spent a couple minutes talking about anything other than dead bodies in our elevator.

Knowing that he was with my dad made me feel a hair better. I thought through how someone could have gotten the knife. It had to be Ed. He must have kept a set of keys. Why? If everything that I'd written off to my craziness—the packages, the phone call from Beth—were all real . . . were they all connected to Ed? Why was he doing this to me? Most of my suspicions I'd kept back during the interrogation. After Nicole's dismissal of Taylor's notes and her disbelief at my story of having been drugged, I wasn't going to risk anything without proof. There was a lot I didn't tell them—like about the phone call from my dead wife. But if that wasn't a hallucination, then maybe they could trace it.

As I came down Avenue A and headed through Tompkins Square Park, I spotted Gretchen Becker in a long fur-trimmed red coat walking a tiny dog and heading toward me. She waved as she approached, and the little dog's legs pumped furiously as they crossed the street. "Peter," she called out. She picked up her shih tzu and stepped over a mound of brown snow.

"Hi, Gretchen." What was she doing outside my building?

"I've been waiting for you. I was hoping that I could ask you some questions about Ann Walsh and her brother. I understand you had quite the night."

"I did, and I'm in no mood for more questions."

"I take it the police have interviewed you."

"Look, Gretchen . . ."

"Before you say it," she interrupted, "maybe we could do some information sharing. She looked around. "But please, let's go inside."

"And you want to help me because?"

"Peter, please. It's not just the story. We have to talk."

"How did you know where I live?"

"I asked Miranda for your address."

"I see." I felt uneasy around this woman who had such a strong connection with Ed. Why did she keep looking around? She appeared as jumpy as I felt. "I don't mean to be rude, but it's been a rough few days and I have stuff I need to do." I turned to walk away.

"Ed was sleeping with her."

I stopped dead. How could she know about my fear that it was Ed's child Beth had been carrying? I caught myself. "You mean with Ann?"

"Who did you think?" She gave me a searching look.

"Does it matter? Where's the proof?" I looked back at her on the other side of a snowdrift, the dog panting in her arms.

"Invite me in." She smiled, and despite my annoyance, I admired her persistence.

"Fine, ten minutes."

"Such chivalry." She deposited the dog into her voluminous bag.

We walked into my building, stepping over crumpled yellow crime-scene tape. *Welcome home*, I thought, as I put my key in the door.

Before I could object, she'd pulled out a small camera and was snapping photos of the open elevator. In front of it were an out-of-order sign and more streamers of tape. I walked over to it, trying to ignore the whir of Gretchen's camera as she framed shots of dried blood.

Images from last night flooded me. Jason's eyes staring into mine. Had I told him it was going to be okay? What a load of crap.

"We have to take the stairs," I said.

"So that's where it happened." Her high-heeled boots kept step with me.

"Yes." When we got to the third floor I surveyed the distance from my front door to the elevator. "Please don't take pictures here."

"Okay." She slipped her camera into her pocket and followed me in. "Nice space."

"Ed found it for me."

She stiffened. "Interesting. The two of you are close."

"Not now," I said. "You said he was having an affair with Ann. Without proof, it's useless.

"How well do you know my cousin?"

"I used to think I knew him. I don't."

Willy emerged from Kyle's bedroom and padded in our direction. He spotted the dog's snuffling head in Gretchen's bag and hissed.

"Let's talk over here," I said, heading toward the front windows. "Did Ann say she was having an affair with Ed?" I asked.

"Not exactly."

"You sound nervous."

"Let's just say I respect my cousin's temper."

"Why's that?"

"For starters, he didn't want me talking to Ann. For some reason she was off-limits. I found that suspect."

"Why?" I asked, playing devil's advocate. "I could see why he wouldn't want her talking to a reporter."

"I'll give you that." She unbuttoned her coat, revealing provocative cleavage beneath a cream silk blouse. Her perfume, a mix of orchids and jasmine, wafted over me. "When Ann told me about the fellowship she was going to get, I had the feeling that it wasn't aboveboard. She wouldn't give the details. She also didn't know that Ed and I were related."

"So?"

"Who has the final say on who gets them?" she asked, her blue eyes staring intently into mine.

"There's a small committee, but ultimately it's Ed."

"That's what I thought." She sighed. And then more to herself, she said, "And why would he give it to a girl who's turning tricks? It doesn't add up, does it? Unless . . . If I'd known it was Ed, I would never have kept it."

"What are you talking about?"

"Ann sent me something. It came with a note that if things didn't go the way she wanted, that she'd give me a much bigger story."

"What is it?" I asked, feeling a sliver of hope.

She attempted a smile. There were tears in her eyes. "It's a condom . . . a used condom. It came in the mail the day after she died."

"Where is it?"

"Safe." She looked down at the floor.

"Why are you telling me this?" I asked. "Why haven't you gone to the police? You need to give it to them."

"I can't," she said. "Not yet. Not until I feel safe. I have a horrible feeling this isn't over. You're a good man, Peter; I don't want to see you get hurt."

As I looked across at her, the light streaming through the windows cast a halo around the fur trim of her coat. I saw fine lines around her porcelain blue eyes. She looked vulnerable in a way that seemed incongruent. "You're scared of him," I said.

Sensing her mistress's discomfort, the dog stood on its two hind legs and licked Gretchen's chin. "Ed is a genius, one of the greatest scientists of our time, but there's darkness in him . . . When I was fifteen, he came and stayed with us in Frankfurt. We—how do you say?— messed around. I was very much in love with Ed. The kind you can only have when you're a teenager."

"Romeo and Juliet."

"Yes, only without daggers and poison." She smiled, and I could picture her as a young girl. "For the two weeks he was there, we were inseparable. . . . You know that story Ed told about his father dying when he was a teenager."

"Yes." I said, wondering at the sudden shift in topic.

"It wasn't long after that, he came. Remember how he had said it happened?"

"Some sort of freak accident."

"It wasn't," she blurted.

The air grew still; the seconds slowed. "What makes you say that?"

"Peter . . . you have to know that I still love Ed. I'm not *in love* with him, but . . . the reason I'm telling you these things is so you'll take care. You have to be careful."

"How do you know it wasn't an accident?" I gently urged.

"If he were to find out I've talked to you . . . I don't know what he'd do. You can't tell anyone," she said.

"I won't. I promise."

"He told me about his father. A very cruel man. I'd only met him once, years before at a cousin's wedding. I remembered being in the narthex of the church, and the Judge screamed at his wife as if she were a servant. So when Ed would lie in bed and tell me about his family, I knew he wasn't lying. I also knew that when he told me about how he felt pushing his father over the cliff, it was the truth."

I found this hard to imagine, impossible to grasp. It's not that the words were confusing, it's just that . . . "You never told anyone?"

"Never. I was fifteen, I was in love with my American cousin, and he had made me promise. I thought it was romantic; he had done it for his mother. He loved her so much and wanted to end her suffering."

As she said that I realized something. "Are you still having an affair with him?"

She looked away. "It's not so simple. Yes, on occasion he'll call me up and come over. I don't count on him, and I've even tried to say no, but the truth is there's something comfortable about what we have. He's been good to me. You may not see it, but there's a tender side to him. When I was in my twenties I got caught in a bad marriage with a man who beat me. It was Ed who got me out, who made certain that Frederick left me alone. He even helped me get my green card."

"The night we met, wasn't that a set up?"

"It was."

"But if Ed and you . . . why would he want to fix you up with me?"

"That wasn't his doing. Over the years Miranda has spoken about you, which is how I discovered your books. By the time I'd gotten away from Frederick, I was a mess—always frightened, feeling like I wasn't much of a person. Your books helped me put it in the past, helped me not be so afraid. I thought that I'm single, you're single . . . that perhaps we'd find something." She smiled. "I've not had luck with men."

"Why didn't Ed object?" I struggled with this information and felt bad that I'd misjudged her.

"That's the way he is. He was probably curious, wanted to see what would happen. With Ed, what's on the surface has little to do with what he's thinking. That's why he comes to me; I'm the only one with whom he's ever let his mask down."

"Does he love you?"

"No." She shivered. "You need to take your son and go back to Cambridge. I hadn't made the connections before, but I see his hand in this."

"There's more, isn't there?"

She drew her coat in like a blanket. "If he knew what I've told you, there's a chance that he would kill me, but I couldn't bear anything happening to you or your son." She paused. "There's one last thing you need to know, and then I'll go. Fifteen years ago Ed bought an emerald engagement ring for the only woman he's ever loved. Miranda wears it, but it was meant for your wife."

26

LIT BY THE GLOW OF a plasma screen in his subbasement office, Ed devoured Nicole Sullivan's ancient file. Tormented by loose ends, he needed something big. The bitch was too smart, too nosy.

The scanned notes from her therapist spanned six weeks

Thursday January 3, 1989

. . . This is the first evaluation for this twenty-year-old never-married Caucasian female.

Chief Complaint: Depression in the context of an unwanted pregnancy.

History of present complaint: Nicole reports that her mood changed following a series of events where she learned that she was six weeks pregnant. When she informed her boyfriend—a man she describes as a famous author—he told her that he did not want a child with her and he revealed that he had lied and was, in fact, married with children. . . ."

Ed imagined Nicole's dilemma, a twenty-year-old Catholic daughter of a detective pregnant in Greenwich Village. It didn't take much to figure out that the father was Carter Walsh. To be sure, Ed had leafed through old Expansion School catalogues and its authors' symposia, determining which Walsh had hosted and which Nicole Luria had attended.

He read on.

Thursday, January 12, 1989

Patient is more depressed. She has stopped attending classes and despite my recommendation that she speak with her parents, she has not. She has decided to terminate her pregnancy. While she denies thoughts of suicide, I believe that she is at considerable risk for self-harm. I have recommended an antidepressant after she terminates her pregnancy.

Monday, January 23, 1989

Nicole showed for her session on time. There was a large bruise on her cheek. She was subdued and told me that she had had the abortion, but did not want to discuss it. She said that she had gotten the money from the man who had gotten her pregnant. They fought and he struck her.

She continues with little appetite and minimal sleep. I recommended that she spend time with her family, but she says that she's too embarrassed and that her father—a police detective—would insist she tell him who struck her. . . .

Thursday, January 26, 1989

Nicole was quiet through most of the session. She is clearly depressed and for the first time agreed to take medication. She mentioned that she had an aunt who did well on Elavil. I agreed to start a low dose, which I will increase by 25 milligrams every other day. I reviewed potential side effects and gave her a week's supply.

The next note had Ed on the edge of his chair, his face inches from the screen. The handwriting, while still that of the therapist, was jagged and less careful.

Sunday, January 29, 1989

I was called to the ER by Dr. Patchett; Nicole overdosed on Elavil. I visited her in intensive care, where she apologized for not having told me that she was intending to kill herself. She admitted that she had asked for

253

the Elavil because of its lethality. While she denied further thoughts of wanting to die, I concurred with the psychiatric consultant that Nicole is at considerable risk for a second and more lethal attempt and would benefit from an inpatient admission on an involuntary basis, if necessary.

Friday, February 3, 1989

I received a call from the psychiatric consultant at University Hospital who informed me that Nicole had been discharged to the care of her parents. When I asked him why she had not been transferred to the psychiatric floor, he reported that both she and her parents were in disagreement with that plan, and that she was no longer in a condition where she could be held against her will. . . .

Monday, February 27, 1989

After several unsuccessful attempts to reach Nicole, I contacted her at her parents' home. She informed me that she would not return to school nor continue therapy. She said that the overdose was a mistake and not something that she would repeat. I asked her if I could speak with her parents, and she refused. I told her that if she wished to contact me at any point in the future, she should feel free to do so. She thanked me and restated that she was not going to continue in treatment.

At this point, I will close out her clinic record. . . .

Ed sat back. The thing that didn't make sense was why would such an obviously intelligent woman have taken Ann's case? Admittedly, in the beginning it would have been just one of those random New York happenings, where the indiscretions of youth pop up fifteen years later, but once she'd recognized her long-ago lover's child, why wouldn't she have said, "No, thank you. Someone else can handle you and your fucked-up daughter."

You kept the case, why? He thought of two scenarios. First, she could do damage control on information that might come up about her past. Second—and this spoke to a woman of great depth—she wanted payback. Ed could appreciate the power of a slow-burning hate growing through the years. What if Nicole

Luria, now Detective Sullivan, had unfinished business with Carter Walsh? He wondered if she was still an artist; he even had a desire to see her work. Did she still paint? Or had she buried that just as he had had to hide his love for Beth?

As he closed the file, his intercom buzzed and his secretary told him that Gretchen was on the phone.

"Tell her I'll call her back." Gretchen was the last person he wanted to speak to. Her impromptu visit with Peter had been a betrayal.

"She said it's important."

"Fine." He'd agonized over the WAV file of their conversation from this afternoon, their voices too low to be clearly heard. The line clicked. "Hello?"

"Ed," Gretchen said. "We need to talk."

"What about?" He heard her dog snuffle in the background and pictured the fussy animal cradled in her arms like a hairy baby.

"I have something I need to give you. . . . It's from Ann."

His fingers clamped down on the receiver. "What is it?"

"Not over the phone."

Bitch. After all he'd done for her this was his payment. "Don't play games, Gretchen. What have you got?"

"When can you be here?" she asked.

He heard a tremor in her voice; she was scared. *What have you done?* "How's tomorrow? One. Your place?"

"That would be fine."

As he hung up, he could barely breathe. Ann had sworn that no one knew about their affair . . . but Ann had lied. *What the fuck are you playing at?*

A crash sounded from outside the laboratory. Ed's head swiveled, he bolted from his chair, and shut down his computer. For a moment he thought it was the cops. He held his breath and heard Ralph joke with the assistants—apparently, the movers had knocked something over. He tried to calm himself, but instead all he could think of were the chances he was taking. Everything was at risk.

He pushed through the door and stepped out into the main lab.

"Hey boss," Ralph greeted him, his face distorted by the thick glass of an analytic scale he was calibrating. "It's finally all ours."

For a moment, Ed wasn't certain what he meant, and then he heard the sounds of feet and swearing men. "Are they done?"

"That's what the foreman told me."

"Good," Ed said. As he stepped into the circular lobby his mind wandering back to the conversation with Gretchen. *What did she have?* Dust covered the lobby floor, and Ed glimpsed two men in coveralls retreating through the tunnels with an autopsy table.

Jeff Corbut, the hospital's physical plant supervisor came over with his clipboard. "That should be the end of it, Dr. Tyson. You want to look?"

"Sure." Ed followed him into the morgue.

"You're getting fifteen hundred square feet. We left the cremation oven, per your instructions, and your assistant said it was okay to leave the old tables."

"Great," Ed said, taking inventory of the antiquated dissection tables, the very ones he'd used as a medical student. The brand-new crematorium, a half-million-dollar piece of equipment, Ed had kept at Ralph's request, as it provided an easy way to dispose of rat remains. "What about those?" he asked, eyeing several forty-gallon drums.

"The idiots!" Corbut said. "They need to go . . . unless you can use a couple hundred gallons of formalin?"

"Why not?" Ed said, just wanting to be done with the workmen. "We go through a ton of solvent."

"Great . . . so if there's nothing else, I'll call your secretary and set up something for next week so we can start the build-out."

"Good . . . and Jeff?"

"Yes, Dr. Tyson?"

"Could you get someone down to install a security door to the tunnels?"

"Same as the one on the stairs?"

"Yes, and as soon as possible."

AFTER JEFF LEFT, ED SURVEYED his new space. He walked to the crematorium and twisted the handle. Inside there was room enough for a coffin. He reached into his jacket pocket and pulled out Taylor's notes. He put them inside, yanked the handle, and turned on the jets. Through the tempered glass window he watched the papers turn to ash. He dialed up the oxygen, switched on the blowers, and sent them swirling up the flue and out over the city.

"Hey, boss, playing with the new toys?"

He started at the sound of Ralph's voice. "You caught me." He wondered if Ralph had seen him burn the notes.

"So this is going to be where it happens." Ralph commented. "I don't know if I've ever said this, but I can't believe how lucky I am to be working with you."

Ed faced his gushing assistant. "It's mutual, Ralph. I could never have done this without your help. How are you coming with the Tumoren synthesis?"

"So close," he said, referring to the task Ed had set him—taking the distilled plant extract and manufacturing the molecule in the laboratory. "Are you ever going to tell me what's in the bottle?"

"I can't yet," Ed admitted.

"It's a fungus, isn't it?"

"How'd you know?"

"You left some contaminants. I ran them through the spectrograph. I'm figuring some kind of mold?"

"Close." He said, picturing the woody mushroom that was a staple of the Krago diet and the source of Tumoren.

"It's going to be a zoo, isn't it?"

"I think so."

"You're going to be really famous. This is so huge. I can't believe I'm part of it. This is history."

As Ralph voiced his excitement and his fantasies of the press coverage and accolades that would soon descend, Ed stared into the oven. He was back in the jungle, deep in a devil's-vine trance. Around him he heard drums and footfalls of the hunter and hunted. He pictured Nicole Sullivan and Peter. They were circling, trying to catch him. His plans had gone so wrong. Peter was free, Gretchen was playing a dangerous game, and the detective needed to be neutralized. Like a leopard surrounded by hunters, he saw a single path to safety.

Attack.

27

I STARTED AWAKE, COLD SWEAT sticking my skin to the leather couch, where I'd passed out. Fragments of a nightmare skittered through my mind. Five dancing women. Could be nice, except these ladies were dead and half dissected. I recognized them: my mother, Ann, Beth, Gretchen, and Nicole. All were at a party and wanted to dance with me. My heart pounded, but it wasn't they who frightened me. It was seeing Ann on a hotel bed; it was so clear. Her eyes—the same as her brother's—conveyed the same sense that she was awake and wanted to speak, but couldn't. She lay there, blood oozing from her wrists. All in vivid color—the quilted bedspread an explosion of red and green cabbage roses. There was someone else. I was trying to see this person's reflection in her eyes, but it was distorted. The harder I looked, the less clear it became.

I turned on a light, and gooseflesh popped on my arms. Willy jumped onto the couch and butted his head against my side. I tried to orient myself. It was Thursday evening. Kyle was with my Dad and I was the suspect in a double murder. Would tomorrow be the day that I was arrested?

I put on a pot of coffee and left a message for Peggy. No way would I be there tomorrow. I sensed that my time was running out. Either I'd be arrested or . . . what? Would Ed come after me? I thought of Gretchen and how she'd pleaded with me to get out of town. I, in turn, had begged her to hand over whatever evidence she had to the cops; I'd offered to go with her. She had said she'd think about it, but her vagueness made me doubt. When she left with her dog, I sensed that I'd not see her again.

My mind was awhirl. It was hard to think, but I had to do something.

As I fed the cat, my thoughts returned to the dream and the bedspread—so vivid—too vivid.

Before I could make sense of it, I grabbed my keys, beeper, and cell. With my hand on the door, I stopped. I retreated to my study, snatched an album off the shelf, and peeled out a picture of Beth, Ed, Miranda, and me at our tenth reunion.

Outside, I flagged a cab. "Central Park South," I said, and I gave the driver the name of the hotel where Ann had been attacked.

The way I figured it, my nightmare was my brain's way of pushing through the amnesia. It was too real. *What had I seen? What had I done?*

"Hey, mister," the driver called from the front seat.

"Sorry." I said, realizing that we'd reached our destination, and that I had spaced. I got out and stared up at the white marble facade of the Park South.

I walked past the doorman and through the revolving door. I felt him watching me, but maybe I was just paranoid. I didn't look back as I took in the deep red carpet and the elaborate chandeliers. It wasn't exactly the dream, but it was close. I went to the elevators, searching my memory. Had I ever been here? I stepped inside and pressed the button for the tenth floor. *Why did I do that?*

The lights moved up the panel of buttons; the door opened, and I stepped into my dream. I stared at the carpet and its intricate pattern of rose and green. I looked up and down the hallway, not certain what I was doing. I saw a cleaning cart halfway down. I went toward it; each footstep on the padded rug tugged at my memory. A vacuum roared from an open room. I stepped in and faced a bed with a cabbage-rose coverlet.

The vacuum stopped. "I'm almost done, sir," a pert cleaning woman said, mistaking me for a guest.

"That's okay." I backed out. As the elevator lurched down I felt as if I might throw up. All doubt was gone; I had been here the night Ann was murdered. *What did I see? What did I do?*

Back in the lobby, I spotted the doorman behind the desk talking with a man in a black suit, probably the manager. They looked at me as I headed toward them.

"Do you know me?" I asked.

They glanced at each other.

"I'm Peter Grainger," I persisted. The doorman looked away. "Please look at me. You've seen me here, haven't you?"

The doorman mumbled something to the manager; who got up from behind the desk. "Sir, if you're not a guest, you'll need to leave."

I pulled the photo from my pocket. "What about him?" I asked, trying to get them to look at it. "Have either of you seen the blond man in the picture? Have you?"

The man in the suit was having none of it. "Sir, I've called security. I recommend you leave."

"What's the problem? Why can't you answer a simple question?" I focused on the doorman and sensed a crowd gathering. "Have you seen me? Have you seen him?"

His eyes darted from beneath the brim of his cap. "You've been here," he admitted. "I don't know about the other guy."

It was an answer, just not the one I wanted. "Are you sure?"

"Mister," he said, as two burly men in dark suits with hearing devices in their ears approached. "Thousands of people go through here every day. I remember you because we spoke. Don't you remember? I gave you a letter from that girl who got killed."

"That's enough, Jimmy." The manager said. He looked back at me. "Sir, you need to leave . . . *now*."

It was clear I'd get nothing else, but what did he mean, that Ann had given me a letter?

One of the security officers made a grab for my elbow. I pulled back, and as I did I noticed a security camera trained on the checkout desk, I turned and saw another one by the front door. "What about your security tapes? Could I see them for that night?"

"Absolutely not," the manager said. "They're with the police; talk to them."

It was a decent idea, and I made a mental note to give the information to Harold. I allowed myself to be escorted out the door, and I wondered if my actions were making things worse. I could hear Harold. *Do nothing.* Easy for him; he wasn't facing arrest for two homicides. There was no doubt I'd been here. I wondered why Nicole hadn't told me. I guess until they charged me she was keeping her cards close.

I walked south and wondered if the cops had the note the doorman had mentioned. What did it say? I recalled Jason and Ann's eyes from my dream. Why couldn't they move? I thought about my toxicology results. "Jesus! If he'd drugged me . . . that had to be it! They didn't move because they couldn't. Ed's been working on paralytic drugs for years. The realization hit hard; they were both wide-awake, watching themselves die, in horrible pain. Tears flowed as I realized what they'd suffered. It also explained a lot, like if Ann was doing better in the hospital why did she die? Because he couldn't let her ever wake up.

As I crossed Fourteenth Street, I knew that the one place I

might find something solid lay two stories below ground in Fleming. Problem was, Ed's security door was beyond my amateur lock picking. And then I remembered . . . the tunnels. There was a chance that if they hadn't completed the morgue move they'd still be open.

I jogged toward University Hospital. Outside the ER I looked across the street at Fleming. I remembered how when I was a resident, if the weather was bad, the tunnels were the best way to get from the on-call rooms to the hospital.

I walked past the ER, trying to remember the route. I found the stairwell next to the cafeteria, and headed down. Even with the renovations, this felt familiar.

The kitchen was to my right. I spotted a swinging door and pushed through. Heat from the nearby boiler room washed over me, and I felt myself slip back in time as I followed the dips and twists in the tunnels. I moved past storage rooms heaped with unwanted furniture and equipment. I paused and heard the faint sound of cars overhead.

Then, in the dim light, I saw a small door on my left. I expected it to be locked; it wasn't. Behind that lay a long corridor lit by bare bulbs and just wide enough for a stretcher. As I walked the hundred yards toward the final door—the stench of preservative stronger with each step—I recalled times I'd had to wait while corpses were ferried to and from the morgue.

I touched the handle and pushed gently. The door cracked open and cool air rushed up my nostrils. I started to sneeze, but stopped myself. The red glow of an emergency sign above the stairs and a ribbon of light from under the laboratory door were the only illumination. It was late, but could someone still be here? I crept toward Ed's lab and pressed my ear to the wall. I heard the hum of machinery and a deeper rumble from the furnace. I reached toward the knob; it turned but wouldn't open. I froze, hearing a woman's voice from behind the door. She was coming closer. I couldn't make out the words, and for an instant I wondered if this were still my nightmare—Beth! She was laughing, there was someone with her, and they were moving toward the door. I froze at the sound of her voice; cold sweat covered me and adrenaline flooded forth.

I looked across the dark room and bolted into the morgue. The laboratory door opened, and behind the door I saw Ed.

"Soon," he said.

I couldn't see who was with him . . . but the voice.

"Yes," she said, but there was no one there. "You're sure this time?"

"Yes." I heard the jangle of keys and a single set of footsteps moving toward the stairs. "By the end of tomorrow, this will be finished."

28

NICOLE SAT IN THE SHADOWS of the Westport Funeral Home, a white-columned mansion, which now hosted mourners—more than she'd expected. The receiving line snaked past the open caskets of Ann and Jason, and took a shuffling turn toward Carter and his youngest daughter, Jennifer, who bore a striking resemblance to her dead sister.

Half hidden by burgundy velvet curtains that surrounded a bouquet niche, Nicole felt old stirrings—the memory of her first love. In the dim light from forty feet away, she could see the man who had enthralled her with such fire about the horrors of the war.

She was grateful that there were so many callers wending past the white-satin-lined coffins. A few were in their twenties, probably classmates of Ann, but most were Carter's contemporaries. One wore an American flag jacket and another a lapel pin honoring POWs and MIAs. His book, she knew, was still in stores, no longer in the front window, but never out of print.

She could just make out Ann's profile, her flawless skin and perfect hair. Seeing Jason's face and remembering his anguish the day Peter had interviewed him, brought tears. *Watch out for Ann.*

In the foyer, storyboards covered with family photographs had been assembled. One picture in particular hit her hard: the family on a boat. Ann and Jason were young. Carter was grinning. One arm was around his beautiful wife; the other held his children in close. It couldn't have been much before their affair, maybe even at the same time. It spoke volumes to the innocent she'd been, to the lies that he'd told and that she had believed.

That she was even here had been undecided until late last night. Hector had been willing. "One of us has to go," he'd said. "I don't mind."

"No, I'll do it."

"Something about this case really bothers you," he'd commented.

It had caught her off guard. She'd come close to telling him, but hadn't. In a weird way, it was because she trusted him that she couldn't. It would only burden him with information that would make him an accomplice. That, among other worries, had kept her up through the night.

Donny's ultimatum was the other biggy. He'd called as she and Adriana were eating reheated lasagna. "I got the papers. We need to talk. Can I come over?"

She'd sent Adriana downstairs to be with her grandmother.

Donny had shown up looking better than a man had a right to, in skintight faded jeans, a T-shirt, and his red baseball jacket. Something about his clothes struck her as odd, too cool for December. "You're sure this is what you want?" he'd asked.

"It is," she'd answered.

"Okay, I won't fight it. But I need to tell you something, and I want you to hear it from me."

It was then she'd made the connection. "You're seeing somebody?" His outfit was a variation on what he'd often worn when he took her on dates. When the jacket came off at a restaurant or bowling alley, it was hard to ignore his well-muscled torso and killer-blue eyes.

"It hasn't gone anywhere," he had told her, as though that made it okay.

"You're taking her bowling?"

"It doesn't have to be like this, Nicole. Just say the word." In his straightforward way, he was leaving the choice in her hands.

"Adriana starts at the Garden School on Monday."

Donny had looked away, as though even mentioning his daughter's name cast a shadow across his face. In that moment, she knew that she couldn't love him. Care for him, yes, but if she was honest, it had never had been love.

"Will you come to see her?" she had asked. "Adriana needs her father."

"Sure . . . What will you tell her?"

"I don't know." She'd even cracked a smile. "It's Jeanine that's going to be hard."

Now, here in a funeral home, it felt right that death and the ghosts of relationships should surround her. She turned as a fresh pair of callers came through the doorway: Peter and Michael Grainger.

Peter gave a faint smile in her direction.

What is he doing here?

He said something to his father and headed in her direction. "Hi."

"I'm surprised to see you here," she commented, wondering if he'd go through the receiving line.

"My dad tried to talk me out of it."

"So why'd you come?" She met his gaze.

"I don't know if I'm supposed to talk to you without my attorney." He smiled.

"You don't have to," she said, trying to resist being drawn in.

"I was joking. Mind if I sit?"

"No." She cleared her coat and pocketbook from the adjacent chair.

He rested his elbows on his knees and looked across at the coffins. "It's a weird tradition, having the dead on display. You have to wonder what kind of effect it's having on her," he said, looking at Jennifer Walsh, whose gaze never moved from her shoes as she passively shook hands.

Nicole looked at the teen, whose face was hidden behind a curtain of straight blond hair. "I can't imagine what it's going to be like for her. . . . So, why are you here?"

"It's a little weird."

"From you this should surprise me?"

"Fine . . . Ever since I became a psychiatrist I've made it a point to go to as many of my patients' funerals as possible."

"That is weird. Why?"

"Lots of reasons. If it's a suicide, I need to see the family and offer my condolences."

"Isn't that risky? Don't people sue psychiatrists when someone kills himself?"

"Yup. But there's something about facing the family. It helps you figure things out, and more often than not, they're glad you came. Although . . . sometimes they're angry and say something cruel, like that I should have been able to stop it, or seen it coming."

"What do you say?" she asked, struck by the ease of conversation with this man she might well arrest before nightfall.

"The truth: that I wish I had."

"So what about today? Neither of them committed suicide." It was so hard sitting with him, just wanting to shake him and ask, *Did you do this?*

"I know," he said, watching as the line shuffled forward. "How's he doing?" he was looking at Carter.

"He seems numb," she said, keeping the second half to herself. *And drunk.*

"A lot of vets here. When I was a resident I did a stint in a VA hospital. I had more than one patient tell me to read *The Jersey Boy* if I wanted to understand even a fraction of what they had gone through."

"Did you?"

"Many times, and I've given copies to residents. I kept checking to see if he'd written a follow-up book. . . . He never did." Peter sat up straight. "Okay, here goes."

"You're going to talk to him? You think that's wise?"

"Not really." he got to his feet, "but like I said; I have to do it." He looked at her. "It's a funny thing about fear; the more you give in to it, the more it takes over."

Nicole watched him as he joined his father, who was inching toward Carter and Jennifer. She thought about what he'd said. He was right, and she admired his courage, but another part of her wondered if he was being truthful. She kept her eyes glued to his back as he approached the Walshes.

At first, it seemed as though they'd pass smoothly through the line. Peter moved in front of Jennifer. He shook her hand and said something. Then he came to Carter. The two men shook, but then something happened.

Nicole leaned forward as Carter looked up. He was still holding Peter's hand. A rumbling murmur started in the receiving line. Jennifer turned and looked at her father, then backed away. A space grew around the two men and it seemed as though Peter were trying to get his hand free from Carter's grip.

Nicole was out of her seat and moving fast toward the coffins.

"I know you," Carter said.

Her breath froze, and for a moment she thought he was speaking to her.

He gripped Peter's hand. Blue veins popped beneath the cuff

of his dress shirt. "She told me about you." His words were slurred.

"Peter." Michael Grainger tried to pull his son back.

"What did she tell you?" Peter asked, shrugging off his father and twisting his hand free.

Carter stumbled and fell back against a showy display of carnations. "This isn't over!" he shouted as a ponytailed vet helped steady him. He looked around, as though realizing where he was. "Get out!"

Peter backed away.

By now, several of the vets in the line had surrounded Carter and were trying to calm him. "Who the fuck do you think you are?" he yelled at them. His body twisted and his face reddened as he tried to break free.

Nicole grabbed Peter's arm above the elbow. "You need to get out of here. Now!" She said, prepared to drag him away if necessary.

"What did she tell you about me?" Peter shouted back to Carter as Nicole and Michael Grainger attempted to push him toward the door.

"That you were fucking her!" Carter spat out.

To Nicole, it was as though the air had been sucked out of the room.

"That's right," Carter shouted, saliva spitting from his lips. "She was fucking her shrink. Just like before! You're all a bunch of fucking perverts!"

Peter stood his ground. "It wasn't me," he said.

A change came over Carter; he stopped struggling, but the men on either side of him didn't loosen their hold. He looked at Peter and then at Nicole. His head cocked slightly and his eyes squinted.

Nicole held her breath, feeling his gaze rake over her.

"Get out," he said.

"Come on," Michael Grainger said to his son, tugging him toward the door.

She could feel Peter's reluctance, but worse, she now found herself face-to-face with Carter. She wondered if he recognized her. Some sort of light seemed to have gone on in his booze-addled brain, but what? Plus there was his accusation, which if true, was the one thing missing from the case against Peter—the motive.

"That was not smart," she whispered to Peter as they cleared the door.

"I tried to tell him," his father said, looking at Nicole.

"I thought it was important to pay my respects." Peter said.

"Uh-huh," Nicole replied. "No other motives?"

"There are always other motives. You know that."

His answer surprised her. "So what was yours?"

"Probably the same as yours." He pulled out a knit ski cap and pulled it over his ears. "I'm trying to figure out what happened."

"Detective," Michael Grainger interrupted, "I don't think my son's supposed to talk with you without his attorney."

"Dad, thanks, but she already knows this. . . . And a hell of a lot more, I'm finding out."

"Still," Michael persisted, but he stopped when he spotted Ed Tyson heading toward them.

"That was very stupid," Tyson said, looking directly at Peter. "Why would you come here?" Then, as if just noticing Nicole, he nodded in her direction. "Detective . . . Peter, I have enough trouble in dealing with this family as it is. I don't want the university getting dragged in."

Peter glared at Ed and then slowly replied. "It's a little late for that."

Nicole caught the flash of something on Ed's face. As though beneath the surface he was smiling. "I don't know what you're talking about."

"Give it a rest, Ed. Ann had an affair with her therapist last year. Everyone here knows it . . . except my dad, who knows it now. She'd moved on to someone else, someone who could take care of her tuition problems. Someone who could—"

Tyson stopped him. "I'd be careful, Peter. Especially without proof. Don't you agree, Detective? One should have proof before throwing around accusations."

Something in his manner caused her to stiffen. "Everything is being looked at."

"Of course." He smiled. "Isn't there a truism about homicide that everything comes out—all of the dirty little secrets, things hidden away long long ago."

"So why did you come?" she asked, trying to figure what it was about Tyson that made her skin crawl.

"Part of my job," he said. "If I didn't come, people would talk. To be honest," he continued, "I'm surprised that *you're* here."

His pale eyes bored into hers. "I had the feeling," he continued, not breaking his gaze, "that you had some connection with Carter."

Nicole's adrenaline surged. That's what this was all about; he knew. While Carter might not have recognized her, Tyson knew. She said nothing as she saw everything start to unravel—the case, her career.

"Anyway," Tyson said, clearly enjoying himself. "I'd love to stay, but it's cold and I need to get back. Good day."

She felt sick as he walked away.

"You okay?" Peter asked. "Don't let him get to you. It's what he does."

"I'm fine." She felt panicked. It almost didn't matter who'd killed the Walsh children, because when her involvement with Carter was revealed, the entire case would be polluted. "I need to get back to the city," she said, shaking off Peter and his dad.

She didn't look back when she found her car in the crowded

lot. She turned the key and gripped the wheel. She couldn't move. Was Tyson trying to blackmail her? Why? What was he hiding? She pulled out her cell. *Please pick up.*

"Hello?"

"Hector."

"What's wrong, Nic?"

"I'm drowning. You got a minute to run the case?"

"Sure. Are you going to tell me why it's freaking you out so much?"

"I can't," she said. "And not because I don't trust you. You've got to believe that."

"Okay, just tell me what you want me to do."

"Run the facts."

"Sure," he said. "Let me close the door. . . . We start with Ann in her dorm room. She gets the call at seven for a date at nine, and off she goes. Cabbie takes her to the Park South where she goes to room 1001, registered to a Mr. John Johnson."

"Have they typed his statement?" she asked.

"Not yet, but what a piece of work."

"Scum," she agreed, feeling her nerves start to settle.

"So we have Mr. Johnson, aka Ralph Wittier, forty-eight, father of three and Vice President of Acquisitions and Mergers for the First Global banking corporation."

They'd interviewed Wittier on Wednesday; he'd been accompanied by a lawyer who'd looked like a linebacker and wore a pin-striped suit. Wittier, on the other hand, was a tiny weasel of a man with sharp features and a retreating hairline, but what he had lacked in height he had made up for in arrogance.

"What do I have to do with any of this?" he'd said, taking the offensive.

"You were probably the last to see her alive. . . . That is, of course, with the exception of her attacker," Nicole had answered, her voice rich with insinuation.

"Is my client a suspect?" the attorney had shot back.

"Not at the moment; he's a witness."

"You don't know that for certain," the attorney had said.

Hector had become the bad cop. "If you keep butting in," he'd said, "it's going to look like obstruction, and I don't believe your client wants any more exposure." He'd turned to the balding vice president. "Correct?"

"Yes." Wittier had begun to sweat.

"So how many times had you seen Ann Walsh?" Nicole had asked.

"She used the name Veronica. I didn't know her real name until I was contacted."

"That must have been a shock," she had said.

"You called me at home!" he'd replied indignantly. "My wife doesn't know about this."

"How many times had you seen her?" she'd repeated.

"A couple, maybe three."

She knew that Wittier was lying. They had already paid a visit to the Imperial Escort Service, which was run by two small-time hustlers—one grossly obese and the other rail thin—from an apartment in Sheepshead Bay, Brooklyn. Hector had dubbed them the creepy twins, but they kept good records. It hadn't taken much arm-twisting for them to hand over Wittier's name and credit card receipts. In exchange, Nicole had not arrested them. She also had no illusions that, should either she or Hector return to that apartment, all traces of the operations would be gone.

"Let's start again," she'd said to Wittier. "You'd been seeing Ann Walsh for nine months—regularly. She must have been quite special."

"I don't have anything to say. I was seeing a call girl. So what? You're not going to pin a murder charge on me. I went straight home after."

"Who saw you when you got home?"

"My wife, of course." He'd looked up at Nicole. Dark pit stains had soaked through his shirt and jacket. "You can't talk to her about this. She doesn't know."

"We don't have a choice," she'd said. "A girl's been murdered, one whom you've been seeing for months. The other thing you need to think about is your choice in payment. I can't imagine the shareholders will be pleased to know what you've been charging on your company credit card."

"You can't talk to my wife, and what I charge is my business." He'd looked toward his lawyer. "You have to stop her."

Hector had answered for him. "He can't."

Wittier had glared back at his attorney. "What the fuck am I paying you for?"

"Tell you what," Nicole had offered, not giving the lawyer a chance. "You can call her now and tell her yourself. Otherwise, we'll do it for you."

Now, parked in her unmarked car outside the funeral home, she tapped her forefinger against the wheel. "So what else did you think of him?" she asked Hector.

"It's too pathetic; he sees the girl for nine months and doesn't seem concerned that she got killed."

"She wasn't real to him," Nicole countered, thinking of the dead girl laid out in her satin coffin. "Like some sort of fast food."

"But why the same burger month after month?" Hector asked. "Yes, pretty, but shelling out that kind of money? What was it about her?"

"Wish I knew, but that was her MO; she collected regulars. You look at the ledgers and she was doing two or three dates a week. Always taking home at least five hundred plus another two for the house. The same names over and over."

"Huh. Then why bother with the creepy twins?"

"What do you mean?"

"She gave them forty percent. Why not keep it all? Especially if you're seeing the same guys. Why bother with the middleman?"

"You got to see her side," Nicole said, needing this give-and-take with Hector to get back on course. "She wanted to keep her business life separate from her school life. So the creepy twins handled the credit cards and set up the dates. That way she was Veronica and no one knew who she was in the daytime. But back to Wittier. He makes it home to the wife and kids a little before eleven; Ann stays in the room . . . Why?"

"She was planning to meet someone else?"

"Correct, which is where things get freaky."

"Don't forget the note to the doorman."

"I know. It's just . . . He was pretty sure that she didn't give him the note until eleven thirty."

"So?"

"So, what's she doing up in the room by herself from the time Wittier leaves at ten until eleven thirty?"

"Watching TV? Turning another trick? Don't know."

"We don't. But Ann Walsh wasn't a girl who sat still; she was doing something. And then an hour and a half later she comes down to the lobby, hands the doorman a note with instructions to give it to Grainger. We know that she called his answering service, and that Peter showed up at the hotel just after midnight. Let's assume he goes upstairs to meet her—that makes no sense. Peter Grainger is a highly respected psychiatrist. What would get him up to that room?"

"Hello?"

"You think he was sleeping with her?"

"I don't know how much sleeping, but having sex . . . maybe."

Nicole felt a surge of anger. "I'm not saying you're wrong, but I'm not convinced. If they were having an affair, why bother with the doorman? Why not just give him her room number over the phone or meet him in the lobby? She wasn't stupid. If she were sleeping with Peter Grainger, why expose him to a doorman? It's too obvious, like she wanted somebody to know that Peter was there."

"The Hansel and Gretel theory," Hector offered.

Nicole stared out as the coffins, surrounded by veterans, were wheeled out of the chapel toward the hearses. "A trail of bread crumbs. But who was she leaving them for? I wish we had the note. . . . What was in it that would get Peter up to her room? . . . You really think he was sleeping with her?" Her breath caught as Carter emerged and was escorted into the lead limo.

"She slept with two shrinks that we know of."

Nicole nodded. "So the first 911 call came at twelve fifteen." It was thirty-seven seconds long and started with a man's breathing, as though he were about to say something and then didn't, followed by the sound of something hitting the carpet, like a body. "The thud is?"

"Ann."

"Maybe, although she's found on the bed," Nicole said. "So either someone else hit the floor—like the caller—or,. . . . And who hung up the phone? Twenty-two minutes later, call number two—the crazy brother."

"Watch out for Ann," Hector said.

"I know . . . and by the time the call gets traced and they figure out which room it's coming from, all that's left is a dying Ann. Which gets us to the physical evidence . . . We have Ann's blood all over Jason. He was probably trying to stop the bleeding, which would account for the pattern on his hands. We have trace amounts of Ann's blood on Peter's jacket. The question is, where did it come from, because he was also with her in the ER early Sunday. So we can't say beyond a reasonable doubt that he picked it up in the hotel."

"But—"

"Yes, I'm getting there. We do have a hair from Dr. Grainger

277

found on the carpet and trace fibers from the rug on his shoes. Which—add in a positive ID from the doorman—we've got him at the scene and in the room."

"So what's the problem?" Hector asked. "Let's get a warrant."

"You're certain?" she snapped. "You sure there are no holes? You sure a judge isn't going to pick this one apart and tell us to come back when we've done our job?"

"What did I say?"

Nicole felt the heat rising in her cheeks. *Shit.* She didn't want Peter to have done this, to be just another perp. "Convince me it's him."

"Okay. Dr. Grainger does a bad thing with his pretty patient. She has a few drinks, gets feeling lonely, and tells him to come see her. He gets there, they fight or maybe she threatens to tell her daddy . . . as she's done before, and he kills her and tries to make it look like a suicide."

"Why would he call 911?" she asked.

"We don't know it was him," Hector said. "It could have been the brother."

"Please."

"Right," Hector admitted. "He would have said something like, 'Watch out for Ann' several dozen times. So you think the doctor called 911? Could it have been Ann?"

"No blood on the phone."

"Also right . . . So if it's not Ann, the brother, or the doctor—who?"

"Well, that's the question, and it's why I'm not eager to arrest Grainger. Like, what was she doing after Wittier left and why would she leave a note? And where does Jason enter? All we can say about Peter is that he was in the room where she was killed. We could justify a warrant; I just think we'd be wrong. Someone else was there."

"You're saying he's being set up."

Nicole watched as the hearses and limos switched on their lights and started toward the cemetery. She thought about Hector's "Hansel and Gretel" analogy. She pictured Tyson and remembered his threats. "It's a whole lot of bread crumbs. . . . So why do they all lead to Peter Grainger?"

29

"RALPH." ED OPENED THE DOOR of his office and looked out. It was late Friday afternoon; all the staff had gone. Only Ralph remained. "I need to talk with you," he said, walking to his assistant, who was busily entering data into a laptop.

"What's up, Ed?"

"I don't want you to think I'm paranoid, but we have a problem."

"What is it?" he looked up, letting Ed glimpse the three-dimensional model of the Tumoren molecule on the screen.

"I got a call from Security. Someone triggered the motion detectors last night. . . . I think we might have made a mistake in submitting the study findings."

"A spy?" Ralph was incredulous.

"Perhaps. Ralph, until we've pushed Tumoren through the FDA, there's a possibility someone will try to steal it."

"What do we do?"

Ed looked at his brilliant assistant, who just today had completed the synthesis. Ed had told him that starting next week they'd set up two final rat studies using the synthetic molecule.

What he didn't tell Ralph—and wouldn't—is that while waiting for the FDA, he'd already selected ten candidates at the cancer center, all of them deserving—mothers and wives, a man with advanced colon cancer, and three young children. "I've been thinking about this, Ralph. You're the only one I can trust."

"Name it."

Ed deposited a thick envelope on Ralph's bench. "I completed the FDA application; it's all here. I was getting ready to express mail it, and—"

"You think someone might try to intercept it?"

"I do."

"What about faxing?"

"Too risky. Same with the Internet. There's only one way, and it's a lot to ask. Would you drive to Bethesda? Maybe take some friends . . . your wife, the kids. Make it look like a vacation. I'm too nervous even to have it go through an airport. This is the biggest thing in medicine since the discovery of small pox vaccination."

"When do you want me to leave?"

"As soon as possible; don't let it out of your sight. Be at the FDA first thing Monday morning, and don't hand it to anyone other than Raymond Albright."

"You're scaring me, Ed."

"Welcome to the club," he replied, shaping his voice to match Ralph's. "When you get back, the word will have leaked."

Ralph stood and took the package. He opened his briefcase and carefully placed it inside. "Can we get more security?" he asked.

"I have them installing the door in the morning. I plan to stay the night."

"I could stay."

"No, I want you on the road. In fact, do you have a copy of the molecule?"

"Of course not," Ralph said, having never once, in more than ten years, broken Ed's dictum against taking restricted materials home.

"It's in that laptop?"

"Yes."

"Take it with you; hide it someplace safe."

"Okay." Ralph appeared shaken. "I wish you'd let me stay with you."

"I'll be fine. Like I said, maybe I'm just paranoid." Ed smiled, and as he did, he glimpsed himself in Ralph's adoring eyes. "One more thing." He pulled his checkbook out of his jacket pocket. "Tell your wife this is a bonus. And when you get back, we'll talk about some real money." He made out a check for ten thousand dollars.

Ralph batted a tear with the sleeve of his lab coat. He took the check and impulsively reached out and hugged Ed, something he had never done before.

Ed stiffened and then hugged him back. He felt Beth's presence watching him. He had played the scene well and could now prepare for the night's real performance.

ONCE RALPH HAD GONE, HE worked fast. Chanting softly and chewing coca, Ed flicked on the morgue lights. Energy crackled through him as he covered a large section of the floor with oilcloth and wheeled a primitive dissection table toward the cremation oven. He slipped Beth's name into the chant and felt her gain strength. Tonight he would work magic.

He climbed onto the table and clipped an expanse of oilcloth to a sprinkler pipe. The fabric hung like a shower curtain, obscuring the tabletop. He jumped down and stepped back. He stopped chanting.

"Yes, Ed," Beth's voice whispered. "Tonight you avenge me."

"An eye for an eye," he replied, looking at the cremation oven.

He had no room for failure; if he did not succeed, they would come for him. The detective, Peter, even Gretchen had betrayed him, skipping town and leaving a threatening note taped to her door with half a latex condom, purportedly from Ann. Although she had fled—he suspected to Germany—any fantasies she had of saving Peter would be too late.

Ed turned out the lights and headed back into his office. He pulled out a fresh coca leaf coated with ayahuasca. He let it rest on his tongue; the acrid mixture mingled with his saliva. He put on a headset and listened to the microphones in Grainger's loft. He heard the sound of two male voices. "Good." Now for the tricky part, the catalyst that would set all in motion.

He slowed his breathing, picked up the phone, and punched in the Westport number. It rang four times and an answering machine clicked on. He let his mind travel over the distance, as though he were walking into the Walsh home, going over to Carter passed out in a chair, and tapping him on the shoulder. *Pick up the phone.*

There was a high-pitched electrical whine as the receiver was lifted.

"Goddamn machine! Who is this?"

"Mr. Walsh?" Ed inquired, his voice warm with compassion. "This is Dr. Tyson, Ed . . . from the medical school."

"What the hell do you want?"

"I just wanted to see how you were doing. I had meant to offer my condolences at the funeral, but it didn't seem like a good time."

"No shit."

"I don't know what possessed him to show up. It seemed . . . inappropriate."

"What the fuck was he looking for?" Walsh's words slurred together.

Ed gently exhaled, feeling the first effects of the drug, a sensation as though his skin were slowly dissolving. "Are you by your-self?" he asked.

"Jennifer's home," he said, "but she doesn't want anything to do with me. She blames me."

"It's not your fault." Ed soothed and coaxed the inebriated man, becoming his friend, his confidant.

"Yeah . . . I don't know what it was about Ann, but we just fought all the time."

Ed felt Carter slipping into a maudlin reverie. *That wouldn't do.* "You're not to blame," he said.

"Easy for you to say. . . . Why are you calling?"

"None of this is your fault. . . . Did you kill her? Did you kill your son?"

"What the fuck? Of course not."

That's better. Ed gently teased the anger to the surface. "How do you deal with the fact that the man who did this is still out there?"

"If I knew who it—"

"You do." Ed cooed like a mother to her child. "Think about it. You were at the funeral. There was a reason he was there, and it wasn't to pay condolences. Think about it." Ed heard the clink of ice against crystal.

"Why are you telling me this?" Carter slurred, his tone suspicious.

"Because you're her father. You have a right to know. But I wouldn't worry, I think the cops will arrest him soon. Of course . . ."

"What?" Carter shouted into the receiver.

Ed let the man's voice rumble through his head and down into his belly, letting it mix with his spirit, changing it and bringing it back up through his throat. He answered Carter in his own voice; it was perfect down to the soft angry slur. "If it were my children, I don't think I'd be able to take it so calmly. The police have a way of fucking up. He has an expensive lawyer. He won't even serve time. If it were my children I'd need to know that they had been avenged. If they were mine."

"He's not getting away with this!"

"There's not much time."

"If I knew where the fucker lived . . ." Carter said.

Still speaking in Carter's voice, Ed fed him the address, had him repeat it back, and then hung up.

He pressed redial.

Carter answered. "Hello?"

Ed shifted the muscles in the back of his throat. He pictured Ann, letting her memory shape the words that came feather-soft through his lips. "Daddy, help me. Daddy, Daddy . . ." He made her sound young and frightened.

"Ann? Baby?"

Ed hung up.

30

"I KNOW YOU THINK THIS is a terrible idea," I told Dad as he stared at the bottle of Amytal on my dimly lit kitchen counter. "There's no other way."

"Peter . . ."

"Look, I can't force you, but I have to do this." I knew that I was using his love for me as blackmail, but my back was to the wall. By tomorrow I could be in jail. "Maybe this is clutching at straws, and maybe I'm not going to like what I find, but . . ."

"Okay." His shoulders slumped. "We could both lose our licenses for this."

"No one needs to know."

"Things have a way of getting out, Peter."

I let him vent as he unwrapped the syringe. I rolled up my sleeve, soaked a cotton ball in alcohol, and wiped it over my forearm.

He drew up the barbiturate and approached me with the needle. "Last chance."

"Do it." I laid my arm across the counter and pumped my fist to pop a vein. His expression tensed as the needle pierced my skin, but I didn't flinch as he slowly depressed and then pulled back on the needle. A pearl of blood formed on my skin. I thought about Kyle, safe in my dad's West End Avenue apartment, and knew this was my last hope. If I couldn't remember what happened that night and find something solid against Ed, I'd lose everything.

"Come on." He led me toward the sofa. On the way he grabbed my leather jacket. "Put this on, it's cold in here. Now, lie down and close your eyes."

I felt the drug as it circulated through my body.

"You're going to start to feel sleepy," he said.

I cracked my lids and saw him lean forward; his head just a few feet from mine. "I love you, Dad." I said.

"I love you too, son." A tear splattered across his cheek. "Now, close your eyes."

I wanted to reach across to him and tell him that everything would work out, but the drug was pulling me down and his voice had started to lull me into a trance.

"Okay Peter," he said, "no matter what, you're going to keep yourself safe, and at any time you can use my voice as a lifeline to come out. Do you understand?"

"Yes." I felt the strangeness of answering without effort, as though my lips no longer needed my brain's permission.

"I want you to imagine a beautiful place. It could be the beach, a favorite park. Can you see that place?"

"Yes," I stared out over the turquoise waters of the Caribbean. It was the view from the hotel in Saint Martin, where Beth and I had gone on our honeymoon.

"Make that place real. See it . . . hear it . . . touch it . . . taste it . . . smell it."

I saw the vibrant fuchsia bougainvillea that rambled over our deck. Waves lapped as they broke across the volcanic rock in our private cove. A tiny green lizard scampered up the slanting trunk of a bent palm that had nearly toppled in a hurricane. I smelled Narcisse Noir, Beth's perfume.

"Hold that place inside your head. Call it home. Say 'home.'"

"Home," I repeated.

"If I say 'home,' you are to return to this place. Do you understand?"

"Yes."

"Good. Now, I want you to go back to last Monday night. I want you to do that now. Begin with dinner . . . tell me where you are."

I drifted and watched as Monday night formed in my mind, like watching a movie. Words left my mouth effortlessly, floating in the air. "I started to get a headache," I said, feeling the dull throb return behind my temples. "It's not that late, but I want to go home. I'm mad at Ed, I need to get away from him, he's lying to me and I don't know why. Gretchen wants to go home, too. She asks me if I'll walk her. She's very pretty, but the headache is getting worse. I feel like I might throw up. I need air. Ed's watching me, he knows that I'm not feeling well."

"Does he say anything?" Dad's voice coaxes, and the movie shifts.

"He's joking with Gretchen—'Don't stay out too late'—but he's watching me. I feel dizzy. It had to be the wine . . . I'm in the elevator now, and Gretchen is talking."

"What is she saying?"

"I hear her and then I don't. Something's not right. I tell her that I had too much wine. She laughs and touches me. . . . We're outside now."

"You just skipped something," Dad said. "What happened in the elevator?"

"I can't see it," I said.

"Take a deep breath and count slowly to ten on the exhalation; as you do you'll find your way back to the time you skipped."

I did as instructed. "I'm in the elevator, Gretchen is telling me about the article she's writing on the medical students. Her hand is on the front of my jacket. Her lips are so beautiful; I lean down and kiss her. The elevator doors open and she pulls back. She's laughing and I laugh, too, it's the strangest feeling. I want to throw up, but I feel so light. We go outside and the air is wonderful; it's freezing cold and it feels as though it's going right through me. She's talking and her words are like music. They have melodies and rhythms, and on the corner of Ninth Street I throw up. She asks me if I'm okay, and I tell her that I feel better. The lights from the cars are amazing, the entire night is filled with sound and color. I have to focus to hear her, and when we get to her apartment, she asks me if I want to come inside. I go up with her and her apartment is filled with flowers and there's a little dog sniffing at my ankles. Her name is Lily and she has a bright red bow on the top of her head. She's wonderful, and Gretchen tells me that I'm more interested in the dog than her, and maybe we should take Lily for a walk. Then we're back outside, and the dog is pulling forward on her leash. Gretchen tells me that my pager is going off, and I wonder why I didn't hear it.

"I take it out of my pocket and there are numbers. I realize that I'm acting odd, and remind myself that it has to be the alcohol; I drank too much. I see the time on my pager and realize that it's an hour later than I thought. And there's a phone number that seems familiar and it's hard to dial. I tell myself to act normal with the operator. She tells me that I have an urgent message from Ann Walsh. I have to call her right away. She gives me the number, but I can't remember it. Gretchen hands me a pen and a piece of paper. I have the operator repeat the number over and over. I lie to her and say that it's hard to hear her over the traffic, but it's like the numbers have a life of their own and want to wander between the phone, my brain and the paper. I hang up, and Gretchen asks me who it was. I tell her that I need to make a call."

"Did you tell her who it was?" Dad prompted.

"No. I walked away from her and Lily followed me. I needed to concentrate. It was the hardest thing to take those numbers and dial them, but I did. I almost forgot why, and then Ann picked up. . . . Oh . . ."

"What is it?" Dad asked.

"She's so unhappy. She's crying. She tells me she has to see me right away. I listen and I know that I'm in no shape to see any patients. She's mad at me and I don't know why. She tells me I had no right to tell him what we had talked about. I ask her who she's talking about, only now she's crying. She tells me that she doesn't want to live and that this time she's going to do it."

Dad's voice seems so far away. I'm drifting away from it. "I'm standing on Tenth Street. I look back and see Gretchen and her little dog. My cell phone is in my hand.

"Where are you?" I ask Ann.

"Park South Hotel," she says.

"What room number?"

"I'm not telling you. You'll send the police. I'll meet you in the lobby, but if I see the cops or an ambulance, I'll do it, swear to God, and it will be all your fault."

"She hung up. 'Ann. Ann.' I look down; Lily is licking my shoe. Gretchen is a few feet away.

"That was Ann Walsh, wasn't it?" Gretchen asks.

"I have to go."

"I walk away and then I run. Gretchen's calling after me, but I don't stop. I run as fast as I can. All I can think about is Ann and that she's going to kill herself and that it's my fault and that I have to get to the Park South and save her.

"I'm sprinting and the cold doesn't touch me. I dodge through the traffic without slowing. It's almost as if I can predict which way a car is going to go. It had to have been more than two miles, but when I get there, I'm barely winded. How is that possible?

"The doorman follows me. He hands me a note. I read it and it's as though it contains messages inside messages."

"What does it say?"

"Nothing. Just her room number—1001."

"But it's as though those numbers are trying to tell me something. The ones seem about to bolt off the paper and the zeroes start to spin like snakes biting their tails. I try to focus; I have her room number. But why isn't she in the lobby? I have a sense that I'm heading into something bad, but I hear her voice on the phone, and I'm thinking she couldn't wait, she's gone ahead and done it, and I'm going to find her dead.

"I take the elevator, the carpet is like a jungle, all wild reds and greens. I get to her door, it's unlocked. 'Ann. Ann.' There's no answer. I push it open and I see her on the bed in a black dress, sitting up against the headboard staring at the door. She doesn't move. 'Ann,' she doesn't say anything. I go inside. 'Ann, are you okay?' I see her belly go in and out, as though she's struggling to breathe. She's crying. 'Ann.' I'm thinking that she must have taken an overdose. I feel her pulse, it's weak, barely thirty. I pick up the phone and dial 911. I hear the operator asking me how can she help, but there's someone behind me. I feel something bite me on the neck. I try to turn, but my legs collapse and I hit the floor. I hear the operator."

"Who else was in that room with you?"

"She's looking at him. Her eyes are still alive, but she's dying."

"Looking at whom?"

"I can't see him."

"How do you know it's a man?"

"He's strong, he's lifting me onto the bed. I weigh nothing to him. He drops me, and all I see are the roses on the bedspread. They're growing, wrapping me in their vines. I hear footsteps and the closing of a door. I can't move. . . . The roses are spreading, they're bleeding, she's bleeding."

"Peter? Peter?"

Oh, God, not again . . .

"Peter? Peter?"

The roses crawl over my body, wrapping me like a spider. Their vines suck the air from my chest, pulling me down. I'm no longer in the hotel. I see the Audi and smoke and Beth's hair through the window. I try to open her door. My fingers claw the dirt. I find a rock and smash the window, my hand bleeds and I see the first flicker of pale orange flame from under the mangled hood. "Help me!" A beat-up Toyota slows. I see the driver. His eyes wide and bulging. "Help me!" I claw at his window, he accelerates, and I see my palm print in blood. "Help me!" I scream and when I turn back to the car it's gone and now I'm driving and Beth is next to me. She's crying, something about the baby. I brace myself, expecting her to say that the child is going to have Down Syndrome or worse—has died. My attention is fixed on her, knowing that whatever it is, we'll figure something out. It can't be that bad. But there's a light coming toward us. A white Toyota careens across the median strip and heads straight towards us. It happens so slowly. I see his face through the windshield, his eyes wide, his hands gripping the wheel; I know that he's high on something. We're going to hit. I turn the wheel hard to the right. We bounce off the road and rip through a guardrail. My foot slams on the brake, a rock wall races toward the windshield. Beth's head cracks against the dashboard. She's bleeding, only she doesn't look like Beth, it's Ann, and there's so much blood, and she's looking at me, staring at me. Someone else is there, trying to stop the bleeding. Dad's shouting "Home! Home!"

AN EXPLOSION RIPPED THE NIGHT; glass shattered. Something stung my cheek and cold air washed over me.

"Peter, are you okay?" Dad shouted. "Home! Home!"

His voice pulled me away from Ann . . . and from Jason. Jason was there—he was trying to save her. I told myself they're dead and that this wasn't real, but when I opened my eyes, there was something horribly wrong.

"Get down, Peter!" Dad shouted, as he yanked the lamp out of the socket, plunging the loft into darkness save for the distant red dots from the answering machine. A breeze blew through the room and it made no sense that he would have opened one of the windows. Why was there broken glass? Why was my cheek bleeding?

"What's happening?" I whispered.

"Someone just shot out your window. Are you okay?"

Adrenaline surged. "I think so." I heard footsteps storming up the stairs. I jumped as a gunshot tore at the security door. There was a second and a third. I thanked God that Kyle was at my Dad's as a siren screamed in the distance. Something hard pounded at the door over and over.

I was on my feet. "Come on," I shouted. "We got to get out of here!" I grabbed Dad's arm and started to run with him through the loft.

We heard another shot as I threw open the door to my study. I heard pounding and the sickening sound of the bolt ripping from the frame.

I yanked up the steel plate that covered the lock for the window gate and pulled back. "Come on." I punched the palms of my hands hard against the wooden window frame and felt it give. "Come on!" I pushed and strained and it finally opened enough that we could make it out to the fire escape. I heard footsteps in the apartment. "Go!" I whispered to Dad. "Get out! Hurry!"

31

EVERY TIME NICOLE DID SURVEILLANCE, she thought about what her dad used to say: "The minute you got to take a pee is the minute your perp decides to make his move. Never fails." True to form, her bladder was aching and for the last half hour she had been sitting in a cold Impala trying to decide whether to drive across Tompkins Square Park and use the bathroom in the Ukrainian diner. If it were Hector, he'd just use a coffee cup.

After their Hansel and Gretel theorizing, they had decided to stake out Peter's loft. If all bread crumbs led to Grainger, it stood to reason that by watching him long enough they'd find out who was leaving them.

She glanced up at the dimly lit windows of Peter's loft and decided that rather than risk her perfect parking spot, she'd sprint through the park to the diner.

She was halfway across when she heard the shot. *Son of a bitch.* She raced back toward the loft, pulling out her cell and pressing for the emergency operator as she ran. Clearing the park, Nicole looked up and saw the light had gone out in Peter's loft. A piece of glass dangled from the frame, reflecting the streetlight. It hung suspended and then crashed to the sidewalk. The front door to the building was wide open and the lock was shredded.

She called for backup. A second shot ripped the night. She unsnapped her Glock, and with gun drawn, entered. She heard something smash against a door and then another shot. Petrified, she edged up the stairs as a fourth shot tore into metal.

As she approached the final flight, Nicole double-gripped her revolver, and with her back to the wall, she sidled up. She felt the floor shake as the door to Peter's loft was kicked in. Peering up the last stairs, she saw the back of a man standing in the open doorway.

"Freeze!" she shouted. "Police!"

He tripped slightly and turned back in her direction.

"Jesus!" It was Carter.

He squinted and stared in her direction.

"Put the gun down!" she ordered. "Do it. Now!"

"I know you," he said, not loosing his hold on the weapon. He seemed confused, and she thought he was going to comply. "Fuck it." He bolted into the loft.

Nicole cleared the last three steps and realized that in the lit hallway she was a sitting duck. Bracing her back against the wall, she inched toward the door. She heard a siren, but knew it would come way too late; whatever was going to happen rested on her.

"Put down the gun, Carter," she shouted from outside the door.

She jumped back as a shot ripped through the doorjamb.

"Fuck off, bitch! Where are you?" he shouted into the empty space.

She realized that he was trying to do two things at once: hunt down Peter and keep her away. She had no choice. She ducked and rolled through the darkened opening. She saw Carter's silhouette backlit by the streetlight. He was a good thirty feet away, his attention fixed on the couches, where she imagined Peter and his father were hiding.

"Put down the gun!"

He turned. She saw the glint of a gun barrel, and knew that at that range and in the dark, there was no way she'd hit it out of his hand. She had to aim for his chest.

"Put it down, Carter! Now!"

"Fuck you, bitch!" He fired wildly.

Nicole squeezed off two shots.

The explosions echoed in her head and were followed by a strange silence.

Carter didn't move. Then his right leg buckled and he fell forward, landing hard on his knees.

She couldn't breathe. He hung there as though he were praying. His torso swayed and then he toppled, his head cracking on the wood floor.

"Don't anyone move," she said as she inched toward him. She saw his gun on the floor and kicked it away. Still holding her Glock, she knelt beside him. "Carter . . . Carter." She pressed two fingers into the side of his neck, feeling for his carotid. No pulse. "Someone turn on a light," she shouted.

Sirens screamed below and footsteps clambered up the stairs.

"Someone turn on a fucking light!" She crouched, frozen in place. The sirens wailed and then died. Blue lights bounced up from the street and flashed around the walls of the loft. "Is anyone in here?" A sickening fear grew with each passing second. "Peter? Dr. Grainger?"

She stood; her right knee throbbed with pain.

An officer called through the open door. "Police, drop your weapons!"

Nicole called back, "This is Detective Nicole Sullivan." She shouted out her shield number. "The shooter is down. There might be multiple casualties." Her eyes had now adjusted to the dark and she looked over the back of the sofa, braced for the worst. "Peter . . . Dr. Grainger."

No one. She saw an overturned table lamp that had been pulled from the socket. She plugged it back in, aware that she was altering a crime scene, but she needed light. She looked down at the floor, which was strewn with glass and turned as the first helmeted SWAT officer came in with gun drawn.

"Detective Sullivan?" he asked.

"Yes," she said, putting her still-warm Glock in its holster.

"Are there others?" he asked as more helmeted officers appeared.

"I don't know."

"Home invasion?" he asked.

"The motive wasn't robbery," she said, not wanting to look at Carter.

"Who is he?"

"His name's Carter Walsh." She looked out the shattered window as an ambulance and paramedics arrived.

"Are you hurt?" the officer asked.

Nicole thought about this. "No." It wasn't pain that was flooding her with a sick tingling sensation. It was an effort simply to move, to try to appear normal.

Her gaze drifted across the street. "Oh, thank God," she muttered. "Thank you."

"What is it?" the SWAT guy asked, coming to stand beside her.

"There are the intended victims. They got out." She started to cry.

32

ED SAT, RIGID, ON THE flat roof of the ladies' restroom on the north side of Tompkins Square. Hidden in shadows and dressed in gray, he was invisible. His eyes sparkled, his pupils dilated from the drugs. His brain hummed and his senses felt heightened. Beth was by his side, swaying in the gown she'd worn the night he had proposed.

He dialed down his earphones as the sirens grew too loud and peered through binoculars, needing to know what had happened. The gunshots had been unexpected. Carter was supposed to be a diversion, a way to get the detective off his back. This was not planned.

Prior to Walsh's arrival he had seen Peter and his father in their loft and heard their muffled conversation. The father was hypnotizing the son.

Ed had struggled to hear Peter's mumbling as he recounted last Monday night. Still, he had not understood how Peter had managed to get out of that hotel room. Probably something to do with Jason Walsh, or Peter's revved-up stress response, but that was water under the bridge, a variable that couldn't have been foreseen.

He turned as a wailing ambulance rounded the park.

Who is it for? Who was hurt? Or dead? Peter could not get off that easily. There'd be no justice in that.

A crowd grew and a stream of onlookers hurried past his hiding place. "Best to move on," Beth whispered, her hand on his shoulder.

"I can't." He stared through the binoculars as a stretcher was hoisted up the stoop. He saw Nicole Sullivan framed in the shot-out window. Fear pulsed through his cocoon of drugs. *She's looking at me.* Then, following the direction of her gaze, he saw it land on two men—Peter and his father. *Good.* But who was the stretcher for?

Just then, a stocky man flashed a badge and stormed into the building. Even from this distance, Ed recognized the medical examiner, whom he'd met at several fundraisers.

Oh my. He couldn't suppress a chuckle. Detective Sullivan must have just shot and killed her ex-lover. *My, my, my.* And giddy at this unexpected bonus, Ed clambered down the chain-link fence and raced toward his Mercedes.

Driving north, he dialed the number for Michael Grainger's Upper West Side apartment. He held his breath and waited.

"Hello?"

"Kyle," Ed said in a perfect imitation of Michael Grainger's baritone. "There's been a shooting at the loft . . . Your dad's been hurt."

"Oh, God. Don't tell me . . ." The boy was in tears.

"Kiddo, we'll get through this. I've asked Dr. Tyson to bring you to the hospital. I told him you'd be waiting downstairs. He should be there in a few minutes."

Ed hung up, reached into his breast pocket, and uncapped a waiting syringe.

33

I CAN'T WRAP MY BRAIN around this; we're alive. I stare up at my building. Dad's next to me, and none of this seems real. Nicole's looking down at us—she's so beautiful. What is she thinking? What's just happened?

The shots . . . but how did she get here so quickly? Was she watching me?

I'm sweating, which makes no sense considering that the ground is frozen and my breath is coming out smoky white. Yeah, the Amytal. Is that why I'm looking at Nicole Sullivan and wondering how it would feel to kiss her?

"You okay, Peter?" Dad asked.

"I think so." I started to say something, and then I saw the ambulance. I looked up at Nicole; she was crying. She must have shot whoever it was that broke in.

So much noise, so much chaos—some of the cruisers, their light bars still flashing, officers setting up wooden barriers and for a second time this week, yellow tape getting stretched across my front door.

A television van double-parked at the end of the block and a film crew emerged. A perfectly madeup Asian woman pointed toward my building.

"You got some fucked-up karma, man."

"You talking to me?" I turned and was startled to see the kid who'd tried to mug me. He looked sick. "What's wrong with you?" I asked.

"Nothing, just cold, man." He was shivering. "That's where you live."

"Yup."

"Nice." His teeth chattered, giving his words a choppy cadence. "You got that whole place to yourself?"

"I have a son."

"Shit . . . he okay?"

"Yeah, he's not at home. Did you see what happened?" I asked.

"I heard it, but there's some weird shit happening."

He had his hands jammed far into his pockets, but what I had first thought was a filthy sleeve I now realized was a grimy ACE bandage wadded up around his wrist. "What's that for?" I asked.

"It's nothing."

"Show me, I'm a doctor."

"It's nothing."

"Fine . . . Carl, isn't it?"

"That's right."

"I'm Peter, that's my dad," I said.

"Are you really a doctor?"

"Yup."

"What kind?"

"Psychiatrist."

"Fuck."

"What?"

"Nothing, I just thought . . ."

"What happened to your hand, Carl?" I asked, hoping that I hadn't injured him last week.

301

"I got cut." A wave of chills set his teeth chattering.

"How bad?"

"Bad," he admitted.

"What's going on?" Dad asked, pulling his attention away from the circus that had formed on Avenue B.

"Carl, this is my father, Michael." I watched as the teenager started to pull his hand from his pocket; he flinched and just nodded.

"Son, you need to get out of the cold," Dad said.

"Yeah." He looked down at the ground and then up at me. There were tears in his eyes. "It really hurts, man."

"Has anybody looked at it?" I asked. "Like a doctor?"

"I can't. They ask too many questions."

"Okay," I said, wondering if he was about to bolt again.

"How long ago did you get cut?" I asked.

"Few nights . . . I didn't know it was your place."

"What are you talking about?" I asked, glancing up at my windows.

"It was in the park, some dude, like James Bond staring up at your place."

"Describe him," Dad said.

"It was dark," Carl said. "I just wanted some money. He didn't have to cut me."

"You mean stab?" Dad asked.

"Yeah."

"Can you remember how he looked? Think hard."

"He smiled a lot," Carl said, "even when he cut me. Like he was enjoying it."

It had to be Tyson. "What color was his hair?"

"He had a hat and something in his ear."

"A hearing aid?"

"No. . . . it was different, and when I first saw him he was checking out your place, like he was listening or something."

I heard a woman call out my name and I turned to see the reporter advancing toward us.

"Let's get out of here," I said.

"We can't, Peter," Dad replied. "They're going to need our statement."

A light flooded my eyes and I could see that Carl was seconds away from disappearing. "Come on." I grabbed his good arm and headed back toward my loft.

We were now being pursued by the news crew.

A patrolman stopped us outside my front door. "Please," I said, "we ran down the fire escape, my dad doesn't have a coat, and I don't want to talk to reporters."

He seemed uncertain. "Okay, stay in the hall," he said.

"Thanks," I said, already stepping over the yellow tape. The elevator opened in front of us and a paramedic came out.

"How bad is he?" I asked, knowing that our would-be attacker had been shot.

"Body bag." He kept moving toward the door.

"Come on." I needed to see the face of whoever had just tried to kill me, and I desperately wanted to call Kyle and make sure he was all right.

"He was blond," Carl said as I closed the elevator gate behind the three of us. I pressed the button.

"I thought you said he was wearing a hat."

"He was, but his lashes were really light and I think his eyes were blue. I just wanted some money."

"Carl, how old are you?"

"Seventeen."

"Try again," I said, "I've got a fourteen-year-old who looks older than you."

"Sixteen."

I looked at him as the elevator lurched to a stop. "Third time's a charm . . ."

"Fourteen," he admitted. "Almost fifteen. When you're fifteen they stop coming after you."

"Who?"

"Social workers and shit. After fifteen they don't care."

I knew better than to press him. "Let's get a look at that hand." My stomach knotted at the sight of the mangled lock on my door. Thank God it had held long enough for us to get out. The reality of what had almost happened, of what *did* happen was too much. I needed to let Kyle know that we were all right. I could only imagine if he turned on the news and saw . . . God only knows.

Nicole met us at the door. "You can't go in," she said. Her eyes were red.

"Are you okay?" I wanted to give her my hand, but stopped myself.

"I should ask you that." She looked at my dad and then at Carl. "Who are you?"

I felt Carl's panic; here the boy had let me bring him in out of the cold and the first thing I did was take him to the cops.

"Who was it?" I asked, avoiding the topic.

"Carter Walsh," she answered hollowly. "I didn't mean to kill him."

"Of course not. You had no choice."

"It was dark."

"It's okay," I told her, not knowing what else to say, glimpsing her despair.

The paramedic returned with the white oilcloth body bag. "Is the ME here yet?"

"Just got here," she said.

"Great . . . any idea how long?"

"Soon."

"You know," I offered, "if you let me inside I can put on a pot of coffee. . . . You look like you could use it."

She looked at Carl, dressed in his throwaway clothes. He was trying not to shiver. "You're sick, aren't you?" she asked.

"I'm fine." His teeth chattered.

She looked at me. "There's a dead body in the middle of your living room; I don't think he should see that."

"I can take him in the back," Dad offered. "He's not well."

"Okay."

"Thanks." I moved quickly past her. It was hard not to look. Carter Walsh lay dead next to one of the pillars in the middle of the floor. A photographer had set up blindingly bright halogen lights and circled the body, snapping pictures.

"I wasn't kidding about the coffee," I said as she followed us back. My real motivation, however, was the phone on the kitchen counter.

"Fine," she said, with the dull expression of someone in shock.

With Dad and Carl safely in the back, I headed to the kitchen. Nicole followed.

I eyed the phone. "Okay if I use this? There are some people that are going to see this on the evening news and I want them to know that we're okay."

"Like your son?" she asked.

"Yes," I said.

"So who's the kid that looks like he's jonesing?"

"His name's Carl and I think he can identify Ed Tyson. Said he was staking out my apartment the night Jason was killed . . . Let me call Kyle and then I'll tell you everything."

"That would be a change."

She was trying for sarcasm, but I could tell she was deeply troubled. I pressed the speed dial. The machine picked up. "Kyle, it's Dad. Pick up the phone. Pick up the phone," I said over the recording. I waited. Even with the Amytal, like high-octane Valium pumping through my body, I felt the tension mount with each passing second. "Pick up the phone." I heard the beep; I glanced at the clock, it was after eleven, maybe he was sleeping and didn't hear it. I hung up. I felt Nicole staring at me.

"What's wrong?" she asked.

"Let me try again." For a second time, I heard Dad's recorded voice, "Please leave a message after you hear the beep."

"Kyle, pick up. Pick up the phone!"

I heard a ringing noise from behind me and watched as everyone in the room reached for their cells. It sounded familiar; it was mine, I must have left it in the study. Hoping it was Kyle, I raced to get it. Nicole followed.

I flicked it open and felt a wave of relief at the sound of his voice.

"Dad?"

"Kyle." I looked through the open door, past Nicole and into the bathroom, where Dad had unwrapped Carl's bandages. Even from this distance I could see the angry pus-filled wound in the center of his hand. Red streaks shot up the kid's arm, and I knew he needed to get to a hospital. "Where are you, Kyle?" I heard the beeping of a car horn in the background. "I tried to call you. Where are you?"

"He's with me."

"Oh, God." It was no longer Kyle's voice; it was Ed. The air left the room, and the lingering effects of the Amytal were blasted by a surge of adrenaline.

"Be very careful, Peter. That is, if you want to see your son alive. Your apartment is fully bugged. I hear and see everything."

I looked across at the bathroom, where Nicole had gone to help Dad clean Carl's wound.

"What do you want from me?" I whispered.

"That's the spirit. For starters, this conversation is between you and me; if you tell that pretty detective or anyone else, Kyle is dead. Do you understand?"

"Yes." I backed into the shadows. "Why are you doing this?"

"I think you've probably figured that out."

"Beth . . ."

"See, you're not so dumb. I want you to think about what you did. Murderer," he hissed. "You couldn't stand it that she wanted me. You killed her because of that."

"It's not what happened." I felt sick, knowing he was serious. I had to find Kyle. I looked away from the bathroom and toward the window and the fire escape. I thought of Ann and Jason, and of Carter—dead in my living room. "Tell me what you want."

"That's easy. To balance the scales—take things back to zero, back to the beginning."

"What are you talking about," I whispered as I eased through the window and started down the metal stairs.

"You have an hour," he said, and I heard a car engine shut off. "That's how long it will take the drugs to stop his breathing. One hour."

"Where are you?"

"Don't play dumb; you were here last night. Your footprints were all over. One hour. Come alone." The line went dead.

34

NICOLE WATCHED AS MICHAEL GRAINGER coaxed the boy's hand under warm water. The stench from his wound was like that of a body left to putrefy in the sun. The stab wound oozed green pus and hot red streaks tracked up his arm. She tried to listen to Michael, his voice so like his son's, as he comforted the sobbing teenager.

"You need antibiotics," he said.

"No hospitals. I can't."

Michael didn't push; he looked at Nicole, as though expecting her to speak. She couldn't. She'd just shot and killed Carter. She pictured him falling to the ground and heard the *crack* of his head on the wood floor. What had she done? She felt dead inside, and no longer cared that when this came out—her involvement, her affair, the abortion, the falsification of her police record—the punishment would be nothing compared to what she would inflict on herself. *Why did he come here?* He was drunk, his children were dead, he wanted revenge. It made sense, but it didn't add up. How would he know where Peter lived?

"Ow!" Carl squirmed as Michael Grainger poured peroxide over the wound.

"Sorry," he said, getting a soft cotton towel and patting the wound as it bubbled furiously where the bactericidal hit the infection.

She looked at the kid and then at Peter's bearded father. "Do you have a picture of Tyson?" she asked, wondering if the kid could identify him. Although she could hear Hector's response— *Yeah right, and who's the judge going to believe—a junkie runaway or dean of the medical school?*

"I'm sure he does," Michael said. "Where is he?"

Nicole glanced through the open door toward the dark opening of his study. "He was talking to Kyle," she said, knowing that had been just a couple minutes ago, but feeling as though it could have been hours. "Peter?" She walked back toward the study. He wasn't there; she shivered in the cold air from the open fire-escape window. "Peter." She headed toward the kitchen, remembering he'd said something about making coffee.

Fred Corley, the medical examiner, was in the middle of the loft kneeling beside Carter's body. He glanced at Nicole, shook his head, and returned his attention to the body.

Her eyes darted around the room. Peter wasn't in the kitchen. She spotted Hector.

"Nic," he headed toward her. "I came as fast as I could. I'm so sorry."

"Where is he?" she asked, her numbness pushed away by surges of panic.

"Who?"

"Peter? Where's Peter Grainger?"

"He's not with you?"

"He was." She circled the loft. "Peter. Peter!" Hector stuck at her side, even as her pace quickened. *Shit!* She opened the bedroom doors.

Michael Grainger emerged from the bathroom with Carl. He looked at her, his expression worried. "What's happening?"

"Where's your son?" she asked.

"I thought you said he was talking to Kyle."

"Oh, God. She grabbed the kitchen phone. "Call him! Call Kyle."

Michael did as instructed.

She watched as he held the receiver to his ear.

"No one's picking up. . . . Kyle, it's Grandpa. Kyle. Kyle! Pick up the phone."

Nicole ran to the study and grabbed a photo album off the shelf. She flipped through the pages, her gaze skittering over the images, and saw for the first time how beautiful Beth Grainger had been. She came to a page from which a picture had been removed, and right above the space was a shot at a formal party. Tyson and Grainger standing shoulder-to-shoulder. She raced back to the group in the kitchen and slapped the album on the counter. "Carl, do you see the man who stabbed you?"

The kid, in obvious pain, squinted and leaned down. "Yeah." With his good hand he pointed to Tyson. "That's him. It's that smile. . . . Fucker."

Hector looked across at her. "What's going on?"

She pulled her partner aside and whispered. "We've been set up. Peter's been trying to tell me all along that it was Tyson. I thought he was just . . ."

"Slow down, Nic," he urged.

"I can't," she said. "Hector, I'm so sorry."

"What are you talking about?"

"It's Tyson. Somehow he knew to get Walsh here. But it's a diversion." She pushed her hand against her forehead, needing to think.

310

"You're not making sense."

"It makes perfect sense. Hector." She looked at her partner dead-on. "I should have dropped this case the minute I knew Carter was involved . . . I had an affair with him in college."

"Oh, shit!"

"It gets worse, and Tyson knows it. I'm so fucked right now, but I've got to find him. I don't know for certain what he's up to, but it isn't good."

Hector glanced in the direction of the ME and the crime-scene team.

"This was all a diversion." She talked fast and kept her voice low. "When it comes out, any half-decent attorney will say I polluted everything. It doesn't matter who killed Ann and Jason. But we've got to find Tyson, and I don't think we have much time. As bad as this is, I think it's just the opening act."

"Okay, Nic. I'm with you, but they're not going to want you to leave."

"I know," she said, and moved back toward the study and the open window. "I'll understand if you don't want to come with me. My career's over, but yours doesn't have to be."

"Oh, shut up." He followed her out onto the fire escape. "So where do you think he is?"

35

WITH HIS MERCEDES HIDDEN IN the shadows of Fleming's loading dock, Ed unbuckled Kyle Grainger, pulled the paralyzed teen from the car, and hoisted him into a mail cart. He had little time, and while things were going well, he needed to stay sharp. The boy had been easy, but if Peter had gotten to him first. . . .

"But he didn't," Beth whispered as Ed rolled the cart through the mail room. He ran his pass card across the security plate inside the elevator and headed down.

Kyle had been easy. Ed had flashed his headlights and the kid had come running.

"Kyle," he'd said as the teenager yanked open the door.

"Just tell me he's not dead," Kyle had pleaded, tears glittering.

"He's not dead," Ed had said, his tone soft and caring.

"How bad?"

"I don't know," he'd admitted, putting a hand on the boy's shoulder. "It's going to be okay. Here, you need to put on your seat belt."

Kyle had reached back and fumbled for the belt, and as he did, Ed had pulled out the syringe and injected him with T2745.

"Ouch." The boy had swatted at the spot. "What was? . . ."

Now, rolling into the subbasement, Ed was finally ready. There would be no more mistakes. He wheeled Kyle into the morgue and toward the waiting table. The floor was covered with oilcloth, the edges of which were held in place by heavy barrels of solvent. He'd even wrapped the feet of the autopsy table in surgical booties as protection against the splatter. He hefted the boy onto the table, careful to not disturb the oilcloth curtain that concealed him from the door.

"I didn't want to do this," Ed said aloud to Beth and to the boy, who could hear and feel everything. "This should never have happened."

He fought back the rising tide of grief, present since the day he'd learned of her death. As he adjusted the boy's lanky body for maximum visual impact, he knew, however, the pain was older. He pictured a young man in a black cape holding out an emerald ring.

Beth glided to his side. "I'm sorry," she whispered. "It should have been you."

Ed checked the small stainless Mayo table next to Kyle. On it lay an assortment of syringes and a tranquilizer gun with a stiff dose of T2745. On a second table lay an unwrapped scalpel, a bone saw, and an assortment of surgical instruments. Just in case, Ed carried a .357 Magnum in his pocket.

He glanced at the cremation oven; its door was open and waiting. By morning this would be done. Like a chef thinking through a recipe, he recalled: *One hour at one thousand degrees Celsius, one hour at nine hundred degrees Celsius, cremains into bone crusher, turn on the blowers, and Peter's sanity, along with his son, would fly, fly away.*

36

I HIT THE LANDING OF the fire escape at a dead run, dangled, and dropped. A sharp pain shot from my ankle, but I didn't look back as I sprinted toward Avenue A, feverishly calculating the quickest way to Fleming. My eye caught on a taxi disgorging two women. I pushed past them, and gave the cabbie the address. "Please hurry."

"What's the rush?"

I reached back, wondering if I even had my wallet—I did. "Forty bucks if you get there in five minutes."

He started the meter. "And they're off."

I braced as the vehicle took a hard left, roared down the blocks, slowed at the intersections, and then zoomed through red, green, and yellow lights.

I was heading into a trap and I knew it, but what choice did I have? *Shit.* It would be just like Ann or Jason or even Carter. I pictured Jason's eyes staring at me in the elevator, and Ann's in the dream. Something about that was important. "Wait!" I shouted to the driver a block short of Fleming. Across the street was a twenty-four-hour CVS. "Right here." I squished the bills into the metal tray and bolted.

I ran toward the pharmacy, racking my brain for old medical facts. Ann and Jason had been given paralytics. Anesthesiologists could reverse those.

As I pushed through the door and headed toward the pharmacist, it hit me . . . edrophonium and neostigmine, both stimulants, could reverse curare-type drugs.

"Excuse me," I shouted to the top of a woman's head visible through the partition.

A dark-eyed woman with a long braid looked up. "Can I help you?"

"Yes, I need edrophonium or neostigmine."

"Oh, dear," she said. "Sounds like a myasthenic crisis."

She caught me off guard. "Yes," I said, remembering that not only were these drugs used to reverse paralysis in surgery, but they were also used to treat severe myasthenia gravis, a disorder of the muscles and nervous system. "It's my son"—I improvised—"and I'm a doctor." I pulled out my wallet and flipped to my license.

"Which would you prefer?" she asked. "I have both."

"Whatever's most potent; he's pretty resistant." I felt the seconds and minutes slip away. I felt like screaming at her to hurry.

"Probably neostigmine, so I'm assuming you want the one-mg-per-cc."

"Yes."

"Do you want a single syringe? It comes in boxes of one, five, or ten."

"Ten," I said, having no clue as to how it came or how it was dosed. I figured that if the syringes were already drawn up, taking one, two, or three probably wouldn't kill anyone. Why couldn't she move faster?

"How long has your son had it?" she asked, pulling a box out of a cabinet.

"It's just recent," I said, "but please hurry."

"Of course." She came up to the register with the box of syringes. "Do you have your insurance card?"

"Sure." I fumbled through my wallet and handed it to her.

"Oh, you work for the university. That's a twelve-dollar co-pay. It'll just take a couple minutes while I get your information into—"

"Look"—I threw a twenty on the counter—"I'll come back for my card." I grabbed the box and ran; I didn't know how much of the hour was gone. I sprinted down the block, past the locked doors of Fleming, and toward the ER.

I ripped open the box before heading down into the subbasement. There were ten plastic-wrapped syringes, a patient-information brochure, and a packet insert covered with tiny black print and big black boxes labeled "Warning," "Side Effects," and "Information on Overdose." I ducked into a linen closet, pulled up my shirt, and jammed the first needle into my side. I pressed down, not thinking about the pain as I pumped the solution in. I grabbed a second one and did the same. I was sweating bullets, and my fingers and toes started to tingle.

I stuffed the remaining syringes into my pocket, and, dropping the box on the floor, I ran toward the stairs. As I headed underground it grew warmer. I turned a corner and banged my head on an asbestos-wrapped pipe. I tried not to think, just to move, but what if I was wrong? I mean, *really* wrong, and this wasn't where Ed had taken Kyle?

I stopped, disoriented. Which way was I supposed to go? Had I just taken a wrong turn? I held my breath and listened, thinking I could get my bearings by hearing the traffic above me. Why couldn't I remember? I had just been here. Then I smelled it. I turned left and not right, and it grew stronger—the stench of death.

The ceilings dipped and a single bulb lit the way. My teeth chattered and gooseflesh prickled on my arms and my neck. I pictured Nicole and wished she were here. I wished I had a gun or something other than my bare hands, but it was too late for any of that. I just needed to get to Kyle. I'd do whatever had to be done. Whatever Ed wanted, he could have. *Just don't hurt Kyle.* I walked more slowly, rolling my feet along the cement, seeing the first of the pillars and the marble floor in the round room outside the morgue and Ed's laboratory.

I took shallow breaths as I edged closer to the end of the tunnel. I looked into the circular room and saw a light from under the morgue door.

I wondered if he were on the other side and if he could see me as I approached. He'd told me to come alone, I had. I was unarmed—save for eight syringes of neostigmine—and I would face whatever lay behind that door.

My hand seemed disconnected from my body as it grabbed the handle. It tightened around the cold knob and turned. The latch clicked and the smell of the morgue flooded across the threshold.

A dim light shone down on the mostly empty space. It was all different from last night. Oilcloth had been spread over the floor and dangled from a pipe in the ceiling.

I felt a horrible desperation; there was no one here. I'd gotten it wrong. I looked up at the clock. How long ago had Ed called? He'd said that Kyle would be dead within an hour. My gaze lowered to the hanging cloth, which was rigged as though someone had been showing slides. I moved closer and saw surgical clamps holding the slick fabric to a pipe. I glanced down to the hem of the oilcloth and glimpsed the legs of a dissection table, but someone had covered them in blue surgical boots, as though preparing to operate.

I reached toward the cloth, and as I did, the fabric ripped from the clamps.

"Kyle!" He lay in front of me, motionless. I reached for him, grabbed for his head, and stared into his eyes. It had all been lies; he was dead.

It was then that I saw Ed holding the curtain and smiling. He held a dart gun in his other hand and squeezed the trigger.

I felt a stinging in my chest and I staggered. My feet tangled in the oilcloth. I felt a tingle spread through my body. I couldn't stop myself from falling; my eyes were fixed on Kyle as I lost control of my legs, my hands, and my arms. The neostigmine wasn't working. Ed had killed Kyle, and I would soon follow.

37

"WE'LL TAKE MY CAR," HECTOR said as he hit the ground.

Nicole didn't argue; Peter and Kyle Grainger were in danger, and she was to blame. "Why didn't Peter say anything?"

"Maybe he couldn't," Hector whispered as they emerged on Avenue A.

Not wanting to draw attention to their exodus, they kept to the shadows and moved fast. He pressed the alarm on his Jeep, the lights flashed, and the doors clicked open. Nicole slid into the passenger side as Hector turned the key.

"Where to?" he asked.

"Tyson's apartment," she said, hating herself for not having believed Peter.

"You going to tell me the rest?" Hector asked, his expression unreadable as he stared ahead, pumped the pedal, and timed the lights.

She owed him the truth. "When I was twenty I had an affair with Walsh. I didn't know he was married, had kids. I was stupid. I got pregnant and had an abortion. I was seeing a shrink because

I was losing it." She glanced at Hector's profile. "I got extremely depressed, and I took some pills and landed in the hospital."

He nodded, "I'm so sorry, Nic, but why didn't you just give away the case?"

"It sounds stupid, but I never said anything about it on my application. You know the part where it asks about a history of mental illness? I checked 'no.' "

"It's not stupid. You wouldn't have gotten the job. . . . Carter Walsh is dead, right? It wasn't your fault Nic, and this other stuff—who cares?" And then he said something that her father used to say, "Always go by the book, Nic . . . except when you can't."

"That's just it," she said, as he pulled in front of Ed's Fifth Avenue building. "Tyson knows, and don't ask me how, but he set this whole fucking thing up."

"Why?" Hector asked as they strode through the lobby, flashing their shields and bullying the doorman for the apartment number.

In the elevator, she glanced at Hector, glad for his strength and his loyalty. Even just telling him about Walsh had made it possible for her to think through the panic. "Something about the timing of this . . . Tyson gives Peter a job, an apartment, helps his kid get into school . . ." She grew silent thinking about what might be happening with Peter and his son. *Where were they?*

"All just a few months ago," Hector prompted as the doors opened.

"And that just a few months after Peter's wife died." She thought about Peter's grief and the story he'd told in his lecture. "She was extremely beautiful, and he really loved her."

"Tyson?"

"Huh?" Nicole paused outside Tyson's door. "I'd meant Peter, but maybe you're right, too." She rang the bell and rapped loudly.

A dark-haired girl who couldn't have been more than eight cautiously opened the door, leaving the chain on.

"Is this the Tyson apartment?" Nicole asked.

"Yes," the girl answered, her pink nightgown visible through the opening.

"We're police." Nicole held up her shield. "We need to speak with your father."

"I don't think he's home."

"What about your mother?"

"She doesn't feel good. She's in bed."

"This is important," Nicole said. "Could we please speak to her?"

"I'm not supposed to let strangers into the apartment."

"We're police officers, we're not strangers, and we need to see your mother. What's your name?"

"Camille."

"Okay, Camille. I also have a little girl, and you need to let us in right now."

The girl pondered, the door shut, the chain rattled, and they were in.

Nicole scanned what she could see of Tyson's home. The apartment was huge, and Ed's taste for high-style furniture was everywhere. As they passed the living room she glimpsed canvases that could have hung in the Met or MoMA.

"She's sick," the girl said. "She gets tired."

"Really? And what does she do when she's sick?"

Camille looked up at Nicole, her eyes large. "She stays in bed."

Camille stopped in front of a closed door, hesitated, and opened it. "Mommy, Mommy."

Nicole peered into the darkened bedroom. "Dr. Tyson? Miranda?"

There was no answer. She and Hector went over to the massive bed and turned on a lamp.

Nicole felt a shiver and wondered if the woman was even alive.

"Has she been in bed all day?" Nicole asked.

"I don't know. I went to school. But she wouldn't get up for dinner, and Betty had to put me to bed, only I wasn't tired. I wanted her to stay, but she said she couldn't."

Nicole gently shook Miranda Tyson's shoulder. "Dr. Tyson."

Miranda's eyes cracked open. "Who are you?"

Nicole reached over and felt the woman's forehead; she wasn't feverish. "I'm Detective Sullivan; I'm trying to locate your husband. Do you know where he is?"

"Who are you?"

Hector pulled the bedside lamp closer. "Dr. Tyson, try to open your eyes."

Miranda attempted to follow instructions and as she did, they saw that her pupils were like pinpoints.

"Are you taking medication?" Nicole asked, looking over the nightstand.

"No . . . no medication. I'm just tired."

"Where's your husband?" Nicole urged.

"What's wrong?" Miranda mumbled, her eyes closed against the burning light.

"I need to speak with him. Where can I find him?"

"Check the lab. He's always there. Something big . . ." She struggled to get the words out.

"Where's his lab?"

There was no answer.

Nicole felt like slapping her. She was taking something, possibly an opiate. Yet, from what little she knew about Miranda Tyson, it didn't fit. Few high-powered physicians had the time to be morphine addicts. "Camille." She turned to the girl. "Where's your daddy's lab?"

"It's in his school, and he has a room there where he grows things."

"Where he has his office with all the windows?"

"No, it's way downstairs. It smells bad, and they keep the dead people there."

Nicole wasn't certain what the girl meant, but there was no time for chitchat. She got to her feet and looked at Hector. "Let's go."

TWO MINUTES LATER, THEY WERE on the street and sprinting toward the medical school. They raced up the stairs of Fleming and pounded on the doors. Hector cupped his hands against the thick glass. "Shouldn't they have a fucking guard?" They ran around the building trying all the entrances. Nicole wondered if she had probable cause for breaking into a public building. What they had were assumptions built on assumptions; the single solid piece of evidence was a positive identification from a street kid alleging the dean of the medical school had stabbed him. *Works for me*, she thought, and she reached back and freed her service revolver.

"Do it." She turned at the sound of Hector's voice and saw a perplexed expression on his face. "Something's burning," he said.

At first she thought he was kidding, fabricating a lie that could be used if they were wrong, but then she smelled it, and it was coming from inside.

"Stand back." She sighted the lower corner of the center door and fired into the inch-thick tempered glass.

38

I'M LYING ON THE MORGUE floor; I can't move. Ed's coming toward me, smiling. He's saying something about Beth. He bends over and his hands dig into my arms as he shoves me back against the wall. I try to speak. "Why?"

He sits me up and his fingers hold up my chin, forcing me to look at Kyle. Bile rises. I focus on Kyle, on his chest; he's breathing. He's alive, but barely. I recognize the effects of Ed's paralytic drug. It's clear that's what he's also given me—and that the neostigmine isn't working.

"Yes, Peter," Ed whispers. "He's alive, but now comes the moment I've been waiting for."

As he talks I realize how stupid I've been. My fear is so thick, even more paralyzing than the drug that he shot into me. I fight it. Kyle is still alive, and so there's hope.

"I wonder," Ed says moving away, "what it will be like for you to see your son dissected before your eyes, knowing that he was awake for the entire ordeal, knowing that he couldn't move, but could feel every cut of the blade."

He walks over to Kyle and picks up something from the metal

tray—a syringe. He turns in my direction. I try to feel the tips of my fingers. I'm able to make them move just a bit, a spark of possibility, maybe the neostigmine is doing something. I can't let him see that, and I do the same with my toes. I know his drug has a rapid onset, so if I'm not totally paralyzed, I've got a shot.

Ed kneels beside me and desperation washes over me as he pulls up my shirtsleeve and prepares to inject me with more.

"This is special," he says.

I see his smile from the corner of my eye.

"These, my dear Peter, are your last seconds in the world of the sane. What I'm giving you now is very potent, the kind of thing that only the most experienced shaman will even attempt, and then only when the surroundings are filled with great beauty. It will take you to other worlds, only in your case, this is your ticket to hell. Look at your son. See how afraid he is. How fragile. Just like the child you took from me."

I feel a prick as the needle enters my arm. His breath is hot on the side of my face. I picture my entire nervous system: my brain attached to my spine, the nerves that send messages out and messages back. Like switching from autopilot to manual, I force my body into action. It isn't much, but I manage to butt my head into his. There's a cracking sound and I feel the pain in my scalp as shocks ripple through my body. Ed falls back on his hands. He stares at me; he looks confused.

The syringe, embedded in my flesh, hangs.

Ed laughs as he backs away. "So that's it," he says, as his smile spreads. "I should have realized. . . . It's the adrenaline."

I don't know what he's talking about. I try to move and nearly topple onto my face. My legs won't work.

He's back on his feet and heading toward his drugs. He's talking to himself. "Just like the rats," he says. "*That's* how you got out of the hotel room. I should have listened to Ralph; adrenaline breaks it down. You need more."

"Move," I shout at myself. "Move!" My fingers claw against the floor, I visualize my biceps and my triceps and the muscles in my forearms; I will make them work. I push back against the wall and get my feet and my legs to support my body. I feel the neostigmine going head-to-head with his drug, pushing it back.

But it's too late. He's coming toward me, aiming the dart gun.

I can't maintain my balance. In desperation, like a fish flopping on a boat, I hurl myself at his legs. I roll as hard and as fast as I can. Pain shoots up my arm, and then my chest connects with his legs. I jam his knees and feel him lose his balance.

A tray crashes to the ground.

The pain in my arm is intense and as I manage to raise my head I see that the needle has broken off in the meat of my muscle. It's an odd pain; each throbbing pulse strengthens the connection between my body and my brain.

Ed scrambles back. "Clever boy, but you're too late."

"No!" I shout, standing on legs that don't feel like mine. At least I'm off the floor; I'm moving. I stumble stiff-kneed into the dissection table, against Kyle. I glance back at Ed, who's still on the ground, and I teeter toward him, trying to build up speed like some stiff-legged Frankenstein.

He's searching around the fallen table. I have to get to him before he can find whatever rolled under there.

"Shit!" He looks at me and abandons his search. He runs back, his hand shoots up the wall. "It's too late." He flicks the switch and the room goes dark.

I listen to the sound of his voice; it seems so far away. Colors and shapes swirl in the blackness. Faces form in midair and I hear a woman's familiar voice calling my name. "Beth?"

There's laughter.

Ed is watching. I feel his presence. I turn toward the laughter and I see the shadowy silhouette of his body against the wall; he's circling.

326

I keep between him and Kyle, but there are others moving in the dark. Something brushes against my leg, like an animal running past.

And there's sound, a whistling hum and voices, and there she is again, calling my name over and over. *"Peter. Peter."*

"Beth?" She's trying to tell me something, but I have to focus on Ed's shadow. He's moving toward me, toward Kyle.

"Peter. Peter. I'm over here." She's singing. *"Come to me, Peter."*

The music is beautiful, like wind chimes. I want to lie down and listen to her voice and to the birdsong that flows from every corner of the room that's no longer a room, just a swirling mass of color and light and music.

Something's wrong. Something is chasing me and chasing Kyle. I have to stop it, to find it. The song changes, shifting, discordant. Where is my body? A wind whistles through me as though my skin and the molecules of my flesh have been pulled apart and I'm nothing more than a collection of atoms spinning in space.

A sick red glow oozes toward me like spreading blood. There's a sparkle of teeth and metal. The energy is sick and damaged. I will not fear it. My body vibrates as my feet glide across the ground. I reach for the sick red mass; it moves back, it laughs. I turn with its every movement, following it across the room, moving it away from Kyle, from my heart.

We dance. A part of me wants to reach out toward the sick mass and make it better. I surge toward it, touching it, feeling the solid flesh beneath the swirl of atoms. I grab tightly and hear the laughter turn to a scream. I see Ed in the dark. His face contorts as he breaks free of my grip and runs toward Kyle.

Suddenly he's gone, but something's crawling on the floor. There's an explosion, a flash of light, and the whirling voices and the music shatter like broken glass.

He has a gun and is aiming it at me.

I hurtle toward him. "No!" A warrior's cry fills the air.

He fires. I see sparks as I barrel into him. He falls back and slams against a fluid-filled drum. There's a swishing noise and a loud crash as the metal container rolls and breaks open. A wave of formalin spills across the floor. The cool solvent soaks my shoes and thick fumes rise into the air, a noxious mix of methanol and formaldehyde.

Ed is on his back, his gun waving in the air. He bats at his chemical-splashed eyes. He staggers to his feet and whirls blindly, his gun extended, trying to locate me.

I duck and move in. I grab him around his waist as a shot whizzes at the ceiling. I tackle him and force his gun hand to the floor. The fumes are in my eyes, they rush into my chest. I clamp down on his wrist and feel the gun fire into the floor.

A blue spark catches in my periphery. A bit of trivia pops through my mind—*formalin is highly flammable and has a low flash point.*

I squeeze hard as his fingers claw at my throat. The gun drops to the floor. I twist back on his wrist, making him release my neck.

Blue heat surges toward us. I push him away. "Move!"

I do. He doesn't.

His eyes shoot open and he grins as he spots the gun about to be swallowed by the spreading flames. He lunges toward it.

Bells clang as I stumble toward Kyle. The fire alarm springs to life, the sprinklers creak, gurgle, and twirl into action, but there's no time.

A bullet whistles past my head and shatters a glass shelf, sending its chemical inventory crashing to the floor.

I reach for Kyle and slip my arms between his long body and the coolness of the stainless-steel table. I heft him into my arms and stagger under his weight.

A burning mass rushes toward me. It's Ed. His clothes are on fire, but it doesn't seem to bother him. He levels the gun at Kyle's head.

"Why?" I back away, not about to give up.

The muscles in his face contort as flames pass from his clothing to his skin.

"She was mine!" He looks to his right, and I see the shadow of a woman in the billowing smoke.

I back away, but Ed seems frozen, staring at what has to be an illusion. He reaches toward her as the flames from his clothes and the melting oilcloth shoot up his body, engulfing him.

Fire licks at my feet, my nostrils burn. I back toward the door, unable to take my eyes off of Ed and the spectral image of my wife, burning like a torch.

Suddenly, Kyle seems lighter in my arms.

Dark smoke billows up, taking human form, as if the room is filled with ghosts.

Something brushes against my cheek, I smell Narcisse Noir, Beth's perfume.

I can't feel my feet and I wonder if they're on fire. I look at Kyle's face and know I have to keep moving.

I stumble out of the morgue and into the circular room at the end of the three corridors. It's filling with smoke. I try to find the entrance to the tunnels, but it's dark and I can't see it. I know that it's just a matter of minutes, maybe seconds, before the smoke and formaldehyde fumes will do what Ed's gun and drugs didn't.

"Move," I tell myself, choking as I stagger toward the exit light over the stairwell. I glance back. The morgue is ablaze, but what makes me pause as I hold my son in my arms is the unshakable sense that Beth is back there, watching me.

Battling through the smoke, I press up the stairs toward the security door at the landing. Each step is a small victory as I try to make my feet, my ankles, and my knees work. Kyle, heavy in my arms, is struggling to breathe; the muscle wall of his diaphragm spasms.

I press his body against the latch and pray that the door isn't locked from the inside, but it doesn't budge. I push harder, unable to catch my breath. It's locked. I can't breathe, my eyes burn.

Glass shatters from above. I turn back, half expecting to see Ed in pursuit, but there's nothing.

I hear distant voices. A woman shouts out my name.

"I'm here," I yell back, throwing my weight against the door. "Help us! We're here! We're down here!" I cough. The smoke thickens and pours out through the vents. It's impossible to see more than a few inches.

The weight in my arms is so heavy.

"Peter, where are you?" It's Nicole.

"Here! Down here." I'm coughing and my arms and legs can't take much more.

I hear banging on the other side of the door.

"It won't open!" I shout, as the words choke in my throat.

"He's down here! Peter, stand back." Shots rip at the lock, it breaks, and I stumble through.

Nicole Sullivan's face appears, framed in smoke. We look at each other and then she sees Kyle in my arms.

"He's alive," I tell her. "He's been drugged." I cough, and she grabs his legs, taking some of the weight.

"Where's Tyson?" she asks, as she helps me up the two flights of stairs.

"I think he's dead."

FRIGID AIR BLASTS MY FACE as Nicole leads me through the shattered glass door. Snowflakes swirl, then land on my cheeks and my forehead. The air fills with screaming sirens and flashing lights. Medics race toward us. They try to take Kyle. "No!"

"It's okay," Nicole says, trying to make me stop resisting the paramedics.

I don't want them to take him. I want to keep walking, to go home, to take my son home.

Kyle is barely breathing, and in the streetlight I see black trails of soot that track from his nostrils to the corners of his mouth.

"Get him some oxygen," someone says, and Kyle is taken from my arms.

"Peter." Nicole's hand touches my shoulder. "Are you okay?"

I can't speak. I watch as they lay Kyle on a stretcher with a bright orange mattress. I stand next to him, my eyes on his chest, and look for movement as the medics snap an oxygen mask onto his face. I'm afraid that if I look away he'll stop breathing. I need to see the condensation of his breath against the clear plastic. "I'm staying with Kyle," I tell her.

"I'll ride with you."

A paramedic tries to give me oxygen and get me onto a stretcher. "No." I wave her away and push my way into the back of the brightly lit ambulance. Nicole walks with me and I give her my hand to help her up.

"What?" she asks, settling beside me on the plastic bench.

"It's nothing." I look into her eyes and realize that she has just saved our lives. Another few seconds and I would have succumbed to the smoke. I'm about to say more when an explosion rips the night. The ground shakes and the windows of Fleming and the buildings on either side are blown out.

The paramedic at the front of the bench looks back, terror in her eyes. "What was that?" She shouts up to her partner as glass showers the ambulance, "Let's get out of here."

I stare at Kyle. Why isn't his chest moving? I reach for his wrist; his pulse is weakening. "No!" Ed had said an hour. I remember the syringes jammed in my pockets and pull one out.

"What are you doing?" the paramedic asks.

"Antidote," I say, not waiting for her approval as I uncap the needle and jam it into Kyle's thigh. I bend over him and put my mouth on his, breathing for him, remembering how I did the same with Beth. His lips are still warm, just as hers had been. I count to five as I pull out a second syringe. "Breathe, damn you." I uncap it and jam it home as tears stream down my face. I breathe into Kyle. "One two three four five." Breathe. "One two three four five." Breathe.

I feel his body spasm, and then his belly shakes, his mouth opens, and he sucks in a massive breath. He starts to shake and then cough. His eyes open. Someone's hand is on my back. Kyle's choking on the air, trying to speak. The ambulance swerves and I topple back against the bench.

The driver's saying something, but I can't hear him as a second explosion drowns out the sirens. The van swerves and lurches onto the sidewalk; for a moment I think we're going to crash. We come to a screeching stop.

"DAD?"

"Kyle." I cupped the side of his face in my hand.

"I heard Mom."

"I know," I said as I looked through the back window and saw how close we were to the hospital. "It was Ed mimicking her." I needed this rational excuse; I knew I'd never erase the shadow in the smoke and the scent of her perfume.

Nicole and the driver helped me get out Kyle, who was still strapped to the stretcher. All around us was a scene of chaos—the baying of sirens hurtling down the avenues, Fleming engulfed in flames, glass everywhere, the snow and wind picking up.

The staff of the ER had flooded into the street, where they watched as the nightmare unfolded. As we approached with the stretcher, two nurses and a doctor ran toward us. I was rambling and trying not to sob as we wheeled inside. "I've given him twenty ccs of neostigmine. . . . He was drugged with a paralytic. He stopped breathing."

NICOLE STAYED AT MY SIDE as they rushed Kyle into an intensive care cubicle and got him started on an IV. I don't know how much time had elapsed, but he was breathing and had fallen asleep.

"Peter?"

"What?" I asked.

"I need to go out and see what's happening." The cubicle's thin curtain did little to block out the pandemonium of incoming ambulances and patients.

"Of course."

She got up to leave. I wondered if I'd ever be able to express my gratitude to her.

"Nicole?"

"Yes?"

"When this is over . . ." I said, standing and letting my eyes leave Kyle for the first time, "would you go out with me?"

"I would."

Before I knew it, we were kissing like two starving people at our last meal. Nicole was heading out into a night of unspeakable horror; I had almost lost my son and my life. The kiss was long and hard and tasted of smoke and tears.

"I have to go," she said, pulling back.

My soot-stained fingertips brushed the side of her cheek. Our eyes held, and then she pushed through the curtain and was gone.

EPILOGUE

I WAS BACK IN MY OFFICE three months after Fleming burned. I was on the phone with Nicole, making plans.

"Argentinean steak house?" she asked.

"No, nothing South American." I didn't want to trigger memories of Ed.

"Right. Japanese?"

"Carl can't deal with raw fish," I replied, pausing to think how strange it was that the fourteen-year-old was now my foster child. Just last month Dad had helped us rough out a bedroom for him in what used to be our laundry room. I was now the parent of two teenagers who'd become as thick as thieves, even volunteering their afternoons at the local drop-in center for runaway and throwaway youth.

"I'm tired of pizza," Nicole said, having come to the same conclusion as I had: with our mixing of her six-year-old, my dad—often with Sheila—and two teenagers, Italian was about the only thing everyone could agree on. Since that night, however, we'd all found ourselves needing to be together, creating an instant family, calling one another multiple times a day just to check in.

"So how's your day going?" I asked.

"Not terrible," she said. "I think they're about ready to close it out, but you never know. I think the mystery condom clinched it," she said, referring to the package I'd received from Frankfurt containing a crumpled bit of latex with the mingled DNA of Ed and Ann. "I just want this to be over," she admitted.

"That makes two of us," I said, enjoying the solitude of my office with the ugly green chairs. I could still picture Ann picking at the threads. The reporters continued to call, but Peggy was an iron wall between them and me. The articles that had appeared following the fire were wildly speculative, suggesting everything from terrorists, to black-magic rituals in the basement of the medical school. Even the scientific community was buzzing about the last papers Ed had submitted for publication. His work had zoomed in an unexpected direction—antitumor drugs. If what I was reading was accurate, there was a strong chance that he was on to something. "About six?" I asked.

"I'll try," she said. "You know, it looks like I can swing the weekend off."

"Really, you want to get out of town?"

"Hell, yes."

A knock came at the door. Still on the phone, I opened it to see Felicia with a mischievous grin. "Nicole, I got to go, we can talk about it over dinner. I love you."

"I love you, too."

"Fine," Felicia said, as I hung up. "Everyone's getting some except me. You're not going to believe what's in the waiting room for you."

"What?" I was in no mood for surprises.

"You'll see, and Peter . . ."

"Yes?"

"It's great having you back."

"Thanks." I left the safety of my office, walked the hall of a thousand therapists, and peeked into the crowded waiting room. Since the fire, the clinic had been overwhelmed with new referrals. We were all working like dogs, helping people cope with the horror and the destruction. Two custodial workers had died in the blaze, the lifetime work of several researchers lay among the rubble, jobs were lost, and the medical students and faculty had to be taken in like orphans by the other medical schools in Manhattan.

There, in the waiting room, clutching a wad of tissues, was a girl who couldn't have been more than nineteen. Her heavy blue eye shadow and black mascara were smudged in thick circles. She looked up expectantly. I smiled in her direction, took note of her facial piercings, and looked at Peggy.

I leaned down and whispered, "This is my three-o'clock emergency?"

Peggy, who's seen it all, whispered back, "She was very insistent. Said she couldn't wait. 'Desperate,' I believe . . . name's Brittany."

I looked at the girl with her black mesh stockings and Technicolor dye job, all pulled together with a Catholic school-uniform skirt, ripped T-shirt, and high-top Keds.

I walked over. "Brittany, I'm Dr. Grainger."

"Oh, Doctor," she blurted as I led her back toward my office. "I don't know what I'm going to do. He was supposed to be with me!"

As she flopped into one of the green chairs, it was difficult to suppress a smile. I nodded and listened as Brittany poured out her heart—how the boy she'd had a crush on since the first day of school had finally asked her out to a party and had then left with someone else. I suppose I wasn't very empathic, but all I could think was how normal this was. I wanted to get up and give her a hug, tell her that there'd be other boys and that she'd get over this, and maybe if she toned down her fashion it might go better. Of course, I wasn't about to do such a thing. So I listened and helped her calm down, and I was strangely happy that Brittany was my three-o'clock emergency, because, this was normal stuff.... Things were getting back to normal, and that felt wonderful.

www.smpl.org